IN
THE
DARK
I SEE
YOU

IN
THE
DARK
I SEE
YOU

MALLIKA NARAYANAN

UNION
SQUARE
& CO.

NEW YORK

**UNION
SQUARE
& CO.**

NEW YORK

UNION SQUARE & CO. and the distinctive Union Square & Co. logo
are trademarks of Sterling Publishing Co., Inc.

Union Square & Co., LLC, is a subsidiary of Sterling Publishing Co., Inc.

This is a work of fiction. Names, characters, business, events, and incidents are
the products of the author's imagination. Any resemblance to actual persons,
living or dead, or actual events is purely coincidental.

ISBN 978-1-4549-5007-3
ISBN 978-1-4549-5008-0 (e-book)

For information about custom editions, special sales, and premium purchases,
please contact specialsales@unionsquareandco.com.

Printed in Canada

2 4 6 8 10 9 7 5 3 1

unionsquareandco.com

Cover design by Melissa Farris
Interior design by Rich Hazelton

For Viv,
who makes everything possible.

AUDREY: NOW

THE DELICATE STEM OF THE WINEGLASS SLIPS FROM MY GRASP. I FUMBLE to straighten it, but the Malbec is already seeping through my blouse. A heady spatter bursts in the air. Memories of waking up morning after morning, the same sickly-sweet stench clinging to my skin, make me queasy. I set the glass out of the way before snatching a tissue from the side table and pressing it to the silk. It's too late, though. A stain will have already bloomed on it.

Another beautiful thing, ruined.

I close my eyes and momentarily lose myself in the swelling trill of Frank Sinatra's "Something Stupid." Then, I scoop myself out of the chair and head to the closet.

A squealing wail pierces through the wall that backs up to Sarah's townhouse. It's been half an hour now. Nicole never fusses for so long. For a moment, I'm tempted to go check on her, but the last thing I want is to talk to Sarah or even be in the same room as her. I ease the blouse over my head and fling it into the laundry basket, a familiar dread filling me. Moving to Shore Drive was a terrible mistake. I should never have come here. I'll keep my distance from now on, from the pair of them.

Nicole lets out an affronted cry, followed by angry hiccups. Then, a limb-shaking shriek rends the air.

My skin prickles. Nicole never cries like this. Unless . . . it isn't Nicole at all. I pull on a clean blouse and rush downstairs. Grabbing the phone from the charging cradle, I slide it into the back pocket of my pants, then slip my feet into the ballet flats by the door and head out.

I trace the wrought-iron railing up the stairs of Sarah's home and knock hard on the door. It moves back.

"Hello? Sarah?" I push the door open and step in, sidling to avoid the entryway console table. "Sarah?" I call out, louder. Nicole quietens, perhaps recognizing my voice. The abrupt silence is eerie. I take tiny, tentative steps into the living room. *Where* is *Sarah?*

"Sara—ahh—"

The next moment, I'm facedown and my nose is pushed into something soft. Dazed, I lift my head and come up for air. It takes a moment to work out that I've tripped on something. After propping myself up, I place a hand on the mound before me. The familiar form—the torso, then the shoulder—is unmistakable. I reach for the face and find Sarah's head twisted away from me.

"Sarah? Sarah!" There's no reply.

I run my fingers along her jaw, then the curve of her neck, and feel for a pulse. Warm liquid oozes on my fingers. I lift my hand to my nose. A metallic odor fills my nostrils. *Blood.* My heart stutters in my chest.

"Sarah, wake up." I reach for her shoulder and shake it hard. "Come on! Get up."

She doesn't move. I gulp and pull back. Something sticky comes away in my hand. As I unfurl my fist, a web of fibers entangles in my fingers and cuts into my skin. It takes only a second to realize what it is. Sarah's hair, tangled, matted with blood.

I cry out and recoil, swiping my hand frantically against my pants. A wave of revulsion turns my stomach. I lean over and dry heave.

Then, steadying myself, I pry the phone out of my pocket.

"Siri, call 9-1-1."

Calling emergency services in five seconds, the automated voice replies, making me jump. Each second is an age. One by one, scenarios flash through my head. Did Sarah fall down the stairs? Was it her scream that I heard? Did she trip and break her neck?

My heart hammers against my rib cage when the call finally connects.

"9-1-1, what's your emergency?"

"She's hurt. My neighbor, Sarah. I'm calling from No. 4, s-sorry, No. 5 Shore Drive, Sleepy Point."

"What is your name, ma'am?"

"I'm Audrey. Audrey Hughes."

"Audrey, is your neighbor conscious?"

"No! Send an ambulance immediately."

"Try to stay calm. Help is on the way. Is there someone else in the house?"

My blood runs cold. *Nicole!* "There's a baby. She's upstairs, I can hear her. Oh, God." *How could I have forgotten about her?*

Dragging myself upright, I shuffle to the stairwell and press on upstairs, my heart pounding in my ears, a desperate prayer on my lips, *please let her be safe.*

"Nicole?"

I hear her fussing in the bedroom. I push the half-open master bedroom door back and place careful steps forward. From the closet, I hear faint music still playing in my house. "Nicole?" I call out. Her cries come louder now that she senses I'm close by.

I cover the distance to the bed and reach for her. Relief floods me when my fingers graze the hard edges of her baby car seat and I find her strapped inside. Her sharp wail as I unclick the belt holding her in and pick her up makes my heart sputter. I cradle her to my chest. "Shh. It's okay. I'm here."

"I've found her," I say to the operator over her cries.

"Is the baby all right?"

I freeze. "What?"

"The baby, is she okay?"

I turn back to Nicole's form, stricken with horror. "I-I don't know," I whisper.

"Can you repeat that please?"

I curse. I should have mentioned it to the operator, first thing. "I'm visually impaired. I can't see if she's all right!"

"The paramedics should be arriving soon, Audrey. Please try to stay calm and stay where you are."

I hug Nicole, trying to pacify her, but she's inconsolable, as though she knows, as I do, that the paramedics will be too late.

Sarah is dead.

SARAH: THEN
4 YEARS AGO

THE FALL MORNING SUN GLINTS OFF SKYSCRAPER WINDOWS INTO LASER beams. I use my palm as a visor and saunter up toward Eighth Avenue, nudging the right earbud further into my ear. It never quite fits, although the left seems fine. I often wonder if the defect is in manufacturing or my physiology. The latter, I guess, grimacing as the putrid collections of garbage in massive industrial containers threatens the toast I've scarfed down minutes before. At the crossing, I glance up toward the traffic light. A reflection shoots directly in my eyes, leaving my vision blotchy. As I cross in the haze of the morning's sharp shadows, still seeing spots, a truck screeches to a stop, inches from my face. A horn bellows. I freeze and stare at the green and white beast, my heart pounding. A split second is all the difference between standing frozen in the middle of the street or being pulped and schmeared across the tar, like cream cheese spread on a bagel.

The garbage truck driver rolls down his window, sticks his head out, and yells, "Jesus, lady! Watch where you're going!"

Someone yells, "Get out of the way!" I place a shaky step back, in time for the truck to peel away. A few feet ahead, the light turns and the truck lurches to a halt.

"Thanks a *lot*," the driver shouts out once more, head out of the window. The shutter of the garbage feed at the back of the truck snaps back like an alligator jaw. The resounding *bang!* makes me jump. A few of the morning regulars pause for a second to ascertain that it isn't a gunshot before resuming their speed walks.

A blast of arctic air smacks everything in its path as wind tunnels down Eighth Avenue. I wince and pull my light fall jacket closer around my waist with icy hands, darting a glance at my watch. My bus arrives exactly on time. I rub my numb hands together as it pulls up. The doors spring apart with a *whoosh*, the pressure brake releasing a blast of welcome hot air. I wave at Rupert, the driver, and try to squeeze myself into my usual corner. Not many look forward to the hubbub of the morning commute. Everyone's in a rush to *be* at work. How they get there is always a source of annoyance. Not for me. The air, heavy with steaming coffee and news ink, fills me with the best kind of anticipation as the bus pulls away.

With only three CPAs and one tax consultant on the payroll in our little company, I won't be climbing up any corporate ladder at Tcheznich & Co., but the clientele is consistent, and Mr. Tcheznich isn't greedy, which is saying something in New York. I'm up for a promotion soon, though, according to Celia, our top grape in the grapevine. She's cozy with the boss, Mr. Tcheznich, a conservative man whose facial tics never extend so far as to smile or frown properly. He bobs his head when he means no and shakes it vigorously when he agrees. We had thought of Celia cozying up to him as a blessing; we might yet work out what our boss thinks. Instead, though, he's starting to rub off on her. She used to be easy to talk to. Now she frown-smiles like him a bit and I've noticed a worrying head-nodding tendency. She doesn't have the neck for it.

By rights, this promotion should have been Celia's. I was the last to join the team, but that's the way these things go. Only one of us can become the senior auditor. It appears she thinks so as well. She didn't spell it out; she didn't need to.

"You're lucky," she said, the vein in her forehead twitching the way it does when she's annoyed. "The boss likes you."

Why do people say that? Such a cop-out when they can easily offer something more gracious. After all, I bypassed the boss's bed and climbed up the hard way.

Celia and Norman are already settled in the conference room when I get to work. I stop at my desk and check my email to find an urgent client request for an internal audit. Armed with a fresh brew, I settle in beside them. My fingers try hard to keep up with my brain. Before long, the pace of Celia's typing increases as she works harder to keep up with me.

Midday, I frown over the scattered paperwork. This is turning out to be the project from hell, my hell anyway. Documents are missing. I've emailed our contact at Fortitude Trading, the client, requesting the missing documents. Of course, Dan is more than a contact now. We're close friends. I could easily text him, but there's a protocol to follow and paper trails to maintain so I email and keep it professional.

My brow furrows when I spot that the reply, a little later, is from John, Dan's colleague at Fortitude.

> Hi Sarah,
> Daniel isn't available and I will be stepping in for him hence-forth. I'll check about the document and get back to you.
> Thanks,
> John Berkley

I stare at the email and wonder why John says *henceforth*. I type a reply.

> Hi John,
> Regarding the documents, Dan had mentioned a second file as well as the one we have requested for this quarter. To speed things up a bit, could the three of us hop on a quick call later this afternoon? Thanks.
> Sarah

I replace things at my desk and neaten up, fidgeting, when a new email arrives.

> Sarah,
> I'm happy to call you this afternoon but Daniel won't be able to join us as he no longer works at Fortitude Trading . . .

I stop here and read it over a second time, the air leaving my lungs in a rush. I read on to see if there's an explanation, but there isn't one.

I sit still as though someone waved a wand and turned me into a statue. When I spoke to Dan last night, he didn't say anything about it. Not a word, not even a hint. After I snap out of it, I step into the breakroom and text him.

> Just heard you've left Fortitude!?
> Call me!

"Everything all right?"

I jump and find myself staring at Celia. My hand goes to my heart automatically.

"Oh, I didn't mean to startle you," she says, with a smile that doesn't reach her eyes.

"Everything's *fine*." I regret my tone immediately. She appears satisfied that I took her bait.

She lifts her chin and narrows her eyes as if she isn't convinced. I shake my head and walk back to my cubicle.

When I look back, her eyes are still on me.

Mr. Tcheznich is a strong advocate for work-life balance—as am I—so I try to head out of the office by five. Today it's close to six by the time I wrap up and get my head around Dan's sudden departure from Fortitude. While I wait for the bus, I'm still going over and over the words from John's email in my head.

Back when I'd just moved to the city, I used to walk home to familiar-ize myself with the streets. Now I know them by heart. I'm aware of which streets to avoid because the sidewalk has been scaffolded to address the inevitable repairs all New York buildings seem to periodically need. Or the best route home so I can stop at the bakery on the way. I can close my eyes and direct a passing tourist to any address within a five-mile radius. My urgency now isn't to devour New York like an open-mouthed tourist, but to live the life I imagined I would when I moved here.

Like myself, Dan was newish to New York, an import from Minne-apolis. It was perhaps what drew us together, being newbies in this crazy, amazing city, and we found ourselves bumbling around town, getting our bearings. On weekends, Dan and I watch plays, hang out at the Strand, laze at Central Park or Madison Square, or check out the exhibits in the Guggenheim or the Whitney.

I hang a right on 21st Street, orange-brown leaves crunching under my shoes, and forge my way among the evening throng, dodging an elbow here and a briefcase there, a weird sensation creeping in. Dan hasn't called me back. Nor has he texted me.

I heave myself up the two flights of dank stairs of my depressing gray building and enter my studio apartment. There's an envelope waiting on the floor. Against the old dark oak flooring, the paper stands out, ominous and white. The only person who leaves me unaddressed envelopes is my landlord. There's been no rent hike yet; he's kept it stable, only springing other unwelcome surprises like his unscheduled visits.

"I gotta keep an eye on my place!" he said the first time he knocked on the door and simply stepped inside before I could ask him who the hell he was. The lease had been through an agent, and I'd never met him before.

"I own da place," he'd said, pointing a fat ringed finger around the apartment.

I was new, I didn't want to antagonize him. I let him in.

"Big mistake," Celia said the next day.

"Why?"

"Because now he'll think he can drop in whenever he wants!"

She'd been horribly right. He's also hinted a couple of times that if I joined him at his biannual pool party and brought along a few of my "pretty" friends, the rent might be cheaper. It's not as though we're in swanky uptown. This is Chelsea. Well, the Meatpacking district, but I'm on the border and Chelsea sounds better if I have to tell someone where I live. But a pool party in the Meatpacking district sounds *wrong*.

I stare at the envelope, an unpleasant, regurgitating taste in my mouth.

Dear Ms. Connelly,

*   *Your current lease will expire on February 2 of the upcoming year. I regret to inform you that renewal will not be possible, and I will need my apartment reverted to me on the second of February. Please consider this your notice. If this notice is ignored, or if I don't hear back from you confirming your agreement to this notice, I will be left with no choice but to evict you as per the agreement you signed on the initial lease documents.*

Anthony D'Angelo

P.S.: My daughter is returning to New York, and she will need this apartment.

I've barely settled in! I only took on the initial six-month lease under the impression that it was renewable annually thereafter. *Dammit!* I crumple up the letter and fling it to the sofa along with my bag. Perhaps I should have brought my pretty friends to his pool party, possibly even thrown in an impromptu striptease. At least I wouldn't be getting threatened with eviction.

I fish out my phone from my bag. Not a peep from Dan yet. It's so unlike him. He wouldn't up and quit his job, one he's been happy at, especially with the promise of a promotion soon.

My call goes straight to voice mail.

"Hey, it's me. Where *are* you? Call me back!"

After placing the phone on the charging cradle, I flop onto the sofa and flick the TV on, my appetite replaced by a sinking churn in my stomach.

I've been saving for years for a decent down payment on a home somewhere far from here, like White Plains or one of those pretty suburbs beyond New Rochelle, but it's too soon. A friend from the upscale CrossFit studio I'd attended back when they opened and were giving free promotional months, said she and her partner had been house hunting for a year and had gotten nowhere. A couple of months aren't enough to find a decent house anywhere at all, and this isn't any old city. This is New York. I'll be lucky if I can find a pigeonhole to rent by February.

AUDREY: THEN
10 MONTHS AGO

"Put your back into it, come on," Jason, my personal trainer, says. I'm distracted. The heavy, rubber air from the equipment in the gym and the pungent sweat laced with artificial tropical fruit sprays makes me think about Sarah.

When I met her, it was the thing that first registered, the smell. A pleasant but intense perfume like the sort you get at airport fragrance showrooms, at the rate of a ransom per ounce. The second she opened her mouth it made sense, like it is *her*. As I press up the weight with my hips, following Jason's hand on my ankle, guiding me, I think about how this scent follows her, like everyone in our neighborhood seems to.

I have it on good authority from Priya Patel from No. 10 that late-twenty-something, blond, sea-green-eyed Sarah is lusted after by everyone. I should have known when I began frequenting the gym in the Paradise Clubhouse that her name will be familiar here as well. Some days I wonder if it's the reason I joined this gym when there's another a couple of streets down. But no, among other considerations, it's also free. Well, paid for through hefty home association fees. And it's closer to home, and that is reason enough. They've assigned me a corner of my own in the massive gym so there won't be any accidental trips. I suspect they're more afraid of a lawsuit, but whatever their reason to go the additional mile to accommodate me, I'm glad of it. Sometimes, just sometimes, I hate that I need this special accommodation. I try not to dwell on it.

Sarah and I even share the same personal instructor. Not very surprising, he's the most popular one here. Everyone wants him as their instructor. And more. Jason is a little too in love with himself and his muscles to notice anyone else but from the way he waxes poetic about Sarah every time I'm in, I assume he shares the neighborhood's collective lust for her.

"Seriously! Have you *seen* that ass?" he asks. He's been on and on about Sarah since our session began. It's probably why I have her in my head.

"Sorry, I didn't mean to—" he says, dropping his voice. People do that often. They ask if I've *seen* something, a simple turn of phrase after which follows a terrible, awkward silence.

"You're fine," I say.

"She's got *the* perfect body, you know. She's healthy, too, not all bones and skin. I've talked to her about being a model."

"You'll find she's already got a job." Though I'm not strictly sure what her job entails; she's a consultant—a catchall title. Once she said she could easily be an influencer if only she didn't hate social media so much. That was surprising. A vanity like hers demands attention and where better than the hotbed for it all—social media? But I've checked. While she has accounts everywhere, she's hardly active and has a pitiful following.

"What kind of a model?" I ask, trying to heave and press up what must be one ton, though Jason here assures me it's only forty pounds.

"Not like a runway model. I mean, a model to showcase my talents as a personal trainer. After she's had the baby, that is." After a pause, he adds, "You could easily model for me, too. Another couple of months and you'll be properly toned. You've got great bones."

After my session, I head to the showers, to scrub sweat off my improperly toned body with great bones. I'll remember to boast about it the next time I'm on a date.

"I've got a Corvette, '63," my date will say. "It's still got great bones."

"Well, so have I," I'll say, and we'll be an instant hit.

There's usually a stall reserved for me, but it's taken today. I find myself in an unfamiliar booth far from my locker. I trace, then map out this new route in my head, and commit it to memory: hang right, stick close to the wall, mind the bench midway, then, in the corner, the stall. A hook to the right, for the towel. A tiny but potentially deadly step into the stall, shower handle at chest height; different from the handicap stall, where the shower knob is lower so someone seated can turn it on.

As the rain of hot water washes away the suds, I think about Sarah, her soft hands, her fluid body, and how she's the least body-shy person I've ever met. Last week, she tried to show me the perfect warrior pose right in the middle of the kitchen while I was unloading the dishwasher. She'd returned from her prenatal yoga class.

"Here." She guided my hand to the flat of her back. My palm against the curve of her spine in her tabletop position, my fingers against her toned bare skin. Through her back, I could discern the thrum of her heartbeats like a pair of little fluttering birds.

On the inside, Sarah is made up of more than what people can see. Strength, determination, lust for life, for fun. Lust. Lots and lots of lust.

After I step out of the shower, I bump into someone right by the bench, my towel slipping off my chest. "Oh! Sorry!" I say, recovering.

"No problem. Are you okay?" the woman asks.

My nipples perk into diamond points in the cold of the locker room. The hairs on my arms prickle. I pull up the towel, picturing a quick rove of her eyes, the easy but telltale casing glance with which women regard other women.

I'm not okay. I've stubbed my toe badly against the metal feet of the bench, but I smile and say it's fine. It's my fault for being distracted. If I hadn't been thinking about Sarah, I'd have heard the woman come up.

I pull on my clothes, grab my things, wave off Tania, the ever-cheerful receptionist, and head home. Outside, the sun is warm on my face. I turn

left and begin an automatic mental check for the markers in each block—
the root sticking out on the second, the dip in the pavement at the end
of the fourth, right by the juniper. I've had to carve these patterns in my
brain after I moved here. Tattoo them in the old-fashioned, lemon-thorn
way, repetition and practice. Six blocks down, voilà, a parade of townhomes in the clearing. Wind channels down the promenade, between
rows of townhomes facing the roads and each other, green spaces in the
center. Beyond, the Hudson ebbs and flows. A waterside walking trail
winds around the river. About a mile in, in a flat clearing, there's a small
lighthouse—more for show than function. Marking the end of the walking path is a trio of metal stumps leading into a hiking trail away from the
river and into the back end of Sleepy Point.

"It's so quiet here. How will you manage after New York?" was the
question on everyone's lips after I moved here. But I relished the change.
The solitude and the memories are all that's left.

There's little traffic and no light stops in between the blocks spanning
the gym and my home, but I halt at the end of every block anyway. Safety
first, always.

It's strange that I never bump into Sarah at the gym. Perhaps our
schedules are too different.

"Hi, Audrey."

From the gruff baritone aged by barking orders, it's Mr. Juno Cane
from No. 3, an elderly gentleman, an ex–army man.

"Hi, how are you?"

"All good, j'you know," he says.

But that's just the thing, I don't know. His name isn't Juno; it's Bob. I
call him Juno because he often adds *j'you know?* at the end of his sentences.

"How's the knee?" I ask. "Are you back to your ballet days?"

"Can't complain, juno? At least I can hobble about now."

"That's great," I say, making a move to say bye.

"I'll be seeing ya. Be careful up ahead, now. It's still all dug up, juno?"

"Will do. See you." I walk on, thankful for the reminder. I sidle onto the road to be safe and make the last couple of blocks home. Lisa and Jack Dodson, from No. 7—a power couple who work in the city but live here—had a water main break a month back. It turned out to be a huge job once they began digging. A fight between the city and the private water company has stalled the fixing. Last week, a six-year-old boy fell into the pit and cracked his head on the old cast-iron pipe. The parents, who were visiting a relative in the area, have threatened to sue the Dodsons, but to their misfortune, both Jack and Lisa are lawyers.

Yesterday, I heard the boy died. His young, unlived life snuffed out over a silly tussle on who is going to pay to dig up concrete.

Today, I've been wondering if his death is some sort of omen. I've only just moved here. I thought it would be safe so far from the city.

I've just typed in my username to log in to my support group, Blinkers-Off, when the *dingdong* of the doorbell sounds and echoes in the house. I frown and have my watch read out the time. Nine-thirty. Who's visiting at this hour? My heartbeat quickens as I follow the stairs down. *Rat-tat-tat*, a knock follows the *dingdong*.

"Hello? Audrey, you home?"

I stand frozen for a moment before I unlock and open the door a crack.

"It's me, Sarah," she says, and pushes the door back. From the way the air shifts and swells with her perfume, I assume she's swishing past me.

"Hi, come on in," I say, but she's already in the living room. I shut the door and take a deep breath before joining her.

"You don't mind if I put up my feet on your coffee table, do you?"

I start to say something, but Sarah carries on: "I swear they're like two ripe watermelons."

There's a scrape; her feet are on the table.

"Anyway, I stopped by earlier. Where were you?"

I fold my arms across my body and turn to face her, annoyed, and, to my astonishment, a little amused. "Out for a walk," I say, seating myself opposite her, in the guest chair as she's taken my spot on the sofa. I want to ask her what she's doing here, but she beats me to it.

"I *had* to meet someone! What a day. This little monster's kicking me so hard I'm thinking of signing up for prenatal kickboxing instead of yoga. Who knew the third trimester was going to be this hard?"

She huffs and adjusts herself on the sofa. The spring squeaks under her.

"Would you like something to drink?"

"Sure, you got some juice?"

"There's some apple juice in the fridge—"

"I don't want to bother you. I'll grab it myself."

"Sure, help yourself," I say.

There's no reply. From the sound of a scrape, I imagine her feet have swept off the coffee table and are shuffling to the kitchen, which is open to the combined living/family room. The fridge door swings out with a rattle and the bottles inside clink. My heartbeat quickens. I gulp back a rising wave of panic. What had I been thinking? I should never have moved here.

SARAH

I cross Ninth Avenue to catch the bus to work, thinking back to my dreams when I first moved to the city, working in some chic concrete and glass office in the financial district. That all seems naive now. My boss doesn't arrive in a limousine. Ours is a lackluster office, walls uninspiring gray on gray with the only window facing a bus parking garage. And it suits me fine, even though my credible job may seem far beneath someone with my pedigree.

Celia has already asked me twice since morning if everything's okay. "You're sighing again," she says. We're both heading to the unisex restroom. It has a single toilet stall and a sink near the door so you must lock both doors for privacy.

"It's my landlord. He's asked me to move out."

"Is he hitting on you again? You can sue, you know? There are laws against unfair evictions in New York. A friend of mine is a social worker if you need help."

Great. Just when I think I've figured Celia out, she offers to help. It's to throw me off, I'm sure.

"N-no. It's not that, although, the eviction threat *was* overkill and unnecessary. His daughter is returning to New York, and he needs the apartment back for her."

"Returning from where?" she asks. She's unzipping her pants by the sound of it.

"Haven't a clue."

Although Celia and I have been working together for a little more than two years, going through the motions of intimacy, like being in the restroom together, still makes me uncomfortable. I turn on the tap so I won't have to hear her. Icy water gushes on my already cold hands.

"You're washing your hands again, aren't you? You're supposed to wash them after," she says, zipping up. The flush goes off. I'm startled by the violence with which the water cascades.

"What are you going to do, Sarah?" she asks, as I walk in and shut the toilet door.

"I don't know."

Later, when I'm on a break, I email Rachel, my real estate agent, and update her on the situation, my gut churning with anxiety over the unfairness of being uprooted when I only just moved in a few months ago.

Still no call or text from Dan. I'm starting to worry. Midday, I take a proper lunch break, even though it looks gray and unfriendly outside. The blast of cold whipping my face is refreshing. I twitch with impatience, and then I give up. I take out my phone and call him.

I sigh with relief when he picks up. "Hi, Dan."

Silence.

"Hi," he says, finally.

"I've been worried. I've been trying to call you."

"I know."

"You've quit your job?"

"I-I didn't quit. I was fired."

My jaw drops open. "What! That's awful! What happened?"

"I don't want to talk about it."

Heat creeps up my neck. I shouldn't have asked him directly. "Are you okay?"

"No, Sarah. I'm not."

It must take so much for him to admit this. Dan is usually as tight-lipped as I am. It's one of the reasons we get along as well as we do.

"Look, if there's something I can do, anything at all, you will let me know?"

"That's very kind."

I suppress a squirt of irritation at his stiff, formal tone. I know what he's trying to do, because it's something I do as well: he's distancing himself. "Hey, I mean it."

"I better go. I've got to meet my lawyer."

Apprehension fills me as I process the subtext: Fortitude has dictated the terms of his layoff and he's been told to seal his lips.

It's unlike me not to have a backup plan. The notice from Mr. D'Angelo has caught me off guard. The result of complacency, I remind myself. I hurry home to view Rachel's response in the privacy of my soon-to-be-ex-apartment, away from prying eyes. I'm not certain why, but Ms. Celia Bundt has taken to looking over my shoulder when she thinks I'm otherwise occupied.

Of late, she's also been slipping in a sly question or two about my past in seemingly innocent conversations. It's worrying. No one likes to be watched or checked on.

> Sarah,
> I've attached a pdf with some apartments I think you'll like.
> Take a look and let me know if you're interested in any. We'll
> have to move quickly.
> Best,
> Rachel

I pour scalding water into a mug with peppermint tea and bring it with me to my tiny but neat desk, where I have the printout of the pdf ready. I look for standard, telltale descriptions, and keywords to avoid.

Unique, for example, means the ceiling will likely be all sloping and slant-ing and you can forget about standing upright. Or *quaint*, which suggests the lights will flicker and the taps will deliver water when they want. You must at all costs avoid *cozy*, where half your body might end up in your neighbor's apartment if you, God forbid, stretch. The worst real-estate tag of all, everyone knows, is a *time-saver apartment*, code for "You can stir a soup pot in the kitchen with a free hand while you scrub your body in the shower with the other."

I can't help but frown when I scan the attached pdf and note that Rachel has picked all shared lets. I'm not one to share. I like my own space, and I'm finicky about cleanliness and hygiene, which isn't ideal if you have a roommate; you can only dictate the terms so far.

Finally, a listing catches my eye. It's a one-bedroom, a tight one-bed from the square footage specified, but the rent looks doable. I haven't lived in anything larger than a studio since . . . well, never, so the thought of a whole bedroom makes me a bit giddy. And it's right up the street from me, on West 20th. I reply immediately, asking to see it.

The floor begins to shake as I hit SEND. It's been happening ever since the new people moved in below, a couple of months ago. I've tried to picture the sort of activity that could cause their ceiling to thump so my floor moves and shakes in turn, as though we're in the middle of an earthquake. Perhaps they jump until their heads hit the ceiling all eve-ning long. Once, when I ran into them on the stairs, I took particular note of the shape of their heads, expecting them to be squashed into four little squares but they looked fine.

The neighbor across from me practices violin in the evenings, a Bach enthusiast. The violinist's neighbor, diagonally opposite to me, is a mas-sage therapist, a back enthusiast. The violin is without a doubt preferable to the wailing from the apartment to my immediate right. The woman there has a baby who, it appears, is displeased with her new life and broad-casts this displeasure at the highest possible octave. Sometimes the violin competes with her—different scales like mismatched songs—at others, it's a duet. Together, the twin wailing is stiff competition to the almost incessant sirens of the city.

However annoying, though, you can't pick your neighbors, can you? Just as you can't pick and choose your family. They are who they are, and you're stuck.

AUDREY: NOW

"I'm not sure what more i can tell you, Detective Greene. I already gave a statement."

A shuttering click startles me. A camera, I imagine.

"Ms. Hughes—"

"Detective? Can I have a word?" someone says. Voices leak from the alien static of police radios. The intrusion of this presence in my home after all that has happened today only disorients me more.

"Excuse me a moment," he says to me. His shoes clatter on the hard floor. He murmurs instructions to the officer who interrupted him.

"We have your statement, Ms. Hughes, but we need you to tell us everything from the beginning."

I nod and wipe my face with the back of my palm.

"What time did you go over to your neighbor Sarah's house?"

"I first heard the baby, Nicole, crying at about eight-thirty. She usually fusses at bedtime, so I ignored it for a while. But later, when she hadn't stopped, I thought I'd go over. That's when I . . . found Sarah." The moment I was in Sarah's house, her blood oozing on my hands, replays in my head. The tea I had before works its way back up my throat without warning. I snatch a deep, shuddering breath and gulp.

"What happened before?" Detective Novak asks. The woman's sandy rasp jolts me again as it had when she first introduced herself to me.

"Sorry? Before?"

"Between you deciding to go over and you finding the body?"

"Nothing."

"Nothing?" Detective Novak prompts.

"Yes, nothing." Even I hear the exasperation in my voice. "I decided to go. I went."

"You simply got up from the couch and went over?"

I roll my shoulders back and sit up straight. "No. I was upstairs, in the study."

"You could hear the baby from there?" Greene asks. Pen scratches on paper.

"Well, no, I was in the closet. My closet backs up to theirs."

"Why were you in the closet?"

Heat floods my face. "I . . . spilled something on my blouse. Some red wine."

"We'll have to take it in," Greene says.

"Why?"

"Do you have an objection? We could get a warrant."

From the moment I found Sarah, a part of me has been hoping that it was an accident, that she lost her footing and tripped down the stairs. But I've only been trying to kid myself because admitting it could be a homicide means opening myself up to more questions, more interviews. It's . . . bad. And dangerous. And I know what the detective is thinking, even though he doesn't say it. Wine. Blood. All the same color once dry. What if I'm lying? What if I killed Sarah, came home, changed my clothes, and then claimed I spilled wine? Of course, a simple forensic test could clear that up, but still. It would waste valuable time in evidence gathering.

"Ms. Hughes? Do we need to get a wa—"

"It's fine. Take it if you must. It's in the laundry basket."

"Thank you," Greene says, then instructs an officer to bag the blouse.

"But *don't* touch anything else," I add.

There's a sudden silence, as though everyone's stopped what they're doing and are looking at me.

"I-I won't know if you move things around and I could fall or hurt myself," I explain.

"Of course," Greene says. From his tone, I can't work out if he's taken my request at face value.

"What happened after you changed?" Novak asks.

"The baby was still crying. That's when I decided to go over. I came downstairs, changed into my ballet flats—an officer took it all away."

"What time was it?"

"Nine or five past nine would be a good guess."

"Okay, so you went over at a few minutes past nine, and knocked?"

"I did, but the door moved back. It was already open." My voice cracks. I gulp and reach for the water bottle beside me. I sense their eyes on me, watching as I sip.

I set the bottle back on the table and splay my palm on the velvet arm of the sofa. "I called out to Sarah, but she didn't answer. I walked in and tripped over something—she was on the floor. I tried to rouse her, but she wasn't responding. I called 9-1-1, then went to find Nicole."

"And where was the baby?"

"On the bed in the master bedroom, strapped into her car seat." I shiver though it's a sultry July evening. "Do you think it's connected to the break-ins?"

"What break-ins?" Greene asks.

"There was a rash of them in the neighborhood a few months ago. A lot of homes were hit. Mine was one among them. And Sarah's. She mentioned at the time she might have seen the intruder."

"We'll look into it."

"Did she report it?" Novak asks.

"I don't know. I told her to, but she thought it would be a waste of time."

"Ms. Hughes, where in England are you from? Your accent . . ."

"Oxfordshire."

"Which part?"

I stiffen. "You w-wouldn't know it."

"Anyway, back to Sarah," his partner mutters. There's a subtle warning in Novak's tone. A signal to her partner that it's late, she wants to wrap this up and go home.

It's what I want as well. I want the chaos to stop. I want not to feel so muddled. I need some quiet to collect my thoughts, to give them a clean, unconfused version of the events.

I yawn behind my hand. "Detectives, would you mind if we continue this tomorrow?"

"Yes, yes, we can. It'll have to be first thing in the morning. We need to talk to you when everything's still fresh in your mind. Ms. Hughes, do you . . . have someone to help you?"

"I'm sorry? Help me with what?"

"There's blood. On you, I mean."

"I may be blind, but I assure you I do know how to bathe." I sigh. "Sorry. I'm very tired. Thanks for your concern, but I'll be all right.

"What's going to happen to Nicole?" I ask, as we shuffle toward the entryway passage.

"She's safe," Novak says.

"She'll need her favorite blanket—the one with the baby monkeys on it—and the yellow teething ring with the rattle."

"Monkey . . . blanket . . . yellow rattle," Novak repeats, halting. From the ruffle of paper, I presume Detective Novak is jotting it down.

"She can't sleep without it." Poor mite. I wipe my cheeks with a sodden sleeve of my T-shirt and blow my nose into a tissue.

"Can you be at the station tomorrow morning, say, eight?" Greene asks when they're at the door.

"Of course. Good night, detectives."

They pull the door shut behind them. Outside, Greene lets out an audible sigh. "Can you believe this? Our only witness to the homicide is blind."

Being stuck with blind little old me must be *so* hard for them, I think, then bite down my irritation and listen.

"I'll tell you one thing," Novak says. "Sight or no sight, there's no such thing as a reliable witness."

"True."

"Although, she does seem genuinely upset," Novak adds.

When both their voices become low, I imagine they're walking away. I press an ear to the door.

"Why do I get the feeling that she's lying?" Greene is saying.

I clap a hand over my mouth and strain to hear the reply.

"What do you think she's lying about?"

"Nothing. And everything."

"You think everyone lies to you," Novak rasps.

A hollow laugh. "That's because they do."

Their voices fade away.

Numb and tired, I stand still while car engines cough and sputter as, one by one, the cops pull away, leaving behind an odd, unsettling quiet. Alone, at last. I head upstairs straight to the closet and strip once more. I toss the clothes into the laundry basket. In the bathroom, I pause, remembering Detective Greene's words. I picture smears of dried blood encrusting my skin and shudder. A long soak in a tub of scented water to relax my taut body is tempting but the thought of lying there, blood leaching into the water, tingeing it pink, sends a chill down my spine. Instead, I step into the shower and pull the curtain closed. I turn the shower knob all the way. Near-scalding water gushes out, massages my neck, and sluices down my spine. Remembering the blood, I soap, then scrub myself with vigor. I'm about to wash off the suds when I hear a small *thud*. After turning off the shower, I cock my head and listen, water dripping from my hair and body, feeling the steam snake around me.

"Hello?" I call out. Another *thud* makes me jump. I did lock the door, didn't I? Did I arm the system? The fear surges into panic as I realize I haven't armed the house after the detectives left. I pull back the shower curtain and am about to step out when there's a whisper.

"Hello?" My voice quivers.

I reach toward the hook outside the shower. There's nothing but air where my robe should be. Goose bumps ripple across my arms and neck. With one hand on the shower frame, I step onto the bath mat. Under my feet, something soft and coiled slithers. I yelp and hop back into the shower, my heart pounding in my chest. I bend and stretch an unsteady hand to the floor. Beneath my fingers, the soft folds of my silk robe are a caress.

My shoulders slump with relief.

"You silly moo." I scoff at myself and hang up the robe on the hook. I shiver as I dab my body with the soft towel. A chill has crept into the house.

SARAH

A SIGH OF RELIEF ESCAPES ME WHEN I SEE AN EMAIL UPDATE FROM
Rachel. Though, as I read on, my excitement at the thought of checking
out the one-bed apartment dims.

> Sarah,
> I'm so sorry but that apartment has been snapped up this
> afternoon. I'll keep my eyes peeled for something similar.
> Best,
> Rachel

Before I can place my phone on the countertop for charging, the
neighbor's baby wails, bleating out like a distress siren.

I'm supposed to be at the theater; I have a ticket to *My Fair Lady,* but I
can't seem to focus on anything besides Dan. Instead, I pack a cheese
sandwich and brave the evening crowds along the way to Hudson River
Park. It's dark and an early-November chill frosts the air. I button up my
coat and stick my hands into my pockets, stuffing my sandwich in as well.
I picture the cheese hardening in the cold. I'm not sure why I thought it
was a good idea to bring a cold sandwich to eat at the windy waterfront,
but old habits die hard. And I've just thrown away a $175 ticket.

The park green looks nearly black in the shadows, where the street-
lights don't reach the leaf-covered ground. In the silence of the swirling
black, my heart begins to thud hard. A girl must watch where she goes
in the dark. Even in a big city thronging with people, things can become
quite dangerous all of a sudden. When I hear footsteps dogging mine,

my pulse quickens. I crane my neck to see who's behind me. An elderly gentleman emerges from the shadows with his mastiff, which drools and snarls. I gulp and walk on, my thoughts settling back on Dan and his predicament. It's no small thing to be fired these days, there's hell to pay with HR. But to be fired on the spot beggars belief. The reason must be something stupidly huge, or frighteningly careless.

The thing is, I *know* Dan. He's way too honest for anything stupid like mislaid or diverted funds. Even with access to millions of dollars managing Fortitude's employee payroll, and their 401(k) funds, he wouldn't be tempted. This is a man who returns the extra cent and never takes a shortcut even if it means a loss of his time or money. They couldn't possibly fault him for unprofessionalism or misconduct—he's a conscientious, good human. Whatever their reason for firing him, I know in my bones, it's got to be a mistake.

"You know why you're here," Mr. Tcheznich says.

"Do I?"

He nods. I worry it's bad news when he says, "Ms. Connelly, I am glad you came on board three years ago. Your dedication, your commitment to detail; it's valuable in what we do, and it's been appreciated. I want you to know that I've been considering an appropriate reward." The morning sun is like a halo behind him. It's almost an ecclesiastical moment after the anxiety I just felt.

"You're to become senior auditor, starting January. I will formally announce it after Thanksgiving."

I'm ecstatic. I'm certain it shows on my face, but I don't care.

"Mr. Tcheznich, I'm very grateful."

He graces me with a rare unconfused smile, teeth and all.

I try to pull a poker face when I step out of his office. Celia is glaring at me. She's dying to know what went on in there. It's absurd; it's as though she needs to know *everything*, especially when it comes to me. I tell Norman and her the news like it's brand-new information and I never had a clue. Norman proposes a toast in the evening, a rare outing for just the three of us; our tax consultant, Ted, is on location in New Jersey for the day. As it's the first time that Norman has taken initiative, I accept right away.

As the afternoon wears on, I regret it more and more. Celia's face looks like thunder. I can't work out if it's something I said or did, but sometime during these past six months, her warmth started to wear off. When she watches me, as she does now with her beady eyes, all I feel is a chill. And with Dan's awful predicament, my much-awaited win falls flat and hollow.

It's a washout when we step out. A slurry mix of rain and ice falling sideways assaults us. Norman opens his umbrella but it's pointless. Within a moment it's upside down.

"Turn up your coat, Norman," Celia says while we wait for a cab.

"Okay," he says, and turns up the tips of his coat collar, obedient. It brings a lump to my throat for some reason.

"The Bowery," I say after we get in, almost moaning aloud for the hot air inside the vehicle. I blow into my hand to warm it up and hope Norman follows suit. He's got a certain innocence, like the way he carries an umbrella if there's even a hint of rain in the forecast, or how he has to be the one to unwrap the new printer paper in that careful, deliberate way of his. I suspect he's somewhere on the ASD spectrum; he's certainly got one of the trademark intelligent, patterned ways for it. We try our best not to coddle him. He is, after all, a well-adjusted, high-functioning adult.

Celia asked me if I was on the ASD spectrum, too, once because she finds my handwashing a bit OCD. I don't know. Maybe I am. Maybe everyone is, on some level—we all have our quirks.

We're strangely quiet for a threesome looking to party, but then socializing outside of work is a rarity. The only reason Celia is even here is that it's work-related and therefore an unspoken obligation. We drag ourselves out of the wind and into the lobby and head to the bar, shaking off the icy rain from our drenched hair and coats.

The music is lively. I realize too late it's a Friday evening, the week before Thanksgiving. We're going to get crushed by tourists. I usually prefer the local bars, where you can be certain you won't bump into them. I'm not sure what made me pick the Bowery, except, I am. I should have ignored Celia, I suppose, and the way she said, "Oh, you'll want to go somewhere nondescript and quaint, I'm guessing?"

She thinks that I intentionally play down everything to meet their level, whatever *that* means. It's so far from the truth, I want to laugh.

"You can get *anything* you want. It's so unfair," Celia had said before things got frosty.

Even as a little girl, I was quite aware of how people would look at me. But blessed as I am in that department, there's a difference—isn't there?—between the way others see us and the way we see ourselves. Sometimes, in the mirror, it's as if two girls are staring back at me. The girl everyone sees, and then, lurking behind her, a shimmering mirage only I can glimpse in the reflection, a second girl. A girl on the run from her past. At times, I'm not even certain which of the two girls I am.

Now we're in this ridiculous, flashy place, an odd threesome, conversation awkward and bodies squished, because I'd disliked her tone. My martini cocktail is already half spilled down the front of my very sensible shirtdress, thanks to someone's errant elbow. Standing with remarkable poise and composure to my right at the bar is an all-leg blonde sporting a hugging dress showing off the right attributes and accessories.

My one splurge for my last birthday had been for the only accessory I'll ever need, a watch. A girl always needs to be able to tell the time. Time to eat, time to work, time to run, and time to run away. I'm younger than the blonde, I suspect, but I feel older. No, correction: I feel like an old soul. My eyes mist when I think of the person who used to call me that. I wish he were still around. He was the only person who ever really mattered.

"Are you okay?" Norman asks.

He's good at noting social cues and asking the right questions, but it still takes a kind heart to want to do these tedious things. I want to hug him. For his kindness. But I don't.

"Yes, thanks," I say, holding up my glass. "Here's to the future."

"You'll be a great senior auditor, Sarah," he says, and wipes his glasses, which keep misting up. It's overly warm in here with so many bodies jammed together.

"Cheers," Celia says, clinking my glass with hers. When I see a wan smile stretched taut across her face, I think she's finally come around, but her eyes are two cold, hard pebbles.

AUDREY: THEN
9 MONTHS AGO

I WAKE UP THINKING ABOUT MOTHER. IT'S SUCH A STRANGE SENSATION. I've managed to successfully shut her out for years. Of late, though, she's been creeping up on me, more often than I either like or can handle. I reach for the robe hanging on the side of the mirror stand, shrug it on, and tie my hair into a pile atop my head with a scrunchie. It's been weeks since I last colored my hair; my roots, I'm sure, are starting to show. It's time to do it again. I pout. I hate the chemical smell of it, but it'd be too easy to let things slide. And then where would I be?

"Boo, what's the time?" I've reprogrammed and renamed the smart device from the generic, manufacturer-installed one. He frightens the living daylights out of me sometimes, speaking out abruptly, telling time or announcing the weather like a helpful poltergeist.

"It's 6:12 a.m.," says he, his weird, monotonous tone making me jump.

It's strange how he can be scary but also comforting at the same time. Something I need especially when I'm thinking about my mother shouting at me to get out of bed. When the truth is, I haven't heard her voice since . . . a very long time. I'm in one of those odd moods today when I dread *and* miss that sharp voice, slicing and dicing at me at times, at other times coddling me, *Let me have at least a pint, love, won't you? Please? For me?* And the inevitable raging screech that would follow whether or not I gave in. I rarely did.

Cruel, cruel girl. Can't do such a small thing for me? I've had to put up with your whining shit all these years.

"Get it yourself," I'd said once. I'd just turned ten. I'd shocked her into silence before her face had twisted and reddened with rage.

How dare you talk to me like that? How dare!—

I'd let her shout, threaten, then whimper, then threaten again to have me flung off to foster care, or to throw me out on the streets, until she exhausted herself into sleep. Later, she'd lie in bed, slick with sweat and grease from unwashed hair and skin, too tired, too out of it to wake up. I'd learned early on to recognize the pattern, the oscillation between the strange, spirited exhilaration and the unprompted rage, followed by the inevitable, discombobulated numbness from steeping in alcohol. Often, I found ways to escape her wrath. Sometimes, misgauging her befuddled awkwardness, I wasn't quick enough. Even now, after all these years, I can feel the sting of her backhand or the lashing of her boyfriend's borrowed belt on my skin. The one good, proper meal was when Gramps brought me something. Otherwise, it was week-old toast. Sometimes, nothing at all. Occasionally, her boyfriend would bring a link of sausages and fling them at my face.

"Here, for you," he'd say with that nasty glint in his eyes. Once, I flung them right back at him even though I was so hungry I could eat dirt. His hand went to his crotch, and for a single, stretching moment, I wondered if he was going to unzip his pants. Then, he took off his belt and beat me until I was blue. I'd pleaded with my mother, cried, screamed. I waited for her to jump in to protect me—hit him or throw him off me. The bottle in her hand was empty by the time my cries died. I knew that day that if I didn't get out of there soon, I wouldn't make it into adulthood. To me, she was Barbara from then on—I stripped her of the one thing she was so proud of—her title. She hated it when I called her Barbara.

But, today, I can hear her lingering, threatening, moaning. *Shh*, she used to say when I first began sneaking in a bottle for her in the morning, still pretending everything was fine. *It's our secret.* I've come to loathe that word. *Secret.* Six little letters carrying the implicit consent to something awful, the bargain of trust for gain. A burden that's yours to carry all your life.

"Boo, play 'Yellow Submarine,'" I say, as I head to the bathroom. The thin layer of grime covering me ever since I woke up feels sticky.

"Piping it up now," he says. He's nice sometimes.

Just one pint, love, I hear Barbara again, pleading with me.

"Go away!"

But she doesn't. She sulks in the corner like she once used to, lingering, like the secrets I carry.

My browser announces that the BlinkersOff website has loaded. I trace my index finger over the raised dots on the keyboard keys and log in. The speech-to-text built-in software is handy and tempting, but our group decided, early on, that we would type since most of us needed to practice our braille.

This support group is more than a resource for vision-challenged people from all walks of life; it's a refuge for lonely people, too. There's always someone to chat with. It's a members-only, gated community for visually impaired people to communicate with one another in a safe environment while simultaneously creating a large collection of audio articles members can access. But, like anywhere else, it's difficult to form friendships with big groups of people, so BlinkersOff encourages buddy groups under their banner.

Back downstairs, I switch on the dishwasher while I wait for the kettle to boil. In the background hum of the motor starting and the sloshing of the wash cycle, I make chamomile tea and bring it up to my desk. A tiny smile tugs at the corners of my lips when I think about our little cluster, Hillary, Becca, William, and myself. A murder of blind crows cawing communally, airing and sharing our collective and private grievances.

Sarah thinks my life falls into place by magic, that the tasks I accomplish in a day—waking up, bathing, prepping meals, cooking food, even cleaning—are simple and easy. I can't begin to explain the workarounds I have for these seemingly easy functions, that there's no express lane or quick master class on learning to live blind. Each little task used to be a herculean enterprise. If I didn't remember the mitt before grabbing a boiling pot from the stove, I'd end up with a burned hand, because I couldn't see it boiling. Then, I learned to orient and center myself. The path from the kitchen to the front door, from the front door to the master bedroom, from one end of the house to the other, all carefully mapped and filed away in a folder in my brain, so I won't stub my toe or run into a wall. I've developed a near-precise method for everything.

"Don't you need a cane inside the house?" Sarah asked me last week when she dropped by for no reason.

"No," I'd said. She'd been very impressed, I could tell.

"It isn't a party trick!" I'd wanted to yell once, but I didn't. It took hours upon hours of orientation and mobility therapy so I could tell direction, walk, and climb stairs, but she won't understand. Few people do, and that's what I realized after I joined BlinkersOff. They do. They get me—they get what being blind means.

It's been less than a month since I met Sarah, but when she sits across from me, chatting away as she does, I'm filled with a strange *familiarity*, as though I've known her for ages. When she began showing up at my place, putting up her waterlogged feet on my coffee table, I wouldn't have believed she'd be creating dating profiles for me three weeks later.

"I'm *fine* by myself." My complaint fell on deaf ears.

"That's a sad thing to say!" she said, in the same tone one would admonish a dog to stop chewing your shoe. "Never say it again." And here she is now, on a mission to hook me up to someone like an IV bag, on Bumble, no less, an oddly well-suited name for someone like me.

"Ooh, *he* looks good."

"If he's got a profile photo on, he won't want to meet me." I scrape the bottom of my foot into a small tub with a buffer-filer.

"Why not?" Sarah is sitting up or has changed positions; her sophisticated, spicy yet slightly floral scent flirts with my nose.

She huffs a bit.

"You okay?"

"I'm a bit winded. My stomach has gotten so big I can't see my toes anymore."

My phone buzzes. It's lying on the desk, next to the laptop.

The quality of the vibration changes. I suspect she's picked it up and is holding it in her hand. Among her many other qualities I've been noting since I met her four weeks ago is zero inhibition. And it's fine. I can accept it, as long as she doesn't touch my cane. I couldn't bear it if she laid her hands on it, caressed it, or tossed it carelessly onto the sofa. It'd be the equivalent of caressing or tossing my limb. To be safe, I always put it out of her reach.

"What does the caller ID say?" I ask amid the buzzing. It's on silent. Siri will otherwise announce it after the first ring.

"Sherman, colleague," Sarah says, and hands it to me.

I decline the call and place it back on the desk. "I'll call him back later," I explain, wondering why I feel the need to do so.

"So anyway, why wouldn't this guy want to see you?" *Tap tap.* I imagine she's rapping her nail on my laptop screen.

"Because he's a seeing person. A regular Joe."

The doorbell rings.

"Oh, who is it?" Sarah asks, as though her evening is the one that's been hijacked.

I shrug, then my stomach drops when I remember what I've ordered. A pinch of irritation laces my blood. It had slipped my mind altogether that it was supposed to arrive today. Strange. I never forget things. It's her. Sarah. She distracts me too much, too often.

"Do you want me to get that?" she asks.

"Would you?" My feet are tucked into warm, luscious-smelling pedi-water.

I hear her shoes out the door, to the right on the passageway, then her footsteps trip downstairs before she's on the landing wood floor.

Once I hear the clear click of her shoes on the entryway tile, I pluck my feet out of the water, use the towel on my lap to wipe them with vigor, and spring out of the chair. I reach for my phone on the desk as I hear Sarah opening the front door.

Priya's "Oh!" resounds all the way up here. She's surprised to find Sarah here, in my house, *again*.

My heart begins to race. Surely I should wait to see if Sarah is going to let her in. But what if I don't get another chance?

My ears perk at their low, muffled voices below. I picture Priya standing outside, looking in, Sarah holding the door ajar, not letting her in. It's one of Sarah's tricks, to hold back, make people feel like they're missing out on something. It looks like Priya isn't going to come in after all.

With no time to waste, I search the desk for Sarah's phone, and once I find it, I place my phone next to it, carefully adjusting it the way Sherman taught me to, and pray I'm pressing the right button this time. A small beep alerts me that the app I've deployed is active. Suddenly, I realize it's fallen silent downstairs—I can't hear Priya or Sarah. *Shit.* What if they're on their way up here? I tense, ready to pluck my phone away.

Then I hear them again below.

"—I don't know what you mean," Sarah seems to be saying.

Priya's response to it comes loud and clear. "I think you know exactly what the fuck I'm talking about—"

What in the world? I strain to hear the rest, but it's lost. They've lowered their voices. Or Priya has gone away. I wait for the door to shut but it doesn't. It makes me nervous. As soon as I hear another small beep, a signal that the app has finished its job, I place our phones back the way I found them and rush back to my seat.

Moments later, Sarah says, "Brian and Priya are such an odd couple." From the sound of her voice, she's standing right by me. Too close.

I never did hear the front door shut. Nor did I hear her come back up the stairs. How long has she been standing here? Did she see me hopping back to my chair? Has she noticed that I'm a little flushed, or did she hear the *splat* when I shoved my feet back into the pedi-water? Or, worst, did she see me handling her phone?

"Classic square peg and a round hole," I say, deciding to play it cool, even though my heart is hammering inside my chest.

She agrees readily. I feel bad. Priya and Brian might be a square peg and a round hole, but that's no reason for Brian to be sleeping with Sarah. But then, people don't sleep with Sarah because they don't couple excellently with their partners. They sleep with her because she's irresistible, even in her third trimester.

She's breathing heavily. It's expected after she's climbed stairs, but I think it's more than the exertion. She's furious.

"What did Priya want?" Hints of curry, along with a faint trail of smoke, waft in the air.

"She wanted to drop off a casserole."

"What was all that about, just now?"

"What?" she asks.

"I heard you two arguing."

"It was . . . *nothing*."

Her tone is too clipped for my liking and despite her insistence, I'm certain I've missed something important. If I press her more she'll only further deny it.

"I can't stand the smell of curry these days. It's so perfumy, like potpourri," she says.

Sarah should be the last person to complain about perfume.

"Funny the things that make me want to retch. I thought I'd be done with all this nausea nonsense by my third trimester. Ugh. I need to

IN THE DARK I SEE YOU

pee again. I went like two minutes ago." A door opens. A light ruffle of clothes pulled down, and then the jet stream of liquid hits porcelain. She's in the bathroom.

"There was a delivery bag sitting outside your door by the way. I've managed to drag it into the passage."

"Sarah! You shouldn't be lifting heavy things."

"Nah. It's fine. What is it anyway? The label on top said it's from Hirt's nursery."

I gulp before answering. "It's dirt."

"What do you need dirt for?" she asks, still peeing.

"For the garden?" I hate the tone of question that's crept into my reply.

"What garden? We have like one rectangular patch of concrete."

"Hence the dirt. For plants."

"But it's winter."

I swallow the irritation that bubbles up without warning. She can be so inquisitive, so . . . meddling.

A flush, then water gushes from a spout for a quick hand wash.

"Anyway," she says. The sound of her voice tells me she's taken up her post at the reading chair opposite the bed. "Back to this guy—his name is Sam, by the way." She twitters on, Sam this, Sam that. I'm only half listening. All this talk of dating has me thinking of McKenzie, *again*, because I have been remembering her a lot lately. Those lips . . . that soul-piercing glance that could reduce me to a puddle of melting butter in seconds. I try to ignore these thoughts about her, but it's like plugging one hole in a dam; the water only comes pouring right out of another. So she comes now where I can't stop her. In my dreams. It irks me that Sarah assumes I date only men, but I can't share McKenzie with anyone. And especially not with Sarah. Some things we must keep for ourselves alone.

"You smell of smoke," I say, to distract myself more than her.

Her dismissive laugh fills the room. "Oh, *that!* I took one teensy weensy puff when I stepped out."

I didn't know she smoked. But then, I've only known her a little less than a month, and she's pregnant. Perhaps she's given it up for the baby. I don't say anything, though. If she wants to smoke, that's her business.

I wait until she leaves to call Sherman.

Calling your colleague, Sherman, Siri announces.

"Hey," he says, after picking up on the first ring.

"Everything okay?" he asks. His voice, one of the few I've been able to recognize from the start, is full of concern.

"Sherman, I–I think I've finally managed to do it."

"Plug your phone in," he says.

I connect my phone to my laptop and wait, drumming my fingers over my desk while he remote-accesses it. I've failed twice before, and time, I fear, is going by too fast.

There's a pause. I hear him tapping. "There's a thin veneer of a simple encryption."

"Really?" I worry it's too easy, that there's more to this subterfuge.

"I guess people get complacent. We're in."

I let out a nervous laugh. "I never expected it to work!"

He tsks. "I did," he says.

If this works . . . no, I'm getting too ahead of myself. There's still a long way to go.

SARAH

IT'S BEEN TWO DAYS SINCE DAN HAS BEEN FIRED. I'M A LITTLE HURT HE doesn't want to speak to me, but in his place, I wouldn't want to speak to anybody right now, either.

I steal a look at Norman, his face scrunched up in concentration. It wouldn't occur to him to be devious even if he had the best of opportunities handed to him on a plate. His mind simply doesn't work that way. He's a straight shooter. We all are.

At least, that's what I once thought about Celia, too, that she's on the straight and narrow. I don't know anymore. But Celia aside, I suppose that's what's eating away at me. It's always law-abiding, line-toeing people like Dan and Norman who get into trouble.

I hunch over the spreadsheet, anxiety and annoyance gnawing at me like persistent, gorging mice. I loathe sitting, watching helplessly, being able to do nothing. It makes me want to break things.

I head up the corridor leading to my apartment, my nose twitching with assorted smells of garlic, curry, and rosemary floating about. I turn to tuck the mail into my bag, pluck the key out of the side zipper, and look up just short of bumping into the large, lumpy frame of Mr. D'Angelo.

I pull out an earbud and hold a hand to my chest. "You gave me a fright!"

He laughs, his too-small pearly teeth showing beneath his gummy lips.

"There you are," he says, as though we had a date and I've kept him waiting.

"Yes, here I am," I say.

"Shall we go inside?" he asks cordially. I can't think of a valid reason not to open the door besides the roiling in my gut when I spot his thick, large-ringed fingers.

"Could you?" I say, motioning at him to step aside so I can open the door. His belly brushes my arm as he moves to step back. Bile flushes up my throat. My fingers shake and the key misses the hole a couple of times while sweat begins to bead on my temple despite the frigid, stale corridor air.

I burst into the apartment as soon as I get it open. He follows suit and shuts the door behind him. He steps inside and surveys the apartment. The door didn't close all the way, I notice, relief flooding my veins. "I'm not sure I received an email saying you were going to drop by . . ."

"No. I didn't email. I was passing by and wanted to check in. You did receive the notice saying I'm terminating the lease without renewal?"

"Yes. Yes, my acknowledgment is in the mail. I'll be out before February 2."

His too-tight leather coat strains when he moves to the passageway coat closet. His ears are redder than mine, I notice when he turns to his side, places a hand on the door to the apartment, and whips something out of his pocket. It glints in the overhead light. Is that a switchblade? He appraises me, turns around with determination, and shuts the door.

I gulp and take a step back.

AUDREY: NOW

THE WAITING ROOM OF THE SLEEPY POINT POLICE DEPARTMENT IS MUSTY
and smells of rancid food and stale coffee. The cacophony surrounding
me is like a dull background drone. Someone is demanding to see a detective in charge. Another is moaning about the bail amount. A bell chimes
at the same time a phone rings. Outside, a car peels away and the siren
blares, startling me. What I need is caffeine. To wake up. I'm in ahead
of time. Detective Greene had asked to meet at eight. I was ready at six.
The moment I stumbled over the body, my face buried in the unmoving,
squishy mound, played over and over like a stuck DVD in my head. I
tossed and turned all night, jumping every time the fridge hissed, ice clat-
tered into the bucket in the freezer, the wind battered the windows, or the
air-conditioning kicked on. *Everything* sounded unusual.

"Ms. Hughes?"

Detective Novak's light floral fragrance permeates the stale air.

"Morning, Detective Novak." The skin on my face stretches with my
tight forced smile.

"Morning. We're ready for you. If you'd come through this way,"
Detective Novak says. I unfold my cane.

"Would you like me to take your arm, guide you?"

"No, thanks, Detective, I'll manage on my own."

"We're heading straight down the passageway two doors to the right,"
Detective Novak says. She lets me trail behind her. The telltale *swish-
swish-swish* of my cane on the floor tells me that the hallway is carpeted.
Here and there, a dull *thud*—the carpet has worn down. As other officers
dodge past us, I feel their eyes on me. Sarah once asked how I know

when someone's watching me. I didn't answer. I didn't need to. A woman always knows.

"In here," Novak says. Inside, she guides me by my arm to a chair.

"Are we in an interrogation room?" I fold my cane into my handbag and sit down.

"Yes, we are. How did you know?"

"It smells of sweat and fear."

There's a momentary silence.

"Kidding. It was a guess," I say.

"We don't have separate rooms for interrogation and witness statements here," Novak adds in a light tone.

"Ah, I see. Detective, may I trouble you for a coffee?"

"Sure."

"Hello, Ms. Hughes," Detective Greene says, as the heels of Novak's shoes click away from the room.

"Morning, Detective."

I glance over in the direction of Greene's voice, then look away.

"If I may, how long have you been visually impaired, Ms. Hughes?"

"I had near-perfect vision until a few years ago. And technically, as we're on the topic, I'm not vision impaired. I have *no* vision, as in, NLP. No light perception."

"If I may, how did it happen?"

"A trauma."

Novak walks in. "Here you go," she says and places it in my grasp. "I'd give it a minute. The coffee here is scalding to mask the dishwater taste."

"Thanks."

"What kind of trauma? I was asking Ms. Hughes here what caused her blindness," he adds for his partner's benefit.

"An accident." The faint scar running down my forehead prickles with the reminder. I wish I'd thought to put on some powder or makeup.

"I'm sorry, that's bad luck," Greene says.

"Luck had nothing to do with it," I say, and gingerly sip the coffee. Novak was right. It's awful. But it's piping hot, and the steam makes me come alive.

"And you can't see at all?" Novak asks.

I shake my head. "I was explaining to your partner that I fall under the rare 2 percent category of people who lose vision. I'm completely and permanently blind."

"So, Ms. Hughes. I'd like to go back to last night," Greene says.

I nod, relieved to switch the topic.

"When did you last see Sarah alive?" Detective Novak asks. There's an awkward silence. "Let me rephrase that. What time did you last meet Sarah before you discovered her body?"

The question stuns me for a moment. A reminder that I'll never meet Sarah again. I clear my throat. "About five-thirty."

"And how did she seem? Was she agitated? Happy?"

I pause to consider. "She *was* slightly on edge—had been for a week or so."

There's silence. I can picture the two detectives silently communicating, exchanging pointed glances, or mouthing words to each other.

"And why was that, do you know?"

I shake my head. "I have no idea."

"How well would you say you knew Sarah?"

"I'd like to think I knew her well. But it's hard to say. How well *do* we know people?"

"But you did spend a fair amount of time with her."

"Before Nicole was born, yes. But I've spent more time with Nicole lately."

"How come?"

"Because I babysit her."

"When do you usually babysit?"

"Weekday evenings. Sarah has a yoga and Pilates class at six at the gym. I'm usually done working by five, so I mind Nicole from about five thirty until whenever Sarah is back."

"What time did Sarah usually return?"

"Seven thirty, some days eight. Rarely, and with prior planning, she'd stay out late. Although, that's more recent since the baby has turned five months."

"Did she usually drop Nicole off at your place or did you go over?"

"My place, mostly. It's more convenient for me."

"What time did you go over to babysit yesterday?" It's Novak who asks this time.

I sip on the coffee before answering. "No, I didn't babysit yesterday. I went over, but Sarah said Nicole was already asleep."

"When was that?"

"About five-thirty."

"Did she cancel her plans with you often?"

"No. Rarely."

"So, you met her yesterday afternoon. What about before then?"

"Well, I saw her the day before yesterday. Morning."

"Why was that?"

Is this their usual style, back and forth, a question from each of them, leaving no time to think? "No reason. She just dropped in," I say, after a pause.

"And *you* went over to *her* house yesterday afternoon, is that correct?"

"Yes, Detective Greene."

"Why?"

I sigh. They've only begun with their questions and I'm already tired. "Sarah was supposed to drop off Nicole as usual, but she didn't. She didn't text me, either, so I went over to see her."

"Was it unusual for her not to turn up when she says she will?"

"Yes."

"Do you have any idea why she didn't come over yesterday?"

"No . . . no."

"You don't seem sure. If there's something, you need to tell us. This is a murder inquiry." Novak's tone is curt.

My face grows hot. "It was none of my business but I'm certain Sarah was on one of her dates."

"One of?"

I shrug. "Yes."

"And who had she been dating?" Detective Greene asks.

I shift in my seat. They're watching me, observing every little twitch and quirk.

"I appreciate you want to stay loyal to your friend, but this is a murder investigation. Please let us decide what is pertinent and what isn't."

I nod. "Of the people Sarah dated, I know some random names, of course. Ben, whom she met at the café down the street, and another called Harry. I don't know their last names. But three of the people she saw on and off live on Shore Drive. Ronnie, for one. He lives in the city with his family but visited her whenever he came down to see his mother, Mrs. Kirsch, who lives in No. 13, in the row of townhomes behind mine. Then there's Brian Hunt. He and his wife, Priya Patel, live in No. 10, the corner townhouse on my row. Brian came by quite often to see her."

"When did she usually meet them, and where?" Novak asks.

"From what I could tell, at Sarah's place. Late nights. Brian has insomnia, or at least that's what I've heard."

"Who else?"

I purse my lips. "She was lonely. And she's . . . she *was* raising Nicole by herself. It can be . . . tough."

"You two were good friends," Novak says. But absurd as it is, it sounds as though she's leveling an accusation. The subtext is clear to me: Is that why you're defending her?

"Yes, I suppose we were."

"Ms. Hughes, can you think of a reason why someone might want to kill your friend so brutally?"

SARAH

I TENSE UP WHEN MR. D'ANGELO'S FAT FINGERS REACH TOWARD THE lock on the door. "What are you doing, Mr. D'Angelo?"

Silence. Blood gushes through my body. My ears begin to ring. Where's my phone? I reach inside my pocket, but it isn't there. My eyes dart to the catchall bowl at the entryway where I've tossed it out of sheer habit, and curse silently. Too far. There's no landline. Only a buzzer for the door, which Mr. D'Angelo's large frame is currently blocking. I'm well and truly pinned. There's no escape. There's no balcony with steps I can reach for and yell out. There's one tiny room and Mr. D'Angelo is occupying a large part of it.

I want to scream but my jaw is clamped shut.

"I wanted to . . ." he begins to say, and takes out the object. I cover my mouth and let out a silent scream, as he reaches for the bolt at the top of the door. "Measure this closet. My daughter always complains there's no room to put her shoes and bags. I'm thinking of knocking it out and making it bigger. For her. As a surprise," he adds, bypassing the bolt and steadying one hand with what appears to be one end of a measuring tape. He yanks it across the length of the closet and makes a note on a tiny notepad and pencil he's whipped out from the other pocket.

"Mind if I have a quick look?"

"Knock yourself out," I say, using one of Celia's favorite phrases, and in a tone so like hers that I surprise myself. All that pounding, gushing blood finally calms as though it has found an outlet, and leaves me dizzy.

He opens the door, sticks the end of the tape to the back, and makes a note of the depth. "Aha. As I suspected," he says, looking pleased.

"I can eke out another six to ten inches in both directions."

Good for his daughter, I think, *and for the tenant after her.* It didn't bother me. I only have two coats, two good pairs of shoes, and three bags.

Leaving him to his business, I step into the kitchen area, fill the kettle and set it to boil. I'm about to ask him if he wants tea now that he isn't about to assault me, and jump when I find him standing right behind me.

"Yes?" It's come out sharper than I intended, but really, the man has no respect for personal space. I couldn't bear it if his belly, or any other part of him for that matter, caressed me again.

He does a double take and steps back at the force of my voice. Good.

"I'm sorry to spring the renewal thing on you. I'm aware you had indicated you would be very interested in renewing your lease after the six months, and I preferred that so I wouldn't have to look for a new tenant every time. But—" He shrugs and throws his hands up in the air.

"Where is she now, your daughter?" I ask, my tone softening. Here's a father willing to do anything for his daughter. Not a man about to assault his tenant even if he did threaten to evict me if I don't vacate his apartment on time.

"LA. She thought she could cut it as an actress; took acting lessons but she says it's too tough out there. People are too 'mean.' You kids, can't take a harsh word. But it's a rough world. Cold. I told her, Angel, you gotta learn to deal with these things if you want to work in the industry. But she says she's done and wants to come back. Eh. What's a father to do?" he says, putting both hands up, very Italian-like. Lucky Angel.

"It's no problem. I'll find another apartment soon, I'm sure."

"About that, I was wondering if I could send someone over, say, the first week of Jan? It'll be in the daytime, of course, no disturbance to you. I'll make sure they clean up."

He looks so excited about fixing a closet for that spoiled daughter of his, red-faced, and skin covered in a film of sheen, I don't have the heart to say no even if I don't like the intrusion. Whether or not I'm here is irrelevant. It is my space. But then, it is his space.

"Okay. But please let me know in advance. I can't be opening the door to strangers."

He throws his large head back and coughs. I picture the germs hitting every surface of the kitchen. I wince and turn my head away.

"Excuse me," he says. I think he's about done when he lets out a cataclysmic sneeze. The kettle begins to wail at the same time, and it's as though the kitchen has been struck by a mini explosion.

He whips out a handkerchief from his breast pocket and trumpets into it. It makes my stomach roil once more.

I fold my arms over my chest and wish he'd simply leave.

"I will email you before they come. Don't worry," he says, and pivots on his foot, and retreats to the door.

"Ms. Connelly, thank you for being a good tenant. Your deposit will be returned in full."

"Bye, Mr. D'Angelo," I say, hoping that's the last of him I'm going to see until I move out. The door shuts with a click. A sudden peace fills the room.

Then I remember the sneeze. I fetch a bottle of disinfectant spray and wipe down all exposed surfaces within the radius of that seismic explosion. It's boiled water but I dump it out, give the kettle a good scrub with soap, refill it, and return it to the stove.

Later, I lean my back against the bed's headboard and prop the laptop on a cushion on my knees.

Rachel,
I've heard from my landlord again. I'll have to move out
before February. I know Thanksgiving's around the corner,

but could you send me a list of any apartments available
at the end of Jan or thereabouts? Thanks. Anything like that
last apartment in your previous list would be a bonus.

Thanks,

Sarah

I set aside the laptop to charge and stretch my neck, trying to work
out the kinks in it. I check my phone to see if Dan has replied to my many
messages. And, at last he has.

> Leave it alone, Sarah. There's nothing you
> can do.

I want to shake the stubbornness out of him, but I get his reluctance
to speak, and his reticence, especially if he's been forbidden from discussing the specifics of the layoff.

I circle back around what I know, the little I know, and arrive at the
obvious conclusion. He's a little like me. No, a *lot* like me. He doesn't
have hordes of friends who would stick out their necks for him, or whom
he can lean on. He's alone and now he's stranded.

AUDREY: THEN
9 MONTHS AGO

I'm on the way back from the corner shop when Mrs. Kirsch accosts me.

"You'll never guess what's happened!"

"Hi, Mrs. Kirsch. How are you?" She's one of those who assume I can recognize someone without introduction. I can, but only when I'm paying attention. Moreover, she smells like she usually does, of vinegar and freshly baked bread.

"Devastated, dear. My home was broken into yesterday."

My neck and shoulders tighten. "That's terrible! Are you all right?"

"Yes, I'm fine, dear. I'd been to the city to see Ronnie and when I returned, the door was open. Bob said I'd been brave to go in on my own, but I wasn't going to wait around for the police. What if the burglar was still there? I could have caught them red-handed."

You're lucky you didn't, or you might not be standing here, talking to me. But I don't tell her that.

I flash a sympathetic smile. "Hope you haven't lost anything too valuable?"

"The necklace is gone."

"Oh no!" Everyone knows about her diamond necklace and its lineage, but she explains again in the same words I've heard before: "You know, it belonged to Mendel's mother. They brought it from Germany before the war and hid it in the lining of the coat. It was a miracle that it survived the journey, and now it's gone."

The necklace and its heritage are all Mrs. Kirsch talks of when she invites you over, and invite she does. Not all together so it'd be a party. She asks people over one by one, walking through the same routine and even offering the same biscuits, depending on when she sends out the summons.

"How dreadful! Was it insured?"

"Between you and me," she says, her voice dropping several decibels, "this is only paste. The real one is in a secure locker somewhere—all my clever Ronnie's idea—but still, it's come as quite a shock. You be careful, now."

I nod, too disturbed to smile.

As soon as I get back home, I set the groceries aside and instruct Siri to call Sherman.

Calling your colleague Sherman, Siri says. While it connects, I pace, annoyed at Siri for repeating the same things over and over, but also comforted to learn what I cannot otherwise know; things I once took for granted because I could *see* who I'm calling, or that the call is connecting.

"Audrey," Sherman says, after he picks up on the second ring. My name trips awkwardly from his mouth. "Everything okay?"

"Not really. There's been a break-in at a neighbor's one row behind me, No. 13."

"Shit. Are you okay?"

"Horrified, but otherwise fine."

"What was stolen?"

"Diamonds."

He wolf-whistles.

"It was paste, though."

"Still. I'll see if I can dig up something on it."

"I doubt it, it's too soon."

"No harm in trying," he says.

"True. Any luck with the phone?"

My heart sinks when he doesn't immediately reply.

"I'm afraid not. The info on it is either stuff we already know or just day-to-day things—messages, calls."

"I knew it was too easy."

"We're still sifting through it all. You never know, something may be hiding beneath the seemingly innocent everyday communications."

"I doubt it. It's as we expected. She's being careful."

"Apparently."

"The money can't have disappeared, Sherman. There has to be a trail."

"She will slip up, sooner or later."

He's right, but each day that goes by erodes some of my patience.

It's frustrating to go over it all again, but when stuck, it's always best to go back to the beginning. I start with the camera feed from inside a bank, which then led us outside to an ATM. From there we found a link to a not-so-swanky Midtown hotel. Smart. It's a great way to disappear; blend in with the tourists. It's after this point, here, when the trail started to trickle down to crumbs. There was a wait, we know from the way the hotel stay was extended, one day at a time. Then the crumbs vanished, eaten away by the chaos of a city so large it can swallow someone up. There's a lot of information to sift through, but I concern myself with what I'm good at: bills, credit card statements, and swipe dates. Three years' worth sits in my head in a large folder I access to recount, reposition, and replace.

This, however, is only one of the many client folders in my head, albeit the most often accessed. I take a deep, cleansing breath and make room in my head for today's task for a new client—always exciting. A new client means a new challenge. After sorting the data Sherman emailed me earlier I have the software read out the spreadsheets to me. I work as I always do; absorb it all at first, then go through it all to find the first row or column that doesn't fit.

Everyone in Paradise Townhomes knows about the break-in at Mrs. Kirsch's even though it only happened hours ago. Her son Ronnie is here, kicking up a storm. Her *clever Ronnie*—as she says every chance she gets, because Ronnie invented a particularly clever screw cap for bottle tops, which he patented and made millions from—is frantic about the safety of the neighborhood. He's already sent out flyers to everyone asking to set up a vigilante team, which didn't gain much traction—no one here has that sort of time or patience. But he's secured a community meeting out of it.

"The whole reason I moved to the suburbs is so I wouldn't have to deal with this nonsense, juno?" says an affronted Bob, standing at my door.

I'm not quite sure how the door to my townhome has become the one to knock on when there's something to discuss in the community. Sarah invading my space I can just about handle. But this everyone-over-to-my-place isn't something I'd imagined when I'd moved here. Or ever.

"I couldn't agree more," I say, locking the door behind me.

"Are you going to the meeting next weekend?" he asks, as I uncoil the elastic wrapped around my cane and reach for the black rubber handle. I roll my wrist in opposite directions to unlock the joints of the cane until the tip touches the tactile paving below my stairs.

"I gather this is sort of mandatory, so yeah, I'll be there, although, I do hate community meetings with all my heart."

Bob clicks his tongue. "You and me both. Nothing but complaints. I can't stand people who complain. It's one of the reasons I like you, young lady. You never complain."

"I don't have much to complain about," I say.

"The trail is dark," he warns me.

"I have a flashlight." I wag it at him and wave before I cross over to enter the walking trail, positioning myself on the map I've created of the place inside my head.

"Why do you carry a light?" Sarah asked once when I headed out for a walk armed with one in my pocket.

"So people can see me."

"And how does that help *you*, exactly?"

People are wrong about Sarah. She isn't rude. Her utter forthrightness is something I treasure. People often pussyfoot around me, not knowing the right thing to say or, worse, worrying that what they say might be misinterpreted. It's all quite exhausting. Sarah never pussyfoots.

"Oh, you're blind, aren't you?" she'd asked the first time we met. "Crap. Life must be tricky."

I'd laughed as I always laugh at the innumerable things she says.

"But I've heard the sex is fantastic."

"Pardon? Sex?" I'd asked, and had cringed immediately. "I mean, is it supposed to be fantastic if you're blind? I didn't know."

"It's the lack of inhibition," she'd said.

"I see." I'd felt a little foolish because I hadn't seen. For me, sex had always been a fumbling, sloppy mess, full of inhibition. Experience didn't improve it. It felt worse because by then I'd worked out how it was supposed to feel. Until I met McKenzie, I hadn't even known what an orgasm felt like.

I cross the road, avoid the evil little patch of loose gravel, and sidle around it until my cane strikes gritty asphalt beneath. I imagine it's grown dark even though it's barely six. I can tell from the slowing of the purr and hiss of evening engines and the quiet of green in the center of the road in between the lanes, as it's been since Halloween. The kids won't come out to play until Easter. Seagulls cry overhead. The occasional *click-clack* of my cane is the only other sound apart from the gusty, winter wind kicking up along the Hudson. My hair flies every which way, heavy long strands lashing across my face. The air is crisp and slightly smoggy from chimney smoke. The smell of half-desiccated wet leaves tickles my nose. A fox terrier's bark is sharp in the distance; I'm close to rounding the lighthouse. From the high-pitched whine, it belongs to the Chambers family, though it's always Meghan, their youngest, who walks it.

"Hey, Audrey," Meghan says a moment or two later. I assume she's by the steps leading up to the lighthouse entrance. I often find her there.

As I round the spikes marking the end of the trail, there's a scrape of a bicycle tire and the squeak of a hasty brake all too close. My heart skips a beat. I freeze in place as I've trained myself to do.

"Whoa, lady, are you blind?" someone wheezes, winded from shock or speed. I didn't hear it come, which means he must have been close to flying. It's too dark; he can't see my cane.

"Are you all right?" I ask, willing my pulse to slow.

"Yeah. I'm fine. No thanks to you."

"This is a walking trail, you know. You're supposed to walk your cycle until you head to the park."

"Thanks, *Mom*," he says. The voice is moving away from me. He's back on the bike.

I turn around and head home, thinking of Juno's suggestion the other day that I should get myself one of those bright vests. Perhaps I should have it embossed with *Blind Woman on the Loose* in neon green.

It's colder still now. Dew clings to the evening, and the wind's whipping faster, my mind whirling along with it as I work my way through all the spreadsheets I've consumed this afternoon. The numbers from each row and column flash up one by one in my head. I tally each as I go along until a sum stops me short. It's only off by one digit, but it makes all the difference in the world. I go through it all again to confirm that I've got it.

The thing with mistakes is that they're often a pattern, mostly unintentional. Now I know what I'm looking for, I can work my way back to when the pattern began.

I feel a thrill, like a current, energizing me. Sex may be Sarah's thing, but sorting through information is mine. It's silly, but it fills me with pride to track, trace, map, and locate it in my head. Of greater importance, however, is the ability to recall it all, and that's *my* secret. Only Sarah has come close to working it out. "The things you remember!" she said only this morning when I asked about something quite mundane. Sharpness and presence of mind are incredible qualities, and when present in someone like Sarah, it's a superpower, too. It's also a little frightening. She enjoys playing dumb, I think she gets off on it, but underneath it all, Sarah is smart. More than once, I've been overcome by an odd sensation that she can see past me; that she can see *through* me.

Perhaps it's only my imagination working overtime. Sarah isn't the sort to keep quiet once she knows something, especially if it's to her advantage. No. I shouldn't worry so much. I should learn to relax a bit, as Sherman says. But dropping my guard isn't easy, and it can prove more than careless. It could become dangerous.

It's only after I've walked past my townhome that I realize I've been distracted. I've missed all my cues: the rosemary bushes bordering the first townhome, then the boxwoods outside Juno's house, then the twinkling and clanging of the wind chimes I've strung up outside mine. Myrtle borders the steps to Sarah's townhome. My feet have caught in the tangled vines enough times for me to automatically sidle to the right of the pavement when I near her house. I stop and put out my hand, wrapping my palm around the curved wrought-iron railing going up to No. 5. I've stopped in the nick of time. A few more steps and I'd have been facedown in the creeping green.

I turn around and walk a few steps, reaching for my home's smooth balustrade, the reassuring clanging of my wind chimes flying in the squall reaching up from the water. If I hadn't been thinking of Sarah, I'd never have missed it. She's distracted me again and she's not even here.

I try not to let it get to me too much because it works both ways. She is equally distracted by me. A quick ruse to send her to the kitchen and by the time she was back, I'd already taken her house key from her bag and pressed it in the tiny but clever little pad I'd hid in my palm, and returned the keys to her bag.

SARAH

SOMETHING HAS BEEN GROWING, FESTERING EVER SINCE I SPOKE TO Dan. He sounded *off.* He's just been fired, so it's not that surprising. But there's more, and I suspect it's something awful. I've pushed him as hard as I can, but he won't tell me anything.

All he had to say was, *Leave it alone, Sarah. There's nothing you can do.*

That's where he's wrong. He doesn't know me, the real me. Telling me there's something I can't do is like a dare. An itch I'll do anything to scratch. So I've decided I'm going to help him even if he doesn't want my help. All day, I've been trying to work out how to go about it.

What I need first is information. Resorting to hacking is a little extreme, but without Dan I'll have to find it myself, assuming Fortitude hasn't already blocked him from accessing his email and documents. It'd be stupid to use my computer or phone to do it, which leaves me with one obvious choice.

I throw furtive sideways glances at the clock on the back wall until at last it's five-fifteen. Norman, as always, is the first to leave. I usually leave next, and the last to leave after Ted is Celia. I've only stayed late once before, when we had the filing incident and all of us, including Mr. Tcheznich, were here until midnight to sort out the mess. So Celia won't be easily fooled if I linger here without an adequate reason to do so.

I peek at her from under my lashes. The vein in her temple is throbbing. I stand up to head to the printer, and one step in, there's a high-pitched whine followed by a *poof* sound and my screen goes blank. When I turn back, the green blinking light on my CPU has gone red.

"Dammit!" I turn around and sit back, making a show of trying to decipher what the problem could be.

"What is it?" Celia is at my side within seconds.

I swear softly.

"What?" she asks. Her face is full of concern.

"I've pulled out the power cord by mistake and the computer shut down before I could save the spreadsheet." I try my best to look dismayed.

"That's all right," she says, solicitous, "there'll be a copy of all your work in the database."

"Normally," I say, looking sheepish, "but I created a file on the local hardware."

"But . . . we never do that. It's like file-saving 101. Always create files in the folders that get automatically backed up!"

Her coffee breath is right on me. I'm slightly nauseated by it, but I don't move my chair back.

"I know," I say in a nasally whiny tone, rightfully abashed. I dart a glance at the clock. "Tch. I'll take care of it tomorrow."

"Is it for RA?" A strange expression is etched on her face.

I nod. As I'd expected and hoped, she points out that Royal Assets and Investments are over in Asia, and in just a few hours when it's still night here, in New York, it'll already be the next morning for them. She shakes her head. "You'd better get it done now," she says, going back to her desk.

"I . . . can stay and help," Norman says.

"That's so kind, Norman, but I don't want to hold you up. I'll be fine, thanks," I say. The corners of my eyes prickle. Norman lives farthest away; if he misses his bus, the next one is hours later, and he'll miss the connection as well.

"Okay," he says. "I'm leaving now."

"Bye, Norman," Celia pipes up.

She sighs as though I've landed a massive problem on her shoulders. "Do you want me to stay? I mean, I have plans, but I can change them."

I shrug and offer her a delighted smile. "Could you?"

Those who don't know Celia as I do might mistake the glint in her eye for irritation. However, I'm not taken in. It's schadenfreude. It makes her happy that I need help. But it makes her happier that I've fucked up. At last, she has a hold over me. She isn't like that with everyone. I've seen her perfectly nice side as well, but there's something about me that brings out this thirst for vindication in her.

"Even half an hour will do. Could you go over the purchase invoices, and I can go over the rest."

"Okay," she says, her tone heavy. It's Thanksgiving week. She wants to be home early.

Phone in hand, she trudges into the breakroom from where I hear a muffled conversation. I rush over to her chair where her bag is hanging, whisper a *sorry* into the ether, and check the side pockets and the zippers.

"C'mon, c'mon," I mutter as I slip my hands into the nooks and crevices of her office purse and my fingers brush everything except keys. Her heels click as she makes her way back from the breakroom and I'm about to rush to my seat when I clock the keys sitting right beside her hat on her desk.

I'm back in my seat seconds before she can spot me.

"It's rebooting now. The invoices are in the first folder," I say.

"I can only stay fifteen minutes," she says, pulling her chair closer to her desk and putting on her glasses. I begin the motions of opening various folders containing checkbooks, sales receipts, bank statements, tax returns, and inventory records. The time flies all too soon and I hear Celia's chair roll back on the linoleum flooring.

"I managed to get about half of it done," she says, her mouth a flat line.

"That's very helpful and I appreciate it," I say with a warm smile.

She nods, but a slight frown worries her brow. She isn't quite convinced. I worry when she lingers for a few moments. But then she grabs her things and heads out.

The door clicks shut, then the upward whoosh of the elevator being called. I wait until the ding, and to be safe, an additional ten minutes. In case she's forgotten something and returns.

The temperature can't be over sixty-five; it's always cold in the office but a bead of sweat is making its way down my back under my blouse. As soon as the office clock ticks to five-fifty, I clutch the keys that have been burning a hole in my hand ever since I grabbed them and head to the boss's office.

If Mr. Tcheznich returns, I'm screwed. I've no excuse to be here. An urgent awareness fills me. Whatever I do, I should do it quickly and get the hell out of here.

People are so careless. Take Mr. Tcheznich, for example: His computer's username and password are stuck to the monitor. Even the seventy-year-old doddering cleaning lady could log in if she wanted to and she doesn't speak English.

Dan is usually meticulous, but all it takes is one instance, a single, careless moment. A few weeks ago, we were at a café, grabbing a quick lunch together. He went to fetch a bottle of water, his laptop screen left open on our table. All the details were right there. Work email password, server log-in username, and password. I didn't mean to see it; it was a swift glance, but here we are.

I attach a USB and launch a VPN. Once the VPN kicks in, I pull up the website for Fortitude Trading and navigate to the employee login. I say a prayer to my teacher before entering Dan's username and password. All the skills I learned seem so long ago, rusty from languishing unused in my mind.

I sit, tense, hoping the login works, that they haven't had the time yet to lock him out. My eyes widen with disbelief when it connects, and the landing page loads. I'm in! I can't believe my luck, but I dare not linger. After a swift glance at the various links, I hit the email tab and pull up all the emails from the day before he was fired. Standard emails a payroll department employee's inbox might have; meeting invites, inter-departmental info requests, two from me, another about signing a card for a surprise birthday of a colleague, an appeal to contribute to a charity Fortitude Trading supports so their team meets the quota and can win the raffle, where the whole team is cc'd.

Nothing suspicious jumps out at me from the emails; nothing hinted at, no code or covert talk to anyone within the company. As I work back to the day he was fired and from my email to Dan, it appears from the time stamp as though he was summoned to the boss's office while he'd been replying to me. There's an unsent draft saved in his inbox, addressed to me. It all looks fine. Ordinary.

I go to the company news tab to see if Dan is mentioned anywhere. It's as I expected; his departure has not made news within the company. The time on my watch says six-fifteen. Time flies when you're doing something illegal.

I'm about to switch off the lights when I hear footsteps in the main corridor outside the office. I jab the power button, disconnect, pluck out the USB, and leg it back to my desk.

There's a knock on the door. I freeze. My heart thuds away at a sickening pace.

If it's Mr. Tcheznich and he goes into his office, he'll find his computer still powering down, and the CPU warm even if the screen is off. And he'll know it was I who used his PC. There's no one else here.

AUDREY: NOW

"Ms. Hughes, can you think of a reason why someone might want to kill Sarah?"

Though I've been expecting this question, I'm stunned to hear them ask it. The weak, now lukewarm coffee turns bitter in my mouth.

"No," I say to the detectives, "I don't know why someone would want to kill her."

"How close were you two?"

"We were friends, I guess. She came over a lot, we hung out."

"Did you fall out with her recently? Any fights or arguments?"

"N-no. We didn't fight."

"Are you sure about that?" Greene asks.

"A neighbor overheard an argument you had with the victim two nights ago," Novak says.

I cock my head to one side. "Then they are mistaken."

"If you say so."

"I *do* say so, Detective Novak. I told Sarah I couldn't babysit Nicole anymore. She's getting too big, you see. I won't be able to keep up with her without being able to see her. She agreed, with obvious reluctance because Nicole is used to me. That's it. It was a discussion. Not an argument."

"You'd be surprised at how little it takes to commit murder," Greene says.

Audrey scoffs. "You think I would kill Sarah over something so silly?"

"Did you?"

"No! I did not."

"Ms. Hughes, Audrey, were you jealous of Sarah?" Novak's voice is gentle, goading.

"Jealous? I'd never been jealous of *her*."

"That's not what we've heard."

I sit back, relax my arms, and train my eyes to where they sit.

"And what have you heard?" I ask.

"That she was popular, a little *too* popular. I could understand if it got to be too much. Being in the company of someone so attractive, so *wanted*, can't have been easy."

"Of course not!" I remind myself that it's their job to bait me, to make me say things I'll regret. I shake my head. "Sarah liked going out, she liked being the center of attention, and, yes, she was popular, but I wasn't jealous. Each to her own."

"So you didn't fly into a jealous rage and kill her?"

"No, Detective Novak. I did not. Look, do I need a lawyer?"

"Why? Do you think you need one?" Novak counters.

"I'm asking *you* that. You seem to be questioning me under the guise of a witness statement. You haven't read me my rights. You haven't offered me the chance to protect myself."

"This is a murder investigation. We're allowed to ask any number of questions that get us the answers. People who have nothing to hide generally don't ask for lawyers. You went over to the victim's house twice on the day she was murdered. And you were overheard arguing with the victim on two consecutive days, including the day she was killed. It might be better if you told us everything you know now. What did you and Sarah argue about yesterday afternoon?"

I'm stunned into silence for a moment. Then I clear my throat. "Who said I argued with her yesterday?"

"You were overheard."

"That's not possible. I didn't argue with her. I'm not prone to having arguments."

"You're arguing with us now."

I smirk. "I'm protesting my innocence. There's a difference."

"What time did you leave Sarah's place yesterday afternoon, when you went over and didn't argue?" Greene asks.

I purse my lips and glare, so to speak, at Greene. "About five-forty, or five-forty-five. I was only there for ten, max fifteen minutes."

"What did you and Sarah talk about?"

I wish I could stop them from ambushing me like this. I could stand up and leave, refer them to the lawyer Aegis will be happy to provide, but no. The detectives are right. It's in my best interest to answer their questions, even if they are annoying and persistent.

"Ms. Hughes?"

"I asked her why she hadn't dropped off Nicole. She said she had other plans and that Nicole was already asleep."

"Did she say what these plans were?"

I shake my head. "No."

"It took fifteen minutes to say why she hadn't dropped off Nicole at your house?"

"First of all, she took ages to open the door. And when she did, she seemed distracted. It took forever to get answers out of her."

"And when you left her at five-forty-five, was Sarah Connelly alive?"

"Yes! She was *very much* alive."

"You said you knew of at least three people with whom Sarah used to hook up with on Shore Drive. Mr. Ronald Kirsch, Brian Hunt . . . who are the others?" Novak asks.

"Matt. Matt Chambers, from No. 19, and possibly Jack Dodson, who's in No. 7, but that's only a guess," I say, relieved they've moved on from me. "Matt lives next door to Mrs. Kirsch."

"And how do you know Sarah was seeing Mr. Chambers?"

"I've heard him, over at hers. He has a distinct voice," I add.

"And was she seeing them all at once?"

"How do you mean?"

"Was she dating them all at the same time, or one after the other?"

"She . . . alternated. It depended on availability and opportunity, I suppose. But she wasn't partial to seeing them exclusively if that's what you mean. But that's not—"

"And she stopped seeing all of them recently?" Greene interrupts.

I wish I could steer the conversation to show them the real Sarah—the Sarah I knew. Right now, everything I'm telling them is painting Sarah in the worst possible light because the truth of it is that people judge. Even a victim isn't exempt. "That's the impression I got, Detective Greene. But I couldn't tell you with absolute certainty. I stopped hearing their voices in her house. She could have easily met them elsewhere."

Novak sighs as though this conversation is irking her.

"How long have you known Sarah Connelly?"

"Nearly ten months."

"And when did you move into No. 4 Shore Drive?"

"About ten months ago."

"So, you've known Sarah from the time you moved in?"

"Pretty much."

"Where did you move from?"

"The city. I used to live in Manhattan."

"And your decision to move away?"

"Too noisy. Too busy. Too . . . everything. I like it here. It's quiet. I can hear myself think."

"Sleepy Point is, well, its namesake," Novak says. "Apart from the usual teen drug issues or your average theft or gas station holdup, nothing serious happens here. That's why this is all so confounding."

"And murder is a very serious crime," Greene says.

"Crime is so often thought of as something that happens to others. May I ask, how did she . . . what was it that killed Sarah?"

"We're still waiting to confirm that."

"What is it you do for a living, Ms. Hughes?" Greene asks.

"I'm an accountant."

"With?"

"A private firm."

"Does it have a name?" I'm suddenly reminded of Sarah. She'd asked me this very question once.

"Yes, Detective Greene. It's called Aegis."

"Must pay well," Greene says.

"I can't complain. I'm well compensated. They pay me enough. I don't have to cash a disability claim every month."

"Oh, I'm sure they pay more than that. That's a fine townhome you live in, with a fancy clubhouse and luxury facilities."

"It is, isn't it? I had a shoe cupboard studio in Manhattan. When I found this house, I couldn't stop myself."

"Back to last night; were there no sounds other than the baby crying at eight-thirty?"

I'm tired and hungry, but I'm the one who found Sarah and they need answers.

"I had music on last night. It was only when I went into the closet that I heard Nicole crying."

"You didn't hear Sarah's back door or garage door opening or closing?"

"No."

"What about later, when you went over, did you hear anything at the time?"

"No. Well, Nicole was crying but I didn't hear anything else."

"You didn't mention the spilled wine when we first spoke yesterday," Greene says.

"I did!"

"Not at first."

"I-I didn't think it was important." Then, after a pause, I add, "It's embarrassing, okay?"

"Are you sure you spilled wine, then changed out of your clothes and stopped by next door and not the other way around? That it was upon your return from Sarah's house that you changed?"

"Yes, I'm sure. It happened the way I said it did. You have the clothes I'd been wearing when I found Sarah."

"You said Nicole kept on crying for a long while?"

"Yes, Detective Novak. She cries often when it's bedtime. I thought she would settle down, as she does. Later, when I went to change out of my blouse, I heard her screeching, and it sounded like she'd been crying rather a lot. That's when I decided to go over."

"If Nicole cries often at bedtime, why did you check on her last night in particular?" Greene asks.

"She's an infant with colic. She's always crying. I went over because I thought Sarah could do with some help or a couple of minutes' break. It can be overwhelming to care for a baby all the time."

"So, you went over at about nine . . ." Greene says.

I'm in a time loop! Just when I think I'm done, they shove me down a wormhole and I'm back at the starting line again.

"I know we've been through this before, but I need to go over it many times, I'm afraid," Greene adds.

I nod. "I understand." I recount it all over again like a script. I went in, tripped, found Sarah, and dialed 9-1-1.

"What did you do while you waited?"

"Nicole was still crying, so I went upstairs to find her."

"Upstairs?"

"That's where the sound was coming from."

"And where was Nicole?"

"I found Nicole in the master bedroom, on the bed, strapped in her car seat. I mentioned that last night to the officer on scene and later to you."

"Did Sarah often leave Nicole upstairs by herself?"

"No. Only when Nicole was asleep. And she always had the baby monitor."

"Sure," Novak says. There's something in her tone I don't much like.

"Detectives, you'll hear lots of things about Sarah, but she loved Nicole to bits. She . . . she was a good mother."

"What was Sarah like?"

"*Like*, Detective Greene?"

"Give us a gist of who she was."

"She was just one of us, you know?"

"How you mean?" Novak asks.

"That she was just like any one of us in the community. And she was a new mother, trying to manage her life the best way she knew. She was a good friend . . . in her own way."

"Do you know where Sarah worked before she began her consultancy?" Greene asks.

"She used to be in insurance, she said once."

"Have you met any of her *fashion consultancy* clients?" Novak asks.

From the way Detective Novak says it, it's plain she doesn't believe Sarah was ever a consultant. "No. I haven't."

"You've never heard one of her clients over at hers? Did she ever mention any names?"

"No. By the time I met Sarah she was heavily pregnant; she wasn't working much, or at all."

"And do you know if she had any other income?"

"I don't."

"Rich family?" Greene asks.

"Honestly, I don't know."

"Have you ever met Nicole's father?"

I shake my head. "I don't even know who he is."

"Sarah never mentioned him?"

"No, Detective Novak. She didn't."

There's a knock. A chair scrapes and there's a low conversation at the door.

Footsteps return to the room. "Well, thank you for your time, Ms. Hughes," Greene says.

"Of course. Are you . . . done?"

"For now. Though, we will have more questions soon. The investigation has only begun."

"I understand." I heave myself out of the stiff-backed chair.

"I'll show you out," Novak says. From the sound of her footsteps, I assume she's waiting by the door.

My cane out, I take a couple of steps. There's a light scrape and I run straight into a chair. I stumble, hurtling forward, and crash into Novak.

"I'm sorry," I say, winded, to Novak. She steadies me and hands me my bag, which fell when I flailed.

"No, *we're* sorry," Novak says, after a brief but awkward pause. "We should have made sure the path was clear."

"No problem," I say, recovering.

They walk me outside, to the cab I've left waiting. As I get in, the wind carries the detectives' voices.

"What's wrong with you? Why would you be so cruel?"

I'm wondering what she means when Greene replies, "I suppose I wanted to make sure she *is* blind. It's uncanny, the way she looks at you when she's talking, as though she can see you."

I scoff and climb into the cab. When I got up from the chair, I'd been certain from the click my cane had made that the path ahead was clear. The chair had materialized in front of me as though out of thin air. I thought *I'd* messed up, misinterpreted the new, strange sounds. But no. Detective Greene slipped the chair right in my path.

He tripped me on purpose.

SARAH

"Hello?" someone says. Mr. Tcheznich's CPU is still whining like a tired puppy. I note with a gulp that I've left the light on in his office.

"Hello?" they call out again. I sag into my chair when I recognize it as belonging to Arnie, the security guard.

He opens the door a crack and sticks only his large round head in through it, like a floating cake pop.

"Hi, Arnie."

"I saw the lights on," he says.

I smile and say nothing.

"Working late?"

"Yep, but I'm almost done."

"Be sure to lock up now," he says, and walks away.

"G'night," I call out to his receding footsteps. There's tapping. I look down to find my hand is shaking and the key I took from Celia is clanging against my desk. I put it back where I found it and lock up behind me.

I'm tempted to message Dan and demand that he tell me everything that's happened, but I fear it won't go over very well. I turn the little I know in my head while I trudge toward the Brooklyn Fare to pick up a sandwich.

Rather than wait for the next M11, I decide to walk home, using the time to exercise my head; take it on a run, so to say. Before Dan, I used to work with his predecessor, Kelly, until she moved on to another department. I don't miss her. I was happy when Dan took her place. He's more detail-oriented than Kelly, something I admire, and it's no wonder we became fast friends. By the time Kelly transferred, it was plain even to her that Dan and I got along better than she and I ever did.

I'm on 21st Street, my thoughts so focused on Dan that I crash into someone. We both say, "Sorry!" catch our breaths for a second, and walk on. He must be a tourist. A New Yorker wouldn't apologize. They simply don't have the time. At the crossing on Ninth Avenue, I wait for a stream of cars to pass by. Across the street, a shop door opens and a woman walks out, hand in hand with a man. I look away but am drawn back to her when she laughs. My eyes widen when I realize it's Kelly. It feels strange, as though my thoughts conjured her here.

The traffic slows and I cross at the same time as they flag down a passing taxi. Head down, I throw a discreet glance. She leans in to him for a quick peck before they name the destination and get in.

As I near my building, it strikes me how different Kelly looks, how radiant. I should be glad for her, I think, climbing up the gray steps awash under the cool low-wattage overhead light. Perhaps she's finally found her niche in her new role. But somehow it annoys me that a person like Kelly has managed to find a comfort zone, maybe even happiness, when someone like Dan, who deserves the best, is in such a fix right now.

Back home, I set water to boil, pluck an Earl Grey from the box of tea, and drop it into a mug. It's hard to fire people these days. They would have had to have a reason beyond question for such a drastic measure. And that doesn't bode well. If this goes further and they sue him, which I assume they will—why else would he have lawyered up so fast?—it could ruin Dan. He'd never be able to get another job, well, not in his field anyway.

A high-pitched whistle brings my mind back to tea. I saunter over to the sofa with my steaming mug, the sandwich on a plate, and flick the channels on my streaming device, mindless. *Gladiator* is playing on some channel, and I watch it for the umpteenth time, distracted. I know all the dialogue by heart. I say the lines along with the actors for a while and then give up.

Rachel hasn't yet replied. February isn't far away.

"What is with you, today?" Celia asks. I should've known she'd be watching me this morning, especially after last evening's fiasco. I've been throwing a nervous glance at Mr. Tcheznich's office since morning. I'm terrified any second now he's going to come barreling out the door and order me into his office for a confrontation. I've never broken into anywhere in my life before, let alone hacking into our client's account. Last night I'd felt like it was the right thing to do, even though for a moment, when Arnie put his head through the door, I thought I was doomed. This morning, in the cold, pale sunlight streaming in from the passageway window, I can't believe what I've done. Knowing how to do a thing isn't the same as doing it. I've never *needed* to hack before, but having the skills and using them are quite different things.

"I might be coming down with something." I also can't stop this dirty feeling from climbing up my legs that if I don't think up some plausible excuse or distraction, Celia will catch me out. I'm not the only clever one in this office. And today, for some peculiar reason, she's watching me more than usual. Drops of cold sweat bead on my forehead.

Midday, I look up to find Mr. Tcheznich's shadow on my computer.

"In my office, if you please," he says, crooking a finger, beckoning me.

Blood drains away from my face. I bumble into his office, sick to my stomach. He closes the door behind me and shuts the blinds.

AUDREY: THEN
8 MONTHS AGO

Jason is brutal today, fooling me into doing rep after rep. "Last one, Auds, then you can take thirty." And I fall for it each time.

"Hey, you."

I nearly drop my dumbbell when I hear Sarah's voice, here, in the gym. "W-what are you doing here?" Heat creeps up my neck when my tone comes out indignant and embarrassed.

"I thought I'd catch a quick swim."

The energy in the room has changed. The runners and cyclists have all slowed. All eyes, I can sense, are on Sarah. I picture her in her tank and maternity tights. *The ones that make my butt look like two just-baked buns,* she claims without a hint of humility. Some of the people here, I'm sure, will add swimming to their routine today.

"I'll catch you later." I leave her to her fans and return to pressing a dumbbell up and over my shoulder in reps to improve my triceps. Jason is happy. "Yes! That's it!" he says, as though my triceps have jumped up and high-fived him.

I head home after a quick shower, an odd irritation rippling through me. This is *my* time, *my* space, and to be upstaged by her, in the one place I'm impregnable, feels invasive somehow. By the time I arrive at my door, I'm simmering with a strange energy.

So much so that I almost don't notice that my door is open.

I would never forget to lock up. I push the door back and take a tentative step, nerves tingling. Two paces in, I stumble over something. My outstretched fingers flex, then bend against the back wall of the passageway. After I'm upright, steady, I put my hand out to the large protruding object on the floor. Angular edges and a soft cushion on top. It's the entryway bench.

"But why should it . . ." I mumble to myself, then clap a hand over my mouth, remembering the break-in at Mrs. Kirsch's. I'm about to step inside to look for signs of an intruder when a thought comes to me. What if the intruder is still in here? The air rushes out of my lungs all too soon, leaving me light-headed and winded at the same time. I need to move but my legs refuse to cooperate. As if in slow motion, I grab my bag and step out. Then, I turn around and lock the door, turning it twice to engage the double latch. If the intruder is still inside, they will need an extra beat to undo the double lock. It's a special technique; they will have to twist the knob left, then right to undo it. Of course, as an intruder, they might be familiar with it, but I do it anyway. Then I scramble clumsily, weaving my cane about until I'm two doors down and knock on Bob's door.

I hear his feet down the steps. He flings the door open and greets me with surprise.

"Is everything okay?"

"No, it's not. Someone's in my house," I say.

"Did you call the cops?"

"No, I've come straight here."

"Hang on," he says. I hear his heavy, lopsided footsteps back up the stairs. The sound of doors opening, closing, then footfalls on the steps again.

"Let them try getting out with this pointed at them," he says, slamming the door shut behind him.

My jaw falls open. "Are you carrying a gun?"

"Yes, now come on."

We march back to my house. "Shh," he says, pulling me to a stop. "Stay here."

"But it's locked. Here," I say, digging into my pocket for the keys.

"Dial 9-1-1."

I nod, wondering if he's still facing me or if he can even see me. "Be careful," I say anyway.

"9-1-1, what's your emergency?"

By the time the cops arrive, Bob's ascertained that there's no one in the house.

Of course, the police want to see things for themselves. They introduce themselves as patrol officers Riley and Rodriguez, then ask us to wait in the living room while they conduct their search.

"You wanna go 'round the back, Riley? I'll start upstairs," a woman with a faint Latino accent says.

"Yep," comes the reply in a slightly nasal, deep tone.

After they're done with the sweep, they cross-check things with each other in low voices in the kitchen before joining Juno and me in the living room.

"There's no one here," they announce. That much is obvious. What kind of idiot breaks in and stays put until the cops show up? Still, it's comforting to hear them say it.

"I told you he's gone," Bob tells them.

"And you are . . . ?" Riley asks.

"A neighbor. Bob Cane."

"I'm assuming you have a license for that," says Rodriguez. I picture her pointing to Bob's gun.

"Of course," Bob says.

"You should have waited for us," Riley says.

"What if he was still in here?" Bob counters.

"That's *why* you should have waited," Riley says.

"So, I should have let Audrey come in by herself?" Bob asks. He can be formidable when he wants to. The army captain in him can't help but peek out once in a while.

"Excuse me," I say. It's absurd, as though this is Bob's house and I'm the visitor.

"And you are?" Riley asks, again. I wonder if he's the junior of the two. I find senior officers like to stand back and observe while the newbies ask all the elementary questions.

"I'm Audrey Hughes. This is *my* house."

"Ms. Hughes," Rodriguez says. I turn in the direction of her voice. "Tell us everything from the start."

I give them a blow-by-blow rundown until the moment they arrived.

"And you didn't see anyone?" Riley asks.

Of course, my cane is still in my bag. Bob shifts beside me.

"I wish I could've, but I am blind—as in I can't see; I have no vision." People are prone to assuming that *I'm blind* is merely a turn of phrase, so sometimes I add the jargon.

There's a pause. No one knows what to say, but then, it's expected; I'm not uncomfortable.

"Why did you think there was a break-in?" It's Riley who asks.

"Because I never leave my door unlocked. Or wide open, for that matter. And the entryway bench had been moved. I stumbled over it."

"There's no way you could've moved it yourself . . . and you know, forgotten?" Riley again.

"Are you sug—"

"No, she wouldn't—" Both Bob and I have spoken at the same time.

"Are you suggesting there's been no break-in?" I ask.

"We won't know until you tell us if something has gone missing. After all, that's the primary reason for a break-in."

I nod. "Fine. I'll check," I say, getting up. "Bob, coffee and tea are on the top right shelf of the high cabinet. Put the kettle on and make yourself a cup if you want."

"Thanks, Audrey, but I'm fine," he says. He's upset. I can tell. I feel bad for having dragged him into all this. I can't figure out why I knocked on his door in the first place.

Rodriguez walks around the house with me as I take stock.

"Anything worth stealing in here?" she asks, standing in my bedroom.

"A silver-plated paperweight should be sitting on the small round table in the corner."

"Yep, it's here," Rodriguez says.

We count off more things. Rodriguez walks beside me, talking at me, asking me invasive, private questions. I sort through my stuff, haphazardly, frazzled.

In the study, I check for the things that matter most, work and personal laptops. Everything else is either dispensable or replaceable.

"So, anything missing?" Rodriguez asks.

We're in the closet. She's running her hands over the hanging clothes, my handbag, and shoes. I want to ask them to leave, and I would if it hadn't been me on the phone half an hour ago, begging someone to come over.

"I guess not."

She doesn't reply. I know what she's thinking: How would I know?

"As far as I can tell, nothing appears to have been taken. I'm afraid I won't know until I need it, whatever it is, and find it's gone."

"You're very organized," she says. Her soft voice rings out from right behind me.

I flinch and turn around to face her. "That, I'm afraid, has nothing to do with blindness. I've always been organized."

She falls quiet. I picture Officer Rodriguez's eyes roving, noting the clothes arranged in color-coded order.

Sarah noticed it straight away. She tried to convince me to rearrange everything based on their use, but I refused point-blank.

"I have a system, Sarah, and it works, so leave it alone."

I've never been so stern with her; from her plaintive silence, I think she was taken aback, but there was no rancor later.

These are, after all, our private choices. The thought brings to the fore the niggling sensation I've had ever since I found the door open. I stifle a gasp that's arisen in my throat. How could I have been so stupid? It should have been the first thing I thought of when I walked in and realized someone had been inside my house.

"What is it?" Rodriguez asks.

"Nothing. A frog in my throat," I say, suddenly annoyed at the presence of three people in my home when all I want now is for them to leave.

We join her colleague, who's chatting with Bob, in the living room.

"Other than the open door, there are no signs of a break-in, miss," Riley says. "Are you sure you had locked it?"

I don't answer the same question a second time. I look up at him, at where he's standing.

"If Audrey says she locked it, she locked it, juno?"

"Look," I say, stamping down the impatience starting to rankle me, "thanks for your help. Now, if that's all . . ."

"Until you report something missing, there isn't much we can do." It's Rodriguez this time.

I nod. "I understand."

"Breaking and entering isn't a crime?" Bob asks.

"Of course it is, but can you prove it? There's no camera around, so we can't see someone in the act. You say your door was open but when Bob here came to assist you, he found the door locked. You could well be making this up."

Silence.

Beside me, Bob's mountain-shouldered, stocky frame twitches. He's working up to give them a piece of his mind, but I beat him to it.

"You think I made this up?"

"Wouldn't be the first time someone's done that," Riley says.

"People do forget things," Rodriguez says.

I want to explain that I don't. I can't. Even if I want to, I can't forget things. Before I lost my vision, I used to have a photographic memory. Eidetic memory, someone had said. I knew it was rare. My mother had laughed and called it idiotic memory. I could remember everything I've ever seen, minute details that other people do not notice, like the fine print, or a byline in a paper. I could recall every detail. I never told anyone, especially in school, or they'd have pegged all my success to merely this ability.

It was strange for a while after I lost my vision. There were no images for my brain to scan. A low panic coils inside me when I remember those initial days, with no confidence to do anything. Without vision, without being able to make and keep the memories in my head, I'd assumed my life was over. In some bizarre trick of fate, or more likely, nature's compensation, my ability to track my vision, to recall everything I've seen, somehow transferred to other senses. I recollect other things now, smells, exact conversations, with utter clarity. Mundane details like which program is on which channel, and of course numbers.

Even without revealing this detail about myself, the officers think I'm weird enough. People don't like surprises, so I act the way I'm expected to act—as a bumbling nitwit.

"That's a lot of help, thanks very much," Bob says.

They take his sarcasm as a cue to leave.

"It's fine, Bob. Thanks for coming, officers, and for your help."

"Such as it is," Bob says under his breath.

"I know this must be frustrating, but there isn't much we can do at this point." Riley sounds annoyed now, like I've wasted his precious time.

"What about the other break-ins?" I ask, as we all head to the passageway.

"Yes, don't you think this is connected?" Bob asks.

"Well, they were robbed; things were taken, valuables. And you said you're not missing anything . . ." Riley says. I've changed my opinion—he's the senior between the two. He seems sour enough to have worked for fruitless years in the police.

"Here," Rodriguez says, tapping my hand. She places a card in my palm. "If you think of anything, or discover something missing, call this number."

"Thanks," I say, as I let them pass me to the door.

Bob and I stand at the doorway while the two of them descend the short flight of stairs.

"What a load of BS," Bob says.

"At least they didn't outright accuse me of lying. Oh, wait. They did. But I imagine they've been on plenty of fool's errands to make them jaded."

"Jaded? They are beat cops, juno? Patrol officers. This is their job. Dumber and Dumberer here are supposed to be helping people."

I can't help but laugh. Juno is cooler than people know. "Though, Rodriguez seemed okay," I confess. "It's Riley that got me all . . . riled up."

"Look, do you want me to stay? Only, I've gotta go somewhere—"

"Oh no, don't let me keep you. I'll be fine."

"You sure? I can call and cancel."

"I'll be all right Bob. You go on now."

"Use the dead bolt," he says, giving my arm a warm squeeze.

"I will."

As soon as I'm by myself, I run straight to the kitchen and put out a hand to the smooth cold quartz countertop. The bowl's still sitting on top, in the same spot I'd left it. Only, now it's empty. And the spoon is gone.

Maybe that's why the intruder didn't take anything. Who walks into a house and sees a bowlful of soil with a spoon dug into it and thinks it's a normal household? They might be the ones in trouble. For all they knew, a serial killer lived here. Or someone as dangerous.

What I can't work out is what the intruder could have done with all that soil. Did they throw it into the trash? Or did they spoon it down their throats, choking at first, then savoring the taste of the dirt in the mouth, as I would have?

SARAH

"Sit down, Ms. Connelly," Mr. Tcheznich says. His preference for last names is something I'm used to, but today it sounds stiff, official, like the tone you'd use to tell someone they're being let go.

"O-okay."

He falls quiet. In the uncomfortable silence, I worry he can hear my heart hammering within its cage like a trapped bird, wings fluttering against steel bars.

"It's very sad, isn't it, when we can't trust our own."

I gulp. I've risked everything, a promotion, a career, and my credibility, and I don't have anything concrete that could put Dan in the clear.

I nod, unable to speak.

"I've received some disturbing news, and this pertains to you."

My vision goes blurry. The room begins to spin around me. I gulp again, trying to gather the nerve to say something before he calls me out and I never get the chance to defend myself.

"I—"

He puts up a hand and cuts me off. "This is about Daniel Sorcese."

I nod again.

"David tells me that they've had to fire Daniel."

I look up, sharply.

"They're trying to keep it under wraps, but I'm guessing you already know. Daniel's replacement has been in touch with you?" His voice is lower; I'm guessing he doesn't want the others to know.

"Yes, yes that's right, John's been in touch."

Mr. Tcheznich looks grave and nods. "So stupid. People never learn." It's at the tip of my tongue to ask what exactly Dan is being accused of, but it feels like a betrayal to Dan. And whatever the accusation, it doesn't matter. I know Daniel can't have done anything wrong.

"Since you've been working closely with him, and he, I believe, is your friend, I thought you should know."

"Thank you for telling me."

"I can trust you to keep this quiet?"

I nod and offer a small, tight smile. I'm about to get up to leave when he says, "Ms. Bundt tells me you're sick?"

"Oh, it's nothing. I'll be fine."

"If you need to leave early, it's fine. Tax season is over, after all, and it is Thanksgiving week."

"Thank you," I say, and open the door.

Celia's eyes are burning a hole in the back of my head. She wants to know what I've been discussing with Mr. Tcheznich. Rather than field her questions, I collect my things and head out after a quick goodbye. Norman looks up, and then glances at the office clock, puzzled. I wave at him from the door, but his eyes are still on the clock.

The cold afternoon air is a delight after the way my nerves have been tingling all day. It's only a quarter past one and I'm beginning to suspect I *am* coming down with something, but I'm not going home.

Today, I'm on the opposite side of the street waiting for the M11. A bus will be along in less than four minutes. The sky is gray, and it looks like dusk already. I try to keep my eyes on the sights and sounds that are always a comfort, the people milling about, and tourists stepping out of shops and museums. Even at this odd hour in the afternoon, there's a crowd. It's what I love about New York.

The bus soon approaches 87th Street. The pull-bell dings. After I get off, I walk past the Belnord Hotel. Two plush brownstone townhomes sit on either side of an older building in desperate need of a face-lift. I shuffle to the entrance and try the door. Locked. I try the buzzer next, but it's broken. Dammit.

A grocery delivery van pulls up. A balding, middle-aged man hauls two large crates worth of fresh stuff out of the back. I pretend to text someone on my phone and mind my own business, like a typical local. He nears the door with both hands full. I wonder how he's going to get in when the door springs back as if by magic. I spy a small key card in his hand when he sidles in. I wait until he's disappeared down the hallway, then catch the door with my foot before it closes.

AUDREY: NOW

THE CAB PULLS AWAY FROM THE POLICE STATION. I'M FLUSHED AND muddled, too warm in the sunbaked car after the frigid stale air inside. I should have told them when I had the chance about last night and how the patio door had shut when I'd been in the shower. If Detective Green's cheap trick hadn't thrown me off my game, I probably would have.

Wicked girl. Always making things up! Mother used to say if I complained or tore open her notion that everything was perfect. But the hazy imprint of her palm on my thigh was there even though she pretended it wasn't and told me that I was imagining it. Just as my back door *had* shut later. The master security control logs the opening and closing of each door and window. And the proof is there in the log. Fifteen minutes past one in the morning, the back patio door had closed. But, how? The police had left by then. Though, sometime after the arrival of the second police car, I lost track of who was coming and going. The officers on the scene, the paramedics, then the forensic team, followed by the detectives, all traipsed in and out. One of the officers could have left the door open by mistake, and the wind could have pushed it shut later. Or someone ensured that the patio door remained open and closed it when I'd been in the shower. But *why*?

It's so frustrating not to understand what is going on. I could tell the detectives now, but it's a bit silly to bring up such an inane complaint when they're investigating a murder.

And I'm not sure I want to go back in and talk to them again. Not after the way they interrogated me. Witness statement, my arse. And that horrible blunt question: *Do you know who killed Sarah?* Heat rises up my neck. I shouldn't have lied. I shouldn't have lied about anything. It's too late now. I can't take back my words.

Back home, after a change of clothes and a quick wash, I slump at my desk. The ergonomic chair does nothing to keep me upright. I sip from a mug of steaming peppermint tea, and then I call my boss.

"Audrey, I got your email. Are you okay?"

"Greg, hi. Yeah, I'm okay, thanks."

"And you found the body?"

"Yes."

"That's . . . terrible. Are you sure you're all right? If you need some time off, it's okay. I understand."

As my boss, he is concerned and is saying all the right things under the circumstances, but we both know what's at stake if I don't keep up with my work.

"It *was* awful. I'm not great but I'm coping. I don't need time off, Greg. It's the opposite. I need to keep busy, to work, or I'll go a little mad."

"Oh. Okay then, work it is. All I'm saying is, we're flexible."

"Thanks, Greg."

I hang up.

I set my tea on the desk and stretch, stifling a yawn.

Today had started at a quarter to four, as it sometimes does. I need a nap, but sleep has become an enemy. It began with waking up in a panic in the middle of the night, remembering. I'd lie awake for a while, as though afloat on some distant ocean, slowly drifting back into the lull of sleep. Over time, it took longer and longer. Many nights, I couldn't fall asleep again. Then I began waking up far too early. Or I'd lie in bed, growing restless, the day shrinking around me, sleep beyond the reach of my fingertips. Now I'm lucky if I sleep for four hours without interruption. With no light perception and the inability to see the sun, it's difficult if not impossible to tell day from night. But I'm determined not to slip into the sleep medication pitfall, and rarely resort to an Ambien. If my doctor has her way, I'd be drugged all the time. Some days, when I can't catch a wink of sleep, I think it might not be such a bad idea.

I'm about to reach for my laptop when a deafening, high-pitched whine nearly knocks me sideways. It takes me a second to realize that it is the home security alarm. I'm stock-still, my heart hammering against my chest like a bass drum. An intruder. I spring up from the chair and hasten down the stairwell before freezing midstep. What if they're inside, and headed straight toward me? I flail and clamor back up the stairs until I can touch the wall of the passageway, and crawl into the bedroom. I shut the door behind me. Amid the piercing shrill of the alarm, I hear the faint trill of my phone's ringtone. The tremor running through my body is uncontrollable as I reach into my cardigan pocket for my phone.

"This is Hoyt Security. Miss Hughes, are you all right?"

"N-no. There's someone in the house. Please, help."

"What's your address?"

"No. 4 Shore Drive, Sleepy Point."

"We've called the police. They should be there any minute now."

"O-okay."

"It's okay, hang in there. Someone will be right with you. Try to stay calm. I'll stay with you the whole time."

"Where are you right now?"

"I'm upstairs, in my bedroom."

"Can you lock the door?"

I reach up on my knees and push in the flimsy button lock on the handle.

"I've l-locked it."

I'm holding the phone between my shoulder and my neck, straining to hear a siren through the blazing alarm. The operator asks me questions to keep me occupied.

"SPPD! Open the door!"

"The police are here," I tell the operator at Hoyt Security before putting them on hold.

"I'll be down there. Give me a minute!" I shout over the din and head to the corridor. I race down the steps, one hand on the banister to avoid tripping. At the entryway, my fingertips graze the number pad. I punch in the code with shaky fingers.

"Front door, open," I command. The door swings open and footsteps barge in.

"SPPD!" Someone shouts again. "Are you okay, ma'am?"

"Yes."

"Ma'am, please stay here while we have a quick look around."

"Okay," I say, and lift the phone to my ears. "The police are here. Can you turn off the alarm now, please?"

A sudden, eerie quiet replaces the chaos.

"Ms. Hughes," a female officer says.

I recognize her voice and slight Latino accent immediately. It's Officer Rodriguez, which means . . . *oh no*. Rodriguez's sidekick, Officer Riley, won't be far behind.

After the way the pair of them treated me a few months ago, I should refuse to let them in. If I wasn't so frightened at the thought of someone lurking in the house, I would shut the door on their faces.

I wish Detectives Greene and Novak had come instead, even if they do doubt every word I say. But they'd hardly send out detectives for something like a run-of-the-mill break-in. For now, I'm stuck with these two beat cops.

"We'll take a look around," Rodriguez says.

"Thanks. I'll wait right here."

"You wanna go 'round the back, Riley? I'll start upstairs," Rodriguez says.

I can't help but feel I'm in a time loop again. The same order of words, said by the same people, in much the same situation, only it's not merely my imagination. They *had* said it right here, in my kitchen, when someone broke into my home a few months ago.

"Yep," Riley says. The side door from the kitchen opens. I picture him walking through the mudroom corridor leading to the empty garage.

"It's clear upstairs," Rodriguez says.

"All clear here, too. The garage is clean. No forced entry," Riley says. "I can't see any signs of a break-in."

My jaw clenches. Did Riley even bother to conduct a proper search?

"Did you know your back door, the one leading to the patio, was open?" Officer Riley says.

I'm so stunned by this news that I forget to reply. All I can think is, *Not again*. Finally, finally, I answer. "That's not . . . it was shut when I checked," I tell him.

"You're sure?" Riley asks.

A sudden burst of energy something beyond anger surges inside me. He doesn't believe me. He didn't believe me the last time, either.

I cross my arms and sigh. "Of *course* I'm sure! I'd know if I left the door open, wouldn't I?"

"And you've had no visitors?" Rodriguez asks.

"Not today."

"Do you smoke?"

I frown. "Smoke? No. I don't smoke. Why?"

"There's a cigarette butt at your kitchen window."

The chill enveloping me has nothing to do with the weather in the house. I gulp. "A cigarette butt?"

Officer Riley's sigh is audible. "Yep, a lit one," he says, in a tone I don't like.

"But I—I don't smoke!" I gasp, wanting to smack myself. I'd smelled the smoke earlier, but had dismissed it, thinking Juno next door had the grill on. "Someone, I can assure you it wasn't me, stood right here, and smoked!" I sound hysterical but I can't help it. The panic I'd felt earlier slams into me once more at the thought of someone forcing their way into my house while I was in the study like a dumb sitting duck.

"I'll call it in," says Riley, while Rodriguez takes a seat next to me and begins to ask questions.

"I'm filling out the report for you," Rodriguez says. "But before that, you'll have to do a full walk-through with me, again, so we can figure out if anything was taken."

I'm always prepared for it, the edgy claustrophobia when someone is invading my space, but when it does happen, I'm thrown off nonetheless. It was only last night that the cops had laid siege to my house and here they are again. I haven't had a moment's peace from the time I found Sarah dead. Now, hours later, another break-in. At least they're filing a report this time. Perhaps they do believe me. When they were here after the first break-in, they all but accused me of wasting police time.

"Yes, of course," I say.

Riley and Rodriguez walk through the entire house as I count off where things should be. By the time they finish the bedrooms, I'm ready for something a lot stronger than tea.

"We'll be in touch." Rodriguez's soft husk is reassuring. "Do you have someone you can call to stay over for a couple of days?"

"No, I'll be fine, thanks." *No, please stay,* I want to beg, but it's a ridiculous notion, especially with Riley around.

After the police leave, the silence is at once soothing and disconcerting, but there's no time to rest. I go to the study and call the security company.

My mind is still a whirlwind long after the silence the police officers have left in their wake. With a large glass of red wine in hand, I go up to the study.

I told Greg I didn't need time off, and now I'm driven to distraction. Where is one safe if not in one's own home? I feel violated all over again. The security system is supposed to protect me. But the ear-splitting wailing of the alarm only freaked me out more. My nerves are on edge, even though I've taken all precautions now. I've changed the security codes after a long, tense call to Hoyt Security. Every door is shut and locked, all windows fastened. I've battened down the hatches.

In a way, I hate this codependence, almost bordering on overreliance, on the security system. All these gadgets are dumbing me down. I want to talk to Hillary and the rest and at once hate myself for it. I'm starting to depend on them too much as well.

The cigarette butts from various parts of the house, as pointed out by Officer Rodriguez, should have been documented, bagged, and taken away for DNA testing had they taken it all with the seriousness I expected. But the evidence was left behind, and I've now thrown them out. I tidy away any signs of the break-in by doing the only thing I can—clean the house to the best of my ability. Over the drone of the vacuum cleaner, round and round the same thoughts buzz in my head. Who broke into my house? Had they watched me? Why? The sheer spiteful malice of leaving lit cigarette butts around the house sends a chill down my spine.

But it's the fact that I hadn't *known* that I wasn't alone, that I hadn't sensed something amiss, that leaves me numb. I'd walked around, clueless, while someone had been here with me *inside* the house, right under my nose, watching me.

SARAH

I EXIT THE ELEVATOR ON THE THIRD FLOOR OF DAN'S BUILDING. MY QUICK strides cover the distance to his apartment, and I knock hard on the door. There's no response. I try once more. Again, nothing. I'm about to knock a third time when a shaky, sleepy voice calls out from inside, "Who is it?"

"It's me, Sarah."

The latch pulls back, metal scraping against the wood of the door, and then the knob turns.

"Wha—what are you doing here?" Dan asks, standing in his robe, his hair disheveled. He scratches his head and looks at his wrist, but there's no watch there.

"What time is it?" he asks, frowning, squinting against the harsh white light in the hallway.

"About two in the afternoon. Aren't you going to let me in?"

"Yes, sorry, of course. Come in," he says, flinging the door wider and locking up behind me.

I follow him into the narrow passageway that leads into a tiny rectangular living room. The east-facing windows filter in afternoon light through the beige blinds, drawn. All I can think is how dank my apartment is with the only window facing north. Dan's living room is a gallery of brightness by comparison, but the place is currently a mess. To the right is a cluttered kitchenette, recycling piled near the sink. Further, on the left, is a bedroom. The bed is unmade. I have roused him from sleep.

As his eyes follow mine, a pink flush creeps into his face.

"I wasn't expecting a visitor." His eyes flick toward a pair of underwear strewn atop an armchair.

"It doesn't matter. Look, I wanted to talk to you."

"One sec." He grabs an assortment of clothes from the sofa, magazines, used crockery, and cutlery from the coffee table, and dumps them all on the dining table.

"Sit," he says, motioning to the sofa.

I take off my coat, drape it on a dining chair, set my bag beside the chair, and take a seat. He runs a hand over his scruffy stubble, rubs his tired red eyes, and stares out the living room window as though I'm not there. I say nothing for a few moments. He's in another world and I'm waiting for him to return to the here and now. I take the time to rehearse what I've come to say.

"Why are you here?" he asks. His voice is like a low tide, ebbing away, retreating. I strain to hear him even though it's quiet out. The Upper West Side is like a different country compared to Chelsea.

"I . . . wanted to check on you."

He looks over at the clock ticking quite loudly over the kitchen entryway. "Shouldn't you be at work?"

"I logged in to your account."

He shakes his head and screws his eyes closed for a moment. "Wh-what account?"

"Your work account."

His eyes are two globes.

"What? Why? How do you know the password?"

"Whatever it is that's happened, why they've let you go, you can't or won't tell me, but I want to help."

"And how does logging in to my work account help?"

"I . . . don't know. I thought I could find something that could help you."

He purses his lips. His tired gaze sharpens.

"And what if you had been caught? They'll think it's me, won't they? I'm in enough trouble as it is!"

Dan's never raised his voice before; I flinch and sink further into the seat.

"You won't tell me what's going on. It left me no choice but to find out on my own."

"And what have you found out?"

Standing by the table, his lean, six-foot-five figure towers over my tiny seated form.

I look away from the glint in his eyes and fix my stare on the window. He's right to be angry with me. I haven't found anything out of the ordinary. Worse, if they find he's logged in to his account after they fired him, it could get him into more trouble.

"Nothing much," I say softly, making myself look into his eyes. "They haven't locked you out yet. I don't think they've told your team what's happened, which means this is an embarrassment for them. And there's only one thing that can embarrass a large trading company like Fortitude. It must affect their dividend payout and the stocks, or the investments in some way."

"Yes, thank you for pointing that out. *I'm* that embarrassment."

"Don't be silly. It's a mistake."

"And you're so sure about that, are you?"

He looks even more exhausted now. And a little exasperated. His arms cross over each other, hugging his lean waist.

I put my hand up like a stop sign. "I am. I know you. You wouldn't do whatever it is they've accused you of. You wouldn't."

He sighs and hangs his head. "It shows you don't know me at all."

I stare at him, trying to absorb his words. Then I sit back. I know this tactic; it's a simple lie to put me off.

"Dan—"

"I'm grateful you've thought to drop by and check in on me and all, but I think it's time you left."

"But—"

"Please, Sarah. I'm so tired. I need to sleep."

He's already shuffling toward the passage, swaying like a palm tree. I've barged in here, uninvited, to tell him I've done something a bit . . . well, *quite* illegal that could get him stuck in even deeper mud than he already is. I should leave but I don't want to. Now I'm here, I want to know what it is he's withholding.

"You can trust me, Dan."

"If there's one thing I've learned, Sarah, it's that I can't trust anyone. Now, please," he says, one hand poised like a frozen tennis swing pointing to the door. The unsaid words hang between us: *Please leave.*

I grab my coat and shrug it on, gather my purse, and follow him back into the narrow passageway. I appraise him up close as I squeeze past him. His watery eyes, murky and gray, look like approaching storms. He opens the door and steps aside as I cross the threshold.

I turn around and search his face. "I—"

"Please just let it go. You can't help me. It's all over now anyway. Think I *am* guilty."

"But what *are* you guilty of? If you'd just tell—"

A puff of wind from the door shutting hits me full on my face.

I put my hand on the door, wondering if I should persist or leave him be. There's no point in trying right now. I won't get anything out of him. I pivot on my heel and head to the stairs. Disappointment licks at me as I take the steps two at a time and descend to the lobby.

Outside, the sky looks silvery and frosty. I stick my hands into my pockets and march toward Columbus Avenue. Once there, I slip into the glass bus shelter. People huddle inside like penguins, necks tucked into their scarves, their feet together, as the M7 bus pulls to the curb.

I look back as the bus peels away minutes later. I was right to come, even if I'm leaving empty-handed. Well, not entirely. I know two things. Dan is lying. And from the way his eyes clouded the second I mentioned trust, it's obvious that Dan is very frightened. Of something. Or someone.

AUDREY: THEN
7 MONTHS AGO

WHEN YOU MOVE INTO A LUXURY TOWNHOME, YOU EXPECT A STANDARD. And except for the break-ins, Paradise Townhomes has met it at every turn so far. Besides the clubhouse with extensive facilities, it boasts movies by the park, swanky catamaran sails on the Hudson, and tailgating barbecue parties. You do not, however, expect mundane activities like community meetings. But everyone's rattled by the break-ins, so a meeting has been called at six this evening, and as the clock ticks on, I get cagey.

A text beeps on my phone. It's from Sherman, according to Siri.

> No second thoughts, I hope.

It's as though he can read my mind sometimes. Despite my insides flipping and lurching like a little sailboat on rough seas, I reply,

> None.

As a distraction, I log in to BlinkersOff, but nobody from the group is online.

I hope Hillary is getting on okay. For someone addicted to love, she's been dating a lot lately, but who am I to call her out on it? She'll be thrilled about my dating profile.

Sometimes, I'm tempted to talk to her about McKenzie and that I've never dated anyone since. Not seriously anyway. An odd evening out with some random guy or gal maybe, but nothing more. I can't seem to, not without McKenzie's face floating around in my head like a reproachful specter. She's spoiled it for me.

The phone chirps. Siri announces, *You have a new message from your boss, Greg,* and then, reads it out.

The client is quite happy with your progress. Well done, Audrey.

Thanks, Greg.

I wait for the *swish* confirmation that my text has been sent. If it weren't for my friendship with Greg, his message, especially as one from a boss to his employee, might come across as a little patronizing, but I know he means every word of it.

I twirl the silicone-encased phone in my hand absently as my thoughts return to Hillary. Part of me gets why she's adamant to carry on dating when it's the one thing that's harming her. It's because she doesn't want to end up alone. She told me as much once. It stuck in my head and got me thinking about how *I* might end up. The answer, when it came to me, was unsurprising.

Once Gramps passed, it was only me. Barbara was absent even though she was there. And when she *was* there, she was a shadow thinning out with the changing light; she barely knew if it was night or day. I can't help but think again of the irony in it. I can't tell day from night, either, now.

I've always known I'd end up alone.

"You're *not* alone," Sherman tells me sometimes when I get a bit too morose for his liking. He's right, He's more friend and family than a colleague, but it's not that. It's growing up all alone that makes me feel this way. A kind of loneliness that clings and never lets go.

Being intentionally late, for me, is as hard as jumping off a cliff. I've had to remind myself quite a few times that I'm supposed to wait until I hear the clap of the next door closing to make my move. By the time Boo says it's 5:50, I'm hopping from one foot to another, annoyance and impatience like twin thorns under my heels. I wait until it's 6:05, and then an extra five minutes to be safe, then run to my kitchen and head to the back door leading to the garage. My garage door opens with a hideous screech from little use. I cringe and hope no one hears it. Before I step out into the shared garage space between my row of townhomes and the row behind, I wait and listen. When I'm sure it's all quiet, I step toward the garage of No. 5 and reach for the pin pad. After flipping up the flimsy plastic cover, I instruct Siri to video-call Sherman.

"Usual numeric order," he says.

I punch in the keycode—not easy to come by.

"Perfect," Sherman says. I sag with relief when the garage door glides back without fuss.

I step inside with care until my knees butt up against the rounded bumper of an SUV. It takes several tries to reach the smooth inner rim behind the wheel to ensure it won't be detected by the plain eye. It's after I hear the magnetic *click* of the tiny GPS tracker sticking to the metal surface that I realize how hard my heart is thumping. I negotiate my way farther in and search for the cool metal handle on the back door of the house. It takes a couple of tries to insert the key I've had copied at the local hardware store and let myself in.

With each second that ticks away, my pulse races. I have no time for hesitancy. I climb up to the second level and begin with the main bedroom. The carpeting softens my steps.

"Sherman?" I say into the phone.

"I'm here," he says.

I pluck out the tripod from my bag and stand it up on its legs, angling it to face the closet. I place the phone on it.

"Okay?"

"No, turn it like seven clicks to your right."

I count and turn the camera a little at a time. "Stop," he says. "It's perfect now."

I fling open her closet door and search around for the pullout shelves beneath the top hangers.

One by one, I open the drawers. Sherman helps me sort their contents. Sherman's doing screen grabs, but those can be limiting, so I snap as many photos as I can with my tiny camera, hoping I'm capturing it all well. I tug open the fifth drawer on the opposite side from where I began and stick my hand in.

The front door opens with a squeak.

My breath hitches in panic. If she catches me red-handed, I'm done for. She could hand me over to the police, or worse—she could decide to deal with me herself.

"Move!" A sharp whisper shakes me out of my stupefied state. Sherman's heard the creak, too.

I force my legs to move and grab the phone with the tripod.

"Your bag!" he hisses.

I blanch, pick up my bag off the carpet, then tiptoe to the back of the walk-in closet. I glide the open drawer shut and reach for the long hangers at the back. After squishing myself as far to the corner as I can, I pull the clothes together.

"Shh," I whisper to Sherman. With tight, uncooperative fingers, I reach for the side button on my phone to ensure it's on silent.

"But you said you'll come over later." Her voice is faint; I picture her in the living room. Is someone with her? But no one replies to her complaint, which means she's on the phone.

Another sound I don't hear is the door shut. I pray it's because she's forgotten something and plans to grab it and head out again. But then her footsteps click on the stairwell. I hear the soft *thump* of her shoes on the carpeted stair treads and freeze. She's coming up.

"How long can the meeting last? There's the whole night ahead."

From the sound of her voice, she's nearing the main bedroom. "I never thought you'd pick golf over me," she's saying.

Her voice sounds close, too close. She's right outside. The closet door opens with a flat *click*. My heart thumps so loudly that I fear she can hear it, too. I clap a hand over my mouth and nose to muffle my loud breaths and press myself into the wall.

"Hang on, Ronnie, there's a call coming through. Hello? Yes? What? Okay, I'll be down in a second."

There's a light ruffle. When the door shuts again, a cry of fear stays frozen in my mouth.

"Ronnie. I've got to go. I'll see you in a couple of minutes anyway."

Her voice comes from the passage outside the bedroom. Her feet thump down the steps. The front door opens. I put the phone to my ear. "She's gone," I whisper.

"Wait," Sherman whispers back. My heart hammers in my chest each second I wait, fearing the creak of the door. At last, the front door slams shut.

Get out, now, he says.

By the time I ensure I've replaced everything as I found it, lock up, and head out to the meeting, I'm hot and out of breath. Sweat trickles down my back and dampens my underarms, even though the December chill is setting in.

Priya and I, the last of the dumbfounded stragglers, walk back home after the meeting. It's all still a blur in my head: the discussion, casual at first before getting heated; people hopping on and off like a not-so-merry merry-go-round; and the sudden rush of voices, gasps, and tuts that left me startled.

"Well, that was a disaster!" Priya says, bringing me back to the present.

I scoff at her understatement. "You'd think people would behave themselves at a community meeting in a neighborhood like ours."

"Men will be men, I guess, but still."

"I don't understand what exactly happened," I say. The debate over the security issue got heated. Sarah, of course, added fuel to the fire. The next thing I know, there was shouting and someone yelled at Matt to stop. And finally, Mrs. Kirsch shoved me out of the way, shouting,. "My son, my son!" apparently to rush to *her clever Ronnie*.

"The *bitch* Sarah is what happened. Did you see the doe eyes she was making at Matt? I mean, Donna was right there! It's *all* Sarah's fault," Priya says. Normally, Priya is too sensitive and mindful to use the did-you-see term with me, but she's all fired up. The rush of hatred in her tone is unsurprising, but the viciousness takes me a little aback.

"Was it?" I want to remind her that Matt had something to do with it, but she doesn't sound very receptive right now.

"You *know* that it is. We were all on the same page! Increased security measures were out after Lisa pointed out that cameras and such are too expensive on top of the HOA fees we're already coughing up. Everyone agreed. Then Sarah *had* to interfere and put that ridiculous idea in everyone's head. A vigilante group circling the community at night, in pairs, no less. I mean, really? From how fast she volunteered herself for these night ops, did no one see through her?" Priya stops and scoffs loudly. "Like she's CIA or something. And no one questioned why the patrol squads should be doing nights when the break-ins happened in the middle of the day."

Priya is right, sadly. No one saw through Sarah's suggestions. "Not to mention, a heavily pregnant woman is hardly the right candidate to go on vigilante surveillance."

"People are blind. Truly," she says. Then she puts her hand on my arm and we both stop walking. "I'm *so* sorry, I didn't mean it like that, Audrey."

"It's okay. I know what you meant." We resume our stroll. "Ronnie did agree readily, didn't he?" I say, thinking back.

"He did! As did Matt. All the men took Sarah's side."

Priya, I've learned by now, is prone to exaggeration as far as Sarah is concerned, but she's right in this instance. Almost everyone had jumped at the chance of some private time with Sarah.

"All except Bob," I remind her. "Still, I never would've expected Bob to get violent. He's more disciplined than that."

"Well, it wasn't exactly a punch, and, to be fair, it was Matt who started it. He should never have said it, should he? He deserved it, if you ask me."

"What *did* Matt say? Mrs. Kirsch chose that very moment to moan about the day she visited her *clever Ronnie*, insisting she'd locked the door."

Priya laughs, after having chorused *clever Ronnie* with me. Then, her tone changes. "After Bob shot down the vigilante idea, Matt said that Bob was too old anyway. And he had the gall to say that if Bob's so frightened of some real action, he should stay home and cuddle a stuffed bear. Bob went red and got all up in Matt's face muttering, 'What did you say?'"

Priya's attempt at aping Bob's gruff tone with her sweet, birdlike lilt makes me smile.

"But how did it turn into a brawl?" I ask, still bewildered by the cacophony that had erupted.

"Matt should have walked away right then, but instead he pushed Bob, who staggered backward. Bob took a swing at Matt in return—pure instinct, I think. Ronnie tried to stop him, and, in the process, Bob got both Matt and Ronnie with that gorilla fist of his. Poor Bob. He looked so mortified; he muttered a rough *sorry* before storming out."

I did hear Bob's apology but without the picture Priya has just painted for me, I was left to work out why Bob was apologizing. "I can't believe Bob *hit* Matt," I say.

"A mean right hook, too."

My mouth falls open. I'm a little impressed with Bob. He's pushing seventy but he took on a thirty-five-year-old and a forty-something-year-old all by himself.

I stop and turn toward Priya when I hear the ripple of the wind chimes outside my home. She's in her own world when I say goodbye.

"I better get back home," Priya says, pulling me into a hug. She sounds small and distant.

"Is everything all right?"

"What? Yeah, yeah, everything's fine. Sorry, I'm preoccupied."

"With what?"

"It's silly. I'm thinking about having a party for my birthday."

"That's not silly."

"It is if I'm thinking about it three months in advance. It's a landmark birthday, though—thirty," she adds.

"It's still not silly," I say.

"My sister disagrees. Anyway, I'll get going. Catch you later."

"Bye, Priya."

I instruct Siri to call Sherman. He picks up on the first ring. It makes me sad and a little guilty but also heart-warmed.

"Audrey," he says, as usual struggling a little to pronounce my name. "Everything okay?"

"Yeah. Thanks to you. That was a close call today."

"You're not clairvoyant. You couldn't have foreseen she'd return so quickly."

I laugh. "Second sight? Wouldn't that be cool? Think of how I could advertise myself. Blind Woman Becomes Seer."

He laughs, too. I love how natural it sounds.

"You know what this means: I'll have to return to complete the job."

"Let's first process what we've got. The GPS is active."

"And the photos and videos?"

He hesitates. I worry if I've screwed up.

"Some of them were a little blurry, but I've managed to sharpen them, so no worries. I'll sort them out and see if anything interesting pops up."

Though I'm disappointed, I'm thankful for his honesty. Having to rely on someone to see if I'm doing my job accurately is upsetting to the point of depression sometimes.

"Hey, I said they're mostly fine."

"Yep, I heard you."

Sherman is always quick to remind me that we are a team, though I know how that goes. All I do . . . all I *can* do is get my hands on information, anything and everything I can find. Of the incessant photos and videos I upload, I know most will be blurry because I go by feel. A combination of sense, calculations of angles, and intuition. After I send it all, it's Sherman's job to sort and analyze, make sure they hold up.

"Don't beat yourself up. I couldn't do what you do even if I tried, and I'm not at any disadvantage."

A stab of guilt twists inside me. I should have told Sherman about the break-in, but the moment went by. And given the close call today, he will want me to drop everything and leave right this minute.

"Sherman? I've been thinking, let's do a few background checks. I'll email you a list."

A smile twitches on my lips after we hang up. Finally, a start.

SARAH

I THINK ABOUT SCHOOL AS INSTANT RAMEN BUBBLES IN A POT. THEY were some of the best days of my life. I never needed to study seriously up until then. University was an eye-opener. I'd looked around, hopeless, wondering how the hell I'd got in. *I* wouldn't have let me in. Somehow with the help of a few willing friends and teachers, there I was.

In my freshman year, I did nothing but catch up on everything I was already supposed to know. It wasn't until the second year that my education began in earnest. I buried myself in my bedroom with books. Only by year three could I even dream of taking an evening off or relaxing over a weekend. Then came the various certifications, but I loved studying, and challenging myself.

All this reminiscing makes me think of Dan again. He graduated with honors from the University of Minnesota. I've never asked him what made him move to New York. I assumed it had something to do with a broken heart. And the phone call he occasionally gets; the one he sometimes cuts without checking the caller ID. In the time we've been friends Dan hasn't dated anyone in New York. Not for lack of options or interest. Passersby often appraise him with that instant "I want you" glance. I've seen plenty of overt and covert attempts to win his attention.

"Not interested," he said to me once, when a sharp gentleman with an angular jaw and a ripped body made eyes at him from over the bar. When the gentleman came over to our table later, under some pretext, Dan told him, "I'm with her."

I didn't deny it. I was *with* him, technically. Even Celia asked me about Dan once. The few times he dropped in or stopped by to pick me up was enough to break through even serious, I-don't-fool-around Celia's imperviousness.

"Anything going on between you two?" she'd asked.

"He doesn't swing our way," I'd said.

"Typical. Drop-dead handsome, apparently caring and nice or why would you hang out with him so much, and gay."

"What about you?" Dan asked me, later that same evening at the bar.

"What *about* me?"

He looked over at the now disappointed, ripped, angular-jawed gentleman and nodded.

"I have boobs. He won't be interested."

"And you're not interested?"

"No. I'm not."

He cocked a manicured brow at me. "Not ever? Or not right now? Cuz I'm pointing out the obvious, but you're stunning, clever, and *very* single."

I'd thought a bit before answering.

"Not right this moment. I . . . want to build a life for myself first."

He had tilted his head at me. "You have. You're more *stable*," he said, putting quotes around the word, "than a lot of people our age."

"Not as stable as I want to be. But someday, when I'm good and ready, I'll date again. Maybe I'll make up for it all and date as many people as I can."

Dan's lips had twitched. "What, all at once? Like, bed-hop?"

"Why not? I have hidden depths, you know?"

He'd echoed my playful laugh.

And that was that. We've never spoken of it since.

I think about him now, still heartbroken and frightened into the bargain, alone in that apartment instead of being home with his family for the weekend. I have to persuade him to let me help him. Tomorrow, I'll call him, and I won't take no for an answer.

As I slurp the last of the noodles, a ping alerts me to a new email that's landed in my inbox. After I wash up and let the bowl and pot drain on a mat near the sink, I glide onto the sofa with the laptop. I open the email app and see Rachel's name on top.

> Sarah,
>
> Here's another list of apartments. Can you take a look and let me know if anything interests you? Sorry, it's taken a couple of days. I caught the bug that's going around.
> Let me know!
> Best,
> Rachel

I open the attachment and scroll through, flicking a glance at the specs sheet she's added with the address, square footage, and the rent. I discard most of the options except two.

The rent for the first option is decent, but I know that street. A pest control truck was parked there not too long ago—rats. I discard that option as well and am left with the only viable one on 23rd and Ninth.

I go over the description.

Natural light flows through this 1 Bed/1 Bathroom apartment with large closets and windows with views of the Empire State Building. Location: on the most convenient block in Chelsea!

The amenities it lists as pluses look too good to be true for $2,850. I close my eyes for a second and realize I'm missing something. Then I get it. Laundry. I review the description. At the bottom of that page like fine print, it says, *Laundry two blocks away.*

I bite my lip. If I do end up there, I'll have to do it twice a week so I won't have to lug a huge load every time. But otherwise, doable. *Plus*, it's a one-bed. I reply to Rachel right away, asking to see it ASAP.

I hope it's still available tomorrow.

AUDREY: NOW

It's the golden hour, according to Boo; the summer sun should be setting about now. But time has become liquid, pouring in and out of my life. The irony of it is that time used to pour in and out of Mother's life, too, in the form of cheap booze. I'm beyond exhausted. It's like jet lag, as though I've journeyed across continents in the past day alone. The inertia is losing steam, catching up to my body.

I can't help but think of Nicole or miss her soft baby skin, and her smell, a mix of baby powder and milk. Poor little bear. No more of her mother's lingering scent, no more *little bear*, and *shmugleywoogley*, and *bubkins*. No one to hear her little bleats and come running.

Every time I remember how I discovered Sarah, on the floor, her head caved in, a flood of fear rushes into my nerves.

Don't think about it, just don't think.

Weary, I log on to BlinkersOff again and find everyone is online and chatting.

I wait for a beat before I type.

AudH:
Hi, all. I'm glad you're all here. Something's happened and I can tell you all in one shot.

DrHilLary:
Is everything okay, Audrey?

AudH:

So, my neighbor, the one I mention sometimes? Sarah?
She's been murdered.

I sit upright, roll back my shoulders, and wait for the screen to explode.

Will-I-am:

Did she get shot?

AcidGurl2010:

What? No way!

DrHilLary:

Goodness! Are you all right?

AudH:

I'm okay, a little in shock. I don't know how she was
killed yet but there was quite a bit of blood.

Will-I-am:

Ooh, gruesome-awesome!

William can come across as rude if you don't know him. But I know his sometimes sharp or out-of-place humor for what it is—bravado. It's a shield he likes to hide behind, one I understand all too well.

DrHilLary:

It's not, William. Don't make fun. It's a serious matter.

AcidGurl2010:

Doesn't this give you PTSD or something, William?

Will-I-am:

Nah. I miss it, tbh. I miss the action, the blood rush.

DrHilLary:

We should let Audrey talk.

AudH:

It's not sunk in yet, tbh. It was so weird. All that sticky wetness. In a way, I was glad not to be able to see the blood.

AcidGurl2010:

Wait . . . did you find her? OMG!

DrHilLary:

That must be so distressing.

AudH:

Yeah. I found her. I walked in. . . . You know what? This might be distressing to hear, so if you're not in the mental space for it, I'll wait until whoever needs to log out.

DrHilLary:

Thanks for being considerate, Audrey.

AcidGurl2010:

I live for details.

No one protests or logs out.

> **AudH:**
> I walked in and stumbled on something and fell
> over . . . it turned out to be her head. It was horrible.
> Blood was everywhere. It was so slick and wet,
> I didn't even know what it was I was touching at
> first; but then I realized, it was a body—her body—
> Sarah's. And all the while, the baby was screaming
> her head off.

My face grows hot with shame thinking about how the shock of finding Sarah made me tune out everything else; the mad hammering of my
heart so loud that it drowned out even Nicole's cries.

> **DrHiILary:**
> What a harrowing experience.

> **AudH:**
> I can't believe she's gone. I'm a little numb. I should be
> hysterical, crying, and I am, sometimes. It's distressing
> and puzzling.

A fresh stab of pain radiates through my body. This is the first time
I'm talking about it to anyone other than the police, my distress over how
I found Sarah and the symphony of emotions I've felt ever since. And
something . . . I can't quite put my finger on what is out of place, why it
doesn't add up. It's aggravating and annoying, but the more I try to grasp
this thought, the farther away it flits.

Will-I-am:
It's natural. When the horror of it begins you can't think. There's blood everywhere, body parts, shrapnel, bullets flying in all directions. It's later, when you least expect it that the details creep up on you, colors, smells, taste, how bright or dark it was, the deafening artillery, shouting, screaming.

I can't imagine the kind of horrors William has seen and experienced.

AcidGurl2010:
It must be so hard, William. I'm sorry.

AudH:
I can't claim I've experienced anything like that. William, you are truly brave.

AcidGurl2010:
Will, I think you're brave too. If I did have vision, there are two things I'd like to have done. Play video games and see colors of all kinds. But I'd never have had the courage to join the army or navy. Air force, maybe. I would rock a pilot suit.

I had no such grand plans when I was a teen, vision, or no vision. I had one goal: to get the hell out of the situation I was in.

Later, Hillary manages to drive the conversation to something more uplifting. Smart glasses, much like smartphones or devices, which people with blurry or little but existing vision could use to help navigate life. It calculates distances so they can avoid bumping into things. Or enlarges menus at restaurants or elsewhere, giving them real-time, usable information. We express our excitement for those who can use it but my mind is still whirring like a mixer. What is it that I'm missing? I can't quite put my finger on it no matter how many times I go over the details in my head.

While unloading the dishwasher, my fingers graze the rounded rubber grip of the chef knife in the top, flatware rack. A memory pops into my head. I'm chopping lettuce. Sarah's standing nearby, chatting away. The moment I discovered Sarah on the floor replays in my head before I can distract myself. My hands tracing the shape of Sarah's head. The oozing sticky mess I'd plunged my hands into, checking for a pulse. It's unbearable now, as though I'd stuck both hands into a bin of writhing, wriggling worms.

I run into the hallway powder room, open the lid of the toilet, and retch. After I rinse my mouth and wipe my face with a hand towel, I brace myself against the sink and stand. Can smart glasses help people who have absolutely no vision? Could they, for example, tell me the toilet needs to be cleaned because I'd been sick and flushing twice hadn't helped? That's the sort of practical, household help I need.

William was right. The memory snuck up out of nowhere. I head back to the kitchen and reach for the knife to put away when the resounding *dingdong* of the doorbell makes me jump.

"Audrey? It's me, Priya. You there?"

I open the door to a rush of warm wind.

"Hey, Priya." I inhale the warmth of lingering cinnamon and clove on Priya's clothing. Apple pie. Priya stress-bakes. There's been rather a lot of casseroles and cakes and pies these past few months, poor thing.

"Have you heard what's happened? It's so awful!"

"Here, come on in." I close the door once Priya is inside. The last thing I need is for Juno to hear us and join in.

"Hope I'm not disturbing you?"

"Not really. Tea?"

"If it's no trouble."

"Not at all." In the kitchen, I grab the kettle and fill it in the sink.

"I need to use the bathroom. I've come straight from work and I'm busting to pee."

"Of course. You know where it is."

I bring a teapot and a few tea cookies on a tray and place them on the living room coffee table. I settle on the sofa. Priya takes the armchair, opposite.

"I can't wrap my head around it. Sarah, gone!" Priya says. From the incredulity in her tone, I can imagine Priya's expression. "Have the police been questioning you as well?"

"Yes, they questioned me last night and again this morning." It's a little unbelievable that the two detectives had been here less than twenty-four hours ago. It's as though it all happened ages back.

"Last night?" Priya asks between audible slurps.

"Yes, I'm the one who found her."

"Shit. That's awful. Look, I know she was your friend, but I can't pretend I'm sorry she's dead."

"She had her faults—"

Priya cuts me off. "It's ridiculous the way the police are treating us. They practically dragged me in from work. It was so embarrassing. And the way they grilled me, I thought I was going to have to lawyer up!"

"They ambushed me as well," I tell her. At least I'm not the only one at the receiving end of their third degree, even though the police made it look as though I'm their main suspect.

"Did you tell them?" I flinch from the sharpness in Priya's tone.

I sit up straighter. "Tell them what?"

"About Brian and Sarah?"

My face grows hot. "I had to. They asked me outright. I couldn't lie."

Priya sighs. "It's all right. I'm not blaming you. I told them, too. Anyway, I've asked Brian for a divorce."

"I'm so sorry, Priya."

"It's not your fault he went running every time she crooked her finger at him. Though I do feel bad for Nicole, poor little thing. Where is she anyway?"

"They won't tell me."

"With Alice, I'd have guessed," Priya says. The cup rattles in the saucer when Priya replaces it on the coffee table.

"Alice?"

"Sarah's sister? The one who lives in Pittsburgh. Or was it Philly? Anyway, I told the detectives all this when they dragged me into the station like I'm a serial killer from *America's Most Wanted.*"

"Hang on, did you say Alice? I thought Sarah's sister was named Grace?"

"I didn't know Sarah had another sister named Grace," Priya says, chewing a biscuit.

The shrill ringtone of Priya's phone startles me.

"Shit, I've lost track of time!" Priya says. "I've got to go. The in-laws are coming over for dinner. I've given Brian an ultimatum; he tells them himself, or I do. Thanks for the chai," Priya says.

I wave her off in the hallway, listening for the chirp of the security alarm after the door shuts. My phone starts to ring. Siri announces it's Greg.

"Hi, Audrey. Sorry, it's taken all day to call you back," he says, after I pick up.

"No problem."

"I'm guessing the cops are interviewing you?"

"Yes. I've spoken to them twice so far. Once at the station."

"And . . . how much do they know about what you do?"

"They know I'm an accountant and the name of the firm."

"Okay, that's good."

"Someone might call you to confirm."

"If they question you further about work, let me know right away."

"Certainly."

"As in, not after the fact. I want you to reach out to me the second they begin asking questions. Take a break, use your phone, message me."

"Of course." *Shit.* I've got to tell him about the break-in. "There's something import—"

"Audrey, sorry, don't mean to cut you off but I've another call coming in and I've got to take it. We'll speak later."

"Sure.

"As always, if you need anything, anything at all, contact Sherman."

"Okay, will do."

Yes, good old Sherman. I sometimes wonder where I'd be without him. What we achieve together, with him managing the data gathering and me analyzing it all makes us the "dream team," as we sometimes like to needle Greg and point out.

Priya's reaction to Sarah's death is hardly a surprise. Who wouldn't hate Sarah if their partner salivated like a smitten puppy when she was around? But as much as I understand Priya's reaction, I can't forget the conversation with Priya only the previous afternoon. Hours before I found Sarah's body, Priya had all but admitted she wanted to kill *someone*, and it doesn't take a genius to guess that the someone was Sarah.

And who exactly is Alice, I wonder, as I spoon warm soup into my mouth.

Sarah had only one sister. Grace. I remember that conversation exactly. Sarah had stood at the island and I'd been washing dishes when she had mentioned her sister, Grace. Sarah and Grace, Grace and Sarah, she'd gone on for ten minutes about Grace's childhood jealousy of Sarah.

Who, then, is Alice? I clutch my thin cotton wrap, pulling it tighter, even though I'd felt warm a little while ago. It'll be two months before the autumn chill clings close to the water's edge. Being the first row of water-facing townhomes also means nothing stands between them and the gale-force winds the Hudson sometimes blows.

My mind is still on Grace when sudden inspiration strikes. I disconnect the phone from the charger and send Sherman a message.

His reply beeps immediately.

That's a great idea. Let's explore it tomorrow.

When I don't respond right away, he sends me another text.

Hey, you okay?

I spoke to him only this afternoon after I got back from the station, but I wouldn't mind talking to him again.

Okay if I call?

Of course!

I hit the speed dial button and wait to hear his baritone fill my ear.

Later, while I'm in bed, I wonder if Priya will be able to maintain her cool when the police question her again, for question her they will. Especially after what I, and no doubt some of the other neighbors, have told them about Brian and Sarah. Right from the time I moved here to Sleepy Point, I've been aware of Priya's intense jealousy of Sarah.

More than anything, I can't forget the way Priya had threatened Sarah. If I hadn't been there at the party, listening, and interrupted when I had, I wonder what might have happened. Would Priya have flung Sarah down the stairs? Had Priya returned last night to finish what she started that day?

I can't quite imagine Priya killing Sarah, but who knows what a desperate person will do when pushed to the limits? Maybe Sarah finally drove Priya past her breaking point, and in a moment of uncontrollable rage, Priya killed her. I wonder if the police are digging into Priya's background. And if they do delve deep enough, will they find what Sherman and I did? After all, she was *nearly* charged with a serious crime once before. I should have told those detectives about it. Especially as they seem determined to frame me for Sarah's murder. Shouldn't I give them other scenarios to pursue?

As suspects go, Ronnie is also a good candidate. A self-made millionaire like him isn't going to take a threat sitting down. Not when his reputation, his family, and even his fortune are at stake. No. He'd do something about it. But would he go as far as to kill Sarah to silence her?

I stretch my back like a bow and turn to my side. It *is* possible.

Then there's Bob. He thundered outside Sarah's door only a couple of months ago, threatening to go to the police. Although I couldn't guess why he'd threaten her, it wouldn't be surprising if Sarah had found a way to get under his skin. Bob has a quick temper, too. Maybe Sarah did or said something to make him see red.

For that matter, both Dodsons are equally viable suspects. If someone made a play for her husband, I suspect Lisa isn't the type to stand by and watch. And if Sarah was having an affair with Jack and she threatened or blackmailed him, I doubt that he would take it lying down. Moreover, as criminal defense lawyers, both Jack and Lisa have an advantage over the others—skills and know-how to get away clean with murder.

Matt and Donna aren't a power couple. They're average people with decent jobs and a family to raise. Donna, with her soft voice and a temperament to match, might not seem like much of a threat, but it's the unlikeliest of people that do the unthinkable things, I, better than most, should know. I wouldn't put it past Matt, either, to do whatever it takes to protect everything he's worked hard to build.

Even with many suspects and motives, it's only a matter of time before the detectives get to the truth. The last thing they are is stupid. The thought relieves me, but as I turn over once more and flip the pillow to its cool side, a small seed of fear starts to sprout inside me.

What if they're a little too good at their jobs and find out the truth, not only about Sarah but about everything? I can't let that happen.

SARAH

EVER SINCE WE WENT OUT TO CELEBRATE MY PROMOTION, CELIA HAS cooled even more toward me. I thought the file goof-up would give her something to gloat about, something to hold over me. But she didn't even smile when she ran into me in the breakroom. This morning, perfunctory *hi* aside, she hasn't spoken a word to me all day. I haven't spoken a word all day, either. My throat's fallen scratchy from disuse.

If it carries on this way, soon the promotion will mean nothing. Working relationships can't afford to be tetchy. And I'd be *her* boss. If she holds a grudge against me, she won't work well. All her focus will be on how to get her own back at me, and I won't be able to call her out on it. She'll do enough of a good job of it. Then the whole company will suffer. I have to deal with this situation before it escalates.

I wave to Norman as he leaves and then grab my bag and coat. "Bye, Celia," I say.

"Bye."

It's curt, but it is said.

Below, I wave to Arnie, brace myself against the biting cold, and head to the bus stop. People huddle and tuck into themselves as a gust slaps us and squalls away. I see the bus approaching. At the last moment, I decide to cross over and take a bus from the opposite side. It's only Tuesday and with the long weekend, I'll be able to see Dan on Thursday at the earliest, but I can't wait. I need to talk sense into him, to convince him to let me help.

The slower evening traffic is grueling at this hour, the same route to Dan's apartment takes at least fifteen minutes longer. The buzzer is still broken but someone has propped the door open. This time I skip the elevator and take the stairs. On the third floor, I cross the length of the corridor, having come up the opposite side to Dan's apartment. A violent sneeze escapes me before I have the chance to cover it with my arm. Wiping off my hands and face with a tissue, I knock and pray Dan's in a mood to talk today. After four knocks, there's no response. I frown. Is he out? I take out my phone and dial his number, holding a tissue to my nose, which has begun to run.

A faint ringtone sounds off from inside the apartment. He wouldn't step out and leave his phone. No one does. If we could all have it attached to our hips somehow, we'd do that, too. No, he's home but he's not answering.

I try again a couple of times. A neighbor opens their door.

"No one's in, lady! Jeez."

They're about to close the door when I ask, "You haven't seen Dan today, have you?"

A quick head shake and the door slams shut.

There's a moan from inside Dan's apartment.

I knock softly. "Dan? It's me. Sarah. I can hear you in there dammit, let me in. Dan?"

When he doesn't answer, the roots of my hair prickle like they do when something's off. I knock again.

Nothing.

I try his number once more. Again, I hear it ringing from inside his apartment. He doesn't pick up this time, either.

I slap my palm on the door. I'm about to walk away when I hear another faint moan and a heightened sense of unease washes over me.

Maybe . . . he's hidden a spare somewhere. I lift the doormat and peek underneath. Nothing. Stretching on my tippy-toes, I reach above the door frame and graze the width of the frame with my fingertips. I'm about to give up when I feel the edge of a key. I'm at once relieved and stunned at the stupidity of trusting a spare key in such an obvious hiding spot in New York, of all cities. *You can take a boy out of Minnesota, but you can't take*

Minnesota out of the boy, he'd said to me once. I jump up a little and flick the key to the floor, grab it and shove it through the keyhole.

"Dan?" I call out as I enter the dark passageway. There's no reply. I walk on, winding right, then left to enter the living room, still full of clutter. I surge ahead and knock on the slightly ajar door.

"Dan? It's me, Sarah. You asleep?"

He doesn't reply, but through the open sliver, I can see his form on the bed. I shove the door back and cover the distance to the bedside as soon as my legs will carry me. On the bedside table is an open pill bottle, the cap lying face-up next to it. Ambien.

And it's empty.

"Dan!" I reach for him and shake him. His weight is dead, and his arms are icy. "Wake up!" I strike his cold, slack face with the back of my palm. He doesn't move. Not even a flinch. "No, no, no . . ." I shake him again before reaching for the phone in my pocket to dial 9-1-1.

I'm in the bland, dank waiting room of Mount Sinai Morningside, waiting to see Dan. He's been pumped, and the doctor said those dreaded words no one wants to hear. *We've done all we can, now it's a matter of waiting.*

I'm tempted to call Dan's parents, but he wouldn't want that, so I hold back. *He's going to be all right,* I tell myself, over and over. He's going to be fine. He *has* to be. It's all my fault. I should have read into his words. He'd said them, loud and clear. *It's all over anyway.* The desperation in his voice had been obvious but I hadn't been paying attention, too caught up in my thoughts of how *I* had failed to find out anything useful.

I'm pacing the entryway when I remember I was supposed to have been meeting Rachel to see the apartment. I text her saying I can't, I'm at the hospital with a friend. She's nice about it.

> It's no problem. Text me later and we'll fix up another time.

By the time I'm finally allowed to see him, a potent mix of adrenaline and anger is gushing into my veins. All I can think of is his slack face, saliva pooled at the edge of his mouth, his comatose dead weight sprawled diagonally, overflowing on the small bed. And his pulse, so faint, I wanted to scream until I frightened it into working again.

"This way," a nurse says, leading me to his bed. "Are you the girlfriend?"

"No. A friend."

She casts a thoughtful glance my way, noting the tremor in my voice. "I'm Kayla. I'll be back in a few minutes."

I drag the only chair closer to the bed and plonk myself down on it, exhaustion catching up to me out of nowhere. I thank my stars I'd had the presence of mind to bring his insurance card along and pray HR hasn't had the time to cancel all that yet. I can't bear to look at Dan's body on the hospital bed. His high-cheek-boned face is gaunt, and the shadows beneath his fanned-out lashes are darker.

The curtain springs open with a trill of the rings against the metal rod, startling me.

It's the nurse, Kayla. She offers me a tepid smile.

"Will the doctor stop by soon?"

"Nah. Dr. Leyland will make his rounds later, tonight. Why?"

"Is he going to be okay?" I point to Dan.

"We won't know until he wakes up."

I'm glad she's said *until* and not *if.*

"He's lucky we were able to intervene when we did," Kayla adds.

If I hadn't found him when I did . . . I shudder.

"Hey," she says, placing a hand on my shoulder, jarring me, "are you okay?"

I wonder why she's staring at me, when I realize, my face is wet, and my nose is leaking again. "Yes."

"Here," she says, grabbing a box of tissues from a tray and handing me the one sticking out on top.

"You may as well go home and get rest. He won't be up for a while yet. Why don't you come by tomorrow morning? We won't be sending him home until then anyway."

I sigh and straighten my slouching body. Home sounds tempting after the last three hours.

"I want to be here when he wakes up."

Her eyes go soft for a moment. "Suit yourself. Meanwhile, he's not going anywhere, if you want to go and grab something from the café?"

She reaches inside her coat pocket. "Here, take these after you eat something. You look like you're coming down with a bug."

She cocks her head at me. "Go on." I take the Tylenol and head to the hospital café, praying they have soup. My windpipe is starting to hurt like a pair of hands are squeezing it tight.

AUDREY: THEN

6 MONTHS AGO

SHERMAN WAS A LITTLE MAD AT ME FOR NOT TELLING HIM ABOUT THE break-in right away, but he's over it. He can't stay mad at me, but it's all I can do to persuade him not to pull the plug on the whole thing. And while it's shaken me up, something I don't admit to him, I'm also confounded. I've been obsessing about the bowl I'd left on the countertop, full of fresh soil. Did the intruder empty it? Why?

As BlinkersOff loads on the screen, I think about why I'm here, chatting with these three people. It's the thing we all have in common besides being blind. Addiction. We each have one, like a liver, or a heart. I know all of theirs quite well by now.

William's addiction is alcohol. I've had rather too much experience with it to fall for that. I rarely go over two glasses of wine. Measured.

Hillary's is a strange one. Of course, *I'm* one to talk, but hers is one none of us believed at first. It's love. Hillary is addicted to falling in love. It's the rush, the high of it. She's married about the number of times Liz Taylor has. And dated even more people, because she kept falling in love. It's legit, though. I've read up on it. It's something to do with the neurochemical and physiological responses. Similar to other types of addictions.

Becca is a recovering acid addict. My mother's boyfriend was on drugs. I've seen how it ravages the body. Worse, I've seen the withdrawal symptoms. Explosive diarrhea, vomiting, the chills. An eight-year-old should be in school, not cleaning up vomit and yellow putrid stool off the floor, but it effectively turned me off drugs forever.

Hillary thinks Becca's username, AcidGurl2010, is only enabling her further and has been after Becca to change it.

Her tagline, as Becca likes to call it, is because acid gave her beyond-perfect vision. While she was high on LSD, she could see colors and visions in her head, twice better than what people with 20/20 vision have.

"It's only a username. It's nothing. *I'm* enabling me," Becca had retorted, and resolutely stuck to AcidGurl2010, in what I thought was a very adult approach.

"Although, the way it used to make me puke sometimes, I should change it to AcidHurl2010," Becca claimed once. "And what's *your* deal?" she had asked me when I first joined them.

"My deal?"

"What's your addiction?"

"She'll tell us when she's good and ready," Hillary had said.

"But it's not fair. She knows about all of us. We don't know anything about her."

"Now, Becca. What have I told you about confronting people?" Hillary had asked.

"That it's the best way to get answers?" Becca had said, not missing a beat.

"No, that it can be off-putting and that it'll make people clam up. This is a trusting, relaxed environment. We should give our new guest the same benefits you had when you first came on, thank you."

"It's all right. It must feel unfair, I suppose. You will learn more about me as time goes on, Becca. I'm not that interesting, if I'm honest."

But their addictions almost seem normal. I worry if, *when* I tell them about mine, they'll fall away from my life, too weirded out by me. Today, I decide to finally explain after we're all gathered online. I owe it to them.

AudH:

I know you must wonder why I am a part of this group.
You've all been extremely patient with me; I thank you
for it. My addiction is called Geophagia

AcidGurl2010:

Wazzat

AudH:

It's the need to eat something claylike, dirt, earth, soil

Silence. I wonder if, as always, they don't know if I'm serious or kidding.

AcidGurl2010:

Wait. Let me get this. You're addicted to eating dirt? Is
that even a thing?

Will-I-am:

Jeez. I thought I was fucked up.

DrHilLary:

That's not a very nice thing to say, William. No judgments.

AcidGurl2010:

So, like, you eat soil? On purpose?

AudH:

Yes.

AcidGurl2010:

WHY?

I want to tell her if I knew the answer, I'd stop eating it, wouldn't I? Hillary beats me to it.

DrHilLary:

For the same reason you're addicted to acid, Becca, or why William drinks, or I keep falling in love. We can't help it. It's an ADDICTION.

AcidGurl2010:

That's disgusting! Since when have you been eating dirt?

DrHilLary:

That's enough questions for one day. We're here to be supportive of Audrey. Our addictions are equally disgusting Becca, so don't be quick to judge. It's brave of Audrey to open up to us like this, so let's take a moment to appreciate that, shall we?

AudH:

Thanks, Hillary. I know I've probably shocked you all, but I'd like to explain. Here's the thing, sometimes we have weird cravings, right?

AcidGurl2010:

Like, food cravings?

AudH:

Yes. Some people like the smell of leather or even to chew on it, some like the smell of gasoline, and some like the smell of rain.

Will-I-am:
Petrichor, it's called.

AudH:
Yes, petrichor. Only, that craving for me is so extreme
that I want to taste it, feel that sensation of it in my
mouth, of water on earth.

AcidGurl2010:
I actually like that smell too. I've never wanted to eat
mud though.

Will-I-am:
You're not making this shit up, are you? Just saying . . .
this is super weird.

AcidGurl2010:
How did it begin?

I sigh. I should tell them the truth. I promised I would, but Hillary
private messages me.

*I'm sorry this isn't going as well as I'd hoped! Please don't be discouraged.
You're not obliged to answer anything you don't want to.*

In the chat, there's a new notification; Hillary's now asking William
for a private conversation. I feel bad it's because of me. He's allowed to
say it's weird because it is. But I understand the need to stick to the rules.

"DrHilLary and Will-I-am will be right back," an announcement says.

AcidGurl2010:
I never knew addictions like these existed.

AudH:

I hear you, Becca. I didn't know mine was even
classified as an addiction.

Though I'd have to be dumb if I didn't work it out for myself given
how often I needed to cram the soil in my mouth, or how many times I've
thought, *I'd do anything for a hit, a single spoon of it.*
A ding alerts me to Will-I-am and DrHilLary's return.

DrHilLary:

I think we've badgered Audrey quite enough for today.

Another announcement chimes. "Will-I-am has left the chat."

DrHilLary:

I'm sorry if we haven't been too supportive, Audrey.
We will do better next time.

AudH:

Not a problem, Hillary. I appreciate all of you taking
the time to ask questions. I can understand this
might come across as weird, or even disgusting. I
think it's disgusting too, sometimes.

AcidGurl2010:

No Auds. I'm sorry. It's not disgusting, or at least only
about as disgusting as my own addiction

AudH:

Thanks, Becca. I appreciate it. Anyway, gtg now, catch
you all later. Bye.

DrHilLary:
Bye, Audrey.

AcidGurl2010:
See U Auds.

Now that I've told them, I'm not sure it was a good idea. It *has* been a long time coming, though, so perhaps it's a good thing. I could tell that Hillary was quite happy I came clean with the gang, so to speak. She's been encouraging me to open up from the start, but I've never been convinced.

There is some knowledge that can be too intimate, too invasive, the revelation of which could irrevocably change the way people look at you. This is my privately suffered shame. No one knew. Now they do, and it's as though I've stripped naked in front of a screen projected to the world.

I want to crawl inside my bedcovers and hide. I promise myself one thing then and there; no one else will ever know about it. No one can ever know. I'd rather die than tell.

I'm in the haze of a midafternoon nap when the doorbell chimes. I sit up on the bed and stretch back, yawning.

"Coming," I call out, putting on a robe over my lounging shorts and tank.

When I pull the door back, Bob says, "Hi, Audrey," not in his usual decibel level but somber.

"Hey," I say, and open it wider to let him in, but he stays straddled near the doorway.

"No, it's fine, I don't want to intrude," he says.

"Is everything all right?"

"No. Someone's broken into my home, too."

"Oh, no! That's awful! Did you call the cops?"

"I did. But they were thoroughly useless."

The same irritation I'd felt when they'd accused me of making it all up pinches me once more.

"Was anything taken?"

He doesn't reply. "Bob?"

"Yes. A photograph. It's invaluable."

"Was it an expensive frame?"

"I don't care about the damn frame! It's the photo that matters."

I'm taken aback by his tone. My face must have shown this, because he goes on to explain, "It was the only one I had of my friend. He saved me, juno, after I took the bullet to my knee."

"I'm so sorry." Yet again the inadequacy of the words hits me.

"What's that smell?" he asks, sniffing.

"What smell?" It takes a second to remember that I'd spritzed on Sarah's perfume earlier when I'd been to her place. I should have showered, gotten that smell off me really, but when she offered it, an odd curiosity got the better of me. About half an hour later though, it started to become cloyingly sweet and gave me a mild headache.

"Oh, you mean the perfume. It's heavy, isn't it? Not my style. It's Sarah's actually," I add, and immediately feel silly. As though I owe Bob an explanation.

"Is it?" His voice is awfully quiet. "Anyway, I'd better get going. I just wanted to warn you. Don't forget to lock your door, and next time, before you open the door, ask who's on the other side!"

He leaves me startled and open-mouthed. I want to tell him off for treating me like a five-year-old, but he means well. I wish the police would catch this burglar who seems to have it in for our neighborhood.

Instead of an Ambien, I picture a single sheep. Tch. I've already covered sheep this week. And pigeons. And peonies and roses and horses and beans. I suck in a deep breath and imagine a strand of pasta on the countertop. Then another, and another.

They slither off the countertop and slide up, up, up my back as they wind around my neck in a death grip. They flex their muscles, constricting my neck until my blood vessels burst and my eyes bulge. "Stop," I say. But the pythons won't stop squeezing, their thick, corded vertebrae tightening around my neck. "Please!" I beg. I sound hysterical. They don't care.

I wake up in the nether world of a dream, half-asleep, half-awake, but fully terrified, gasping, choking on a cough. I yank back the covers and jump out of bed, unentangling my body from the fabric, scared numb.

It's only a dream, I tell myself. But I'm left light-headed and on edge. I wonder if I should call my erstwhile therapist, Dr. Khan. I can still hear the woman's posh, cut-glass enunciation.

Dr. Khan was primed for life, an "Oxbridge girl." I was accepted on a hardship grant, subsidized accommodation, and freeloaded on über-rich students who were happy to indulge the likes of me in turn for favors, prepping them, even tutoring them on occasion. We had even been "up together" as she might say, but I didn't *know* her; our paths never crossed. Our kind never mixes. She's upper class, upper cut, upper crust, upper everything.

The likes of her would hardly know a poverty- and deprivation-addled hood called Northfield Oak at the fringes of the most elite institutions in county Oxfordshire. Not that I told her about my past. I had other, important things to discuss with her. Whenever I closed my eyes and sleep took me, I dreamt someone was strangling me. I'd feel the strength in those fingers, squeezing, tightening. I would wake up gasping, wondering if my neck was still attached to my body. Sometimes the dream would begin with someone chasing me. Around and around, we'd go down the same streets and intersections, I'd see the same shops while I ran, panting, the dead weight of terror slowing me down until he caught up with me.

When the nightmares worsened, she'd suggested counting would help me fall asleep.

"Does it work?" I'd asked. She'd already told me I was *too aware* of my surroundings to relax.

"It's like hypnotizing yourself into sleeping."

I want to call her right now and tell her that she's wrong. Nothing is safe anymore, not even pasta.

There's a *thud*. A door has shut. It's Sarah's door by the sound of it. I frown. After the stupid dream, I managed to fall asleep only some time ago. Who's visiting her so late? She screams holy hell if I as much as text her after nine. I tiptoe into the master closet and put on the headphones attached to the listening device on the wall. I wince when the bass buzzes in my ear and adjust the treble to compensate. There's moaning, and a sudden, small *thump*. I wonder if she's hurt when someone says, "Come to papa."

The voice is unmistakable.

"Rooowwr."

A burst of intense heat blooms in my chest and creeps up my neck. After listening for a few seconds longer to ensure I haven't misheard, I scurry out of there.

Back in the bedroom, I peel back the bedcover and drag my body under it. The rhythmic thudding from next door makes me cringe.

Sarah, for being a new mother—Nicole is about five weeks old—has resumed her social life. Yesterday, she dumped Nicole in my lap because she simply had to get out of the house. Dumbstruck, I babysat even though it isn't something I've ever imagined doing, and not only because I'm blind. I protested, pointed out the obvious, that she should pick someone who could *see* the baby.

"Nah, you'll be fine. It's not like she can run around, she's only weeks old. All she needs is her bottle and to be burped and to sleep."

"Just feed her, clean her, and put her to bed? Easy, then."

She missed my sarcasm entirely. "Just check that she's breathing, though. She's so quiet, sometimes. It makes me worry."

She came back to pick up Nicole, not drunk, not slurring, but with a new fragrance on her. A mix of sweat, sex, and her expensive perfume mingled with a man's aftershave—and smoke. A familiar aftershave, but I don't judge, Sarah is free to do exactly as she pleases. It's the world's oldest trick—blame the woman—but people forget something important: It takes two to break a bed.

But I wonder what Mrs. Kirsch would say if she saw her clever Ronnie now, playing matador at the cattle show on the other side of that wall.

SARAH

THE INTERMITTENT MACHINE BEEPS AND STERILE AIR OF THE HOSPITAL have lulled me to sleep. As I rotate my neck, stretching, my eyes adjust to the harsh glare from the overhead lighting. Dan's still asleep. I yawn and look at the time. Nine-twenty. My back is taut from the uncomfortable straight-back chair. I stretch, then slip my hand into Dan's bag and retrieve his laptop. I enter his login credentials, shocked to find they still work. A shrill ringtone shatters the clinical silence.

I dip my hand into my pocket right away, only to realize it isn't the ringtone of my phone. My eyes dart to Dan's face but he's still in la-la land. There's a blue light peeping out from his laptop bag. I stick my hand in and grab his phone to silence it when I see the caller ID. GERRY, LAWYER.

I stare at it for a brief second before pressing Dan's phone to my ear. "Yes?"

"Um . . . May I speak to Dan?"

From the way the rumbling baritone hesitates, I'm certain he's pulled the phone away from his ear to check he's dialed the right number.

"Are you his lawyer?"

"Yes. Who is this?"

"I'm Sarah, Dan's friend."

I explain where we are.

"Jesus! Is he okay?" he asks.

"Yes. He will be."

"Can I speak to him?"

"He's asleep right now. I'll let him know you called when he wakes."

"Okay."

"Before you go, may I ask you something?"

"Yes?"

"Is Dan being sued? Are you representing him?"

"That's two questions but I'll answer. He's not yet being sued."

"But he likely will be?"

"It depends," he says, clamming up.

"Look, I want to help him. He's a very good friend."

"Until I have Dan's consent, I can't tell you anything."

Dammit.

"Hello?" I say but the disconnect tone beeps in my ear.

Not yet, he'd said. I should be relieved. Instead, I'm angrier at the unfairness of it all. A mere week ago, Dan had a job. He was happy, up for a promotion. All credibility and hard work down the drain in three days. And Fortitude is responsible. Someone at Fortitude, at any rate.

The doctor, when he comes at about ten at night, is all business. Kayla explains I'm a friend. Code for: She's not a relative. They check pulse, take temperature, shine a light into Dan's sleeping eyes, and look at the charts clipped to the bottom of the bed.

"And you're the one who brought him in?" He graces me with a glance.

"Yes."

"Had he been depressed of late?"

I shake my head. The conversation with Gerry makes me clam up. If they sue Dan, anything I say now could come back to bite him in the proverbial ass.

"Any sudden events? A breakup?"

I want to scoff. A breakup is never sudden. It is a slow, painful death, a gradual decay of the heart, I want to say, but I shake my head again.

"Had he been on sleeping pills long?"

"I'm sorry. I'm afraid I don't know. You'll have to ask him."

The doctor mutters something to Kayla. I hear the word *stable* and want to sob with relief.

"He's going to be asleep for some time. We've pumped most of it out of his system, but the stuff in the bloodstream will have to travel the course." He sounds definitive now.

"And he's not going to have any damage?"

The good doctor narrows his eyes at me. "We'll know more once he surfaces."

I nod. He shakes my hand and marches out, to the next bed.

Dan has slept right through it all. I take my place on the chair near the door like a sentry and watch him. The nostrils of his pointed nose flare with every inhale. His full mouth with bow-shaped lips is embossed into a square, handsome, angular jaw, one I'm tempted to punch right now.

It's almost four-fifteen when I wake up to stretch my neck yet again, and I note that Dan's hand has moved from its last position. I sit up straight, to ease the knot in my back. My phone slides off my lap and clacks to the floor. I wince and bend to pick it up when there's a full, noisy sigh, the sigh of someone who has slept long and deep. I'm caught between slapping him awake and letting him linger in this numbing peace, which will be gone once he wakes up with full cognizance.

I slip into a fitful sleep. Just as I'm chasing it deeper, someone says something. I'm in my cubicle and Celia is standing up, sneering at me from hers. Norman is trying to get my attention. Sarah, he calls me, but I'm still staring at Celia staring at me.

"What is it, Norman?" I murmur when I hear my name again. I wake up and find myself splayed out on the chair, half sinking to the floor. Dan is staring at me with bewildered goggle eyes.

"Sarah? What . . . ?" He looks around, first uncertain, then growing grimmer, noting the hospital gown, the IV attached to his arm, and the machine monitoring his heart rate and blood pressure.

He closes his eyes again, purposefully this time, and covers his face with his free hand.

He starts to say something, but his voice is dry and cracked. I reach for the cup of ice on the table beside him, a plastic straw poking out. He stares at me for a moment before letting me slip the straw through his mouth.

He looks down, unable to meet my eyes.

I fold my arms across my body and stand over him, silent, glaring. A single, massive tear rolls down his cheek. It melts me. I reach out and press my palm to his arm.

"You're okay, Dan. You're going to be fine."

He nods, still unable to look me in the eye.

"Is there anyone you'd like me to call?"

He shakes his head, utter misery stamped on his tired gray face.

"Is it so bad? Can't you tell me?"

He sighs and turns his neck, casting a pained glance at me.

"Dan!"

He flinches. "I've been a—." He begins to cough again.

Should I be pummeling him when he can barely speak? Then I remember his slack face and limp body a few hours ago. I thrust the glass with shaved ice in front of his face and slip the straw into his mouth again. He sips deeply and gulps.

He pauses, breathing heavily, then says, "I've been accused of embezzling."

It's what I've been suspecting, but to hear Dan pronounce it gives it a cold, tangible form. *It shows you don't know me at all* . . . No. He was bluffing.

"Two days ago, you were trying to convince me to believe this ridiculous accusation. Tell me, if you truly wanted to steal money, don't you have to be alive to spend it?"

He looks down again. "I never said I took it."

"Not in those words. But you said I don't know you. And you're so wrong. I do know you. You would never steal money from *anyone*, let alone your employer."

"Even if I was in deep financial debt?"

I lift his chin to make him look at me. "Even more so. *Tell* me."

He looks startled, then he sighs. "I had a boyfriend, back in Minneapolis. We'd been together ever since I came out, after high school. We were supposed to move to New York. I'd get here first and he'd follow a few months later. But the plan fell apart as soon as I left. He got into trouble, did some stupid things, and did time for a couple of months for something petty. After he got out, he broke up with me."

Dan pauses and looks away, staring at the beeping machine counting his increasing pulse. "I suspected it was because he'd met someone else, although he never told me that in so many words. I was heartbroken, but I understood. Something happened to him in prison. He changed. Completely. The bitter man who came out of prison was someone I didn't recognize. I tried so hard to get him back. Once I realized he wasn't kidding about us, I still tried to reach him. Not to be together, you understand, to get Tom, the old Tom, back. It didn't work. He began getting into even more trouble. Started gambling."

Something twists in my gut. I can guess what Dan's going to say next, but I let him say it in his own words.

"Tom lost *so* much money." He scoffs and looks at me. "Money he didn't have. At the time all I could think was that I was responsible. If I hadn't chased some dream and moved here, he would never have gone to prison."

"You loaned him money, didn't you?"

Dan nods. "It's amazing how quickly it all goes. I kept giving a little here and a little there. I've next to nothing left now."

His pulse is close to 95, but I don't want him to stop.

"They're saying I've stolen hundreds of thousands of dollars and unless I return every cent, they're going to sue me."

"What proof do they have?"

"That's the thing; they won't tell me! Whatever it is, it's apparently irrefutable. I couldn't believe it when David called me into his office, sat me down, and asked me, cool as you like, where I'd hidden the money. And there I sat, like an idiot, not the faintest idea what he was talking about. The CEO came into the office next and tried a different tactic. Spoke kindly, said he understood if I was tempted, et cetera, but if I told him where the money was, it would be better for me. How could I tell them what I didn't know? Before I knew what was happening, they had someone collect my things from my office and escort me out of the building. David shook his head and handed me the card of a good lawyer."

It does sound awful. But there's something else, too. It's the look in Dan's eyes. Haunted. He hasn't told me everything.

"Being accused or even fired for embezzling is one thing, Dan. But it's a leap from there . . . to swallowing a bottle of sleeping pills!"

He blanches and looks down, at the linoleum-covered gray floor. "Y-you won't understand."

"Try me."

"It's family. It's complicated."

"Isn't it always?"

He returns my wry smile with his own, and nods. "My dad's a pastor. When I came out, I didn't know what to expect. He's progressive and all, but things are always different when it comes to your own. But *he* surprised *me*. All of them did, my parents, my brothers, and my sister. My dad looked me in the eye and said, *I'm glad you've figured it out, because we've always known.* They were nothing but supportive."

Warmth blooms in my chest for a family I've never met but feel as though I already know. "Then what was the problem?"

He sighs. "It was Tom. From the start, they didn't like him, not even my sis, Heather, who can get along with anybody." Dan's gaze shifts to the floor. "I fought with them, said some u-unforgivable things, that they secretly hated me for being gay, that they're too stuck up to be happy for me. Eventually, we stopped talking at all because I continued dating Tom despite what they thought. Then Tom went to prison. Heather called me when she found out."

"And said what? *We told you so?*"

"No. It was worse," he says, smiling sadly. "She didn't say anything. Just that they missed me. And we went back to being who we were as if nothing had happened."

"It's worse—isn't it?—when others can see the thing you can't, even if it's staring you in the face."

He nods. Then it dawns on me. "They didn't know that you kept in touch with Tom after prison?"

He shakes his head.

"I should've listened to them. If they found out that I'd kept in touch with him, helped him, gave him money . . . And now with this charge of embezzlement hanging over me, even if they don't believe it, the whole community knows my dad and our family. People will talk." His eyes mist up.

"That's the way it goes in small towns," I say.

"The very thought of facing them was . . ." He starts to choke. "I couldn't—"

"Hey." I put my hand on his arm and squeeze. "It's going to be all right. Don't think about all that right now. Things will look better once you've slept properly and your head clears."

By the time I call in sick, I don't have to lie. Mr. D'Angelo's germs have caught up to me. Mr. Tcheznich sounds quite convinced when he says I should stay home. He's a bit of a germophobe himself. The thought of being sequestered with me oozing, sneezing, and coughing in that tiny office isn't bearable.

"I'll be back," I tell Dan.

"Hey, get back to work. I'll manage."

"I've already called it in—it's Wednesday and this is Thanksgiving week anyway. But I need to go home for a bit. I'll see you midmorning."

He holds my glance with a long, silent one of his own and nods.

"Sarah?" he calls out when I'm at the door.

"Yep?"

His eyes are rimmed red again. "Thanks."

I offer a reassuring smile but as I walk out of there, it drops off my face. If I were a cop or someone from Fortitude, I'd be building a case against Dan right now with everything he's told me. And the fact that he tried to take his own life will only highlight his guilt. The final nail in his coffin.

AUDREY: NOW

THE *BBRR BBRR* OF THE PHONE VIBRATING AGAINST THE BEDSIDE TABLE awakens me. It's a few rings before I'm coherent enough to answer.

"Hello?" My voice is gruff and thick from sleep.

"Ms. Hughes, I wondered if we could speak."

"Detective Greene? What time is it?" I ask through a yawn.

There's a muffled, "Shit!" before he says, "It's 5:45. I apologize, I didn't realize it was this early. I've woken you up."

"No problem. How can I help you?"

"Ms. Hughes, Audrey, would it be all right if I came down?"

"Now?"

"In a little bit. Say, eight? I heard about the break-in. I'd like to look around if that's okay."

"Sure. I'll see you at eight, then."

"Sorry to wake you up, again. See you."

"Hello, Ms. Hughes," the detective greets me when I open the door a few minutes past eight.

"Hello, Detective. Come in."

He steps inside and follows me into the kitchen.

"Coffee?"

"Yes, please," he says. "But first, may I have a look around?"

"Sure. I'd use this door." I point to the service door at the end of the kitchen. "It leads to the mudroom and then on to the garage."

"And here's where they found the cigarette butt." I point to the window above the sink.

"I'll be right back," he says, and makes for the door.

I reach for the tin sitting on the counter and drop measured scoops of coffee into the French press. The door to the garage opens and closes. The alarm on the security app chirps, letting me know the door has been opened. The microwave timer comes on when I hit a preset button for four minutes. I hear the thump of his shoes on the concrete garage floor. At least he's being more thorough than Rodriguez and Riley. The alarm chirps again after the door closes once more. Detective Greene's shoes clatter toward the tiled kitchen flooring.

"There don't seem to be any signs of forced entry," Greene says.

"So they told me." I stop the microwave timer and reach for the French press.

"How did you know the timer was done?"

"Habit. I've done it enough times. I plunge the filter downward, steady, even.

"Forgive my directness, but you seem to function quite well, for a—"

"Blind person?"

"Yes," he adds.

I like that he doesn't walk on eggshells around me. It's refreshing. "Back when I first lost my vision, I couldn't even make a cup of tea without either spilling it or burning myself. It's taken practice and a *lot* of hard work to function."

I place the French press on the island, along with a porcelain creamer. A cloud of rich java hangs in the air. "Here." I hand him a mug. "Help yourself to more if you like."

"Thanks. So, Audrey, tell me about Sarah," he says. There's a slurp followed by a sigh.

"I thought you were here about yesterday's break-in?"

"I am."

I should have known better than to trust he'd come all this way and not pass up another opportunity to question me. "What do you want to know?"

"What was Sarah like?"

I sit back in the bar chair. "Some might have found her appalling. Her honesty was hardly ever shy of rudeness, but she called a spade a spade. Sarah was one of the most talented people I've known."

"Talented in what way?"

"She could do anything. Be anyone. She could imitate someone after meeting them once. It was brilliant and frightening."

"She was well-liked?"

"I know people like to think that of the dead, but the truth is that Sarah didn't care who liked her and who didn't. Most people were awestruck by her. Men," I say, gulping a sip, "couldn't resist her. They were fireflies to her light."

"Men?"

"Men like Brian, like Mrs. Kirsch's Ronnie." After a pause, I add, "I might have failed to mention this before, but I heard Ronnie threaten Sarah."

"When was this?"

"Less than a month ago. I only overheard them through the closet upstairs."

"What was it about?"

"I think, and this is only a guess, she was blackmailing him. Money or she shows some photographs to his wife."

Greene falls silent.

"Oh, I meant to mention something when you in—" I almost say *interrogated me*, but catch myself. "When I gave my statement. I can't be certain this is relevant, but Sarah asked me to track down someone for her."

"Track down?" Greene asks.

"Yes. Someone she'd lost touch with, Adam Briggs."

"And why would she ask you to do it, not do it herself?"

"I got the feeling she had already tried and failed."

"And she thought you were qualified to do it?"

"I have a nose for this sort of thing."

IN THE DARK I SEE YOU

"Do you, now? And did you find him?"

"Yes. He's in Boston. If you have a pen and paper . . ."

"Always," he says.

"1289 Fernwood Drive, Charlestown, Massachusetts 02129."

"You have a thing for addresses, too?" Greene asks.

My lips curve into a small smile. "Apparently."

"And what was Sarah's relationship with Adam?"

"An old boyfriend, Sarah said. He moved away. She lost touch. I don't know why she was looking for him."

"Thanks for letting us know. Anyway, about the break-in . . ."

"Yes?"

"It's quite odd."

I'm unprepared for the quick pinch of irritation. "Don't you believe me?"

"I do. I believe you."

I sigh. "That's an improvement. Officers Riley and Rodriguez seem to think I'm making this up. Possibly for attention."

"They said that?"

"Not this time. But when my home was broken into a few months ago, Officer Riley certainly implied it. I got the impression they think I was wasting their time. Anyway, you were saying there's something odd about the break-in?"

"They should have taken you seriously. The break-in is a weird mix of professionalism and amateurism."

"What does that mean, exactly?"

"I don't want to scare you, but it's not a good sign."

"You are scaring me, but I'm easily frightened these days."

"If the alarm hadn't gone off, you might have never known the house was broken into. And nothing was taken?"

"As far as I can tell."

"As I said, I don't want to scare you, but from the number of cigarette butts left around, this intruder appears to have spent time in your house.

They might have even watched you. Is there any reason you can think of why someone would do that?"

I'm cold again. A mental image forms: I'm in bed, face slack, body tucked beneath a comforter, and someone is standing at the base of the bed, silent, watching. I shudder.

"No. I can't."

"You said you're an accountant, for Aegis?"

"Yes, that's right."

"What sort of an accountant?"

"Would you excuse me for a second?"

"Sure."

In the toilet down the hallway from the kitchen, I put my phone on silent and type a message to Greg.

> Detective Greene is here. He wants to know more about what I do.

I start the tap water running and wait for the phone to vibrate.

I put the phone to my ear when the buzz of Greg's reply comes, hoping the detective hasn't heard it. A monotonous voice reads, *Give him the bare minimum. No specifics.*

Of course, Greg doesn't want me to talk about clients. Anonymity is everything in our sphere. I wait a few seconds before flushing and then open the tap again.

"Would you like some more coffee?" I ask, before sitting opposite Greene again.

"No actually. I have to leave."

"Oh, okay. Is everything all right?"

There's a sigh. "No."

The very air around me has changed. "What is it?"

"Thanks for the coffee."

He's standing up now, ready to leave. His evasion only confirms my fear. Something's happened and it's bad. I can sense it in my bones.

"It's not clear whether the murder and the break-in here are connected, but we're going with the assumption they are. And that could mean that you might be in danger. I'd advise caution."

"What would you like me to do?"

"Could you stay with a friend or a relative for a couple of days?"

"No, Detective Greene. I'm afraid I don't want to."

"It's for your own safety."

"I understand, but I can't let them run me out of my home. And this isn't pride, by the way, or at least, not in the way you think. I *need* familiarity to survive. I know my own home from one end of the door to another. I'd be stumbling around if I went somewhere totally new. It'd be very unsettling."

"Then at least take general precautions. Lock your door, et cetera."

"That sounds very reassuring," I say with a tight smile.

"We've been in touch with Hoyt Security. They say there's no sign anyone other than you opened and closed the doors until that patio door opened after the alarm was set. But I'd get them to come, check things out."

"They are going to." The doorbell rings. "I think that's them, now."

"Thanks for your time, Ms. Hughes, sorry again to have woken you up so early."

"No problem." I walk him to the door.

"I'll be in touch. If you think of some detail, even if it seems harmless or insignificant, or remember anything useful, don't hesitate to call us."

"Useful?" Something about the detective's tone makes me uncomfortable.

"Like Ronnie."

I flush and nod as I open the door to two men.

"Ms. Hughes, we're from Hoyt Security."

"Can I see your IDs?" Detective Greene asks.

"And who are you?" one of the men asks Greene.

"I'll show you mine if you show me yours," Greene says.

In the intermittent silence, I assume they're handing over their badges or IDs. The sun doesn't prickle my skin; it must be a cloudy day, but the warmth of summer rushes into the house when I let them in.

"We'll be running some tests to check out the system, Ms. Hughes. Don't let us keep you. We'll find you when we're done," of them says to me.

I return to the island, their presence soothing *and* annoying, unable to get Detective Greene's words out of my head. *This intruder appears to have spent time in your house. They might have even watched you . . .*

I'm tempted to call and tell Greg that I want to get out of here this instant. I pluck my phone from my pocket and twirl it in my hand. No. It wouldn't do to go running to my new boss at the first sign of trouble. I need to wear my big girl trousers and sort it out myself. I hate to think this way but for the first time since those initial days, I wish I had *some* vision. Five percent. A teeny bit of light perception, even. It's better than *nothing*.

Right now, I'm a sitting duck. An easy victim. Someone could walk right in to hack me to pieces, and I wouldn't see them coming.

SARAH

THE BAGEL IS SANDPAPER. IT SCRAPES AWAY AT THE INSIDES OF MY THROAT as I try to chew and down it with some coffee that may as well be gravy or dishwater. My taste buds have gone numb. Damn Mr. D'Angelo.

I chase the flat breakfast with another cold pill and grab a bag with a change of clothes, my kit, and my laptop. Then I head to Dan's place in a cab and keep it waiting below while I pack a clean set of clothes into an overnight bag from his closet, then head to Mount Sinai. As the blocks pass by in a blur, I lean my head against the passenger side at the back and close my eyes.

"Hey, lady."

I startle when I hear a stranger's voice.

"We're here," the cabbie says.

My chest rattles and I step back and cough into my arm before handing him the fare in cash I'd remembered to grab from home at the last moment.

"Thanks," I say, and hold out my hand for the change, but he's already gone, taillights blinking in the gray morning.

A weird fog not unlike jet lag descends on me as I walk into the antiseptic-laden atmosphere of Mount Sinai's waiting room to take the elevator.

Upstairs, Dan's sitting up on the bed, a nurse taking his pulse. I wave the bag at him as I enter.

"Clothes."

"Time I got out of this miniskirt."

"It suits you," the nurse says, and winks at me.

"Let's get you out of here, shall we?" I say to Dan. "Are you cleared to go?"

"Yep," he says, scratching his stubble with his free hand.

"What about the tests they were supposed to do this morning?"

The nurse sticks a thermometer in his mouth when he opens it to answer. I cringe when I think about how far the pills might have traveled, and all the possible damage they could have done.

"He's ready to get outta here," the nurse says to me, while he sits awkwardly.

The thermometer beeps a few seconds later. She takes it out of his mouth. "97.6," she says.

"So there's no problem? No lasting . . . damage?" I trip on my words, having tried to choose them too carefully.

"You're going to be just fine, aren't you?" she says.

He looks appropriately penitent.

The nurse glances first at me and then at him. "A word before you leave," she says to him.

"Sure," he says.

"In private," she adds.

"She's staying," he says, pointing at me.

"Suit yourself. Now, I'm going to be honest. I don't want to see you back here, you got it? Talk to someone, anyone, a friend, a professional, a priest, whoever."

Dan's red-faced and staring at the floor. I feel awful for him. Almost. But the right things are being said, even if not by me.

She shuts the curtain behind us so Dan can change.

"Girlfriend?" she asks me.

I shake my head. "Friend."

"Make sure someone stays with him for a few days?" She's lowered her voice. "Family member, or a good friend?"

"Is he not fully recovered?"

She throws a sharp, meaningful look. "People who've failed often try again, so you'll want someone to keep an eye on him."

"Of course."

Then she cocks her head, her mouth curving into a sly smile. "I wouldn't mind keeping both eyes on him. If George Clooney and Cary Grant had a love child . . ."

I shrug and shake my head. "He bats for the opposite team."

She pouts. "Lucky men. Boo for us. Anyway," she says, and rattles off instructions for the next few days.

"Thanks," I say. She waves me off and heads to the next bed.

When he flings back the curtain, he looks much better than he's done these past few hours. Shades of his rugged, all-American handsomeness peek through, even if the jeans are hanging on him and the fitted shirt looks a whole size larger now.

The nurse tilts her head and wags a finger at him as we head to the elevator.

"I deserved that, didn't I?" he asks, as we walk to the elevator.

I nod with vigor. "You did."

We're both silent in the cab. Me from an aching body and throat, and having slept so little, my eyes shut of their own accord. And him from sleeping too much, his body slumping under the weight of everything that's happened these past few days. Time, I think as I drift in and out of wakefulness, is such a strange measure. This week could have been a whole age.

We're both asleep when the cabbie wakes us. My head has lolled off on Dan's considerable shoulder.

"Five more minutes," I say.

"This isn't a spa, lady. Wake up," says the cabbie. I sit up startled, then mortified, and shake Dan awake.

"We're here," I say. After I pay the cabbie, we both exit the cab, slow and doddering like two dimwitted chickens.

We're stretched out on the sofa, his legs on the coffee table, mine tucked underneath my body in a semicircle. We're watching the old *Mission Impossible* TV series. He gets only air channels so it's either that or *Matlock*. An

hour in, the words run into each other and everything around me shim-
mers beyond my grasp, blurry.

"You're burning up," he says, touching my forehead with the back of
his palm. My eyes are slits, swollen with heat. Everything is out of focus.

"Mm," I manage to mumble with my sore, aching throat, before sloping sideways.

"Hey, hey," he says, getting up and pushing my form across the sofa.
His eyes, I can tell, are droopy, too. Sleep isn't done with him. He layers
coats and blankets on me.

"I'll make some soup," he says in the blotting dusk light, but I'm out
cold soon after.

The whole of the following day I lie on his sofa, in and out of consciousness. Blips of him flitting about checking my forehead, fuzz and
pill like the threads of the fabric in the back of the upholstery. I'm now
intimately acquainted with his sofa. The noisy spring that's somewhere
between the second and third cushions *boings* every time I move. The
clean scent of Febreze on the arms and the backrest wafts through in fits.
I doze in and out as my fever breaks and returns.

"Should I take you to the ER?" he whispers during one of my brief
clarity-edged moments.

"We just left one. I'm not going back. Hate hospitals."

He stands back and purses his lips. "No one *likes* hospitals."

His further reasoning is lost on me as I drift into another bout of
virus-induced sleep.

It's Saturday morning when I'm finally able to sit up. Dan finds me,
the new fixture on his living room sofa, staring out the window.

"You're up!" he says. He looks about as battered and spent as I do. My
stomach lets out a coiled rumble.

He smiles. "Eggs?"

"I'll go wash up first, shall I? There's a distinct smell in this room and
I'm afraid it's me."

A slow hot shower later, I head to the table where Dan's set plates. The place looks larger now that he's cleaned up.

"Not exactly a Thanksgiving meal." He thrusts a plate of steaming scrambled eggs and toast in front of me.

"More?" he asks, after I gobble it up within a matter of minutes.

I shake my head and sip some blissful breakfast tea. At least it doesn't hurt to swallow anymore. My voice has gone all coldy and nasal, but that's to be expected after a bug like the one I had.

"We're going to figure this out, you and I, and we're going to sort it." I sound like a stranger to myself.

He begins to say something. I put up my hand and shake my head. "I won't take no for an answer."

"But you could get into trouble, too," he says, his ocean-deep eyes wide with concern.

"It doesn't matter if I do. And we'll be careful, won't we?"

He sits back, his large frame somehow squeezing itself into what looks like a toy chair underneath him.

There's a spark in his eyes when he turns to look at me, something I've been waiting to see. Hope.

AUDREY: THEN
5 MONTHS AGO

"You should be careful," Sarah says, wrapping my thumb snugly in a Band-Aid. "What are you cooking anyway?"

"Not cooking, making a salad."

"Why do you need to chop salad?"

"I like my lettuce in bite-sized pieces."

"Why?" she says, tossing the adhesive backing in the garbage can, evidently, from the way the can clangs shut.

"So I don't have to stuff them in my mouth like a big moo-cow."

"You're funny!" Sarah says. She says that often. Sometimes I worry she doesn't know that I'm kidding.

"You can't eat this anyway," she says.

"Why not?" With my right index, I prod my finger encased in the tight Band-Aid.

"Cuz there's blood all over. I'm tossing it."

I sigh. "Yep," I say. The bowl scrapes off the island. I pick up the cutting board and dump it in the sink.

"Anyway, it's not as if you're going to eat it."

I freeze for a moment, as though my whole body has undergone a sudden paralysis. "What?" It's an effort to open my jaw.

"I only see you make food. I've never once seen you eat."

"Don't be silly. Of course, I eat. And Jason, by the way, thinks I need to lose five pounds."

Sarah sniggers. "Jason's a drill sergeant obsessed with thinness and toned bodies. He's bad for body image."

"That's so true," I say, filling the sink with hot water. "He's one complaint away from a body-shaming class."

There's a muffled mewl from the corner of the room. Sarah tenses in response. It's the change I've noticed ever since she's become a mom. Before, she was always relaxed. Now she's in *mom* mode, limbs and boobs coordinating to feed the little monster.

"Hi, sweetheart, did you sleep well?" she asks.

The answer is a pinching, outraged wail like she's screaming, *How dare you ask me any questions? Can't you see I'm hungry? Nipple! Gimme nipple!*

"Aww, my little munchkins . . . Mommy's coming."

The baby bag zipper opens. I hear shuffling while I soak the knife and chopping board in hot water, adding a few drops of liquid from a bottle under the sink.

"Eww . . . I smell bleach," Sarah says, seconds later.

"Sorry." My hand tenses for a second before I cap the bottle and shove it into its allotted spot.

"But that's your chopping board."

"I know. It's to decontaminate the blood."

"That stuff is dangerous! You'll end up ingesting it in tiny doses and die of poisoning."

There are a million other ways to die, I want to say, but I bite my tongue.

"So," she says, sighing. A percussive grunt, and gulp, like a *k-ah,* interrupts her. The little one is suckling.

"Ben has texted me. Ben from the café I told you about last week?"

"O-kay?"

"He wants to meet. I've said no, of course. Oh God, I keep forgetting I'm supposed to hydrate right before I feed."

I open the fridge, reach for a bottle of apple juice in the door, and hand it to her. From the *glug, glug,* I picture her guzzling it down.

The pace of the little one's suckling sound has quickened, too, I notice. This tiny apple hasn't fallen far from the tree. Will she also grow up blond and green-eyed? Will she have a perfect, *toned* body like her mother? And break hearts like her? Or become a manipulative liar like Sarah?

"You'd like Ben. He's handsome. But I don't think he's the kind of guy you'd date."

"And what kind is that?"

"Brawny. Cuz you'd be the brains in a relationship."

I sigh and resist explaining all the wrongs in that statement. A memory assaults me out of nowhere, me on top of him, his chest-hair stubble grazing my sensitive skin, the feel of his thick arms twining around mine . . . a lifetime ago. "I do like brawny men. I had a boyfriend once, big, like a quarterback."

"Why did it break off?"

"Because you're right. I realized I needed him to use his brain more."

"Tsk," she admonishes as though I'd made a terrible mistake.

A whiff of Sarah's perfume assaults my senses as she twitters on about Ben. It makes me light-headed. I step up into the barstool near the counter and sag into it. She wants to meet him, I can tell. It's her tone. She always uses that tone when she wants to be emphatic and deny what she's very well about to do.

In the time I've known her, she's done a lot of things she's emphatically denied.

"What's up with you anyway?" Sarah asks, sighing again. She must be tired. Feeding the baby is a full-time job, but she never complains. "I never understood all the fuss these new moms make, dropping their top and whipping out a throbbing boob anytime, anywhere. But now I *totally* get it. Mommy would drop everything to feed you, my little bubkins, my shmugleywoogley. Yes, she will, yes . . . she . . . will . . . mwah mwah." She smooches the little one, murmuring gibberish only the pair of them understand. There's a corresponding squeak and pigeon cooing.

"What do you mean, what's up with me? Nothing," I say.

"You look tired. One would think you were the one losing sleep over the baby. You've got bags under your eyes. Whereas I still look fabulous on four hours' sleep."

"It's work." It comes out feeble. It's so uncharacteristic of me. I'm never feeble. Correction, I never *used to be* feeble. But now . . .

"Seriously?"

I don't tell her that I haven't been sleeping well. She doesn't know half of it. "I like what I do."

"Where do you work anyway?"

"A small firm. You wouldn't know it."

"You're funny," she says.

"How do you mean?"

"You always act like everything is such a mystery."

I tense up. "What?"

"*A small firm?*" she says, imitating me to perfection. "Does it have a name?"

I try laughing, but it falls flat to my ears. "No mystery. It's called Analytica."

"*I've* never heard of it."

I smile and shrug like I've made my point.

"And what is it you do?"

"Research. Boring, clerical research."

"I'd never have taken you for such a nerd."

I want so much to tell her it wasn't by choice, but I let her chatter on. It's after she leaves that I wonder how much longer I'm going to have to keep up the lies, the pretense. It's exhausting.

Mayonnaise squirts out of the bottle when I squeeze the center. Birthdays are still on my mind as I spread it on soft, fresh sliced bread and fold in thin slices of cold ham. The corners of my lips lift when I think of how excited Priya is about her party.

It reminds me of my birthday and the smile slides off my face. I wasn't planned, expected, or welcome. Barbara used to remind me of this fact, quite often followed by a sharp sting on my cheek. I had been the starver of the oxygen in her life. She'd had plans until I came along and quashed her dreams.

The phone rings. Siri announces that it's Sherman.

"Hey," I say, after I pick up.

"You okay?"

"Yeah, why?"

"You're sounding . . . like you're deep in thought."

His warmth shakes off my gloom. "Nah, I'm good. What's up?"

"About the background checks—"

"Everyone's got a boringly normal past?"

"Almost."

"Tell me."

"It's Priya."

"What?" I set the butter knife into the sink and wipe my hand on the towel.

"Right?" he says.

I share his disbelief. "Let me guess, shoplifting?"

"Nope. She was charged with assault."

"What!" From the start, I've imagined Priya as someone with spunk, the kind that might've aged her parents a bit prematurely. But I'd never have numbered violence as one among her traits.

"Yeah. She punched a fellow student her junior year, a girl called Katlyn."

My jaw drops. "Whatever for?"

"I can't be certain because the charges were dropped but I snooped on her social media profile from back then. Katlyn had apparently flirted with the guy Priya had been dating at the time."

I pull back an island chair and flop into it. "That was what, five, six years ago?"

"Seven."

"Poor Priya. History repeats itself rather cruelly."

"Everyone else appears to be quite clean apart from a couple of parking tickets, and the like."

I'm rattled by this discovery about Priya. It's the unlikeliness of it that surprises me. Then I remember my mother's angelic, innocent face and her quick, sharp hand. No one could reconcile "poor Barbara" with the bruises that often covered my body. One never knows.

"Oh, before I forget, Priya loved her gift."

"I'm glad," he says.

I hang up after promising to touch base later.

"You don't have the right clothes," Sarah proclaims. She's invaded my bedroom again, browsing my closet, and, I suspect from her tone, with disgust.

"It's only a birthday party," I say. I hate the defensive edge that's crept into my voice. "I'm sure a pair of jeans and a nice top will work."

"You can't see, but I'm glaring at you right now. A top and a pair of jeans? You're not going to the mall. This is a party."

I know what's got her back up. It's because I'm invited to a party when she isn't. Everyone from our row as well as a few from the back row have been invited. Everyone except for Sarah is going to be there.

From the sudden warmth that bathes me, I imagine she's switched on all the lights in my master bedroom. I hear rustling. She's choosing between outfits, pulling off their plastic dry-clean covering. Nearby, Nicole's soft, sated breathing is a comforting rhythm. I imagine her little face, scrunched up in sleep, lips pursed into a pout.

"I do have dresses."

"Yes. I've seen them." She laughs a little unkindly. "Mine are better. Like this one. It's a pretty salmon pink. It'll look great with your hair." Her flat pumps slap the wood floor of my bedroom with a thwack like she's turning on a ramp walk. She's parading them for me, which is silly, not because I can't see but because I'd look ridiculous in her clothes.

"And this," she says, walking toward me again, "is a deep red."

I run a mental price check on the dresses, the shoes, and the makeup as she rattles off designer names. I imagine her whipping out credit cards and swiping with absolute abandon.

"Never mind," she says. "The red won't go with your coloring. You're too pale."

"It's winter."

"I'll have to bronze you up a bit," she says, ignoring my weak protest.

It's a waste of time. These clothes, *her* clothes—all this tight, clingy stuff—are not made for my body. I tell her that I like my cardigans and sweatshirts, but she rolls her eyes at me again, I know; I can picture her doing it.

She gasps, startling me. "This is *the* one. It's jewel-tone green. It'll bring out the jade in your eyes and complement your lovely dark hair. It'll pair well with my black wedge," she adds.

Sarah and I take the same size in shoes. She insists we're the same dress size, too, but I suspect I'm one size bigger. Jason thinks so. He's trying to mold me into Sarah's image.

Today he said he wants me to build my triceps like Sarah's. Last week, he singled out my abs. "Your first rib bone is too low and juts out a bit," he said, poking into my bone, making me giggle. "Hers is kinda high, you know? It sits right under her breast. It makes it easier to arch into the waist."

"So rude of my rib to stick out. Maybe I should have it removed," I said, hiding a smirk.

"Yeah, right," he said, agreeing with me at first, then hesitating. "That might be a bit extreme. I'm sure we can work around it."

Now Sarah's trying to squeeze said rude rib into her green dress, so she can zip up the waist.

She pats my belly. "Suck it in for a sec," she says. I do as asked. She zips the metal teeth together.

"You're so lean," she says, patting it again. "Mine used to be concave, I swear, but not anymore," she whines. "I look like Humpty Dumpty."

I can't bear her protesting and complaining. It's at the tip of my tongue to tell her to shut up when I feel the hem of the dress I've worn slide up.

"Don't you wax?" Sarah's voice rings out from the floor.

"Sarah!" I exclaim, turning away from her and tugging on the dress, pulling it down urgently.

"What? It's only me," she says. I can tell her eyes are on me.

"Wax?" I sound dimwitted again. She often makes me feel as though I've left my brains behind somewhere like a forgotten bag in some shopping cart. It's so like her to intrude, to infringe on my privacy. My blood comes to a sudden boil, and it leaves me a little dizzy.

"Yeah, wax. Like down there. You know, your foo-foo."

"What for?" I pause, trying to keep my voice level to hide my anger. "Like me, it's never going to see daylight."

"At this rate, maybe not," she adds. Her tone is too wry for my liking.

"This scar," she says, as she powders my face, tickling my nose with a feathered stroke of a brush, "you can get it removed, you know? Or lightened?"

My muscles tighten, turning to stone as though I've stared straight into Medusa's eyes. A thousand thoughts, like little snakes, trickle into my head all at once. I have too much to say about it and too little. In the end, I choose silence. Talking can be dangerous. I've come too far to face setbacks.

"Relax." She taps my shoulder and applies another feather-stroke to my face.

"Are you done? I need to get going."

"Almost. Don't move. Your eyes are *so* clear," she says, as she puts on eyeliner. "I can see the ridges and grooves inside. So pretty. Such a shame you can't see how you look, honey." The delicacy with which her hand cups my chin makes me want to cry. Damn her.

"Anyway, I'd better get going, too." She gets up suddenly. There's a scrape; I imagine she's grabbing Nicole's baby carrier.

"I've got to get ready," she says.

"A date?" I ask.

"Sort of. Let's just say it's a surprise."

"For whom?" I ask, confused by her tone.

She giggles. "Oh, no one in particular."

I don't like the sound of it. She's up to something.

SARAH

DAN WANTS TO RETURN TO LA-LA LAND. ALL I WANT TO DO IS TO PUT UP my feet and drink tea and brandy all day and binge-watch TV. But there's work to do. We need a plan, and we don't have a lot of time, according to Gerry, who is still reluctant to talk to me. The company is giving Dan one week to return the money. After that, he can bid adieu to any remaining goodwill.

"I have two theories," I say, with my laptop open.

Dan looks up from his screen, squinting in the diffused afternoon sun filtering through the window. He stifles a yawn behind his palm.

"Go on." He brings his laptop to the table, where I've made myself comfortable.

"Either someone has hacked into Fortitude from outside and diverted funds to their own account—"

"Or someone from within the company is responsible," he completes for me.

"The latter makes more sense. If someone from outside stole money, why would they bother with leaving a false trail? If they've managed to get into the system without anyone knowing, they can get out as easily. Whereas, if someone from inside Fortitude hatched a get-rich-quick scheme, then they'd have to leave a fake trail, to deflect away suspicion from them."

Dan nods, chewing the corner of his full, bow-shaped lips. "And the bastard set me up," he says, eyes flashing.

"Let's *find* this bastard."

He nods and stands up, stretching his body, lifting his arms until his fingers graze the ceiling. I'd need a stepladder to do the same. He sniffs his armpits and grimaces.

"I need a shower."

"Sign me into your laptop first?" I've made a big show of asking when I got into his laptop without his permission before; but now he's up and fine, it's only manners.

His fingers fly over the laptop's keyboard. I pull up the org chart and sort out the who's who of Fortitude, flexing my fingers stiff from clenching them for two days. Next I bring up various tabs on my laptop and enter search words into each, *how to embezzle and get away with it, the most successful embezzlement schemes*. And other equally shady-sounding keywords.

By the time Dan is out of the shower, I've whittled embezzling information down to three common but key factors:

1. The average age of a person who embezzles is 48 years old.
2. The percentage of people who commit this type of crime tips more to women than to men (51 percent versus 49 percent, respectively).

And lastly, and not comfortingly,

3. Finance and accounting are the most common job functions of embezzlers (about 37 percent).

Dan stares at my notepad and raises an eyebrow.

"Read it and weep." I point to the gurgling printer, which shoots out the few noteworthy successful schemes people have managed to pull off.

He speed-reads, then taps the first, and wolf-whistles. "Genius," he says, reading on.

"Right?"

I shouldn't sound excited, but the information is too delicious. Then I look at Dan devouring it all and sober up a little. He's being set up for someone else's so-called genius.

We each enter notes into the spreadsheet I've created on my laptop. If they seize his laptop as well, he'd only be in more trouble. Documents with titles such as Embezzling 101 and Best Embezzling Schemes of All Time won't help prove his innocence.

"If someone sets out to, it's easy enough, isn't it?"

I nod and gulp the soup.

"The possibilities are too many." He shakes his head.

"That's true, but when it comes to stealing, as imaginative as one might be, there will always be a trail. It's a matter of looking for it."

We both stop for a second and look at each other. We know what we need to do.

There is only a limited amount of information accessible from outside, via an employee's laptop. Moreover, it appears they've finally realized they're still granting him access. We're locked out. There's only one way to find the sort of details we need; we need to get into the system from the inside. Our grand plan to come up with a solution falls apart an hour later when Dan and I both fall asleep on the sofa.

"Why are you house hunting?" Dan asks, after I get off the phone with Rachel, who informs me that the second apartment I'd narrowed down to see is still available.

"My landlord's given me notice. He wants the apartment back."

"But you only moved in a few months ago!"

I sulk a little and update him on why, when I stop and sit down all too suddenly.

"Are you okay?"

"What? Yeah, I'm fine. I've just thought of something . . ." I chew my lip and try to work it out in my head, fast-forwarding to seeing the plan play out.

He raises both well-manicured thick eyebrows at me.

"But there's no time for anything so elaborate. It will need months and we barely have a week." I sigh and slouch back into the curve of the sofa again.

"Are you even going to tell me what it is?"

I shake my head. I go back over the org chart.

"Okay, one . . . no, two possibilities. First, I rekindle my nonexistent friendship with Kelly Fergusson and hope she'll indulge me. I'll have to first think of a good excuse to get in touch with her."

"And second?"

"Option two, I reach out to Dr. Anne Hatchet, whom I'd met at an AICPA summit last March."

Dan's eyebrows rise. "You know Anne Hatchet, our HR director?"

I nod.

He whistles and raises his index. "Option one sounds easier—you already know Kelly well enough." Then he makes a face.

"I know," I say, returning his pouty frown, glad we're on the same page. It's a unique talent to get irritated by just about everything, and Kelly mastered it. On a good day she was bristly, on a bad day she'd make me want to poke my eyes out. But I shouldn't generalize. Maybe she was going through something at the time and I caught her at her worst. After all, she did appear quite happy the other day. But I look at it from her point of view. And I shake my head.

"What?" Dan asks.

"If the roles were reversed and Kelly suddenly acted like we're bosom buddies, I'd be suspicious. Whereas I know Anne Hatchet independently. We connected. Maybe I could reach out and say I'm networking to keep my options open?"

Dan stares at nothing and works his jaw. "Option two it is. But you'll have to get her to invite you to her office. Tricky," he says, pursing his lips.

"And quickly at that," I add.

"I'll think of something," I say, later, as I stuff my used clothes in the small travel bag, readying to return to my apartment. "Thanks for letting me stay. Do you think it makes more sense if I'm here for a couple of days?"

His glance is searching, then knowing. "Worried I'll try to knock myself off again?"

"No," I scoff. "It'll make it easier to show each other what we're working on, rather than email."

He says nothing and continues to stare at me; his eyes are so clear, it's as though he's staring through me.

"Look, I'd invite you over to mine but there's only one bed and the sofa in my place won't even fit one half of you."

He shakes his head as if to say he can't believe we're even having this conversation.

"Unless you're leading a secret double life as a contortionist, in which case you're welcome to stay at mine. Which is it going to be?"

"Fine. You can stay," he says. He isn't too convinced, but I'm relieved when he doesn't fight me on this.

Celia glances at the clock when I sling my bag on the coat hook at 8:05 a.m.

"Monday morning blues?" she asks. I'm usually in five minutes earlier.

"Nope. Stayed over at a friend's place."

She raises both eyebrows meaningfully. "You must be feeling *much* better then?" she adds, knowing full well my voice still sounds gruff and throaty.

"Yep," I say. I'm glad we're back on terra congenial after the tension these past two weeks. But I know it will shatter again, after Mr. Tcheznich announces my promotion, *officially*, which I can't help but roll my eyes at. We're four people. Everyone already knows I'm being promoted, so why he needs to do it formally is beyond me, but that's the kind of person he is. Formal.

"Hi Sarah," Norman says, standing up.

"Hey," I say, wondering if the mood fairy stopped by this morning and waved her magic wand.

It only occurs to me later that this is the first time I've taken a sick day since I began working here. It *is* an event.

As expected, Mr. Tcheznich announces it without fuss. I'm to be senior auditor come January. Celia and Norman want to tag along at lunch. Norman because he's happy for me, Celia so she can glare at me until I melt from the lava heat of her affronted gaze.

"Sorry, I've got to take care of something," I say, and leave them at the building doorway.

I sit at a café I know they don't frequent and type out a careful email to Dr. Hatchet. It must sound professional but urgent enough. Yet it can't come across as alarming, as though I'm desperate for a job. In the end, it takes me twenty minutes to arrive at what I think is the perfect short set of words to persuade her to see me at her earliest convenience.

Celia throws me quizzical glances all afternoon long. She knows something is up; I'm too transparent for the likes of her. Midafternoon, I run into her at the coffee station, unavoidable in a tiny office like ours. She chews on her bottom lip and narrows her hazel eyes at me while I choose a pod and drop it into the coffeemaker.

She's quiet, watching, and all of a sudden her eyes widen like a light switched on in her brain. "You're not pregnant, are you?" she whispers, fierce and close.

"Of course not. Whatever gave you that idea?"

She shakes her head and walks away still chewing her lip.

I smile at her retreating figure. Good. Let her keep guessing. A tiny flutter of anxiety flips in my stomach at the same time. She's still watching me. I need to be extra careful. Especially now since I'm about to, as Mr. Tcheznich would put it, *engage in criminal activity*.

It's past four when my phone dings, alerting me to a new mail. I peek at it to see Dr. Hatchet's name in the sender field. I let it sit there until I'm by myself on the evening bus over to Dan's.

I hold out the open email to him as soon as he opens the door.

"She's replied! I'm going to see her Wednesday."

He's quiet. A little too quiet.

"What's happened?"

His face falls. "They *are* going to sue me. They've started proceedings."

I clap a hand over my mouth. "Oh, no."

"At least I'm not being arrested."

"Why aren't they arresting you, though?"

Dan cocks his head and raises an eyebrow at me.

"Of course, I'm super glad they *haven't*, but if they fired you it means they have evidence they can file."

"If they filed a police report, they'd have to go public, and it'll be on record—bad for their image. So they've done the next best thing. Slapped me with a civil case."

AUDREY: NOW

IT WAS STRANGELY COMFORTING TO HAVE DETECTIVE GREENE OVER, followed by Hoyt Security. But the silence they've left in their wake is potent. It's left me jumpy and alarmed by even the smallest of everyday groans, whirs, and thuds of a running household. It's tempting to log in to BlinkersOff, to go crying to them about the break-in, about how the police are treating me like a suspect even though they claim I'm not. But the very thought of explaining anything right now is exhausting. I lean back in the chair and stretch. What I want after the last two days is the feel, smell, and taste of fresh soil in my mouth. It's all Sarah's fault, even if she's dead. All the stress, setting me on edge, pushing me, making me want things I shouldn't. What I need is a dose of fresh air.

I'm on the walking path, waiting for my phone to connect. When it does, finally, a voice says, "Greg Timmons."

"Hi, Greg."

"Hi, Audrey. What did the detective want? Did he ask you any more questions?"

"Yes. But nothing related to work."

"The client is nervous at the turn of events. This places us in a delicate situation, especially now that the news is in the papers."

"I agree, this is a bad turn of events. There's also another matter. It's what I wanted to talk to you about earlier."

"Oh?"

"Someone broke into my house again."

There's silence at the other end. I can almost hear Greg's cogs turning.

"What's been taken?"

"Well, nothing as far as I can tell, but someone was here. They left cigarette butts behind."

"What do the police think of all this?"

"The detective is convinced they're connected, the murder and the break-in. But I can't see how or why. The culprits were never caught. Maybe they're back for more."

"We can get you out if you think you're unsafe there."

"No, no. It's fine. I picked this place."

"Doesn't mean you have to suffer through it. This business is very disturbing. There's something . . ."

This is new. Greg never hesitates. By the scale of his hesitation, he's about to ask something intrusive.

"The police . . . won't tie anything back to you, will they?"

"Greg, are you asking if I did it?"

"Of course not!" I'm about to reply when he follows it up with, "Did you?"

I let out a little sigh. He's obligated to ask me. "No. I didn't."

"Good. Now, if you need anything, you will call me?"

"Thanks, Greg. I'll be fine."

The walk calms me a little. Back home, I wash my face, cold water making it prickle, and come alive.

A sharp knock on the front door resounds through the house. *Why don't people use the doorbell?*

It rings three times in a row, as if in answer.

"I'm coming!" I switch off the house alarm currently set to stay-home mode and turn the doorknob.

"Ms. Hughes? It's Detective Novak. You had better come with me."

"What for?"

"I'm afraid we have more questions."

My pulse starts to race. "Right now?"

"Yes, now."

It must be past eight. I try not to show her surprise. I try not to display any emotion at all when on the inside, terror is clawing at me.

"Do I have time to change my clothes?" I ask, faint.

"I'll wait here," Novak says.

I nod and head upstairs. Novak's tone is *off*. Dread sinks into my bones. What I've been fearing from the moment I discovered Sarah dead is happening.

The police have made a huge discovery, something that could break the case wide open.

SARAH

"Mr. Tcheznich, I'm trying to help Dan in any way I can. He's meeting his lawyer on Wednesday. I thought I'd go with him. I know this is a bit last-minute, but I may I take off Wednesday afternoon?"

He gives me a stern, appraising once-over. "You think he's innocent?"

"Yes."

"But David said they have a boatload of evidence."

"Then they are wrong. I know him. He would never steal."

He looks up sharply. "What do you plan to do?"

"Appeal to his lawyer for help, a way out. Sniff out anything that might help him."

Mr. Tcheznich's shakes his head slowly. "You're going to do this no matter what I will advise you to do." His lips twitch.

I nod.

"One afternoon. That's it. After that, I need you here, full-time, present and accounted for."

"Thank you, Mr. Tcheznich."

I have no vacation days left this year; I took it all to move a few months ago, so I'm at his mercy, but he's kind.

Celia, I know, is bursting to know why I'm meeting with the boss again this week. She gives me her *I know you're up to something* glare when I return to my chair, but I don't have time for her games today.

I rush after work to meet Rachel at the corner of 23rd and Ninth. A redhead wearing sunglasses and a smart, electric-blue puffer coat waves at me as I walk up to the building.

"Hi, Rachel."

"How's your friend? Is everything okay?"

"Yes, yes. All well." I shield my eyes from the glare of a setting sun to look up at the historic building. Sometime in the last century, it's been made over into rental apartments. The prehistoric air-conditioners wedged into the windows should be off-putting, but they excite me. My current apartment has central heating, also included in the rent, but they turn it on at their whim. We're left to fend off brutal winters with meager space heaters.

"Shall we?" Rachel says, dangling the keys at me.

I follow her up the steep steps and take in the quality of the carpeting; it's decent. Not new, but it appears cleanish. The hallways are white—a definite improvement over the dank gray of my current building. As advertised, the ceilings are high. It was built before New York became what it is today, where space, both horizontal and vertical, comes at ridiculous premiums.

I'm a little winded when we get to the fourth floor, but then my breathing has become ragged ever since I've had the flu. She fiddles with the key a minute, then flings back the door. I'm greeted by a flood of light spilling through the massive window even though it's evening and the sun is waning. The apartment's whitewashed, exactly as I like it. Rachel leaves me to it. Phone in hand, she stands at the window, where sheer curtains have been pulled back to showcase their full worth.

The kitchen, a proper one unlike my current kitchenette, is in the front of the apartment. Beyond is the living room. Off the rectangular living room is a passageway at the end of which are the bedroom and bathroom. I want to push up my jaw after it falls—the bedroom is *big*. My puny sofa bed will squish into one corner. I can upgrade to a proper full bed, maybe even a queen!

I peek into the opposite doorway. The bathroom is okay. Not grand but clean and functional. Back in the living room, I'm already picturing my sofa against the back wall. And I can finally get that reading chair I've always wanted. A midcentury rosewood chair like the one I'd once seen in the East Village Vintage Collective.

I look out the considerable window and spot the Empire State Building in the distance. I've counted four closets, as promised, and *a* view of the Empire State, although they promised *views* of it. The light inside is fantastic; a girl could take up painting here! And the location is very convenient.

"Like it?" Rachel asks.

I want to throw my hands around and hug her but do no such silly thing. "Where do I sign?"

"I knew you'd be sold. C'mon. Let's head out. I'll email you the contract. Read it over once. The minimum lease is one year."

"Perfect."

I'm smiling ear to ear as I knock at Dan's door forty-five minutes later, dinner in a brown bag, and a bottle of wine in hand.

"What are we celebrating?"

"My new apartment."

He opens the bag to sniff.

"It's chicken tikka and naan."

"Mm-mm." He places the bag on the kitchen counter. He's cleaned up after the mess we piled up over the weekend on top of the clutter already present before.

"Where's the apartment?"

"On 23rd and Ninth." I rattle off all the *pluses* mentioned in the ad.

"So, what's wrong with it?"

I flash a wry grin. "The laundry is two blocks away."

He gives me an *aha!* smirk.

"But it's fine."

"*That* good?" he asks, placing the naans on a tray and shoving it into a toaster oven.

"Huge windows! Massive. But the real bonus? A separate bedroom."

The chicken revolves in the microwave. Dan sets the table while I put away my coat and bag. It is nice to have someone to come back home to, except this isn't my home. It's Dan's. The unfamiliar domestic scene almost leaves me nervous. It's silly. I should feel relaxed. I'm at a friend's place. I've just scored a fantastic apartment. And landed a promotion. But something, some unnamed menace, makes me uneasy. Someone set out to hurt Dan. They targeted him and it's worked.

He's looking better, less gray, but the impending lawsuit has dimmed that glimmer of hope I got a peek of two days ago. After dinner, I settle in with my laptop and browse my old files where I've stowed my erstwhile CVs.

"Why's your résumé out?" he asks, surveying the documents I've laid out on the once again clean dining table. I'm a good influence on Dan.

"I'll need it for tomorrow."

He nods. "Can I help?"

I start to shake my head, but one look at him and I know he only wants to keep occupied.

"I need to know what sort of people she's networked with on Linked-In. Could you check it and note anyone in trade, finance, or corporate?"

"What's your plan?"

"I'll have to convince her that I'm looking to do something new. I'll have to go with one or two names she already knows, so she knows I'm serious, that I've done my homework."

"And after you're in her office?"

"We'll get to that. First things first, I've got to appear legit."

Dan nods and looks away. "Hey," I say. "It'll be fine."

"I'm sorry, Sarah."

"What for?"

"For having to sit here and waste time updating things that don't need updating."

"We're all supposed to update our résumés once a year or two. It's been three since I've done mine."

"You have an answer for everything, don't you?"

"I do. Now read that and mark it, c'mon. We don't have a lot of time."

AUDREY: THEN
5 MONTHS AGO

I'm late and it's Sarah's fault. She kept me waiting on purpose, I'm sure of it. Only, I don't know why. I try to shake off my strange, edgy mood before ringing the doorbell.

"Hi, Audrey," Brian says. He reaches for my hand, then gives me a neighborly hug. A rush of cigarette smoke hits my face. And along with it, his aftershave, something I've often smelled on Sarah, lingers in the air.

"Come through. It's a mess here, watch your step," he says, and leads the way. From the sound of it, the party is already in full swing.

"Brian, Priya says to put more beers in the cooler," someone says. The voice sounds familiar, but they don't introduce themselves.

"I'll be one sec," Brian says.

"Sure."

"Hey, Audrey, it's Lisa." I'm glad she's announced herself. It's hard enough to recognize voices one-on-one but I find it a near impossibility to distinguish voices in a crowd. The dulcet tones of music, the cackle of laughter, the *pop* of opening bottles, the clink of glasses, and the aromas of hops and fruity wine explode in the air, overwhelming my senses.

"Priya's in the kitchen. May I," she says, and puts a hand on my arm. I take it and follow her to the living room.

"It's so lovely. She's put up white, black, and gold paper globes with pretty solar lights inside," she says. "And there are tiny star-shaped lights across."

In my imagination, the space looks cozy and twinkling.

"There are loads of people already."

I imagine it's the usual mix of coworkers, family, and friends.

"Audrey!" I hear Priya call out. "Hi," she says. She sounds closer now. She places a hand on my arm. "Happy birthday, you," I say, and pull her into a hug. I hand her the bag I've slung on my wrist.

"Oh, you shouldn't have," she says. "You've already given me a gift!"

"No such thing as too many gifts," I say, laughing.

"I'm wearing it, by the way. I love how it looks! Audrey's gifted me these earrings," Priya says to Lisa, presumably.

"That's so pretty," Lisa says.

"I'm glad you like them," I tell Priya.

"They're perfect," Priya says, planting a small peck on my cheek. "Come, come, meet everyone," she says tugging my arm.

"Thanks, Lisa," I say when she lets go.

"Hey, I'll be by the bar they've set up at the back of the kitchen if you want to find me later," Lisa says.

"Sounds good," I say, trying to play it cool when my eyes have misted up a little at her thoughtfulness.

Priya is like a little twittering bird next to me. Her excitement is infectious. I didn't get a chance to do anything special for my thirtieth, but for my next landmark birthday, I promise myself, I'll have a grand party. After all, I do have a lot to celebrate, whatever people may think.

"Ash, this is my friend Audrey, the one I told you about?" Priya says. "Auds, this is my sister, Asha."

"It's Ash. Pri's always talking about you—Audrey this and Audrey that. Great to finally meet you," she says.

"Likewise," I say, and hold out a hand. Asha takes it and gives it a warm shake.

"And these are my coworkers, Katy and Victoria," Priya says.

"Hi, nice to meet you," I say. I have no clue how a graphic design office looks, but I grow wistful picturing the three of them in an industrial loft with high-res monitors and cool computers, brainstorming boards poised strategically, and wide-format printers sputtering.

"I'm Vic," one of them says. I detect a slight, possibly eastern European accent, softened over years of living in America. "Otherwise known as Yeti," she adds with a little laugh. I wonder if it's an inside joke.

"Hey!" the other woman says. From her tone, it's a protest. "At least you don't have to wear heels like me to show you're an adult. Vic's an ex-hoops player. Pro level," she explains for my benefit, I think. "And I'm Katy," she adds.

Someone calls out to Priya. "C'mon. Let's get you something to drink," Vic says to me, taking my arm where Priya left it. I get an idea of how tall she is when my arm grazes the waistband of her jeans and find that it's almost at my chest level.

They walk me to the living room. "Oh no! Who put Jackie in charge of drinks?" Katy says.

"Everyone's going to get *so* drunk," Vic says softly. "Jackie's Brian's sister," she informs me, though I already know this.

The reek of hard liquor hits me hard. "I'll stick to something soft," I say.

"It's a party!" Katy says, laughing. "Have a beer."

She's right. I'm walking back home. I can risk one drink.

Cheers erupt when Priya cuts the cake. Lisa tells me it's a wedding-like tiered cake wrapped in dull gold fondant and white icing, with delicate lilacs trailing down from the top tier like an errant vine. We sing the birthday song in total disharmony. I can only picture the joy on Priya's face.

I imagine Brian feeding the birthday girl some cake, people egging him on between claps and hurrahs.

"Happy happy!" a voice calls out, loud and clear amid the fading cheers.

I almost drop my drink when I recognize it.

A hush falls. I'm not certain if it's only in my mind, but it's awkward.

"Hi, Sarah," someone says. It sounds like it could be Connie, the woman who lives in the row of townhomes behind us, but I've only met her once so I can't be sure it's her.

"What is *she* doing here?" Lisa, who's standing next to me, asks. I'm confused by her tone for a moment. Why would Lisa know or care that Priya hadn't invited Sarah?

When the answer comes to me, the beer I've sipped goes down the wrong pipe. My stomach sinking, I turn to Lisa, who thumps my back, trying to get me to cough it out.

"You okay?" she asks. If it didn't sound so awfully rude, I'd ask her if Jack is also having an affair with Sarah. I can guess what her expression at spotting Sarah here must be like if Priya's usual reaction to Sarah is anything to go by.

"*Hi*, Brian," Sarah says, her voice dripping honey.

I've got to give it to Sarah. It takes guts to show up at a party where you are persona non grata and irk the host by greeting the very husband you've been shagging. I'm cringing *for* Priya. A world of hurt and anger washes over me as it is, doubtless, washing over Priya, too.

"Sarah." Brian's voice is clipped. I can't tell if he's scared or annoyed.

"Happy birthday, Priya," a man says.

"Hi . . . Kevin," Priya says. Brian echoes her. Priya sounds confused. *What on earth is going on?*

"Here, for you," Kevin says. I imagine he's handing Priya a birthday present or a bottle of something for the party when Priya says, "Thanks! Brian, would you put this with the rest of the gifts?"

She's gracious. I don't know if I'd have the presence of mind to be nice if it were me, but then, perhaps it's her tactful way of sending Brian away from here. Away from Sarah.

"I—I wasn't aware that you knew Sarah," Priya says to Kevin, I presume. They sound closer now. They're moving toward us—Lisa, myself, Vic, and Katy. It sounds as though she's leveling an accusation, but maybe I'm the only one who reads it that way. His small laugh sounds like that of a child caught with his hand in the cookie jar. "I don't. I stopped for directions and walked in with her. She sort of . . . insisted."

"Oh," Priya says. I can't help but think she sounds relieved but also annoyed at Kevin's gullibility. But then, what could he have said if a pretty woman insisted on walking into a party on his arm?

"I can't believe she has the gall to show up here," Katy says, not bothering to lower her voice. I wonder if she's talking to me when Vic replies: "How shameless can a person be!"

So I'm not the only one who's aware of the unarguable animosity between Priya and Sarah.

"Some people are too shameless for their own good," Lisa says. Her tone is dark enough to confirm my earlier suspicion: Jack, too, has succumbed to Sarah's charms. I wonder at how the mere presence of one little person can leave such contempt and anger in its wake.

The party is back to its glory. The chatter of people, clinking of glasses, laughter, and music fill the air once again. And but for the taste of the beer, which has turned bitter, I'd go back to enjoying the vibe, too.

"Hey, Audrey," Sarah says. By the tension around me, I imagine Vic, Katy, and Lisa looking daggers at me as though they're saying, *You traitor. How could you?*

"Sarah," I say, but it comes out flat and point-blank.

Her bell-like laugh, one I've come to associate as her reaction to something entirely inappropriate or cheeky, fills my ears. I can usually put up with Sarah's insolence, her utter and unabashed snatching of everything life offers as though it's her birthright. But today it stirs up a dangerous emotion I've long stowed away. Hatred. It mixes into my bloodstream like poison. I'm affronted *for* Priya. For Lisa. For everyone whose life Sarah has razed to the ground then steamrolled over.

"You didn't think I'd miss this!" she tells me, as though she's read the question on everyone's lips.

I down the beer in one gulp. It's fine, I tell myself, I'm going to need it tonight. Katy, Vic, and Lisa are all deathly quiet. Or they've distanced themselves from me now that I'm guilty by association with Sarah. A dull fuzziness I never associate with myself muddles me. *I knew you'd get there eventually*, my mother says in my head. I push away all thoughts of her. I can't deal with her as well as Sarah.

"I thought you had other plans?" I ask Sarah.

"I thought so, too," she says, "but this is much better!"

For whom, I want to ask but the thought remains in my head.

"Who do I have to sleep with to get a drink around here?" she asks.

My hand tightens around my glass. She giggles again. I've got a sudden, frightening urge to smash my beer glass over her head and stop that giggle in its tracks.

"I don't know. You're the expert on that."

"Ooh. *Meow*." Her little cat purr is aimed at me. But it's her fault. She brings out a side of me I hate.

"Where's Nicole?" I ask.

"Oh, I've left her with Mrs. Kirsch. I've left a couple of bottles I pumped earlier."

At least she's trying with Nicole. I hadn't expected her to, somehow. Motherhood, it appears, has brought out a side to Sarah, something soft and resembling nurturing, that has taken me by complete surprise.

"I needed a break from the nonstop crying and feeding. And I thought seeing Brian could cheer me up."

The warm surprise I'd felt a moment ago dissolves like bubbles in a fizzy drink. An awful, sick *crunch* causes a stir and a hush around me.

"Oh my gosh, are you okay?" Lisa is asking.

It's me she's talking to, I realize, when there's a sharp sting in my hand, above my thumb, and in my palm. I've crushed the beer glass I've been holding. The jagged edge of a shard buries itself deeper into my palm when I flex it to test how bad it is. I bite my lip to stop crying out from the shooting pain.

Lisa, or Katy, I can't be certain, calls out to Priya.

"It's fine, I'll take care of it," Sarah says.

Amid the sharp throbbing in my hand, something weird and horrid creeps in. A new numbness that frightens me. So much so that I don't even argue with her. Of course, I don't want *her* to help me. But it might be for the best to keep Sarah contained with me, so she won't wreck the rest of the party.

"No, *I'll* take care of her," Priya says, taking my arm and forcing Sarah to let go. The air around us is so thick that one can take a knife to it.

"C'mon," Priya says, urging me. I grab my bag with my cane and walk with her as she tugs me forth into the passage, to the base of the stairwell. I wish I could read her mind. Did she hear what Sarah said about wanting to see Brian? Did the others?

"What's happened?" someone asks. I realize it's Asha, from Priya's reply.

"Look, why don't you leave this to me and get back to the guests?" Asha says. Priya refuses, but Asha won't hear of it. In the end, I follow Asha up the stairs, the spring of soft carpet treads beneath my boots.

"We've got to clean it," Asha says. She's a doctor, a pediatrician. I'm in good hands.

She runs the tap in the sink and grabs my hand. "This will sting."

I gasp when a gush of icy water hits my hand and a deep, throbbing burn starts prickling in my palm.

"Shit, a small shard is stuck here. I'll need tweezers. Don't move," she says, and leaves the bathroom.

In the haze of the pain, my disbelief over my reaction washes over me in little waves. Brian's not even *my* husband. I hear rummaging in what I assume is the main bedroom since Priya's house is the mirror image of mine.

"Got it!" she says, and returns to the bathroom. She tears something open. I grimace when the sharp odor of a disinfecting wipe stings the air. I imagine she's wiping the tweezers with it.

"A small pinch," she says.

She banters about cuts and what's the easiest way to let an infection set in and fester. There's a rude but quick prick in my palm. I suck in air from between my teeth.

"Sorry, but it had to come out."

I try to touch it, but she swats my hand away. "Nuh-uh, no probing. You'll need to change the Band-Aid at least once a day, or if it gets wet. And if it starts to feel off in any way, or smells funny, you're going to go see a doc immediately, got it?"

I nod, wincing when she sticks a Band-Aid over it.

"The laceration isn't large enough to need stitches," she says. "When was your last tetanus shot?"

"About three years ago," I say.

"That should do. You okay?"

"Yeah, thanks."

"I'd better go check on Priya. You coming?"

"You go ahead. Now that I'm here, I'll use the restroom."

I lock the door after Asha leaves and brace myself against the sink for a moment, relishing the quiet. The awkward tension since Sarah showed up seeps out with every passing minute.

"Auds, all set?" Sarah calls out, startling me. *And here she is again. Not a moment of peace to be had.*

"Be out in a sec."

"Let me in," she says.

I sit to pee, but her presence outside is inhibiting. In the end, I zip up and flush anyway, making a show of it.

"At last," she says when I unlock the door after washing my hands.

"Couldn't you find another bathroom?"

"Ooh, snarky, aren't we?"

"What are you doing here, Sarah?"

"That's a funny question to ask someone in a bathroom."

"You know what I mean."

"I was bored if you must know," she says, after a beat.

"That's no reason to crash a party."

"When did you get all stuffy? Oh, wait . . . you always were," she says with a little laugh.

I sigh, unfurl my cane and make my way along the upstairs passageway until I reach the stairs. I'm about to head downstairs when I hear Sarah say, "What are you doing?"

I'm about to answer her when Priya says, "Do you think I'm blind?" Their voices float toward me from inside the bedroom.

"I don't know what you mean," Sarah says, but she doesn't sound blasé as she always does. There's a tone that's crept into her voice and it sounds unfamiliar. Fear.

"Don't play dumb with me, Sarah. You know very well what I mean."

"Let go of my arm," Sarah says.

The silence is loaded as though it's ready to hit the target. "Priya, let go, you're hurting me!"

I picture Priya's strong little hand around Sarah's arm, squeezing until her fingers leave a bangle of fury. "Priya?" I walk toward the bedroom and say the first thing that pops into my head: "Brian's looking for you."

"Stay away from us. Leave Brian alone!" Priya says under her breath, but I hear the hiss of her anger from behind the door.

"Coming!" Priya says. I walk back to the top of the stairs and wait for her, thinking of the assault charge. If Priya could punch someone for flirting with her boyfriend, I can only imagine what she'd do to Sarah for sleeping with her husband.

SARAH

I drag on my best pants and a smart white shirt. My hair in a neat bun, bag in hand, résumé in a folder, I flick a nervous glance at the mirror. I look gray. And tired. I dab some concealer under my eyes, but that only makes them look puffier. The rouge looks like two distinct circles on my cheeks but there's no time to fix it. I sigh and step out of the bathroom.

"Don't forget, 1:15, on the dot," I say to Dan, who looks like he hasn't slept a wink all night, either.

"I won't," he says. He hands me a sticky note.

"Anne Hatchet's username and password," he says.

My eyes round with surprise. "How on earth did you manage that?"

Dan goes a bit pink. "You remember Brandon, from the next building?"

"Brandon, the guy who has had a crush on you since the day you joined Fortitude?"

Dan nods. "He swung it for me."

"This is fantastic! It'll save me so much time." I reach up and squeeze him in a hug.

"It'll be fine," I say again when we pull apart.

He nods.

"I'll call you when I'm heading there," I say. "Keep your phone charged."

I look up at the clock every hour on the hour at work, counting down the hours, then minutes until I have to leave. I've finished the day's full workload. I don't want to give Celia any excuse to run to the boss with a complaint, even though he's the one who gave me half a day off. It's my diligence for which I'm being promoted in the first place. And attention to detail, he'd say that as well. I make sure every last *i* is dotted and *t* crossed before I power my computer down and head out.

"Where are you going?" Celia, the self-appointed boss of me, asks.

"Out," I say, not looking back to see her reaction.

I call Dan from the cab. It's only a few blocks to Fortitude but I'm too nervous to walk. I want to be there at 1:00 p.m. on the dot.

"I'm on the way," I say after he picks up. "Dan?"

"Yes, I'm here."

His low voice adds to my nerves. "Please don't say you're having second thoughts?"

"Sarah, I'm not sure you should be doing this. If you get caught, that's your career down the toilet, too, along with mine."

"Too late. We decided, and I'm going."

"Then promise me one thing."

I look out, counting the blocks with one hand as the cab moves through midafternoon traffic in Midtown.

"What?" I ask, absent-minded.

"If you're uncomfortable at any point, you'll get the hell out of there."

"Okay."

"No, promise me."

"Fine. I promise. Now hang up and remember, 1:15 p.m. She's a stickler for time."

"Yep. Sarah?"

"Yeah?"

"Nothing."

"Dan, I'll be fine. You'll see. It'll all work out."

In my lap, the paper Dan has handed me with Anne's username and password is almost in shreds from constantly twirling it in my hand ever since I got into the cab.

*   *   *

I step into a café around the corner from Fortitude. Grabbing a peppermint tea and a banana, I find a quiet corner to go through all the information in the folder I've tucked into my bag.

I've reassured Dan with confidence that's now deserted me. A million things could go wrong. Anne could be called away on some important meeting and she could delay, but that I can manage. I'll wait; I'll let Dan know so he can wait for my signal first. Or she might call me into a conference room instead of her office. That would be disastrous. But not as disastrous as being caught snooping on her computer in her office. I've let Dan's energy mingle with mine. I felt so confident this morning.

At 12:30, the café door opens and Kelly walks in. Damn. Damn, damn. I try to sit back, fade into the background, but she spots me and walks straight over. "What are you doing here?" she asks casually.

I gulp. "Meeting a friend."

"Anyone I know? Oh, is it Dan?"

Luckily for me, she looks distracted. "No. I—"

"How's Dan holding up?" she asks, peeking into her bag, ostensibly looking for something.

"As well as can be expected, under the circumstances."

She shakes her head knowingly. "He should have owned up. That would have made it easier for him."

"But he's innocent. Why should he own up to something he didn't do?" I snap back.

"That's not what everyone's saying, Sarah." She looks at me sadly, as though I'm misguided. Over the anxiety churning inside, a flame of anger bursts. Bad news always travels fast.

"He's innocent. And I'm going to prove it." I feel triumphant when her head snaps up with surprise.

"How? You got evidence?"

For a moment, just a fleeting moment, I worry that she knows something that I don't. What if I don't end up finding anything that could help prove Dan's innocence? I decide to call her bluff anyway. "No. But I will, soon." The 12:45 alarm I've set on my phone goes off. "I'm sorry, I need to go."

"See you," she says, her eyes following me out.

I cover the two blocks to Fortitude's HQ, annoyed that I let her get to me. But talking to her has put a fire in my belly. Soon everyone in Fortitude will be thinking the same thing as Kelly. I've got to get this right and prove Dan's innocence quickly, before his reputation is completely shredded.

Seven minutes later, I've received a sign-in badge and been instructed on how to get around. I take the elevator up to Anne's floor and wait in a reception room outside her office.

I rehearse details in my head, flick my wrist upward and glance. It's time. I knock on the door.

"Come in," says a familiar voice.

"Sarah Connelly," Anne says, standing up from her chair to take my hand in a firm clasp. No one would believe she is fifty. Thirty-five, maybe. A young thirty-five at that. Certainly not the mother of two grown, working adults. She preserves herself well.

I smile, warm, despite my nerves. "Hi, Anne."

"Please." She points to the visitor's chair on the other side of the modern desk, the top of which I note, is almost as neat as my own. I'm glad I wore my hair back; she likes neatness and my long hair in waves would appear untidy.

"Thanks for getting back to me so swiftly, I appreciate it." I set my bag on the floor.

"It was a surprise to hear from you, a pleasant one," she says. "From your mail, I grasped a sense of urgency?"

To the point, I remember that about her. But then, so am I. It's one of the reasons she picked me to be on her team as well as part of a training session at the summit.

I pull back my smile a bit and nod, peering at her sharp gray eyes.

"Well, yes. I'm at a crossroads I didn't anticipate. I've been with Tche-znich and Co. for three years now. I've been offered a promotion sooner than I could have hoped for."

"And you want to check your options before you accept."

"Exactly. Once I accept, I can't jump ship soon. It wouldn't be right, which puts me out of the market for at least a couple of years."

She nods. "You like it there?"

"Yes, yes, I do. It is small, though."

"I see," she says, reading between the lines—there's no more room to grow. "How may I help?"

I nod. "I've had little time to think this through, but I'm convinced I should be doing something else with my skills."

She cocks her head to the right. "Like?"

"I'd like to try something new."

There's a knock at the door. I flick a glance at my watch. 1:15.

"Excuse me," she says, and then, "Come in."

A woman's head peeks in. "Sorry to disturb you, Anne, but there's a call for you."

Anne's brows knit. "Can't you put it through here?"

"I'm afraid it's on my dedicated line."

"Have them call me back, please," she says.

"They insist on speaking to you right away; it's urgent . . ."

Anne's shoulders drop. She looks at me. "Hold that thought, I'll be right back."

"Of course."

I wait for the door to shut before dashing over to the other side, where her computer screen is still on. I plug in the USB I've brought and copy all files to it. While the process begins, I click the mouse until I'm in the folder that holds this quarter's update. I glance at the door before clicking through to the employee payroll portal. She's too smart to keep usernames and passwords lying around, but I've come armed. I enter the login details from the sticky note Dan handed me. At last, I'm in. One by one, I navigate and grab screenshots of all the information I can find, saving them all on the USB.

"So strange," I hear Anne's voice too near the door. I scan the progress bar: 98.6 percent. Heart hammering in my chest, I urge the files to be copied sooner. Meanwhile, I poise the mouse to set the screen back to its original state . . . 99 percent, then 99.5 percent.

By the time the door opens and Anne strides in, I'm back in my seat, the USB concealed in my fist.

"What should I do if they call back?" the lady who interrupted us earlier asks Anne through the half-open door.

My face, I know, is flushed red from the heat flooding my veins. Sweat trickles down my armpits. I slip the USB into my pocket, wishing her chair would stop its slight, telltale rotation.

She huffs. "Ask them to make sure they've got the right Anne first!"

Her head shakes as she covers the distance to her desk.

"Everything okay?"

"I've had the strangest phone call. Ever."

I look up to see the incredulity in her eyes. "Sorry," she says, sucking air through her teeth.

"I can come back some other time if you like?"

"No, no. It's fine. I hate interruptions. So, you were saying you want to do something different. What do you have in mind?"

I'm palpitating in the cab, the pressure catching up to me. I take out my phone from my bag with a shaky hand and call Dan.

"It's done. Dan?"

"Yes, I'm here."

"Did you hear what I said?"

"Yes, I did. Did you get everything?"

"Whatever I could find. I'll see you in half an hour."

After he opens the door, I barge in and flop on the sofa with the bag, coat still on, and rest my head back.

"Oh, God, I can't believe I did that!"

He stands quiet, looking at me. He's being patient. If I were him, I'd want to tear out my throat to hear every word of it.

I sip the water he has handed me and recount everything that happened once I was inside Anne's office.

"Good timing! You kept her on long enough. What on earth did you say to her?"

He stands, arms crossed, and grins. The grin turns into a little laugh, then he's holding his stomach and stooping over.

"What?"

When he looks up, his eyes are watery.

"I told her that her son and I—my name is Tom, by the way—are pregnant and want to marry."

My mouth opens but no sound comes out. "Her straight, about to marry the woman he loves, son?" I ask finally.

"Yes, him. I claimed I'm Josh's lover, but Josh is denouncing me because he's so deep in the closet he doesn't know he's gay."

I start laughing with Dan, simultaneously feeling a little guilty. Poor Josh. Anne didn't believe Dan, hopefully.

"And you're pregnant?"

"Not me, obviously. But we've found a surrogate who is, and all our dreams are about to come true. If only Josh will listen to reason and not go through with his sham of a marriage with that woman. Before that, I gave her elaborate, intimate details about my, well, *Tom's* relationship with her son. How we met, how we fell in love, the whole hog."

He's looking a bit abashed now. "I hope the lies were worth it."

I pluck out the USB from my pocket and wave it at him.

"Let's find out."

AUDREY: NOW

DETECTIVE NOVAK'S TIGHT VOICE AND RETICENCE ARE FRIGHTENING. MY fingers fumble as I strip off my slacks and sweatshirt before slipping into a pair of jeans. I drag a thin cotton long-sleeved T-shirt over my head followed by a warm cashmere cardigan. It was freezing in the police station the last time.

A few minutes later, seated in the snug passenger seat of Novak's sedan, I feel a lurch when the engine starts. My insides churn. "Has something happened?" I ask.

"Apparently," Novak says.

"Sounds ominous," I say in turn. There's no reply. The car ride is quiet, but I'm happy to let Novak think. Or at least, that's what I assume. For all I know, she's watching me. Scrutinizing me. I can't help but wonder what has happened. What have they discovered?

At the station, they direct me to a different room from the one I'd been sitting in the previous time. A sweat tactic. I want to laugh. I'm blind. There *is* no familiarity to lean on. Everything's always new and strange. Breaking into a cold sweat from fear of the unknown, the dark, the unseen, is a regular occurrence for me.

There's no time for tittle-tattle; no time to request a cup of tea or coffee. Two chairs scrape and then a door shuts.

"Hello?" I'm talking into a void. There's no reply.

They've shut me in. Alone. Another tactic to loosen my tongue, perhaps? But there isn't much time to wonder. The door opens soon enough, and two sets of footsteps stride in.

"Hello, Ms. Hughes, thanks for coming in on such short notice."

"Hello, Detective Greene, no problem."

There's a ruffle of papers and the slap of something on the metal-topped table between us. I picture folders full of witness statements, interviews, and other facts they've gathered. For although they seem to question only me, that is far from true. They've been questioning everyone in the neighborhood, even Tony from the corner shop and Jason from the gym, according to Bob, who ran into them when they'd summoned him a second time for questioning. But I know that I look far from innocent myself. As the detectives had pointed out the last time, I'd been to Sarah's house twice that day. And I'd been the one to discover Sarah's body. If they accuse me of murder again, in the interest of self-preservation, I should tell them about Priya and how she'd threatened Sarah. Twice.

"Has something happened?" I ask again.

"There's been a . . . development," Greene says.

"Ms. Hughes—"

"Audrey, please."

"Audrey, do you know a Ms. Kelly Fergusson?"

"Why?" My voice sounds strange, foreign.

"Because the body *you* found isn't that of Sarah Connelly. We've identified the deceased as Kelly Fergusson."

"Wh-what?" It comes out as a croak.

The suspicion that something was off, which has been gnawing at me from the moment I discovered the body, clears in a moment. I realize now what I would have known right away if I hadn't been in such an awful panic. Apart from the blood, there'd been no smell on Sarah that night. No perfume. I've grown so accustomed to Sarah's intense scent. She bathed in it. After each of Sarah's visits, it lingered on my furniture, and even on my clothes and hair when Sarah hugged me. Hints of Sarah's perfume should have percolated through the awful metallic stench of blood. But it had been missing.

Words form and dissolve before I'm able to voice them. How can I explain this to the police without deepening their suspicion that I've been lying to them? Truth is often stranger than fiction. They might not believe me, and I'll only be digging myself into a deeper hole.

"I don't understand. Where's Sarah, then?"

"We thought you might know the answer to that."

I scoff. "How should *I* know?"

"You must know something, Audrey," Greene says. "You've been Sarah's neighbor for nearly a year. You may know more than you think you know. Have you ever heard her mention Ms. Kelly Fergusson before?"

"No. Sarah never mentioned that name. To be honest, Detective Greene, she never talked much about her past."

"We'll be honest, too, Audrey," Novak says. "We've spoken to many people here in Sleepy Point and no one seems to know anything about Sarah's past. Where she lived before she moved here, where she worked or used to work. Her social media presence is almost nonexistent. Why is that, do you think?"

My heart starts thudding faster. Inside, it's as though a thousand little birds, all tangled beaks and ruffled feathers, are trying to take flight at once. I take a moment to dampen it down, to calm myself.

"I often got the feeling that she moved here, to Sleepy Point, to start over with a clean slate."

"Until the slate was wiped, there was a whole life. You're saying you didn't know anything at all about her life before?"

"To your point, Detective Novak, I've only known her for about a year. She moved here well before I did. Whatever was in her past, she buried it quite deeply by the time I got to know her. And she wanted to keep it that way."

"Did you never ask her *anything* about her life before? Not even who the baby's father is?" Detective Novak's husky rasp fills the room again after a momentary silence.

"No, I didn't. Sarah never mentioned Nicole's father and I never asked her; it was none of my business. But she mentioned that she used to be in insurance. Oh, and that she'd been in a bad accident once."

There's furious scribbling.

"Did she say what sort of an accident?"

"She didn't, Detective Greene. But she did—does—have a scar. It was at the base of her neck, at least, that's where I think it is. She said it took her ages to heal."

"Did she mention a hospital or clinic?" Greene asks.

I pause a moment, then shake my head. "No."

"Was Sarah a golfer?"

"What? A golfer? No. She wasn't." I'm about to ask why they would want to know such a curious thing, but Detective Greene interrupts me.

"Tell us again, from the beginning, what happened the night you found the body."

I sit up straight and begin again. By the time I've recounted it all with Novak and Greene interrupting me at each turn, trying to trip me up, making me repeat details out of order, I'm ready to drop into bed right then.

"It's strange," Novak says.

"What is?" I ask.

"It's just . . . in my experience, neighbors rarely form close friendships like yours and Sarah's."

"Why?" I say quietly. "Is it so hard to imagine Sarah would want to be friends with someone with a disability?"

"No, that's not it at all—what I mean is, women are likelier to form closer friends with a coworker or someone they went to school with or grew up with. Someone with whom they have things in common."

"Perhaps. When I moved here, in a way I left everything familiar behind. It was the same for Sarah, I suppose. We were . . . *are* similar ages, too. Our friendship might appear strange to someone, but we did become friends . . . despite myself."

"What does that mean?"

This is turning out to be more like an hour with a therapist than with two police officers. They're starting to skirt too close now.

"Well, I moved here looking for a quiet life, as I've said before. Sarah sort of blew into my life. She opened me to possibilities I'd closed off for myself ever since I lost my vision, like forcing me to date again."

"Audrey, do you have any idea where Sarah might be?"

I shake my head slowly. "No. I have no idea at all."

"Are you sure she didn't mention a friend or a relative?"

"I'm certain. She's never mentioned anyone, except the name I gave you, Adam Briggs."

"And you're certain you're not holding anything back?"

I bristle. "I've been helpful from the beginning. I've told you everything I know."

"Is that so?"

"Yes, Detective Novak."

"Then how come you haven't told us what happened at the party?"

I gulp. "What party?" I ask weakly.

"You know very well. Priya Patel's birthday party. Word is, it got pretty violent."

I can't help but scoff. "*Violent* is a bit dramatic, not to mention false."

"That's not what we heard."

"What do you mean?" I ask, trying to sound calm when inside my heart is hammering in my chest.

"That you were so distressed by her presence that you threw a beer mug at her."

"What? Th-that's an outright lie! You've got it all wrong."

"Then give us your version of the events," Novak says.

I want to kick myself. I walked right into that one. "Why would I be angry with Sarah? It isn't my husband she's sleeping with. It's Priya's."

"And the glass you broke?"

"*Tch.* I have a disadvantage, if you haven't worked that out by now. I merely misgauged the height of the table and the glass broke. In *my* hand. I'm the one who got hurt. No one else."

"Be that as it may, someone overheard you and Sarah having a pretty nasty argument a little later."

I think back to that evening. All I can remember is how livid I'd been with Sarah that I couldn't stand to be around her.

"That wasn't *me*. It was Priya, if you must know. I was upstairs after Asha, Priya's sister, saw to my hand, and I was about to come downstairs when I overheard them in Priya's room, so whoever told you it was me Sarah argued with lied."

"What did Sarah and Priya argue about?"

"What do you think, Detective Greene? Brian, of course. Priya said something like *Leave us alone* or *Leave him alone*, I'm not certain, I couldn't hear properly."

"But Sarah was overheard pleading, to let her go, as though someone were hurting her."

"Okay, yes, *maybe* in the heat of the moment, Priya might have held Sarah's hand a bit tightly, but can you blame her? As if ruining Priya's birthday hadn't been enough, Sarah flirted with Brian, in front of us."

"Why haven't you mentioned all this before?"

"You never asked. It was so long ago. Anyway, how does it matter? If the woman whose body I found isn't Sarah, it hardly has anything to do with Priya, does it?"

"Let's get this clear, once and for all. *We* decide what's relevant and what isn't. You tell us everything you know or face charges for obstructing justice."

"Look, Detective Novak, I didn't intentionally hold anything back. It's just . . . everything's been happening so quickly."

"It's been two whole days since you discovered the body and called 9-1-1. You've been questioned ample times since then; you've had plenty of time to tell us everything you know."

"It might be routine for you to find a body every couple of days, but I assure you, there's nothing ordinary about stumbling onto a dead body for me, so forgive me if I'm still in shock."

Silence envelops the small room. I'm exhausted, as though I've endured a marathon. It might only be two days since I found Sar—the body, but it feels as though an age has passed since then. "Is that all? May I go home?"

"You may after you answer one more question. We've found a GPS tracker under Sarah's car. Do you know why someone might be tracking Sarah?"

I gulp in a mouthful of air and shake my head. "May I leave?"

"For now," Novak says.

Detective Greene leads me out of the room and into the entrance. "I'll be right back," he says.

While I wait for Greene, I can't help but think that Novak's initial niceness toward me has disappeared. This new brusqueness makes me shudder. Is it because she's a police officer and it's her job to suspect everyone, especially in a murder inquiry? Or is it the sort of scorn that familiarity often engenders?

"Detective?"

"Yes?" Novak answers.

"Sarah would never have left Nicole behind. Not voluntarily."

"Are you saying she's been kidnapped?"

"I have no idea. All I know is, there's no way she'd have abandoned Nicole. Something awful must have happened."

"What?" Greene asks.

I shrug. "As you said, *you're* the detectives."

SARAH

As the director of HR for Fortitude Trading, Anne has enough information on her computer to make my mind spin. Dan and I enter all the information into various spreadsheets. The past year's financial data is split into quarters. The employee payroll records, including their 401(k) plans. Next is the shareholders' information. Everything is systematic, orderly.

It's after midnight when I look up. Dan's eyes look glazed.

He looks up over the papers in his hand and rolls his eyes. "This is nuts. We'll never get through all this by Friday, let alone figure it all out."

"It's late. Leave it. We'll continue tomorrow. We will get through everything. I promise."

A new mail notification chimes.

I swipe my phone screen to the email app and open it. It's Rachel, the estate agent.

> Sarah,
> I've attached the contract. There's one caveat, they want someone to move in right away. Not sure how flexible your landlord is. I'd check with him if you're keen on this apartment. Let me know if you have any Qs.
> Best,
> Rachel

I cringe at the thought of writing to Mr. D'Angelo. Maybe *I* should drop in on him unannounced; it might catch him off guard. Or it might get me assaulted, I think unfairly. I decide to call him instead. I put a reminder on my phone for 1:00 p.m. tomorrow and shut the laptop screen.

My brain needs time to process all the information I've guzzled over the last six hours. Dan's right. It's not enough that we have most of the pertinent information. The important part is working out the tiny bread-crumbs left behind.

I unfurl the sheet, lay it on top of the sofa, tucking it where I can, and place a pillow at the top.

"I'm off to bed," I say.

Dan rubs both eyes with his index fingers, then yawns. "I'd better pack it in, too. I'm pooped."

I pass a silent prayer to the property gods as my phone rings. I pace the breakroom, well, break-cupboard, so it's only three or four paces before I make a U-turn.

"D'Angelo," says a gruff voice.

"It's Sarah Connelly, Mr. D'Angelo. Do you have a minute? You'd said in your letter I could contact you if I had any questions?"

"Yes," he says, huffing into the phone.

I imagine that heavy, moist breath on my neck for some reason, and wince. I shake off the disgusting image from my head. "I've found an apartment to move to, Mr. D'Angelo, except they want someone to move in as soon as possible. Since you needed the apartment early to make some renovations, would it be possible to end my lease early? I can move to the new place in December?"

"I'll have to check and get back to you."

"Hel—"

There's a click. He's disconnected.

I glare at the phone.

"Expecting an important call?" Celia asks from the door.

"Nope. All done," I say and step out the door before she has the chance to stop me. She's getting antsy now. I'm not sure it's a good idea to let her frustration with me build and build until it explodes like a volcano. I'll take her out for a drink next week. I don't have to; she's the one who's playing silly office politics with me. I wonder, though, how I'd feel in her shoes. If I'd waited for a promotion only for the new girl to come in and swoop it up from under my nose. I return to my desk and stare at the screen, aware that her eyes are still on me.

I'm so distracted on the evening bus to Dan's, that I almost miss my stop. I use the spare keys Dan lent me to let myself in. Plugging my laptop into the outlet at the kitchen wall, I recollect all the information I'd crammed in last night while it powers up.

When I begin to type out my theories, I'm certain of one thing. If Fortitude claims to have irrefutable proof against Dan, there will be a trail that led to him. It's the most important layer of deception set by the person who framed him. People often think setting someone up is easy. Depending on the scheme, it can be, or it can get convoluted, and unexpected. Both need careful planning and great timing, though.

First, I have to identify which kind this is, but I'm starting to see that Dan is right. The volume of information we're privy to now is monumental. It could turn out to be nothing but a distraction. We could waste valuable time sifting through it all and come up with nothing. And they could still charge Dan with a crime he did not commit. And he could be held liable as well.

I take a blank piece of paper and draw a map, marking a starting point of employee X, the embezzler, and join it with a straight line to Dan. Then I drag a horizontal line across it, dividing the page into four quadrants. The beginning of the horizontal line marks the scheme deployed by X. At the other end is the missing money.

There are two things at play here. One is the money stolen by X. The second is the scheme to set up Dan. They are two separate schemes that connect only at the end. I type out scenarios for both, beginning with motive.

Is Dan a scapegoat chosen at random? Or did someone single him out and lead him to the slaughter? I go over Fortitude's financial statements quarter by quarter. Then I pull up the employee payroll and 401(k) screenshots and check those against the employee count from the org chart. Along the way, I cross out all contractors and temps. They're more likely to nickel-and-dime the employers, a receipt for an extra buck here and there. To pull off anything on the scale Dan is being accused of, you'd have to be a full-time employee.

According to his lawyer, the money Dan has allegedly stolen has been siphoned off over the last six months. I create a separate sheet for that and begin combing through every single occurrence in Fortitude, going back eight months. If the money began disappearing six months ago, a comparison chart starting eight months back—examining the intricate, minute differences between two nearly identical fact sheets side by side— might tell me what I need to know.

"Sarah." Someone shakes me.

"Not now, I'll be there in a second."

"Sarah, wake up."

Eyes blurry, I blink and stare up at Dan, looming above me. I've fallen asleep at the table.

"What time is it?"

"One in the morning."

"Where have you been?" I yawn and stretch back. "Sorry, I didn't mean to sound like a nag. I was worried."

"I messaged," he says, a sheepish flush reddening his face.

"Ah. My phone is on silent. Never mind. All okay?"

"Yep. I ran into a friend and we got chatting and ended up at a bar."

"Here," I tell him, dragging his arm with one hand while reaching for a sheet of paper with the other.

His eyes round. "You've found something? Already?"

Before I can reply, he says, "Shit. I should've been here, helping."

I shake my head. "You've been cooped up here for nearly two weeks. You needed the break. Anyway, look at this," I say, tapping on the paper.

His eyes narrow as he takes the sheet from me and sits on the couch, seizing every word as fast as possible.

"And now this," I say, handing him another sheet.

He looks at the header and gives it a thorough once-over. He sits back, cocks his head, and looks up at me.

"Can you see it?" I ask, unable to hide the excitement from my voice.

He shakes his head. I snatch both papers back from him before he can protest and grab the highlighter from the table. He's standing next to me, watching as I circle two figures.

"See it now?" I ask, turning to him.

He stares at me wordlessly and takes the sheet from me. He nods but I see the confusion in his eyes.

"The simplest way I can explain it is that our embezzler was siphoning off funds from employee loan repayments made against their 401(k)s. It's like what Edith Chesterton managed to do. Remember our second case study in Embezzling 101?"

"There are fail-safes that catch these things. Software and basic accounting practices."

"Yes, but the genius here, Dan, is that it isn't all one linear transaction. Three different parties are involved here. One: the payroll accounts managed by a third party; two: Fortitude's internal accounts; and three: Fortitude's fund management accounts. Our embezzler is manipulating the spreadsheets in the transitional phases. If you overlapped all three spreadsheets, for example, you'd be able to see the minute differences. But no one party has access to all three spreadsheets, so they're each none the wiser. To tally the numbers and avoid suspicion, minuscule amounts from various other employee accounts have been deducted. The only way to trace this would have been a full audit, which is what I'm guessing David did before even consulting us."

Dan nods.

It strikes me only now that the reason Fortitude was stalling in handing over the documents after we began the audit is that they'd already found the discrepancy internally. "It's clever, really. Interest payments have been rerouted and added to it all as well. The total is pretty monumental, but the delta in each instance is small enough to be overlooked. Look at the date." I point at the top of the sheet from six months ago. "Now multiply that number by the number of days until four weeks ago."

He grabs my shoulders and shakes them. "You're a genius."

I bite my lower lip. Time to deliver the bad news. "That's only the how. We still don't know who."

His smile freezes. He lets go of me, hands dropping to his sides.

"This is the proof they have as well. Only, they think you're responsible for it."

"Shit, we don't have time. I'm done for," he says, sinking back into the sofa.

"We have until tomorrow evening."

He scoffs. "Tomorrow evening will be here like *this*." He snaps a finger, hard.

"That's why we don't have time to waste. Now, here's what we know," I say, holding out a chair for him to join me at the table.

"Someone at Fortitude is responsible for regularly updating gross wages and required withholdings from employee paychecks. This same person will also be responsible for updating the net amounts to be withdrawn from Fortitude's general account. Now think. Who is this person? You've worked with them. You *know* them."

Dan stares into the wall behind me, letting air out of his rounded mouth as he zeros in on this information.

"I'll have to think about this."

"Think—" I say, stifling a yawn, "and let me know. I'll have to log back in to Anne's account to access the system to reverse-trace the crumbs they've left leading to you."

"You're so sure they have left crumbs."

"The one thing management will be super finicky about in a large company like Fortitude is paperwork. The second paperwork goes missing, it'll raise a flag. So, like a good little worker bee, the embezzler would have submitted and logged records on time, dotted and crossed the *i*'s and *t*'s. As secretive as this person wants to be, they would have had to file information or misinformation. That's the only way to get away with it all."

"You've thought this through."

"Yep."

He looks at me thoughtfully. "God save the world if you went over to the dark side."

It's on the tip of my tongue to make a flip *Star Wars* reference, but the seriousness of everything is crackling around us like electricity.

AUDREY: THEN
4 MONTHS AGO

A RHYTHMIC, FURIOUS *THUD THUD THUD* ROUSES ME FROM A STATE OF languor. "Boo, stop the music." The coffeehouse channel to which I've fallen half asleep shuts off. In the sudden afternoon silence, I listen as my heart marches on to a strange beat.

Thud thud. I jump. Then I recognize the sound. Someone's banging on a door. I trip down the stairs, my right hand on the railing, tiptoe to the door, and put my ear to it. I think it's Bob's banging when it comes again, *thud thud thud*, louder this time.

"Sarah?" It's Bob. "Let me in!" he's growling. Or saying. I can't tell the difference with him sometimes. Either way, he sounds frantic.

"Open the *fucking* door, Sarah!"

Nope. He's angry.

Her response is faint. "What do you want?"

"Let me in."

"I'm about to head out, okay? Can't it wait?" Her voice is clearer now. She's stepped out or opened the door.

"No. It can't. Either you deal with me right now or with the police later, your choice."

What on earth?

"All right, all right, there's no need to yell, jeez," Sarah says. The door slams shut. She's presumably let Bob in.

Once he's inside, their conversation is too muffled to comprehend. I strain to spell out individual words, but I recognize Bob's tone for what it is—a threat. I run upstairs to the closet wall and listen with the head-phones, but it's muffled. Her closet door must be closed.

I'm filled with dread and disappointment. Is no one at all safe from Sarah? I never thought Bob would fall for her fake charms. Or perhaps I have it wrong. The more I think about it, the more I'm convinced I'm wrong. There's no doubt Bob is furious with her, but I can't think what's got his back up, enough to threaten her.

Sherman checks out the photos I've emailed him. While they load on Photoshop, he scolds me over my second near-miss this morning. I under-stand his fear. I had only fifteen minutes to get in and get out of Sarah's house, but I remind him that I'm not here only to babysit and be the shoulder to cry on when things go wrong in this neighborhood.

"Anyway, I hope it's clear enough."

"It's a bit blurry. I'm sharpening the image. If that doesn't work, I'll hand it to Peter—our graphics guy. But it's a great find, Audrey."

"See? Good thing I went back."

"You're going to give me a heart attack one of these days if you carry on like this."

"I got away and what's more, I found what we needed."

He sighs. "I'll keep you posted."

"Catch you later."

At last, I think, after I hang up. We're getting somewhere.

There's a sharp knock on the door.

"They got me, too," Sarah says, after I've opened the door a crack. It's silly to be careful *after* the burglary. I blame Bob and his little outburst at my doorstep about opening the door with care. A sudden flutter of fear unsettles me. Did I remember to put the soil bowl in the dishwasher? The last thing I want is Sarah poking and prodding, asking her intrusive questions again. There are only so many lies you can tell a person before they start to sniff the air and feel that something is off.

Sarah also assumes, as she always does, that I will know it's her. She's right. I do. It's the smell of her soap and that perfume, of course. But it's also her energy. And we have our own unique scents that mingle with the stuff perfumers bottle, and it becomes a signature. Like DNA, which I've been thinking about recently.

"Who got you? Come in," I say, pulling the door back in time for her to waft past me. There's a scrape. She has placed Nicole's carrier on the coffee table.

I've tried to stay out of her life as much as possible since then. I don't trust my mouth or my anger. I haven't forgiven Sarah for crashing Priya's party. I'm not only mad at Sarah, but I'm also livid with Brian for putting Priya in such a position. And I'm a little miffed with Priya as well for blaming it *all* on Sarah and treating Brian as though he's a wind-up toy with no agency over his actions. But it appears that Sarah has taken Priya a little to heart this time. I haven't heard Brian's voice at Sarah's once since.

"Did you hear what I said?" she asks.

"Sorry, I was away with the fairies."

"Someone's broken into my home."

A familiar dread pushes into my veins. "What's been taken?"

There's no reply. "Sarah? What is it?"

"I don't—I just don't understand it," she says.

"What's to understand? It's hardly a surprise, is it? It's been happening for months now."

"Yeah," she says absent-mindedly. "But it doesn't make any sense." There's bewilderment in her voice, as though she never expected it to happen to *her*. Typical of Sarah to think she's too special to be robbed.

"Has anything been taken?"

"Nothing of value is gone—jewelry, watches, gadgets, all still there. One of my old bags is gone, though. Luckily I don't use it much anymore. But it's weird."

"What did the cops say?"

"I didn't bother calling them. What are they going to do, after all? Last week was Bob. He called the cops, a lot of good that did."

That's true. Calling them over certainly had been a waste of my time. It was as though I'd invited them over only so they could insult me.

"Did they leave the door open?"

"Nope."

"How did you know someone's been in, then?"

"Things had been moved around. Plus, I thought I saw someone loitering around."

I gape open-mouthed before I find my tongue. "You *saw* someone? Where?"

"Not clearly, but I thought I saw someone speed-walking away from my front door."

"Shouldn't you tell the police?"

"That's what Bob said, too. I think it's a waste of time. He isn't convinced. I told him if he's so eager, he should call them himself. He got all huffy like he does when he can't boss people around."

"Is that why he came around? What was all that about yesterday afternoon?"

Silence. "What?"

"I heard him banging on your door."

"Oh, that!" She laughs. "That was nothing."

I don't believe her for a minute. Bob doesn't go around yelling at his neighbors at random. It's definitely *something*. But she doesn't want to discuss it with me, so I return to the favorite topic in the neighborhood.

"I hope they catch this stupid burglar red-handed, and he gets hard labor for it."

"Ooh, that's a bit harsh," Sarah says. She's over at the sofa by the window; I can tell by the distance of her voice.

"It's not. This is an invasion of privacy. The thought of someone standing here"—I wave a hand around—"uninvited, touching my things, going through my stuff is a personal violation. It's the message behind it all that gets to me."

"What message?"

"I can get to you where you are. You're not safe in your own home."

She wolf-whistles. "I've never seen you this fired up."

"Well, I don't like feeling violated. Moreover, it's not safe for them, either. What if the next home they break in, someone is in, and armed? Juno has a gun. What if he'd been home? He wouldn't have hesitated to use it."

"This *is* America. Most people have a gun," she says.

I stop to consider that a moment. "Do you own one? A gun?"

"No. Do you?" she asks. A smooth lie, right to my face. Sherman would have had me remove it from where I found it, at the back of the third drawer in her closet dresser, but I'm glad I left it. I've come too far to risk spooking her.

"Nope," I say. "Anyway, I'm about to pour myself some wine. Shall I get you a glass?"

"I can't. It's Nicole's feeding time and I haven't prepumped."

She's quiet as she settles on the sofa and feeds Nicole.

"How do you cope?"

"Pardon?" I've been in another world while Sarah's brain train has been chugging on. I've got to catch up. "Cope? What with?"

"Everything. Being blind. Being single. Life."

"I don't know. Sometimes I think I do; at others, I'm sure I'm failing it all spectacularly. Every day is different."

"I'm sure people tell you you're brave all the time. But you are."

"I have to be. It's not as if I have a choice."

"I'm sorry," she says. She's in an odd sort of mood today. I wonder what's brought it on. I'm not certain I like talking like this with her.

"I know," I say.

In a way, her apology is funny, like it's a karmic joke, but I know she means it. She isn't sorry she's brought it up; she's sorry I must live like this. I should be angry, and I always am, a little. It's never too far beneath the surface of my skin, my rage, but it ebbs and flows along with the current of my present life. I don't let it eat me from the inside, gorge itself and grow fatter and uglier. It could easily, if I let it. There are moments I'm ashamed of when I've let it get the better of me, but then I remember I've unwittingly trained all my life for my present circumstances. Every time Barbara's bony fingers landed on my face, every whipping doled out by her various boyfriends, every push to the ground at school has all been one giant preparation for what I'm facing now, so *I* don't become what I've always hated.

So I won't become my mother.

"It's 5:30," Boo informs us like I've programmed him to, after Sarah once scolded me for her losing track of time and missing her class.

"Thanks, Big Ben," I say, grateful for the interruption.

"No problem," Boo replies.

"Are you heading to your yoga class now?"

"Yep. You couldn't watch her, could you? I've brought all her things, so you don't have to come over. Extra diaper in the front zipper, backup pacifier in the baggie, inside left zipper, along with the teething rings."

How stupid I've been not to have seen through her! This is usually the time I babysit Nicole, but since the party, I've stopped that as well. So this isn't a random visit. She timed it just right, so I won't say no to watching Nicole.

"'Kay, see you later," she says. The door shuts behind her and the alarm chirps.

"It's just you and me now, lil' bear," I tell Nicole as I grab the handle of her baby carrier and trudge upstairs to the study.

I'm on the phone with Sherman.

"Nothing yet from Peter. He's working on it, though, so it's a matter of time."

"What about the trace?" I toy with my hair, curling and uncurling it around my finger.

"No change in the patterns."

I sit up. "C'mon, there has to be something!"

"Nope. The usual café, car, grocery."

"Dammit!" I yell. "Sorry."

"Hey. It's fine. Something will come up, hang in there."

We chat about this and that and I hang up, hoping something changes soon or all this effort I've put in, well, *we've* put in, would be for nothing.

SARAH

THE SIX O'CLOCK ALARM RINGS OUT TOO SOON. EYES BLEARY AND HALF open, I see Dan slumped over the table. One of his hands dangles, almost touching the floor. The other is bent, a makeshift pillow under his forehead.

I steal into the shower and let hot water massage my still-tired muscles. Before I've even stepped out, a mental countdown has begun. Everything I need to accomplish before evening and the hours left in which to do it. I pair my purple shirt with my black skirt, pull on tights, tie back my hair into a high ponytail, and dab on some mauve lipstick. Then I shake him awake.

"What—" he moans, groggy. Then his head snaps up. "What time is it?"

"6:45. I'll have to head out in ten minutes. Any further ideas?" I ask, tapping on the printouts still spread out all over the table.

He scrubs his eyes and stands up. His over-compacted body stretches back to true form. Joints click and muscles protract as he bobs and reaches upward with his arms. "Gimme a minute," he says, and plods toward the bathroom.

I put on the kettle and scoop coffee grinds from a glass jar into his coffeemaker. The dense, almost oily aroma of coffee grinds spreads through the small room.

He returns and sinks back into the chair.

"Last night you said it had to be someone who had access, possibly even maintains the payroll records. And they manage the spreadsheets sent to Picard National and Penny Bank as well?"

I nod and rinse a mug in the sink.

"I've gone over everything, every piece of information we have. There are three possibilities, but keeping in mind the demographics, it narrows it down to two."

"Who?"

"Maria Springer and Doug Fernshaw. Maria is the one who updates everything, and Doug is the one who puts everything together. But . . ."

"What is it?"

"It would be impossible for one of them to have messed around without the other knowing. It's Fortitude's fail-safe. They split the responsibilities so no one person will have access to everything. In this case, for example, it will be Maria who creates the spreadsheets. But it will be Doug who sees to the disbursement of payments and will check records against it."

I nod. "But there's a simple workaround. Most documents today are saved in shared spaces, something both of them will have access to. After one of them has saved it, how long would it take for the other to get in there and make a couple of minute changes? And this is where it's the easiest—once you think something is complete, checked, edited, and good to go, you're not going to check it later, again. Why would you?"

Dan nods.

"Even if we do find them, how do we prove it was them and not me who did this?"

"Leave it with me. Anyway, I'd better go now. If I have to get off early, I don't want to be late going in as well. Coffee should be ready in two," I tell him, as I put on my coat and grab my bag.

"Sarah?" he says when I open the door.

I turn around. His eyes look haunted. I would be scared, too. There's no time and I have so much left to go through and assess.

"It'll be fine. You'll see."

On the bus over to work, I reassure myself that I haven't lied. I will get to the bottom of it all, one way or another.

I'm the first to get to work. Celia blows in ten minutes after I do, her face covered in a thin sheen of sweat. She must have run to avoid being late. No wonder it irks her so much that I've got the promotion when she's the one who is usually first to get into work and the last to leave, and not merely for show. I wave and offer a hurried *hi*, letting her settle in. I'll ask her out for an after-work drink next week, settle things between us. She doesn't return my smile. Her brow is furrowed as she looks at her watch and pulls back her chair. She might be accustomed to working out my every little action and reaction, but in this tiny office, I've been able to tell these things too. Today, for example, she's got something on her mind. And she's avoiding meeting my eyes. She's found out something; something that's to her advantage. One might mistake that furrowed brow for worry, but I know better. It's concentration.

A worrying thought comes to me. What if she knows I met Anne? It's a small world. Then I rally. So what if I met up with Anne? It isn't a crime. I'm overthinking everything because I feel guilty.

In a way, I'm glad Celia's preoccupied. It means she won't have the time to watch me.

When I peek up from my cubicle, Norman and Celia's heads are both bent over something. I change the direction of my monitor in one swift motion to face north. The cubicle partition will cover half the screen and the other half will be covered by my own back. I nudge along the CPU on the floor as well, so the connecting wires don't strain. Once I'm sure my screen can't be visible unless someone's standing directly beside me, I pull up all the appointments and tasks on my roster. One by one, I get through them as fast as I humanly can. At a 10:45, I message Dan. I need him to connect to Fortitude's WiFi so I can get into the intranet. It has to be now because Anne's out of her office, at an appointment across town, so she won't see the activity on her computer I'm puppeteering remotely.

He texts back:

I'm in

Once I get Anne's computer to grant me full access to the system, I run a decryption program to get past company usernames and passwords. While it runs, I mull over Maria's and Doug's profiles.

According to her HR file, Maria is fifty-six years old. She's been with Fortitude for thirty years and has been promoted up from when she joined as a lowly secretary back in the late eighties. She certainly fits the profile.

But Doug's fits perfectly as well. Women may account for 51 percent of embezzlers, but that still leaves a sizable percentage of men. He's put in fewer years than she has and has had relatively less training as well, but is exactly where she is and earns more than she does. I mean, who can blame her if she has a grudge? It's all so unfair.

As soon as the decryption is complete, I analyze Maria's files. Next, I go through Doug's files.

Maria's the one who creates, maintains, and submits the employee 401(k) loan amounts. Fortitude must hold these back from the employee paychecks each month.

Whereas she doesn't have access to the disbursement files; only Doug does. So if she managed to create a false trail of employee headcount there, Doug won't spot it, even if he pores over his spreadsheets. Not with access to only one of the two spreadsheets.

Because *that's* the key. Two separate spreadsheets sit in two different folders without overlap. Until an audit, it's only an assumption by Fortitude Trading that the spreadsheets match. But either of them could have gotten into the system to manipulate them. They work together and likely have their passwords stuck to their monitors. It's no help. All this shows me is that both of them have equal access.

A flick of my eyes to the clock; it's eleven-fifteen already. Time to try a different tack. I check the logins into the back-end systems to see who has gained access to the particulars over this past year through the individual IP addresses.

As soon as I see the dates and times they transferred the disbursed money from Fortitude's corporate funds to a bank account, I'm certain I've found who it is. Looking at it as a whole, a pattern emerges. I frown when I note that the number of the bank account in which the money ends up has been partially withheld.

The click of Celia's shoes sends alarm bells tolling in my brain. I hit the start button and D together to bring back the home screen.

I text Dan:

> I think I've got it! Call you in five

"What is it?" I ask Celia without turning around.

"Have you tallied RA's expense ledger for this month?"

"Yep. It should be in the folder on the server."

"Hmm," she says distractedly, sauntering past me. Then, a thought makes me go cold. What if . . . No, Celia wouldn't do this. Would she? Why? Why would she frame Dan? And the trail clearly leads away from her . . . I'm so caught up in this thought that I waste a few valuable minutes over it before I bring myself firmly back to the here and now. I need to first finish the track I'm on before exploring wild theories.

I spy her heading to the toilet, grab my phone, and leg it to the breakroom.

"I know who it is, Dan," I say, as soon as he picks up.

"Who," he says, his voice low, dark.

"It's Maria. Maria is our embezzler."

AUDREY: NOW

Detective Greene is quiet on the drive back to my house. What is it about car rides that make him and his partner go into silent mode?

"Were you able to find Adam, Detective?"

"Detective Greene?" I say, when he doesn't reply. For a bizarre moment, I wonder if the car is driving itself and I'm all alone in it.

"Oh, sorry, I shook my head."

His honesty disarms me. "That's all right. I'm sure it happens often with people I talk to."

"No. We haven't found Adam yet. Most people think solving a murder is all in a day's work when in reality a simple DNA test takes as long as two days. Information gathering takes a long time. And we're only on day two of the investigation."

I nod. "People expect magic." And it would help if people didn't lie. But they all, including myself, do. And that's perhaps what makes me nervous at the very thought of talking to either of these detectives. I've been lying from the start and it's only a matter of time before they discover it.

Greene parks the car outside my townhome. It's been a long night. The shock of discovering that the body isn't Sarah's but Kelly Fergusson's hasn't worn off yet. Something has gone terribly wrong. What was Kelly doing here? How did she end up dead? All I want to do is flee to the safety of my home. Except, home isn't safe anymore. The thought makes my blood crawl with fear. I'm angry as well. Where is one safe if not in one's own home?

"Tell me about the break-ins you had last year," Greene says. "Both your and Ms. Connelly's homes were hit?"

"People were still moving in. It was chaotic. The construction was still on, some of the homes at the end of the lane didn't even have the windows put in yet. That's when it began. Mrs. Kirsch's home in the lane behind us was broken into. Mine was hit after, and then Mr. Cane's, then Sarah's. I—"

"What is it?" Greene asks when I stop short.

"It's strange, but I always suspected that the breaks-ins weren't random, that it was someone who knew us all well."

"You think one of your neighbors was breaking into the homes?"

"I . . . I don't know. It's a feeling I got."

"Why?"

"Because they seemed to know what was valuable. Not monetary but actual sentimental value to the owners. Mrs. Kirsch's necklace is an heirloom. My pen, a parting gift from a colleague. Bob, Mr. Cane's, photo frame, silver, a keepsake of a buddy he'd lost in the service. You won't get much if you pawn these."

"You'd make a good detective," Greene says.

I click my tongue. "Missed my calling, didn't I?"

"You're certain Sarah never mentioned a friend or a relative here or in the city? Even an acquaintance she could be hiding with?"

I shake my head. "She didn't. Why are you so certain she's bolted?"

"Why are you so certain that she hasn't?"

I shrug.

"Then what do you think happened?"

"I haven't a clue, Detective, but Sarah would never voluntarily leave Nicole behind."

I unclick the seat belt, fumble to find the lever, and push it up to open the door.

"Detective, I hope you don't mind me asking, what was it that killed Sar—Kelly?"

There's no reply. I wonder if I've overstepped the mark. Curiosity isn't a good thing, and it always catches police attention when someone takes a little too much interest in investigations. But as I'm the one who found Sarah, well, Kelly, I can't help but think I have a right to know.

"A golf club," he says, haltingly.

Without warning, the memory of cradling the bloody head, and the way sticky, matted hair had come away in my hands, flashes through my mind. A cold, prickly shiver passes over me, as though someone had walked across my grave. It dawns on me then why Detective Novak had asked if Sarah is a golfer.

I nod. "Thanks for the ride."

"You're welcome."

I exit the car, take out the cane from my bag, and unfold the length of it. The bottom clicks on the ground. Then, after waiting for a beat to listen for traffic, I cross the street, grateful that Detective Greene hasn't mollycoddled me. People often grab my arm or shoulder and force me to match their movements, their pace. I might never get used to that.

The Hudson is slushing along, the water a little rough. The tinkling of the wind chime outside my home reaches my ears. Instead of comforting me, it leaves me disoriented. If I'm standing right outside my home, the chimes should be louder.

I cock my head back to the direction where Greene is parked. He has pulled up further ahead, outside Sarah's townhome instead of mine. It could have been an honest mistake. But no. I'm certain he's done it on purpose. It's his job to suspect everyone and everything, I suppose. Still. These kinds of games annoy me.

I pass No. 5 and saunter toward No. 4. My cane clanks against the tactile concrete, and the reassuring melody of my wind chimes sounds loud and clear. Putting out my free hand to the railing, I climb up the five steps to the entryway. From my purse, I take out the house key and am plunging it in when I feel the hairs on my arm stand up. Someone's watching me.

Panic begins to churn inside. I turn around. "Hello? Is someone there?"

It's silent. A light breeze ruffles my hair. I shake myself, feeling silly for actually expecting an answer. *You're being paranoid.*

As soon as I let myself in and arm the system, the phone rings. Startled, I jump, then answer it, irritated with myself for being so spooked.

"This is Phil from Hoyt Security, Ms. Hughes."

"Yes!" It comes out incisive, barking. It's not *his* fault that I'm afraid of my own shadow, I remind myself.

"There's no problem with the system in your home," he says, after a pause. "The hardware checked out. If there was an intruder, we would know."

"What?" I'm unprepared for the disappointment that slams into me. This is like Rodriguez and Riley all over again! I was so sure Hoyt Security would find the proof . . . Then my mouth falls open. Of course! Why didn't I think of it before? "What if they knew the codes?" I ask.

Silence.

"We can pull up the video that's built into the pin pad of the master interface. It only activates whenever someone enters the code. The coverage is only from the master unit house at the entrance. There are no cameras in the other units by the back patio door and upstairs, but we'll be going through it again and we'll let you know if anything shows up."

"If something does turn up, could you email it to Detective Alan Greene of the Sleepy Point Police Department and copy me in?"

"Sure."

I hang up, biting down the urge to scream. Maybe I *should* have listened to Sherman and had Hoyt Security put up hidden cameras all over. With all the technology available to us, it might seem a bit cavalier that I didn't go for the state-of-the-art stuff. Right now, it could have helped me figure out who broke in, but in the process of watching everyone who comes and goes from my house, I'd be watched, too, and the thought of someone's eyes on my every move . . . I shudder. Sometimes the things that are supposed to keep us safe are the most dangerous of all.

*   *   *

I head to the closet, peel off the clothes from my tired body, and step into the shower. The grief—tinged with both guilt and relief, weighing me down ever since I discovered the body—is gone, replaced by a mix of simmering rage and confusion. Thoughts whirl around my head. Where *is* Sarah? Did she kill Kelly Fergusson? Why would she? Is that why she ran away? Why did she leave Nicole behind? And *what* was Kelly doing at Sarah's house?

I slip into a pair of boxers and a clean T-shirt for bed, thinking about everything I haven't told the detectives. Not held back but *lied*, I correct myself. They're bound to find me out eventually, but I can't worry about that right now. I've got to use what little time there is to figure things out before the detectives do. And then I'll come clean.

SARAH

"Dan? Are you there?" I ask.

"Sorry, I'm here. It's just . . . I can't believe it. I mean we discussed the possibilities last night and seeing names on paper is one thing, but I know Maria. It's so hard to believe."

"I know. I'm sorry," I say.

"What should I do?"

"For now, nothing. Let's turn over what we have to Gerry."

"Except, we don't have any proof yet because we haven't traced the money back to her?"

"Shit," I say. "Okay, what about . . . confronting her?"

Silence.

"How do you mean?"

"Stop her when she leaves the building and confront her with what we know."

"You think she'll come clean?"

"We've got to get her to incriminate herself. All I have are logs from her computer showing you logging in. She can easily lie and say you used her computer after she left work. It'd be very difficult to disprove."

"Unless we can find the money."

He's right, I know. But that's also the trickiest part. Without further details, I wouldn't be able to pinpoint the account number to which the money is being transferred.

"Look, get her out of the office by five. I'll work something out."

"What are you going to do? Sarah?" he adds when I fall silent.

"It's better you don't know. As it is, there's plenty you now have to lie about."

"Sara—"

"Dan, it'll be all right. Trust me."

"If you get into trouble . . ."

"I won't."

"Hey, let's go out for a drink next week. Catch up? It's been a while. Sorry things have been busy. I've been apartment hunting," I tell Celia.

"Sure," she says, in that tone of hers.

I'm not sure if she buys my excuse, but I can't care about that right now. It's nearing four.

I leave quickly. I'm early enough to join Dan in the corner café where he's been holed up all afternoon.

His eyes widen with surprise when he spots me entering the café. A bell dings when I open the door. It's already lit up for the holiday season. Snowman paper chains hang at the doorways. A frosty cloud is set up at the window, with the poster of a caramel-topped drink and a real candy cane stuck on it. It smells of pumpkin spice.

I wave at him and stop to order a double shot of espresso. There's a tremor of fear and tension in my hand as I pry the credit card from my wallet. The cashier notes it but looks away, as though embarrassed. A deep flush creeps into my face. She must think I'm a drunk.

I grab the drink she hands me, and head to the table where Dan's looking about as nervous as I am. "I thought I was meeting Maria alone."

"No. I changed my mind. It's better if we meet her together."

I knock back the scalding espresso. A jolt of caffeine tingles my body. "Let's go," I say.

We head to the south entrance of Fortitude and hang back, near the street.

"I feel like a stalker," Dan says.

"We are, but only in this one instance," I say. "Keep an eye out. We can't afford to miss her."

Dan grows quieter as the minutes pass. The doors begin to revolve, expelling Fortitude's employees into the wintry dusk.

"Tell me about Maria."

He frowns and flicks a look at me. "What do you want to know?"

"What sort of person is she?"

"Conservative."

I read between the lines. Dan's sexual orientation isn't something he advertises, but people notice things. In Dan's case, it might have been the lack of a girlfriend despite his obvious charm and good looks. I don't generalize usually, but sometimes people of Maria's age process the information in front of them and arrive at certain conclusions to suit their view of the world.

He stiffens when a woman in a maroon coat and sensible winter boots steps out of the doors. She's chatting with another woman, who laughs and waves goodbye.

"There she is."

"C'mon," I say, linking my arm into his.

"We're going to follow her?" he asks, aghast.

"We can't talk to her here, surrounded by other employees. You will be seen. Now, quick," I say, urging him to walk on. "Pull your hat down." He's too good-looking not to be recognizable by his colleagues.

He mutters something unintelligible and walks on. I march to keep up with his long stride. We slow down when she comes into view directly ahead of us.

She's about to turn onto Park Avenue when she comes to a full stop without warning. We both freeze. Dan turns to his side, his gaze on the traffic. I continue to look dead-on at her. She pulls out something from her handbag and resumes walking.

"C'mon," I say, dragging him like a reluctant pet.

"She's going to see us."

"She will, but not yet."

Ahead, the pedestrian traffic slows us all down. She half stops again, as though searching through the crowd. It sends an uneasy shiver coursing through my body. Then she spots someone and halts, pulls out a hand from her coat pocket, and hands the item to them.

She's giving a hobo money—a familiar hobo, by the look of it.

"Old-fashioned but good-hearted," Dan adds.

A frown begins to crease my forehead.

"Good-hearted? How?"

"She organizes all our fund-raisers and charities. She heads the US for Hunger drive run by Fortitude."

Some distance ahead, Maria stops and turns around. I grasp Dan's elbow and pull him back.

"Now's the chance," he says.

"It's not her."

"What? But you said . . ."

"Yes, the login evidence points to her. But it doesn't add up. A person who embezzles isn't also going to stop to give out free money to the homeless."

Dan's looking at me with incredulity. "Not even if she's just gotten a few hundred thousand dollars richer?"

"No. Not even then. Greedy people steal. They won't spare a penny. From what you've told me about her, Maria doesn't fit that bill. I need to look at the charity she chairs, but it'll likely be run by a third party and she'll only be Fortitude's liaison with no access to the funds."

"What are trying to say?"

"Maria's not our embezzler."

Dan sucks air through his teeth. "Shit. It's Friday evening and we don't even know who's stolen the money, let alone where it is."

I look up at him with dread. I promised to work everything out and I've let him down. I've failed him.

AUDREY: THEN

1 MONTH AGO

"Uff!" I moan and massage my jaw with my fingers.

"Are you having a heart attack or something?" Sarah asks. I've been so caught up in my head that I've forgotten Sarah is home, my home, with Nicole, who is asleep in her carrier.

"No."

"Is it work?"

"Of course it's work!" When there's no reply, I think *I've* startled *her* for a change. "I'm not usually prone to tantrums."

"Ha! You call this a tantrum? Sweetie, I've got to teach you a few things in life. But what is it?"

"I'm . . . having a day."

"What are you trying to do?"

"Never mind."

"What? You think I can't help? I'm not just a pretty face. I'm smart, you know."

"I'm sure you are. This is technical stuff, though. I wouldn't be able to tell you anyway."

"I bet you're great at it."

I laugh. "And what are you good at?"

"Lying."

I tilt my head up. "Sorry?"

"Lying. It's a talent. It's art."

"And what do you lie about?" I ask, still typing.

"This and that."

"Do you ever lie about important stuff?" I'm not sure what's made me ask, but now I have, I'm curious.

"It depends. What are you trying to *do* that's so complicated, anyway? Research is like googling stuff, isn't it?"

It's a simplistic definition, but she's right in a way. "Mostly. But sometimes it's more involved."

"That's so cool, Auds. Do you know, like, how to hack an account and stuff?"

I stop and look up in the direction from where Sarah's voice emanates. "That's a long jump from research."

"You didn't answer my question."

I cock my head at her. "A little."

"Tell me, I've always wanted to know: What's the difference then between hacking and tracing?"

"They are two completely different things, or they *can* be."

"So, say if I wanted to find someone, could you like put a trace on them or whatever, online?"

I get tingly all over. Why is she asking me these questions?

"I'm *not* a hacker or coder. I'm an investigative researcher, which means I find things on and offline. And I'm not a tracer, but yes, technically, I *can* do that."

"You clever thing! Is it illegal?"

"It depends."

"On what?"

"On circumstances. Tracing can be legal, depending on how you do it. If the information is freely available on the internet and it's a matter of finding it, it wouldn't be illegal. Hacking, though, is illegal."

"But that's only if you get caught!" she says, her glee-filled giggle filling the room.

"The second you have to enter a password that isn't yours, you're entering dangerous territory."

"Have you ever done it?"

I nod. "Once, low-level stuff. I didn't get caught, but it wasn't the right thing to do. Why?"

"Auds, I want you to find someone for me." Her voice is too near all of a sudden. I jolt back.

I'm not sure I like where this is going. I should have caught on sooner; at some point, the innocence of the questions has been lost. We're in a very specific territory now, one shepherded by her.

"I've made it awkward, haven't I?"

"Look, why don't you tell me what it is you want and let me decide?"

I can tell she's excited; her breathing has changed.

"You'll probably laugh if I tell you," she says, but her tone isn't light.

"Go on."

"There was this guy a few years ago."

Here it comes.

"I could never pin him down. In the end, he moved away. To California, I think. I can't be sure," she adds when I fall silent.

"When was the last time you were in touch with him?"

"That's the thing! He's gone and blocked me everywhere," she says.

For a moment, I think she's hurt, but no. She's angry.

"What happened?" I don't like pushing, but she's the one who started it. I was minding my own business, working.

"I think it got too intense for him. He wasn't ready for commitment."

"And you were?"

"Yes. Stupid, isn't it? It's not as if I haven't been bitten before. But something happened a few years ago, and it . . . changed me."

Her voice has taken on a faraway quality like she's sitting with me but is on the cusp of another world.

"What?" I ask. It comes out a whisper. I shouldn't like to force a confidence, but at the same time, it's as though I *have* to learn this intimate detail about her.

She's sitting right next to me, but she's now fully in her world, crossed over. It's the quality of her absence.

"Something I haven't spoken of since to anyone. I was in an accident."

Her admission has stunned me frozen. She says nothing after, either. The silence, as it stretches on like a rubber band between us, is oppressive. It'd be disrespectful to interrupt and ask the unseemly questions everyone always wants to ask at such times.

"It's how I got this," she says, reaching for my hand. I haven't yet mastered the art of not flinching at an unexpected touch. It creeps up on me, makes me gasp, miss a beat. I manage to seize a deep breath as she grabs my hand and isolates my index finger cocooned in her hand, as a child would, and leads it toward her.

My finger grazes an abrasive, raspy texture, like broken leather.

"It's a scar," she says. She lets go and I shrink my hand back like a hose attachment to my body.

"It must have been nasty."

"It took ages to heal."

She's far away again. I can almost sense her shutting down. Before I can decide if I should push her, just a nudge, she says, "I used to have a bit of a different life, before."

"How's that?" I ask. Inside, I'm cringing. Even *I* can hear the too-casual tone in my question.

She laughs, an out-of-place, nervous laugh. "You'll think it's so cliché, a small-town girl from a rough neighborhood looking to make it big in the city, make enough money to buy a house somewhere nice. The dream, you know?"

"But it all worked out; you got your dream?"

"Kind of. But . . . it made me rethink things a bit, have a bit of a personality change. Sometimes it's like I've *totally* changed. So, anyway, can you find him or not?"

"I'm not saying I will, but if I do, I'll need details, the more the better. His full name, his last job, and his date of birth, where he went to school, anything at all you can tell me."

She lets out a piglet squeal. "You're going to! I know you're going to. Can't wait."

"I said I *might*. No promises."

"Shall I note down the details?"

"Not here," I say, when she grabs my work laptop.

I reach for my laptop from my desk and enter my details after it powers up.

"You type so fast. How do you know if it's accurate?"

"The laptop will alert me if it isn't. I know the keys by heart anyway."

I navigate to and open the notepad and hand it to her. "Type it here."

She takes it from me. Minutes pass and the *click-clack* of the keys continues. "Are you writing down his autobiography?" I ask.

I can almost feel her glare in the silence.

"What's BlinkersOff?"

I'm rendered speechless for a moment. Then I gulp. "What?"

"There's a tab opened on your browser. What's Gee-o-pa-Zia?"

"Nothing for you to worry about," I say, and snatch the laptop back from her.

"Sounds like kinky porn."

I cackle, not prettily. "Porn? And what would I do with it?"

"What everyone does with it."

"I don't need porn to have a *ménage à moi*."

"So if it isn't porn, what is it?"

I want to say more, but this isn't the right time. There *is* no perfect time to tell someone you're so mentally broken, you need help to get through the day, sometimes even to get out of bed. This is too serious a topic for one of Sarah's silly moods.

"Don't you have to be somewhere?"

"All right I'm going. I know when I've outstayed my welcome." From the familiar scrape of the baby carrier being dragged over the coffee table, she has picked up Nicole, who fusses, then grows quiet again. I wonder if Sarah rocks the carrier as I do, to lull Nicole back to sleep.

"I'm simply reminding you, as a friend, that you have to be somewhere," I say. My lips twitch despite myself. I simply can't remain mad at this girl. Even though sometimes, I am. Sometimes I'm mad at everybody. At life. But especially at Sarah. But she doesn't need to know that; however honest she is with me, she also lies through her teeth.

So can I.

The chill of the frigid late-spring breeze on my face is numbing. A gloved hand resting on the railing, I stare into the night and listen. The water assaults the banks with relentless violence. I imagine shadows swirling all around, like the thoughts swishing around in my head. It leaves me endlessly waiting for answers, forcing me to revisit a past I can't afford to forget. And yet, there's nothing more I want sometimes than to forget it all.

I turn to the walking path, tightening my grip on my cane as it hits the asphalt. There's hardly anyone around at this hour; it makes it easier to navigate. I've only thought that when footsteps clatter behind me. I go rigid in automatic response. I don't have a flashlight with me; they can't see me.

I turn around. "Hello?" There's no response. The footsteps draw closer. My lungs tighten and my heart falters in my chest.

"Is anyone there?"

"Audrey, it's me, Priya."

I slump with relief. "Oh, hi," I say.

She sniffles. "What are you doing here at this hour?" I'm not sure I like her concerned mother-hen tone.

"Taking a walk. You?"

There's no reply. She's lost in thought. She's got my arm tucked in hers. Her pace is easy; I match it, letting my cane hover in the air as I walk on, guided by her.

"Are you okay?" I ask.

There's a deep, shaky gasp. "You know, don't you, Audrey? About Brian and Sarah? You've known all along, haven't you?"

"I—"

"I'm *not* stupid," Priya scoffs. "I *know* Brian's been having an affair with her."

My ears go hot. I'd been right to think Priya has known about the affair from the beginning.

Priya sighs. "I thought she'll tire of him soon and it'll run its course, or at least stop after I confronted her; then he'll come to his senses."

"I don't know what to say."

"You could have *told* me as soon as you suspected. I thought you were my friend."

My face feels hot all of a sudden. "I wasn't sure, honestly. I did suspect something of the sort when I heard his voice at Sarah's house, once or twice, late at night. But without proof, I couldn't worry you. What if I was wrong? I'm *so* sorry, Priya."

I'm sad but relieved when we reach my door. This is making me too uncomfortable. It's so like Sarah to make me complicit in something I never wanted a part of. Another secret I don't want to keep.

"It's so . . . cruel. Why do people think they have the right to take what isn't theirs?"

I want to tell Priya that I know that I understand the sheer unfairness of it all so well.

"I don't know, Priya," I say. "Hey, it'll be all right," I add.

"No. It won't." Her voice is so small, I want to pull her into a hug. "I'll see you later, Auds."

                              *   *   *.

All I seem to be doing these days is nannying, I think, as I stand at the door yet another evening with Nicole on my hip and wave off Sarah. "Say goodbye to your mom, the breaker of hearts," I say softly in her tiny ear.

I wonder how my continued friendship with Sarah might seem to Priya. She'd sounded so miserable a few nights ago when she'd asked me if I knew about Sarah and Brian. I want to tell Priya that *her* friendship means a lot more to me than I can let on. That I don't *want* to be friends with Sarah, but that would beg more questions I can't answer.

I sigh and shut the door.

Inside, I head upstairs and seat Nicole on my lap for a burp. "Your mom's off to her barre class, to get her pre-you body back," I say, nuzzling her baby-soft neck. She lets out a contented sigh.

We're in the only room with a soft covering on the cold hard floor, also the safest for a baby. I can set her on the rug, play with her and not worry about anything getting in the way. I've blind-proofed my house, which, as it turns out, is pretty safe for babies, too.

I set her on the rug, then pull the cushions off the sofa and create a fort around us. Nicole gurgles. She's happy to be free. From under my desk, I grab a box where I've stowed away the latest package I've ordered ·from an online store. I unpack it and take out the silicone-edged cards, on the back of which there's writing and on the front is a corresponding picture or color.

"This is blue," I say, praying they've labeled it right as I read off the back with my index finger. "Like the sky," I read, frowning at the same time. "Well, the sky isn't always blue, is it? It's gray, sometimes white, sometimes a gradient of orange or pink when the sun is rising or setting, and inky at night. Let's see what else they have," I say, turning around and reaching for the box.

She coos like a playful owl while I read the labels one by one, to make sure they're not lies, or poor Nicole will grow up believing all this garbage.

I arrange them back in the order they came in and turn around.

"Shall we do orange next?"

No gurgle. Sometimes, she just watches me. I wonder what she sees, how much she understands. Early on, I used to get worried when she wouldn't coo or gurgle when I'd speak to her. Sarah was paranoid about Sudden Infant Death Syndrome, so I kept an eagle eye on Nicole, well, so to speak.

Out of habit, I put out a hand to her tiny body to feel the reassuring murmur of her heart.

My hand touches the rug. The space she was lying in is empty.

She's gone.

SARAH

In the cab on the way home, I deflate like a week-old balloon. "I'm so sorry, Dan."

"Will you stop apologizing? You've found out so much! More than I ever could have."

"But it's useless!" I throw my bag on the cab floor. Inside the tiny, glassed-off sedan my voice sounds like a quaking volcano. The cabbie flicks a glance at us through the rearview mirror.

"It's not! Look, we'll turn over everything we've got to Gerry."

"And say what? Hi Gerry, here's all the information we've gotten by hacking illegally into the company that's suing Dan?"

Dan lets out an exasperated sigh and cocks his head at me. "No. We don't have to tell him how we got the information. We could say a friend helped us and leave it at that. The important thing is for him to know there's an alternative line of inquiry so he can pass it on to Fortitude. He can show them the breadcrumbs that lead to Maria."

"But if it's not Maria, they'll string her up next and she'll be crucified instead of you!"

His bright eyes from a moment ago look uncertain now.

"I fucked up," I say, shrugging.

The sharp trill of my phone's ringtone startles us for a moment.

"It's my landlord. I have to take this," I tell Dan, and slide the green answer button.

"Ms. Connelly, this is Tony D'Angelo here. I'm afraid I can't let you terminate the lease two months early. One month is doable."

"But I'll have to pay rent on two apartments for December!"

"I'm sorry, it's the terms of the lease agreements. It's all there; you signed it."

I think back to the agreement I signed not four months ago and realize that he's right. I did agree to it but that doesn't stop the hard bitter disappointment.

"Fine," I say, and hang up.

"He's not agreeing to early lease termination?" Dan asks.

I shake my head and look at him. "He isn't willing to let it go two months early. A month he says is doable."

Dan's lips are a flat line. "What are you going to do?"

"I don't know."

We're quiet the rest of the way.

"Can you stop here?" I tell the cabbie when we're on 30th and Tenth.

"You're going home?" Dan asks.

I nod. "I'm not good company right now."

I want to retreat into my soon-to-be ex-lair and lick my wounds.

There's a sharp *rat-tat-tat* on my floor. Is the family downstairs practicing clogging upside down on the ceiling tonight? The rhythm makes my head want to shrivel and retreat within its shell like a frightened tortoise. It's not been a minute since I stepped inside; not even a moment's peace to be had. Serves me right to want to move to a big city and hope for quiet. I take out my laptop from my desk and power it up.

After it springs to life, I email Rachel a copy of the signed contract. Who knows when I'll manage to find another one-bedroom with such a view? Rachel responds instantly, congratulating me and expressing her surprise at my agreeable landlord. I send a quick reply, disabusing her of the notion and expressing my dismay at having to pay double rent for December. She e-mails me right back.

Welcome to New York.

I sulk as I absent-mindedly stir some stew in a pot.

I'm tempted to go for a walk, get some fresh air, but I don't want to see the happy faces of hopeful tourists. I flick the TV on and skim the guide. *The Odd Couple* is on the classics channel. I think of the past week, me bunkering in Dan's living room. We're an odd couple, too. The phlegmy cough I let out only irks me more. I ignore it and stare, droopy-eyed, at the screen, where Oscar's presence is beginning to annoy Felix and he's regretting the temporary move-in.

Celia is following me around. Dan and I are following Maria to the stop and Celia is shadowing us. Norman is waving his umbrella at me from behind Celia. She's a good person, Dan's telling me and through the watery haze, I can't figure out if Dan's speaking about Maria or Celia. I turn up Norman's collar and look up to find Anne Hatchet. I know you hacked in with my username, she says, her eyes flashing at me.

Behind her, Kelly is standing with her arms crossed. I was better than Dan, she tells me, but you prefer working with him, I see. It's not like that, I say.

Sleep falls away, as though dropping off from a high ledge as I wake up with a start. I stare into the dim light of the overhead low-wattage fixture in the living room and blink as my eyes adjust to it. I freeze as a thought begins to expand in my head. Then it solidifies from its loose, liquid state to something with firm, hard edges.

I drag on a pair of leggings, grab my keys, wallet, phone, and coat, and lock the door behind me. Below, I hurry into the quiet, cold night to flag a passing cab from Eighth Avenue.

"Where to?" the cab driver asks.

"Eighty-first."

He nods at me to get in. I pull the door open and slide in. The thoughts come at me like a blitz attack all at the same time. My heart hammers as I try to work out the one clear idea that's starting to emerge. How stupid I've been! It's all been there in front of me from the start, the evening I saw her arm in arm with a man, shopping bags from boutique stores in her hand, then the taxi to the Waldorf, how happy she looked.

I pay the guy in haste, use the keycard Dan lent me to access the main door, and scale three floors. I knock and knock until Dan flings the door back, and blinks at me.

"What—is everything okay? What's happened?"

I barge in. He shuts the door behind me and follows me into his living room. "Sarah?"

"Dan. I've been so wrong. It's not Maria."

His eyes brighten, then sharpen. "Who then? Doug?"

"No. We've been looking at this all wrong. I've been a fool. When I logged in this morning, I was so focused on finding what I was looking for, I missed something obvious!"

Dan stares at me. "What?"

"It's the other logins! And one that shouldn't have been there. It's Kelly, Dan. Kelly Fergusson's our embezzler."

Dan's jaw drops. "But—"

"Her logins were recorded. I ignored them at the time because I was so focused on Maria and Doug's login activities, but I clearly remember seeing it now. She had access to everything."

"But why?"

"She fits our profile, too, to a T. She's forty-six. And I should have seen it in the org chart but dismissed it because I was focused on Maria and Doug. She didn't get a promotion when she moved on. When you took over her position, she was moved laterally. Same pay grade as the previous position—your position."

"She should have been promoted. She's been with Fortitude for years."

"Maybe that's why she stole. She felt like she was owed?" I plonk myself on his sofa. "Did I tell you I ran into her at the café on the day I met Anne?"

Dan shakes his head.

"She had the nerve to tell me that you should have owned up, that it would have made your life easier."

Dan's eyes flash. "It was no secret she hated me. I mean, she could have made my transition smoother, but she didn't. I remember wondering if she was intentionally complicating things for me. But I was new, and she made out that I was finding it difficult to slip into the role because I wasn't good at my job."

"We've got her footprints in the system, but we need proof. We need to show where the money is," I say.

He nods and lets out a puff of air. I look at the clock—it'll be the right time to call in a favor.

"I have a friend who could help," I say, and pick up the phone.

"But it's three in the morning!"

"I know," I say, and step into Dan's bedroom as though it's mine and shut the door behind me.

AUDREY: NOW

Morning coffee steaming in the mug in one hand, I have Siri call Greg.

"Hi, Greg," I say after it connects, and he picks up.

"Hi, Audrey."

"There's been a development."

"Gimme one sec," he says. There's the sound of keys clacking, then a furtive, "Excuse me," then huffing. I picture Greg at the office. It's early but he's in.

"Sorry, I had company. Tell me."

"The body I discovered, it's not Sarah Connelly."

Silence.

"Greg?"

"Whose is it?"

"It's Kelly Fergusson."

Silence. "Hello?"

"Audrey, there's an incoming call. I'll have to call you back."

"Sure."

I'm not sure how much more bad news I can give Greg before he pulls the plug on this task, *mission*, that I'm on. On top of that, the question that's been looming in my mind since last night: Where is Sarah? If the body is Kelly's, then where the hell is Sarah? What has happened to her? Why did she leave Nicole behind? Why was Kelly at Sarah's home in the first place?

The doorbell chimes. I jump, even though I suspect that I know who it is. Only two people ever ring the bell. One is Priya, and the other, Bob. I disable the alarm and fling the door back to find both of them outside, urgent greetings dribbling from their lips.

As they follow me into the house, I suppress a spurt of irritation. I haven't had a moment's peace from the second I stumbled onto that body. One after the other, the police, a burglar, and now visitors. Will it never end?

"This is quite bizarre," Priya says, after I've ushered them both into the living room. I've been expecting a blowup this morning. Sherman warned me that the news has caught up with the events.

The page-one headline of the *Sleepy Point Daily* says, "Woman's Body Discovered in Upscale Sleepy Point Identified."

"Who was this woman, Kelly Fergusson?" Priya asks. From the *tap-tap*, I picture Priya's fingers drumming the crisp paper.

"How should I know?"

"The murder weapon was one of Ronnie's golf clubs, I've heard." Priya shudders audibly.

"They've said that in the papers?" I would be shocked if they did. It's too early to divulge details like that publicly.

"No. I heard from Donna Chambers. She saw Ronnie when she went to pick up Matt from the police station. And he told her that the police have been hounding him."

"And where is Sarah?" Bob asks.

"She's bolted, of course. She must have killed that poor woman," Priya says.

I'm about to answer Priya when Bob says, "I have to say, it doesn't surprise me. She was a smooth liar and was up to no good."

"We figured if anyone knew, it'd be you. You were her best friend!"

"Look, I don't know anything, okay?" I say, exasperated.

"I hope they catch the bitch!"

Priya's vehemence silences us for a moment.

It isn't fair. It's not even eight in the morning. Far too early to be grilled in my own house by neighbors, as though the police interrogating me this way and that isn't enough.

After the two of them leave, I slump on the sofa, as though squashed under a steamroller. The silence is too oppressive suddenly. Next door, there's no baby wailing. No Sarah prattling on about something. No sounds. All is quiet in No. 5 Shore Drive. It's at once reassuring and frightening. As someone who relies on sound for nearly everything, the lack of it is like being in a vacuum.

I head to the kitchen, open a cabinet on the far right, and reach for a large zip-top bag on the bottom shelf. I yank it out with a huff and place it on the counter. I grab a clean bowl from the dishwasher. *Tch, I never do that.* I always empty the contents and place everything back on the shelves where they belong. *Maybe just this one day.* I reach into the bag, scoop two ladlefuls of its contents into the bowl, and zip the bag closed. I lift the spoon and let the earthy, slightly damp taste fill my mouth, becoming wetter as I chew and saliva pools in. I gulp the first bite and gag, then slow down.

That's disgusting! AcidGurl2010 had said; she was right. They were all right. It is.

As if by some psychic phenomenon, my laptop chirps—someone from BlinkersOff is online. I'm not in the mood today. If it's Hillary, she'll try to talk me out of it; she'll give her unsolicited but good advice, and today I fear I might fling it back in Hillary's face.

A chorus of whispers crowds my head. The body I found, the bloody head I'd cradled and cried over, never belonged to Sarah; Sarah is missing, in the wind. The rising panic and confusion ever since the detectives delivered the shocking news rush up to my throat until I shake with rage. Hot tears trickle down my face. I grab the bowl and hurl it against the wall. The loud crash of shattering porcelain drowns out my animal growl of frustration.

SARAH

It's Saturday when my eyes open. I'm on Dan's sofa again. It's nearing nine but I don't want to wake up. I can hear him shifting inside the bedroom. I huff and sit up.

"Where are you off to?" Dan asks when I gather up my things.

"Home. I've got to pack. I'm moving to the new apartment next week."

He nods. "Look, do you trust your friend to trace this account in time?"

"There's no one better suited to find the proof we need to nail Kelly than a finance security architect who locks up the back-end servers of banks for a living."

Dan wolf-whistles as his eyebrows shoot up. "You have some interesting friends."

I smirk.

"I'll message you as soon as I know something. Meanwhile, what are you going to do if Gerry gets in touch?"

Dan stares thoughtfully, then shakes his head. "Nothing to do. Civil suits take time.

We don't state the obvious, that in addition to suing him, Fortitude could at any moment file a criminal charge and have him arrested.

I open the door to my apartment and frown. It's a mess. Inside, I pick up the fallen pillow from the sofa bed, fold the sheets, and look around. My minimalist approach means there will be fewer things to pack. I let my eyes rove the space and mentally number the boxes I'd need. In a way, this is perhaps for the best. I might be able to make do without hiring a moving van. If I have the keys to both apartments, I could swing by on weekends and haul stuff a little at a time. That would also eliminate the need to pack and unpack. I tally the number of open boxes I'll need and factor in my two suitcases.

The phone starts to ring when I'm pushing around scrambled eggs on a plate, lost in thought.

"Hello?"

"Sarah."

In a second, it's as though I've free-fallen into some other world; one where everything's sharper, brighter, and where even time is nothing. Mac always has this effect on me, even after so many years. "That was quick!"

"This is child's play."

I smile. "It would be, for *you*. Tell me."

I scribble down everything. "Don't you want to know why I've asked you to track down this account?"

"Nope. The more you tell me, the more I'll have to deny."

Our laughter fills the phone.

"Remind me again why it is I'm in New York and you're still in that dump?"

"It's the unfairness of this world. How have you been?"

"Okay. Not too shabby."

"You're languishing all by yourself there, aren't you? I can picture you, alone in some dank, dingy apartment."

I laugh. "Myself and my lonely existence are fine, thank you very much. Although, I am moving to a swanky place soon." I want to add so much more, but I end up saying, "You should visit. It'll be fun."

There's silence. I can picture Mac reading into everything I've said. "Hello?"

"I'll think about it."

"Thanks for doing this."

"I'm glad you thought to call me, if at least under the pretext of seeking my help."

"It's not a pretext. I'm helping a friend."

"Hmm. Lucky friend. Anyway, I've got to go now."

"My love to Liz. How is she?" I ask. Then I regret it. Maybe I shouldn't have asked, but it's something to say. I don't want to hang up.

"The same."

I know my love will not be passed on. No one wants to tell their current lover that their ex-lover passed on their love.

"'Kay, take care."

"Sarah. Bye."

I reach for the red call end button, but the phone's dead. I dial Dan's number.

"I've got it."

"Wow. That was quick."

"That's exactly what I said. Anyway, you should call Gerry and set up a meeting with him today. We should hand over everything we've got now."

"I'll call him and ping you the deets."

We're pacing up and down 50th Street past Radio City and Rockefeller Center, waiting for Gerry to meet us. The air is a mix of perfume, roasting chestnuts, and chocolate from the Godiva store nearby. It's packed; there's a live chef training event. Tourists line up outside for the free chocolate-dipped strawberries once the training is over. Dan and I ogle at the glittering display of a jewelry store through the street window, fully dressed up for Christmas. Fake frost hangs between gold watches, as though the gilt-edged beauties are gifts descending from heaven. Judging by Dan's reaction, they are. I press his arm to step inside the store. He's rooted in the spot.

"Safer to ogle from here. I'll get suckered into buying something if we go inside," Dan says. "Also, I'm broke."

"Not for long."

He presses my arm. Rockefeller Center is lit up. They're putting up a massive tree. The skating rink is full capacity. "A Baby Just Like You" is playing all around us, as though the music is being piped through invisible speakers. But I'm starting to become antsy.

"Where is he?" I flick a glance at my wrist. It's past six. Gerry was supposed to have called us half an hour ago.

The smell of molten chocolate wafting over from Godiva makes my mouth water.

Dan takes out his phone. "He's at Bar SixtyFive, up there, in the Rainbow Room." He points to the top of the Rockefeller Plaza.

We squeeze ourselves onto the escalator from the first level to the mezzanine to take the elevator up. Once upstairs, we're led through, into the heart of the glassed-off room with sweeping views of the Manhattan skyline on all four sides. The view is dazzling. The winter sun has been swallowed by the glittering city lights spearing the sky. Dan raises a hand and waves at someone at the far back of the room.

"This is Sarah. Sarah, Gerry," Dan says once we're at the table.

I offer a hello to the curly-haired, heavyset man with a sizable belly. I shrug off my coat, sling it over the back of the plush velvet chair, and take a seat facing the skyline.

We get down to business as soon as the drinks arrive. Dan's brought printouts and I've brought the rest on a memory stick.

"Here's where the money is," I say, handing him a folded sheet of paper from the folder Dan's carrying.

Gerry's eyes are nearly glazed over by the time he's gone through all the information with which we've bombarded him. For a lawyer, he's slow to grasp it all. I want to be so distracted by the views, the glasses clinking, the ambient music. I want to wonder why it is I've waited for a friend to be sued to visit such a spectacular place. I want to forget about everything and drown myself in a vat of the exquisite margaritas in front of us. But Gerry is looking overwhelmed, and I'm tempted to whack him over the head with my purse for being so thick.

Dan fixes me with a wouldn't-you-know-it glare before we walk Gerry through everything again. *Slowly*. First, Kelly's scheme to embezzle and when it began. Then how she managed to use Dan's logins in the fileshare system, but how she forgot to wipe her own system logins through which we've caught her. Lastly, the account to which she's transferred money, even the exact amount of money that's accrued in there over the last six months.

"But how did you come by all this?" Gerry asks, wiping his thick lips with the inadequate cocktail napkin.

"Does it matter? What matters is, we can prove it."

Gerry nods, stuffing an oyster into his mouth.

"This," Gerry says, pointing to the folder on the table, "looks like we have enough to prove your innocence. I'll go through everything and get in touch with Ike Fletcher."

I look at Dan.

"The lawyer representing Fortitude," he explains.

Gerry looks at his watch. His hour is up. "I'll keep you posted," he tells Dan, tapping his phone.

We shift our behinds and move so Gerry can squeeze by us. He puts out a hairy hand for me to shake before he leaves.

"Not the sharpest knife in the drawer, him."

"Don't let his manner fool you. He may seem absent-minded, but he's supposed to be quite brilliant."

"I'm sure his fees are brilliant, too," I say. Dan smirks. The check arrives as though on cue. I grab it and slap my credit card on top.

"Hey," Dan protests, offering me a weak smile. "I still have *some* credit."

I ignore him and hand both back to the waiter.

Dan eyes the two remaining oysters on the plate. He picks it up and offers it to me.

I shake my head. "All yours," I say, and raise my glass to him. "Here's to getting your life back."

He slips an oyster into his mouth, swallows, and raises his glass, clinking it to mine.

"Here's to having a friend like you," he says.

"Let's finish these bad boys," I say, pointing to our glasses. Dan raises an eyebrow at that and takes a deliberate, savoring sip.

AUDREY: THEN
1 MONTH AGO

NICOLE'S MISSING. MY HEART FALTERS IN MY CHEST. "NICOLE?" I SAY, feeling silly. It's not as though she's going to reply, but she often babbles back, so I try again. Nothing. Silence. I begin to panic, my heart beating out of whack as I call out again and again to Nicole.

I go on all fours and put my hand out, but under my fingers, where she should have been, is nothing but the soft shaggy rug. In the eerie quiet, my blood runs cold, picturing her at the top of the stairs. I'm about to shout out to her when I remember, I'd closed the door leading to the passageway. Relieved, my shoulders drop for a moment before they tense up again. Where could she have gone? I continue calling out to her and crawl a few paces from the office room, through to the French double doors, and into the master bedroom. I hear a tiny *Mmm* and move toward it. When I find her pudgy, silky-smooth leg beneath my fingers, I cry out with relief and gather her in my arms. Sometimes I wonder if she and her mother exist solely to make my life hell.

"Hi, sweetheart," I say, cradling her. "When did you learn to crawl, hmm? You gave me quite a scare, you know."

She gurgles. "Oooom," she says, plaintive.

I strap her firmly back into her carrier, which I've parked close to me. She's not going anywhere now, but she wants to sit outside, I'm sure, and survey her surroundings from her new, expanded domain. Something I can't quite grasp twists inside when I realize I can't watch her anymore. Sarah will have to cough up for a real babysitter—one who can run after Nicole and keep an eye on her.

"Your mommy will be on cloud nine," I tell her, rocking the handle of the seat. "But we'll have to tell her about your little stunt, won't we?"

"Bababa," she says.

"Right. Boo, play some nursery rhymes for our little lamb," I instruct my main man.

"Piping it up now," he says.

I sigh. "Yes, that's right. He's starting to repeat himself," I tell her.

She babbles back conversationally but I can hear the edge creeping into her voice. Sarah should have been back by now.

I sit with my hand patting her warm body, the reassuring *thud-thud* of her chest beneath my fingers.

Then I call Sherman and update him on the latest.

"It could be the lead we've been waiting for," I say.

When it falls silent, I picture him furrowing his brow, thinking.

"The West Coast?" he says.

"Yes. I'll email you the details."

"How did you manage to wiggle it out?"

"Ha. Trade secrets," I say, laughing. "It sort of fell into my lap. Patience always pays off."

"This is great work, Audrey. I'll chase it down."

"Sherman, I have a feeling this should be a priority."

"Noted."

I hang up, a strange, almost foreign sensation trickling into me. Excitement.

I get a message from Sarah:

> Be back in half an hour

Nicole's getting hungry; she's fussing more.

"What shall we do while your mom's out?" I ask Nicole, but she's not amused. I take her out of the seat and lay her on my lap to comfort her.

Her little, fierce fingers grab my top and pull at it. I open the baby tote and reach for a teething ring to distract her, but she wants nothing to do with it. She's unhappy. She's letting me know by pulling my hair and screaming at the top of her lungs.

"Shh," I say, hugging her. "I know, I know. Your mommy will be back soon, okay sweetheart?" I start to hum a tune.

We're both still for a moment. I can't remember the last time I hummed. Then she wails again.

It's *another* half hour before Sarah is back.

"Sorry, sorry," she says. I hand over Nicole, who is crying blue by now.

"I'm back, Mommy is back," she says. The soft ruffle of her chiffon top tells me she's pulling it up to feed.

"Everything okay?" I ask. Something's off. She's sweating a lot; I can tell from the slickness I felt on her arms.

"Can you watch Nicole for a little while longer? There's something I need to do."

"I've got to work," I say. "How long?"

"About an hour. She'll fall asleep now, soon anyway."

"Fine," I say.

"You're the best, Auds," she says, plants a noisy kiss on Nicole, and sets out again.

"You're welcome," I say, after the door closes.

"When are we going to tell her that this can't go on, eh?" I ask Nicole, who smells of milk. She's drowsy; her response is a long sigh and an incorrigible gibber.

"C'mon, let's get you washed."

"It's only me," I say, knocking on Sarah's door. At last, she's back home.

"One sec!"

When the door opens, she's huffing. I try to think of a reason for it but come up blank. I haven't heard anyone over at hers for some time.

"Here." I hand Nicole over to her mother. Sarah grabs the baby tote bag with the other hand.

"I need to—" I start to say.

She places a hand on my shoulder. "I'm heading out on an errand. Can this wait?"

Nicole's ability to crawl is something I need to discuss with Sarah, but she sounds too rushed right now. "Okay, but I do need to talk to you."

"Cool. Need anything from the supermarket?" she asks.

"Nope. I had stuff delivered today, thanks."

"I'll see you later," she says. I climb back down her stairs, swing right, and curve into my stairs. As I shuffle to the left to grab the handrail, I sense her watching me.

Her door shuts a little after mine.

I open my laptop and power it up, unable to shake the suspicion that Sarah's putting me off. Her tone was odd. I've lived next door to her for nearly a year now and she's never once offered to help shop. Her voice was high and tight like a violin string.

In the kitchen, I grab a bowl, ignore the intense hit of self-loathing, and fill it with two scoops of soil. I put a spoon in it and take it upstairs. In the study, I fold myself into the computer chair. Through the closet, there's a *thump*. Is Sarah back from the store already? Or had it been a ruse to get rid of me? The strange feeling I had earlier is back, like she's deliberately avoiding me, and it leaves me with an odd taste in my mouth.

As I log in to BlinkersOff, I recognize that taste for what it is. Anger.

A woman lies on a bed, writhing on the sheets in her lacy underwear while another moves on top of her. The woman on top snakes her hands up over the other one's body until it rests around the throat.

I'm sitting on a chair, watching them. I flush with embarrassment and wonder why I'm there. I'm about to get up and leave when I hear a gasp.

I turn around and look despite not wanting to. The woman below is choking, her neck is being squeezed.

"Stop!" I shout. When she turns around, startled, the face I'm staring at is Priya's. And beneath her is Sarah.

"You know why Brian sleeps with me, don't you?" Sarah says, cackling, laughing, maniacally.

Priya's face twists with anger. She puts her hands around Sarah's throat again and squeezes. Sarah's eyes bulge and she starts to choke on her tongue. I run toward them to stop Priya, but I trip. When I look down, Sarah is beneath me, choking, and my hands are tightening around her throat.

Someone screams. When I turn to the closet mirror, it's Priya's face I see. Her mouth is shaped like an *O,* her eyes frozen with horror.

I awaken with a jolt, my heart speeding like a runaway train. It's only a stupid dream, I tell myself, wiping sweat beading on my upper lip when I hear a raised voice. I freeze for a second, wondering if I'm still asleep and if this is another dream. I pluck the skin on my arm. "Ow," I say, when it hurts. It's real. Someone's talking or shouting. Is there someone here, inside the house? Then it strikes me, the sound is carrying from the closet. There's someone over at Sarah's. I slip out from under the comforter, pad over to the back of the closet, and slip on the headphones.

"You can't do this, Sarah!" The tone is low, quiet. I recognize it instantly.

An outraged, grating laugh. "What do you mean? I can do what I want. And what's more, if you don't pay up, I'll—"

"I wouldn't make idle threats if I were you. You don't know me, Sarah, you don't know what I'm capable of."

"You'd better pay up, Ronnie, or do you want me to send your wife some lovely nude photos of us? Yeah, I didn't think so. Now keep your voice down. My daughter is sleeping."

The voices turn low, indiscernible.

I saunter over back to bed and pull the comforter over me.

"Oh, go away. Go away and leave me alone!" I say to them. I hug my pillow and wish someone *would* strangle Sarah so I could return to the hard-earned lull I'd fallen into an hour ago.

SARAH

"COULD YOU STOP AHEAD ON 21ST?" I ASK THE CABDRIVER.

"You don't wanna come over?" Dan asks, wiggling his eyebrows. I'm a little tipsy. The Rainbow Room has that effect on everyone, because Dan's a bit buzzed too.

I flick a finger on Dan's arm. "Daniel S. Sorcese, is that an indecent proposal?"

He laughs, holds up a paper bag with an open bottle of rum inside, and wags it at me.

"I propose we finish this bottle and wake up with cement for heads."

"Tomorrow," I say, yawning. "I'm wasted enough tonight."

He nods. "Good sense always prevails, I see. Are you sure you don't want me to drop you below your building?"

"It's only a block down," I say, picking up my purse from the seat. "I could do with the fresh air."

"As the lady says," Dan tells the driver, who pulls up at the corner of 21st Street and Seventh Avenue.

"G'night," I say, bending down to peer into the backseat of the cab. "Be good."

"Do I have to?" he asks, clicking his tongue.

A laugh escapes me as I shut the door and sling the purse over my head, across my body. I wave at him as the cab pulls away.

I walk into an archway created by scaffolding over the sidewalk. It's a still night. The wind has died down. My mind's still buzzing. As the night grew on, the buildings began to glitter in the inky sky. Sipping on a third martini, when I'd looked out, it had almost felt psychedelic.

I duck under the construction poles and canopy to cross the street. I hope everything we've turned over to Gerry is more than enough to clear Dan's name. Who knows, maybe he'll be able to sue them in turn for wrongful action, but I doubt he'll go that route. Dan will be relieved enough to have his good name back. He'll move ahead, likely in the same job even as planned. And I'll move to the new apartment. I'll start over, I promise myself. No more shutting myself away alone. I'll get out there, date—

It happens so fast that it takes me a second to understand what is going on. Someone's hand is squeezing my neck, hard. I'm suffocating. He pushes me along the street and shoves me against the side of the building. I flail along like a rag doll, gasping, choking, trying to draw in air through my nose. He's pressing his body to mine.

"Wallet. Now," he says. His beady eyes are staring straight into mine. His face is less than an inch away, mouth almost on mine. His breath is foul, sour. My eyes bulge as his grip tightens around my throat.

I start to see spots. "I can't—bre . . . breathe," I try to say, but he doesn't let go. He parts my legs with his knee. I start to choke from the rising panic. *No, no, no, please, not that*, I plead with my eyes.

I fumble with my purse to reach for the wallet inside, but the clasp won't give.

"Hand it over!" he shouts, spittle flying into my half-open eyes. He pinions me against the wall and twists my right arm behind me so tight that my shoulder dislocates with a sick crunch. I cry out in pain.

His free hand snakes to my rib cage. I cringe at the feel of his gloved hand so close to my breast.

"Here," I croak, pointing to the purse. I can't move.

His face twists with anger. "Rings, jewelry, everything!" he says into my ear. His grip over my mouth loosens.

"There's money inside. Here, take it," I say, trying to undo the metal clasp of the purse from the side, with my left hand.

"Bitch!" he screams, and goes for my watch, which he unclips with practiced ease. Then he grabs the steel strap of the purse so hard that he starts to drag me along behind him. The metal cuts into my neck, making me gasp.

"Wait!" I shout, but he's trying to run with me dragging behind him. "Wait!" I yell again, but he's on a tear to get out of there.

There's a violent jolt as the purse gives way. The force of it pushes me facedown to the ground. Numb from the shock of the fall, I lift my head, open-mouthed, in time to see a pair of headlights flash down the street.

"Sarah!" someone calls out. A scream stays frozen in my throat as the car comes straight at me. In the split second all I can think of is that I don't want to die. Not like this.

There's a flash of searing pain before everything goes black.

AUDREY: NOW

THE PHONE RINGS. SIRI ANNOUNCES THAT IT'S MY BOSS.

"Hi Greg," I say, after I pick up.

"Tell me, what's happening?"

I roll my shoulders back, sit up and begin. No wasting time with Greg.

He's quiet after I've laid everything out on the table. He needs time to think things through.

"Did they ask you about Kelly?"

"Yes. I feel bad, Greg. I've lied, to the *police*. And it gets worse. Sarah is missing."

"This is bad. Missing how? Like, have they put out an APB, or more like a search party?"

"No idea."

"Do they think she's responsible?"

"They won't tell me anything, Greg. All I know is that she's disappeared."

"What do you think has happened?"

"I couldn't say. My instinct says if she was planning to leg it, Sarah would never leave her baby behind. It all feels wrong, like something terrible has happened."

"I think it's time you told the cops everything."

"Not yet. There's something I need to do first."

"I've trusted you so far, Audrey, but the second I think you're in danger, it's game over."

"I'm so close. I can feel it. We're too damn near to give up. I need a little more time to find one last detail. Then I'm done."

Greg sighs.

"It's not for me alone. It's for the client, too. I'm guessing they're still interested in seeing this through?"

"Of course," Greg says. "But it isn't their call alone. You have a say too."

"I know."

"But you won't give up. Not now."

"How can I, Greg?"

"I can't blame you for not giving up. I'd do the same in your place, but it doesn't keep me from worrying."

"I'll be careful. A new avenue has turned up. Sherman thinks it could lead somewhere."

"One more week. And then you're either out or you tell all."

"Done."

I'm exhausted. I didn't lie to Greg. I *am* close. One detail, one tiny tidbit away from finding out everything.

I'm in the bathroom when the phone rings. After I dry myself and step out, I play the voice mail.

"It's Detective Greene here, Audrey. Can you call me back when you get this message?"

I have Siri dial back. "It's Audrey, Detective Greene," I say, after the operator transfers me to him.

"Could you come in later, say, six p.m.? We'd like to go over a few things with you."

His words seem innocent enough, but it's his tone that I read into. They've discovered something, and whatever it is, it isn't good.

I change out of my sheer cotton dress and put on a pair of white linen slacks and a blue polka-dotted frilly shirt. I wind my long hair around my hand, tuck it into a knot at the top of my head, and slide a hair stick through it. I schedule a ride for 5:40 to the police station. Then I grab my office chair by the arm and drag it back.

When the phone rings, Siri announces that it's Sherman.

"Hey, free to talk?"

I stand up and stretch. "Yes."

"You're not going to believe this."

My head is tingling. "I think I will. Tell me."

"You remember those accounts we flagged way back?"

"Yeah?"

"One of them was accessed a few minutes ago."

"And?"

"We've found the money. We had the account frozen immediately, of course."

My legs give way. I sink into the chair. "Do we know who accessed the account?"

"We do."

When he says a name, one that's been on my mind an awful lot recently, my eyes fill without warning and a tear rolls down my face. At last. All the wait has been worth it.

A reminder pings on my phone. The computer chimes. A reminder that it's 5:20.

"Shit," I say, wiping my cheek. "I've got to go now. The police want to speak to me again."

SARAH

A STRANGE, TOO-RELAXED SENSATION LEAVES ME HEAVY, LIMP. THERE'S intermittent beeping. A soft voice begging me to wake up. A stern one yelling at me because I've overslept, that I've missed work. Then, a familiar one cajoling me. "Please, it's time you woke up."

"Later," I say. I want to sleep more. It's comfortable and warm.

"She's saying something!"

There's a crash, a door opening, and the swift clicks of footsteps.

"Welcome back, Ms. Connelly," someone says.

This is a strange dream.

"Wake up, Sarah."

I try to answer, but my mouth feels as though it's filled with cotton.

"Sarah?" he says.

I know that voice. It's Dan. I start to move when someone puts an arm on mine, stopping me.

"Ms. Connelly, you're in Mount Sinai Hospital. You've been in an accident."

Stop, stop, I want to tell her. I screw my eyes shut. I try to stop it but it's too late, and the memories, like the car, meet me head-on: the man pinning me against the brick wall; the purse catching on my neck; a car tearing straight at me, headlights flashing, blinding; the sickening crunch after I felt as though I'd exploded from the inside out; and my face ground into asphalt, a fleeting moment of awareness and then nothing.

"He got my purse, he's got it!" I sound hysterical, and unlike myself.

"Shh, Sarah. It's okay."

When I open my eyes, Dan's familiar figure hovering over me is comforting.

"I—okay," I say, unclenching my body, softening into the bed. "What's happened? Why am I still here?"

"Dr. Ford will be in shortly." The woman with tight red curls makes a note on a chart at the bottom of my bed.

"Who are you?"

"I'm Fiona. I'm a nurse."

"Can you tell—"

"I'll be back in a bit. Try not to move," she says.

Her footsteps thud on the floor. She's gone. After she leaves, I see that her warning was needless. I can't move my arms even if I want to, sheathed in casts as they are.

There's a crunch.

"Here," Dan says, pushing something under my nose. "It's ice."

"To think we were here only last week, and I was feeding *you* ice," I say.

"No, Sarah." His voice is quiet. "That was a while ago. You've been here for three weeks."

My jaw wants to open, but it locks.

"But that's not possible—you *just* dropped me off, in the cab. How can—"

"That was three weeks ago."

"I don't understand."

"You've been . . . unconscious all this time."

It's then that I hear the strain in his voice. My head reels even though I'm already horizontal. Three weeks. I've been here, lying half dead for three weeks.

"Oh! But they won't know at work—"

"They know."

I sag into the bed, a cold numbness washing over me.

"How did I get here?"

A fleeting memory of a figure in the distance lit up in the back glow of the headlights of a car. *Help*, I'd shouted.

"You don't remember, do you?" Dan asks.

"No," I say, but immediately remember a small detail. His voice, in that darkness, was another little comfort I'd hung on to. "You found me."

He's quiet. I can't imagine how that must have felt, watching a car run over someone. "What made you come back?"

"You'd left your phone in the cab. I realized that a couple of blocks later and turned around. If only I'd seen it earlier. I—"

"You can't think like that. How could you have known?"

He sighs, then falls silent.

"What's that smell?" I ask. There's a close, heavy lilt in the air. It's comforting and nauseating at the same time.

"Flowers."

I look over at the table in the corner of the room, its small surface overrun with bouquets. "From your colleagues."

"Shit!"

"Are you in pain? Should I fetch Fiona?" First-name basis with the nurse. He's been here often.

"No, I'm fine. I've remembered something. I have to move out of my apartment. I'm supposed to hand it over by the end of December."

"It's taken care of."

"Who?"

"Don't worry about all that right now. It's done."

I can't fathom it. I'm so tired, my eyes seem to close by themselves.

There's a sniffle in the silence. "Dan?"

"I'm here," he says, snorting into a tissue.

"Hey. I'm fine," I say. "Only a few broken bones. See?" I say, trying to lift my arms. I stop when it burns as though on fire.

"Don't, Sarah."

I grow sober when his voice cracks. I always do this. Make fun. Of things. Of myself; it's not his way, though.

"I'm sorry."

"What for? I should be the one apologizing. If I'd dropped you home, you wouldn't be here."

The guilt in his eyes is too much for me to bear. "Hey, it's not *your* fault!"

"It's not yours, either," he says.

But he's wrong, I know the second he says it. It *is* my fault. I was buzzed. I should have known better.

"Shit! My credit card!"

"I canceled it—found the paperwork at your apartment. It's only the one card, right?"

"And a debit card," I say.

"I–I didn't find the paperwork for it."

"You wouldn't have. It's well hidden. There's a folder in my old carry-on suitcase. It's in there. Would you call the bank to cancel?"

"Of course."

"Oh, and here's your phone. It's charged. I better get to that bank card right away. I'll be back in a bit." He slips the phone into the palm of my hand. "You have a lot of voice mails."

"Dan? Thanks."

"Don't be silly."

The door closes. It's cold. And apart from the beeping machines, a deathly silence cloaks the room. He'd been in a bed much like this one, and I'd been the one watching his chest rise and settle, worrying about what would happen if it didn't rise again or if that would be his last breath. How can it be a month ago, when in my head it still feels like it was only last week?

My attacker stole more than my money. He's stolen three weeks of my life. Weary, I tap the screen to play the first of many voice mails. It's from Anne.

"Sarah? It's Anne Hatchet. I've been thinking about our conversation, and I have an idea. Call me when you get this."

Shit. I'd completely forgotten about Anne and the blatant, straight-faced lies I'd told her. Should I call back and explain? By instinct, I know the answer—no. I'd burn a valuable bridge if I did. At the most, I could tell her I changed my mind, that I'm taking the promotion after all. She might buy that.

I play the second saved voice mail. "Sarah? It's Celia. Where are you? Call me when you get this."

There are many more messages but I'm too tired. And it comes to me suddenly: I didn't ask Dan about the lawsuit. Did they drop it? Was he exonerated?

It's nearing Christmas and New Year's, when things are always a bit slow. Come January, they'll be back in top gear and full speed. If all goes well, I should be able to return to work in January.

By the time the next voice mail from Mr. D'Angelo plays, my head begins to throb. Exhaustion hits me hard.

AUDREY: THEN
3 DAYS AGO

When Sarah shows up at my door, holding Nicole's carrier, I've forgotten I'm the one who wanted to see Sarah last night. From the way she trudges in, sighing, I suspect that she's had a long day.

She sniffles and yawns loudly. "You wanted to see me?"

"It's Nicole. I thought you should know that she began crawling the other day."

"Yeah, I know. She started crawling about ten days ago."

I'm at once proud of Nicole and angry with Sarah for keeping something so important from me.

"You should have *told* me! She crawled away from me, Sarah. I wasn't expecting her to. I lost her for a moment, a *brief* moment, but still! Luckily, the master bedroom door was shut."

"Hey, you found her, didn't you?"

"That's not the point!"

"There's no reason to freak out; it's not as though she can get very far. And if you were *so* worried, you could have called me."

I snap my jaw shut, feeling my vein pulse.

"Look, I think you had better find a nanny, a proper babysitter, to watch her from now on."

"I thought you liked watching her." Sarah's voice is a whine.

"Of course, I do. But she's getting bigger. Soon I won't be able to keep up with her. I can barely look after myself some days."

"I see."

She doesn't see at all. It's her tone; she's miffed.

"Is that all? I'd better get going then."

"Sarah!"

"What?"

"What's wrong? You're being weird."

"You want to stop watching her and I'm being weird?"

"I'll see you tomorrow," I say, and walk her to the door. I can't argue with Sarah when she gets like this.

"Fine."

The door slams behind her. I sigh and reach for the stairwell railing to go back upstairs.

I'm listening to an episode of *Maigret* on TV when it comes to me so suddenly that I choke on the chips I'm chewing. I *know* why she's being so furtive! I lick the salt off my fingers, reach for the phone, and speed-dial Sherman.

"Hey, what's up?"

"We may have a problem."

"Why? What's happened?"

I explain the strange feeling that's been slowly sinking into me the past few days.

"The game is up, you think?"

"I don't know, but if it is, we've got to act quickly."

"I'm hoping to hear from the team tomorrow. Will keep you posted."

"We may not have the time, Sherman. Could you follow up with them like right now, and ask them to hurry the hell up?"

A moment of silence ticks in my ear.

"Got it." He understands.

It's now or never. Our little pigeon will fly the coop at the first hint of a spook, and spooked she is. I worry if I've been responsible for it in any way. I voice this concern to Sherman.

"Look, we can't worry about that right now. Sit tight. I'll focus on get-ting the info ASAP."

*   *   *

"I got snarky last night," Sarah says. It's midmorning. I'm glugging down
the post-gym power smoothie I've divided in half to share with her.

"You did."

It's the only apology I'll ever get from her, so I take it.

"But that's not why I wanted to see you. You wanted me to find
your friend?"

There's a gasp. "You've found Adam!"

"I have."

"Oh, you're so clever!" she says, throwing her arms around me, startling me. "Where is he then?"

"He's in Boston."

I reach for the drawer in the built-in desk opposite the island and
retrieve a piece of paper. I hand it over to her, a shiver of anticipation tingling my spine. "Here. That's everything I could find."

"Thanks," she says. She sounds distant, as though she's already jour-
neying to Boston in her mind.

"Everything okay?"

"Yeah. It'll be good to see him. Maybe I'll surprise him."

I reach up in the air with my hands, feeling my muscles stretch after
the ringer Jason just put me through.

"You've lost weight," she says. In the sports bra and a pair of leggings, she can see rather too much of me. From her tone, I understand it's
an accusation.

"It's a natural consequence of going to the gym," I say. She scoffs.
Nicole gurgles at the same time; I see *she* gets my humor all right.

"And how are you, sweet bear," I say, peeking into the carrier.

"Mmm," she coos back.

"She likes you," Sarah says. There's something in her tone I can't read.

"She'd better," I say lovingly.

"How are you anyway?" Sarah asks, as though we haven't met in months.

"O-kay," I say.

"No, *really*. Are you coping well here?"

I wonder what's brought on this inquisition.

"Yeah," I offer haltingly. "The same. Why?"

"Was the move worth it?"

"Worth what?" I open the fridge to replace the packet of spinach I'd taken out to use in the smoothie.

"The unfamiliarity, for one. You must have had a life before you moved here. Friends, work. What made you leave?"

The hairs on my arm shoot up. Sarah's never shown interest in my past before.

"New *is* always unfamiliar. No one moves to seek the same things, things they've experienced, or people they've met."

"That's what I'm thinking, too. New, unfamiliar, something different, you know?"

"Are you planning to move?"

She laughs. "Of course not! Why would I move? We're happy here, aren't we, my little bub? She's got such a grip, this child. She grabs my hair or my arms like a nifty little thing. She scratched my face today, the little devil. But mama's got concealer, hasn't she? Yes, she does. Yes, she does," she says, planting a kiss on Nicole by the sound of it. "Shit! I've forgotten I have somewhere to be. Better run! See you later, Auds."

"Bye, Sarah. Bye, you," I say to Nicole.

She squeals.

"That's right." I blow a raspberry. She giggles.

"All right, let's go," Sarah says, grabbing the carrier.

I sigh and rest my head against the passageway wall after the pair of them leave and the door is shut. I'm growing fond of Nicole. Too fond.

*   *   *

"It's done," I tell Sherman.

"Now we wait and watch."

"Not hard at all."

He laughs. "Now's the best part," he says.

I hang up and return to my desk.

I pull out the folder in my head. It's bursting at the seams with every-thing I've been adding over time. I see most of the links now. It's a pattern that's starting to emerge. In the center, though, there's a blank space, a missing link. It's what Sherman and I have been after. It ties into every thread, like the one central piece in a jigsaw puzzle that makes sense of all the little pieces. It's right here, almost within my grasp. I hope Sherman is right, that this will turn out to be the best part.

If only I could *see* it all. I shouldn't wish it, but I can't help it some days. I hadn't lied to Hillary and the rest of the gang. I do get so angry sometimes. Congratulations, Dr. Khan, it cost thousands of dollars, but you got me to say it. *I'm angry. I'm so angry.*

My memory makes up for it; I should be happy, but it only makes me angrier still that I can remember *everything.* All the painful little details most people would be happy to forget.

It scares me a little when I go down this burning road. It makes me want to think and do awful things.

SARAH

"WHEN CAN THE BANDAGES COME OFF?" I ASK THE DOCTOR. HE LOOKS ageless, like he could be forty or sixty. He has that professional, clinical look doctors seem to develop over their careers. When they look at you, they don't see *you*, they see the parts they've sliced, snipped, and stitched back.

"It depends on how quickly you heal, Ms. Connelly, but I wouldn't worry about all that right now."

"I've managed to— Oh," Dan says, stopping at the door.

"Hello," Dr. Ford greets him.

"Hi, Dr. Ford. Is everything all right?"

"I was telling Ms. Connelly she should try to relax and eat well." Dr. Ford turns to look at me. "Once you're able, you can move; in fact, you should, under our care, but please don't try to rush the process."

"But I could be here for weeks!"

He offers me a wry smile. "Are you in a hurry to go somewhere? You have a misaligned spine, broken ribs, a cracked skull, severe concussions, internal bleeding, and bruising. And that's just the start. Want me to go on?"

I have no smart retort. After the litany of injuries he's rattled off, I realize he's right.

"How does the head feel?" the good doctor asks.

"Like someone's taken a jackhammer to it."

"Morphine is a click away."

"I can manage for now. I'll press the happy button if it gets worse."

"Ms. Connelly, you have undergone some serious trauma. We've already had to perform three surgeries. I want you to appreciate the seriousness of it."

"Yes, Doctor," I say, feeling absurd, like I'm a little girl with pigtails atop a doctor's desk, feet dangling.

"Hear that?" Dan asks, after the doctor leaves the room.

"I can't believe he's told me off like I'm a child!"

"If you insist on behaving like one . . ."

I glare at Dan.

"About your debit card, I've called the manager at the bank. There's some news."

"Okay. What is it?"

His hesitance makes me uneasy. "I—" he begins when my phone rings.

"One sec," I say, and answer it.

"Sarah! There you are. It's Anne. Hatchet. I've been trying to reach you. Anyway, listen, I've set up an appointment for you to meet a friend. In the field you're looking to get into, he's one of the top people. He can meet you next Monday evening if you're free. I've emailed you the deets."

"I—"

"Hello? You there?"

"Anne, something's happened. I've been in an accident and I'm in a hospital."

"Oh! I'm so sorry. Are you okay? What happened?"

"I can't—" Moving my lips takes monumental effort all of a sudden. The phone falls away from my hand as sleep overtakes me.

There's an insistent, annoying beep. It's getting louder.

"—crashing!" someone shouts.

Oh, go on. Fix it! I try to shout at them to get on with it so the noise will stop, but my jaw is locked again. My whole body feels heavy and numb.

"Clear!"

I'm with Mac. We're hand in hand on a beach. "Come away with me," I say.

"I *am* away with you when I should be with Liz. I can't do this anymore, Sarah. I can't be with both of you."

"Go, then," I say, my voice echoing down an interminable corridor. Mac walks on and on, a never-ending escalator carrying away the remnant of my love.

"—flatlining!"

"Clear!" A high-pitched whine followed by a door slamming.

Mac turns around. Witch-dark eyes stare at me. I want to open my eyes and peer into them.

"She's back," someone says.

"Shh! Mac is about to say something."

"Who is Mac?" someone asks.

"Sarah? Sarah Connelly?"

The escalator blurs, then disappears. Mac vanishes.

"Sarah Connelly."

"What!?" I ask, annoyed.

"Welcome back to the land of the living."

"Wha—"

"This is Dr. Ford. We lost you for a bit there."

My head is a block of concrete. "What happened?" I sound as though someone stuffed cotton in my mouth.

"You had an intracranial hematoma."

"What's that?" I slur through the haze.

"There was internal bleeding. We had to open you up to stop it. You're just out of the surgery."

"Hmmm. She's out, in the recovery ward." A familiar voice is saying to someone. A vacuum swallows up the rest of their words.

It's dark. "Who's there?" I ask.

"It's Dan, Sarah."

"How long have I been sleeping?"

"Since after the surgery."

Surgery? I have a vague, hazy memory of a dream and a doctor waking me up to tell me something . . . about a hemorrhage.

"I'm so glad you're okay," Dan says. He sounds awful. I want to see him, but my eyes are too heavy and swollen to open.

"Me, too," I say. It isn't merely my voice I don't recognize. It's as though I've floated away from life. Like I'm adrift on some distant island, alone.

"It's okay, Sarah. You're going to be okay. It'll all be fine."

He sounds *off*, like he's trying too hard to convince me. Or himself.

"What is it? What's happened?"

"There's . . . don't worry about it. It can wait."

From his tone and the way he's hesitating, I immediately know that whatever it is that's happened, it's bad.

"Dan, just *tell* me. I feel helpless lying here, weaving in and out of consciousness. Please."

"The bank manager called me back about your debit card."

Even before the words leave his mouth, I know what he's about to say.

"Someone used it to withdraw your savings the day after the accident."

"What? How much did they take?"

When he doesn't reply I know it's the worst possible news. "They took everything?" I ask, after what feels like an age.

His voice drops. "I'm *so* sorry, Sarah."

"B-but they'd need my signature and things for that! They can't just give it all away to anyone who walks in to withdraw it!"

"I asked that. No flags went up because according to them, *you* withdrew it. You provided them with all the relevant documents and your signature matched."

My head reels. "What? How is that even possible?"

He falls silent.

"Dan?"

"It's my fault. I should have realized it when I needed to access your apartment for the insurance info and couldn't find your keys. But it didn't strike me then."

"Shit! My keys combined with my address in my purse . . . but that's years of savings!" I cry out. "All gone," I whisper, all of a sudden too tired to speak.

"If only I'd thought to check. But you were in surgery, and I couldn't think straight . . ."

"It's not your fault, Dan."

It's all gone. Everything I've worked for, so I'd have a secure future, one where I wouldn't have to worry about my next meal or making the rent, all the holidays I never took, all the things I didn't buy. Every hard-earned cent—saved by walking, not taking cabs, or eating out at lavish, posh places—is all gone.

All taken by someone else. Dan won't understand, even though he lost all his money, too. Whether or not he thought of it that way, he has family and friends to fall back on. I have no one.

"You're not alone!" Dan says.

I'm mortified when I realize I've said it all aloud.

"You still have a good job. And you'll make it all back. More. You're so smart, Sarah. There's nothing you can't do. Please don't worry about money right now."

"Speaking of, I completely forgot to ask. What's happening with Fortitude?"

"It's all sorted. Gerry took the evidence to David, who confronted Kelly. She's admitted to everything: plotting, stealing the money, framing me. They've dropped the lawsuit against me and have offered me a promotion. It's everything we were hoping for."

"Oh, Dan. I'm so glad."

AUDREY: THEN

1 DAY AGO

WE'RE WALKING SIDE BY SIDE, PRIYA AND I, BACK FROM THE CORNER store. It's sweltering. Sweat is running down my back and into my underwear in little rivulets. Priya is awfully quiet. I wonder if it's only the heat bothering her.

"You okay? Priya?" I add when she doesn't reply.

"Oh sorry, I shook my head." She sounds like a sad little girl.

"That's all right." A sudden strange urge to mother her overwhelms me. She's so tiny. I knew that the first time she hugged me. I'm not a big girl myself but her head about grazes my shoulders.

"Audrey . . . have you ever . . ." She sniffles like she's got a cold.

"What?"

"No, never mind."

"Go on, what is it?"

"Have you ever thought you might be angry with someone, so terribly angry you could kill them?" She sniffles again. I was wrong. She's crying.

"Hey, what's brought this on?"

"It's . . . nothing. Forget I said anything."

There's an edge to her voice that makes me nervous.

"What do you mean?" She doesn't reply. "Priya?"

"Brian wants to move out."

I wish I could see her, look into her eyes and read the meaning in her words. It throws me off-balance. It's not healthy.

"I—I have to get going. I'll see you later, Audrey."

Back home, I worry that I know exactly whom she's so angry with that she could kill them. I can't forget the desperation in her voice. Any more than I can forget something I'd overheard months ago, at her birthday party. Her fierceness with Sarah, and the way Sarah had pleaded with Priya to let go of her hand.

The *off* feeling I've been tamping down this week is back.

You're like a wild gale packed into a tiny box, Mother used to say when I'd go all quiet. Even back then, I'd never show what I felt—anger, desperation, disappointment. *Mark my words, one day you're going to blow up and it'll be ugly.*

Today, a familiar darkness descends on me. It grows and grows until it snowballs into a meteor ball of black hot tar, fire spewing from it. How dare she? How *dare* Sarah break up Priya's family? Who does she think she is, snatching whatever she wants without a thought to the consequences? Two more lives ripped apart by her ruthless greed and lust. Poor Priya. What chance does she have against Sarah's mercenary piracy?

The groan of furniture moving next door only adds to my irritation. I haven't heard a thing from her bedroom for a while. Not a peep. No cattle show. No rodeo, no sound at all. Until last night. I assumed, stupidly as it turns out, that Sarah stopped her recklessness and her shenanigans ever since Priya confronted her.

The nonchalance of it all grates my gears. Sarah isn't even serious about Brian, I can tell. I can't stop thinking about Priya and her despair. Maybe I should intervene. After all, as Priya pointed out, I'm her friend, too. What sort of a person sits idly by and watches their friends' lives being ruined?

The rising mercury isn't helping, either. I've thrown open the windows, but instead of letting out the stuffy air, the blistering heat from outside creeps into the house. By the time Boo announces it's time for Nicole to come over, I'm tetchy. I've agreed to continue watching Nicole until Sarah can find a babysitter with decent references. It's after 4:00, then 4:30, then 5:00, and yet no sign of the pair of them. Finally, at 5:40, I give up and march over.

I knock for the fourth time on Sarah's door, growing impatience buzzing in my head like a swarm of infuriated wasps. Where the hell *is* she?

Finally, the door opens.

"Oh, it's you," Sarah says, as though I'm the last person she's expecting to see. It disorients me before I remember why I've come.

"It's late. Didn't you say you wanted me to watch Nicole today?"

"Oh. I forgot to text you to say never mind. She's asleep."

I'm in no mood for her power games. The sun is searing on my back. The bits of exposed skin burn and prickle. "Can I come in?"

Silence. "One sec," she says. The door shuts. It feels absurd standing on the outside landing like some pestering door-to-door salesman.

The door opens again.

"I'm about to step out, so make it quick."

She sounds hassled.

"No yoga today?" I ask. I'm near the entryway table. Sarah is blocking the space ahead from the sound of it.

"No, something's come up."

"All okay? You're sounding odd."

"I'm in a rush."

"There's something I want to ask you—"

"Can't it keep?"

The buzzing in my head gets louder. "No. It can't. Look, I'm not one to interfere, normally, but . . ."

"Just spit it out," she says.

The irritation I've been holding at bay rushes at me at once. "*Fine.* I know you've been seeing Brian. Priya's Brian."

"O-kay . . . so?"

Her casual admission only irritates me more.

"Well, is it serious?"

"How do you mean?"

"Are you planning to be with him . . . long-term?"

She scoffs. "Why would I want to be with Brian, of all people?"

"Then what are you doing with him?"

"And this is *your* concern how?"

"For goodness' sake, Sarah, I couldn't care less whom you sleep with, but can't you see how miserable Priya is? Or are you so caught up in your own selfishness you can't see the lives you ruin? Stop toying with people!"

"I stopped seeing Brian nearly a month ago, not that it's any of your business what I do with my life."

The weight pressing on my chest all day is suddenly unbearable.

"Don't *lie* to me, Sarah! Just don't."

She goes quiet for a moment.

"And what about you, Audrey, and the lies you've been telling?"

Air whooshes out of my lungs.

"What?"

"You've been hiding things from me, too. You've been lying from the start, haven't you?"

"Whatever do you mean?" My voice has taken on an odd, distant quality. A sound I don't like.

There's a wail from upstairs.

"I'd better see to her." Sarah's too-close voice startles me.

"What? But—"

"You need to leave right now, Audrey. We'll talk about this later, okay? Now, just go."

Back home, I shut the door behind me and march upstairs, shaking with adrenaline and something else. Something too ugly to name. I pant as though I've been running when it's my mind that's been racing all over.

I pace the study, muttering to myself, replaying the conversation over and over in my head, the way every word we uttered exploded around us in her narrow passageway. By the time I pick up the phone to call Sherman with numb fingers, it's almost half an hour later. Time, gone. Lost, like a set of keys carelessly misplaced.

"Hey, Audrey." Hearing Sherman's voice releases the panic I've been holding at bay, and it slams into me like a speeding train. I wipe away sweat from my upper lip and plonk myself down on the sofa in a huff.

"Hi." I hate the tumultuous quaver in my voice.

"What's wrong?" he asks, immediately.

"Something awful has happened. . . . I've done something stupid."

"Tell me." There's a strain in his voice, one I've never heard before but instantly recognize. Fear.

I step out of the shower and reach for my clothes, proper ones, like a blouse and pants. Not the lounging pajamas I'm always wearing these days.

"What's done is done. Forget it all and take the evening off. Do something fun," Sherman said.

Fun. Such a distant, foreign concept. But I'm determined to salvage my evening. Have *fun*. I open the dresser drawer and reach for the perfume that reminds me of McKenzie.

A tiny, angered bleat seeps through from the closet wall. Nicole's fussing. I ignore it and saunter back to the study.

"Boo, what's the time."

"It's 8:30 p.m."

"Play me some Sinatra."

"Junior or Senior?" Boo inquires.

"Surprise me."

"Fly Me to the Moon" starts to play as I trip downstairs to set some water to boil for the pasta.

I hum along, my hips swaying as I twirl. By the time I dunk the spaghetti into the sauce and toss it in with olive oil, Boo is playing "Something Stupid." It makes me tear up thinking of McKenzie, how I miss her and how I've avoided talking to her for so long. I pour a glass of wine and take it up to my desk with the pasta.

Thoughts crowd my head once more as I twirl the noodles around the fork. It was a mistake, a terrible mistake moving to Shore Drive, here, in this house, right next to *her*. I should pack up and leave. Sherman thinks that's a good idea. But it's brought me right back to what I want to forget. Forget it like it never existed, like *she* never existed. Sarah.

After a few bites, I leave the pasta on the desk and slide into the armchair with the wineglass. I take a sip and savor it. Smooth warm notes of the wine coat my tongue. *And then I go and spoil it all by saying something stupid like I love you* . . . Frank and Nancy Sinatra croon in my ear.

I love you. I sing along and splay my hands out. The glass jostles and tips over my blouse. The cool Malbec sinks through the silk.

SARAH

I'M ON THE PHONE WITH ANNE. SHE'S BEEN A SURPRISING, WARM SOURCE of comfort. I'm not without friends, after all. But, as a friend, I can't lie to her. I make myself come clean and tell her the reason for my visit to her office.

"I see. Well, I don't know what to say."

She sounds stiff. But then, I'd expected it. "I'm so sorry, Anne. I was trying to help a friend, and I didn't know whom I could trust at the time. As you now know, they've dropped the charge against Daniel and arrested Kelly Fergusson."

"So you're not looking to do something new?"

"I don't think I'm up for anything new right now. I think I'll be comfortable getting back to the life I knew. Sorry I wasted your time."

It's too quiet. I wonder if she's hung up. "Anne?"

"Sarah, we'll talk about this later; trust me, this isn't the end of it." The words are serious, but her tone is light.

"You're going to make me pay you back, aren't you?"

"Forever."

I smile.

"But first, I want you to hear me out. Do you remember that appointment I said I made for you? How about if you kept it? I still think you might be great in that role. He's eager to talk to you. And when I tell him everything you've accomplished with limited resources at your disposal, I know he's going to be even more eager."

"But—"

"No harm in talking."

"Okay," I say. But only because Anne's insisting, even after I've lied to her face.

"Good. I'll set something up for tomorrow if that works."

"Anne?"

"Yeah?"

"Thanks."

I call Anne again, now that I've finally spoken to her contact.

"How did it go?" she asks.

"Honest answer? Better than I expected. I like the role. It's quite different from what I've been doing, but I can pick it up with some training."

"I'm glad. This could be good for you. A good direction for your career."

"Only, I'll need a bit of time. I don't know when I can go home and resume life. And I'll need at least three weeks more to wrap up at my current job. I owe them that."

"That should be fine. This is more a role creation than a position filling. I'll discuss it—" There's a knock on the door. The door opens.

"It's Dr. Ford, Sarah."

"Anne, can I call you back? The doctor is here."

"Of course. Bye."

I set the phone on the table beside me. Dan's pulled it forward so I can access it without reaching too far.

"Today's the day. Let's take off all the dressing and see how you're doing, shall we?"

I can't believe it's been another two weeks since the last surgery. Time has blurred into the number of steps I take, my food input and output, blood pressure, and such banalities of existence. Except for the visits from Dan, the highlight of my day is the sad tapioca pudding from the hospital cafeteria. Life really is down in the dumps. I've been counting down the days to this one. Being unable to handle even basic functions after I hemorrhaged was not even briefly amusing. The bandages have been nothing but a literal itch I can't scratch. Dan came close to handcuffing me to the bed so I wouldn't fiddle with it.

"Ah-ah," Dr. Ford says, when I touch the stretched crepe around my head, a new addition since the last surgery. "Patience."

"Not my strongest virtue."

The nurse pushes her usual trolley, the one that screeches like a banshee. I hope I never have to hear it again. It's enough to haunt my nights for the rest of my life.

"How are the headaches?"

"Still there, but more manageable."

"It's to be expected after the knock you had, and after the surgeries. But they should abate soon."

"Define *soon*," I say, wryly.

"Weeks, months. I'm afraid I can't give you a definitive answer."

My head feels like it's submerged underwater and I'm gasping, reaching for air. It's felt like that ever since I woke up from the last surgery. There's been no clarity of mind, of thought, of memory. Some nights, when I lie awake, I'm convinced the accident happened years and years ago. Some days, I wake up and think the attack happened minutes ago and that I've just been brought here.

The doctor has my head cradled between his hands as he bends over me.

There's a scrape. The nurse is on my left side. Her strong, antiseptic smell is unmistakable. I sigh as he begins to peel off the layers.

At last.

AUDREY: NOW

I'M SEATED ACROSS FROM THE TWO DETECTIVES. FROM THE MUSTY SMELL likely from dampness in the ceiling, I'm back in the room where they first interviewed me.

There's a click. Detective Greene states the name of the witness—my name—the time, and the names of everyone present for the record.

I'm not strictly an eyewitness, *am I?* But I don't correct them.

"Thanks for coming in, Ms. Hughes."

It's back to Ms. Hughes. No familiarity. This is bad.

"Has there been a development?"

"Ms. Hughes, you've been lying to us from the start, haven't you?"

My jaw drops.

"Lying, Detective Novak?"

I've always hated questions like these, the ones the police can manipulate a person into answering. It's like a lawyer asking a suspect in cross-examination, "Did you stop beating your wife?" forcing them to give a simple yes or no answer.

"We've been checking up on you, Ms. Hughes," Greene says.

"Why?"

"It's routine. We check everyone's background."

"And a good thing, too," Novak says. "Any record we could find of you begins only four years ago. We even checked social media and immigration. There's no record of an Audrey Hughes fitting your description, entering this country. Not four years ago, not ever. There's no social security trail, either. Can you explain this to us?" Novak's rasp has a dangerous edge.

I gulp. They're going in for the jugular. A double attack. No Good Guy/Bad Guy. That's all done. All the pretense has fallen away.

"For the tape, the witness hasn't answered the question," Novak says.

"I need to use the restroom, if I may?"

"Sure. Detective Novak, kindly escort Ms. Hughes to the ladies' room."

"Why? Are you worried I'm going to run away?"

"No. Because you can't see and you might not know where it is," Novak replies.

I flush and nod. "Fine. Lead the way."

"Detective Novak is leading the witness out of the room. Pausing the tape."

How things have soured, I think, as the pair of us make our way to the restroom. For a moment, I wonder if Novak is going to follow me into the toilet as well the way she's shadowing me. But when we reach the entrance, Novak closes the door after me.

Inside, I find a cubicle farthest away from the entrance. I close the door, take out my phone and make a call.

Greg doesn't answer. I leave a message. "Greg, the police are interviewing me again. I'm going to tell them everything." A heads-up in case I need a lawyer soon.

I flush, wash my hands, and step out.

I follow Novak back into the room and settle into my seat.

"For the tape, Ms. Audrey Hughes and Detective Novak are back in the room."

"So, where were you four years ago?" Novak asks.

"I've told you. In Manhattan. Look, is this an interrogation? You haven't read me my rights or asked me if I want a lawyer present, but you're recording me."

"Do you? Want a lawyer present?"

I shake my head.

"The witness is shaking her head. Can you tell us yes or no for the record?"

"No, I don't want a lawyer. I haven't killed anyone."

"As of now, you are a witness. If you continue lying to us, this can become an interrogation," Novak says.

"Fine. I'll tell you everything."

"Good," Greene says. I'm sure the detective is used to people confessing. And mine is a confession of sorts.

"As I've said before, I'm a forensic accountant with Aegis."

"No. You said you were an accountant. Not a forensic accountant. What exactly does it entail?"

"My job is to analyze numbers and find a pattern in the minute details. I look for anomalies, anything that doesn't fit."

"So, it's a bit like finding Waldo, with numbers?"

I smile at his analogy and nod. "Except, sometimes, I have to find Waldo by figuring out that Waldo is missing from the picture."

Greene wolf-whistles, as though he's impressed.

"How is this relevant to who killed Kelly?" Novak asks.

"If you let me explain?"

"Go right ahead," Novak says. I don't need vision to know that she's sneering.

"My job, primarily, is to find our clients' missing money."

"And who are these clients?"

I smile. "Discretion is everything in my line of work. Aegis also works on government contracts, so there's only so much I can tell you without a warrant, which you'll have to take up with my employer. What I *can* tell you is I've been tracking someone for the past year to find large sums of money that were stolen from our clients."

"Thank you for explaining your job. Now we'd like to get on with ours. What does all this have to do with Sarah?"

"Everything. Sarah's the person I've been tracking."

"So you're saying Sarah stole money from these clients?"

I nod. "And from me, personally, she stole a lot more. You see, my real name is Sarah."

"So, hang on, your name is *also* Sarah?" Novak asks.

I shake my head and take a deep breath. "You don't understand. I'm the only Sarah in this context. *I'm* Sarah Connelly."

SARAH

I'm asleep when the door opens later.

"Surprise," a man says. "See what I've brought."

I sit up and grip the side of the bed. "Who is it?"

"Wha— Sarah, it's me, Dan."

I turn and sniffle into the pillow.

"Go away."

"But—"

"Go away!" I scream. "Leave me alone!"

A nurse comes running. A pinch in my arm. I hear a muffled exchange between Dan and her as I fall away, feeling as if I'm stepping off a narrow, tall cliff. A dreamless sleep steals me away to a faraway land. When I wake up, my brain feels as though it has gone blank.

"Sarah?"

It's Dan. Again. "I'm so sorry. I'm so, *so* sorry," he says.

I can't hold back. He grabs my hand and hugs me as my deep, racking sobs echo in the room.

"It's over, Dan. It's all over. I can't live like this. I can't live blind."

He doesn't say anything. He keeps on holding me until all the fight has gone out of me and I sag back into the bed.

"Things may seem hopeless right now. But there *are* plenty of people with little or no vision in this world who live full lives. You can, too. I'm not saying it's going to be easy. But you *can* find a way, Sarah, I know you can."

"I can't. You don't understand," I say, my voice cracking.

"Then explain it to me."

"I have . . . had an eidetic memory. I've survived all my life because I remember everything I see, Dan. And now, everything I've seen is a mere memory. I'll never see again. Ergo, I'll never make more memories."

He goes quiet for a second. "How much exactly have you stored up in that head?"

"Everything I've ever seen. I mean, also paid attention to."

"Wow."

"No! Not wow. No more wow. It's all done." The hysteria assaulting me ever since the bandages opened comes rushing back. The intracranial hematoma caused permanent damage to my optic nerve. I have irreparable blindness.

Dan has no comeback. He knows I'm right.

Life as I knew it is over. Then I hear my mother's sharp, tinny voice: *I was right. You'll never get anywhere. You'll see.*

Shut up. Shut up. Shut. Up, I say, but I can picture the triumphant glint in her eye. The pithy, strangled moan that leaves my mouth sounds like the cry of a wounded animal.

AUDREY: NOW

THERE'S A TINY, AUDIBLE GASP FROM NOVAK, I CAN TELL FROM HER coffee breath.

"Go on," Greene says.

"Back when I was living in the city, I got mugged one night. In the tussle, I was dragged onto the road where a car hit me. While I was in the hospital, someone accessed my bank account and emptied it. It was only after I went home, months later, that I realized that I'd lost more than the money. Someone had stolen my identity as well."

I pause here a moment. It's been such a long time since I've said this aloud. Now that I have, I don't feel liberated at all. But I've begun, and I need to keep going. I must tell it all. "A friend recommended I change my name and start over—identity theft cases are rarely caught. I agreed. I had little choice. I couldn't even get a new credit card or a bank account in my own name. A year after I recovered from the accident, I started working for a new firm—Aegis. My job was to trace the money Aegis's clients had lost. Through luck or coincidence, a client and I had one thing in common. Apart from our money, someone stole our identities as well. The track led to the woman you've known as Sarah Connelly."

"So if you're Sarah Connelly, who the hell is she?" Novak asks.

"Her real name is Grace Foley. She's from Harrisburg, Pennsylvania."

"How did you track her?"

"Our first breadcrumb was a blurry image of her on a bank's security camera. From there, the trail led to a hotel in Midtown, but we lost her after that. We knew Grace had a partner, but the only available trace led us to Grace first."

"So you *did* move here to be close to Sarah, well, Grace," Greene says.

"Yes. There's no law against moving, last I checked."

"And you've been plotting to kill her all along."

I wish I can physically quash the triumph in Novak's voice. "Of course not! What do you think I am? A psychopath?"

"One doesn't need to be a psychopath to kill. Anger is enough," Greene says.

I sit up straight. "I *was* angry, at first, but by the time I moved here, the anger slowly ebbed away. You must understand, it was three years after the accident when I found Sarah and moved here. By then, I'd made a new life for myself. It wasn't easy, it's still not easy. I am blind. I will always be blind. But I wouldn't kill someone because of it. Moreover, killing her wasn't the way to find my client's money—or mine."

"But you moved here. That shows intent."

"You think I simply upped and moved here? I had to learn to live again. From scratch. It took countless hours of therapy and mobility training. It was months before I had the confidence to step out with nothing but my cane to guide me on the streets of New York. In the end, when I did find her, curiosity got the better of me. I wanted to know what she was doing with my money, my identity—who she was and how she was living as Sarah Connelly. I had no intention of befriending her. I *have* told you that before. But she inserted herself into my life and I thought I could use it to get what I wanted—the money she stole from me and Aegis's clients."

"How does Kelly Fergusson tie into all this?" Greene asks.

"I knew Kelly from my previous job. She used to be my contact in a company called Fortitude. She moved on and I worked with her replacement, Daniel Sorcese, until Fortitude accused Dan of embezzlement. I knew Dan well enough to believe he was innocent, that he was being framed. Together, Dan and I tracked down the real embezzler—Kelly Fergusson."

"How did she know that it was you who caught her?" Detective Greene asks.

"I told her." I cringe when I think back to my gloating response that morning on the way to Anne's office when I ran into Kelly, and how I walked right into it after she baited me. "At the time I didn't know who was trying to frame Dan, but I did tell her I was going to find proof of Dan's innocence. And Kelly still had a couple of friends in Fortitude. After she got out of prison, it wouldn't have taken a lot for her to ask around and put it all together."

"And how did she find you, well, Grace?" Novak asks.

I shrug. "The same way I did, I suppose. Grace made the mistake of using my social security number and my ID for rent and other things, and someone as smart as Kelly could have easily tracked it down."

"And she turned up to confront you?"

"I guess. But when she showed up, she would have instantly known that the Sarah she had tracked down was an imposter."

"That's just an assumption. We want facts."

"I can't tell you what I don't know, Detective Greene."

"Are you even blind, Audrey?" Novak asks, after a heavy pause.

"Do you think I'd lie about something as serious as that?"

"Maybe. After all, you've lied about everything else."

Novak's sarcasm isn't unexpected, but it stings. A part of me knew if I told them the truth about who I am, or used to be, they'd suspect me of lying about everything else. "You couldn't put yourself in my shoes for a second, even if you tried. But if you did, you'd see how, despite everything, I've only helped."

"How can we believe anything you say? This could be another elaborate story about working with Kelly and saving your friend," Novak says.

"Talk to my friend Daniel, and Fortitude, the company that first accused him, then withdrew it. Ask my old colleagues, my employer."

"Oh, we will. But we still can't be sure you didn't kill Kelly Fergusson."

"I didn't."

Novak scoffs audibly. "And we take your word for it?"

"I'm innocent. Do your jobs. Find out what happened, and you'll see that I'm telling you the truth. Or would you like me to find out *for* you, Detective Novak? Your partner here thinks I'd make a good detective. I've even given you that number Sar—Grace was so desperate to get her hands on. Adam Briggs? I'd try contacting him ASAP if I were you."

"He's the partner you say Grace was working with?"

"Yes."

"How did you find Adam if he'd gone underground?"

"With some difficulty. Adam is an expert at covering his tracks—he's been doing so for a very long time. I can't be sure when exactly, but we suspect soon after my identity was stolen, the two of them split. From the way Grace spoke about him, I got the impression she has been trying to find Adam for some time as well."

"Why?" Greene asks.

I shrug. "I suspect she was running out of money. Or maybe she was starting to get spooked."

"And how did you find Adam in the end?"

"Grace gave me an old address of his, which enabled us to track his current whereabouts to Boston. However good people are at covering their tracks, they always leave some evidence behind. A trace. All it took was one detail to find him."

"Once you found him, why did you give her his details at all? Why not track him down yourself?"

I pause to take a breath. "From the beginning, we suspected that Grace was the only one who could lead us to Adam. It's one of the reasons I took the risk of moving so close to her. I hoped once that she had his details, they would talk, or meet, and we could learn more about their history, and where they've stashed all the money."

"Do you think Adam has something to do with the murder of Kelly Fergusson?"

"I don't know. Nothing in his profile suggests he's been violent before."

"And what do you think has happened to Grace?"

"I honestly don't know. As I said before, though, if she had planned to run away, she would have taken Nicole with her."

"What I don't get," Greene says, "is what does all this have to with the break-in in your house?"

I shrug. "I don't know, either. I'm waiting for the security company to go through the tapes from the camera they've installed. I'm hoping they can find something on them that'll point to who the intruder was. I've asked them to email you whatever they find."

I sit back. "Now, if there's nothing else, I'd like to go home."

"We may not have enough to charge you right now, but don't leave town, Audrey."

"I wouldn't dream of it," I say, returning Novak's tone.

SARAH

I'M SO USED TO THE ANTISEPTIC, DISINFECTANT SMELL OF THIS ROOM AND the hospital by now, it's almost starting to feel safe. But Barbara's voice lingers in the silence. I can't remember the last time I thought of my mother or dreamed of her. I think it was before I moved to New York. Life here is so conducive to people like me—people who want to forget. The city sucks you up. All you can think of is work, evenings out, weekends in the city, absorbing everything it has to offer like a sponge. No more of that. There's nothing but silence now. It's why I hear her in my ear, laughing, saying that I'll never amount to anything, that I'm an ungrateful, useless girl.

"Go away," I say to her now, as she whispers once more into my ear.

"Sarah, it's me, Celia."

I've been so lost in thought that I didn't hear the hospital room door open.

"Oh."

"I—I came to see how you're doing."

"Okay, considering . . ."

She's moved closer to me. I can smell her no-nonsense, soapy freshness.

She places a hand on mine. It's warm, and although it startles me, it's comforting.

"You're going to be okay, Sarah," she says. Gentle. Her tone is too gentle. She hands me a tissue to wipe my face. I'm crying. Again. I can't seem to help it. And I hate it.

"Dan's told me everything—I made him fill me in."

My hollow laugh fills the room.

"I wanted to let you know that I-I'm sorry."

"What for?" I ask, blowing noisily into the tissue.

"For giving you a hard time. For keeping tabs on you. I was so sure the only reason for your promotion was that you were sneaking behind my back to get the best clients."

"What? Is that what you thought?"

"Ever since you landed the RA account, I thought you were up to something. I mean, they're *huge* and I was supposed to be handling their audit, but it was assigned to you."

I sigh. "For the record, the only reason I took it on is that you already had a lot on your plate, and with the time difference and deadlines, it might clash with your personal life, daycare, and early mornings." I don't add that Mr. Tcheznich asked me to do it as a favor to her, that he understood she was a single parent and didn't want to overwhelm her.

"I know, Sarah. The boss explained everything when I confronted him. It seems so silly now, all the petty office politics."

We don't say the obvious, that the promotion means nothing now. Not if I can't see, and if I can't work. But she promises to visit me and leaves me without too much fuss, which I appreciate. The door closes behind her, leaving me with nothing but my thoughts. And I can't help but feel it's a bad sign if even Celia is being kind to me.

I'm being taken to my new apartment, Dan beside me like a sentry. I regret picking an apartment so high up in a building without an elevator. But I need to learn to walk again. Climbing four sets of stairs in a busy building and navigating people, pets, children, and even bicycles will be good practice.

Neither of us has anything to say once we're inside. I can only imagine the views from the window for which I picked the apartment in the first place.

Dan has been indispensable. But the longer I depend on him, the more frightened I'll continue to be of everything. We don't know how much we rely on vision until it's gone and the world is nothing but a black void. Sometimes, I can make out vague forms in the hazy, foggy brightness of the city.

"I can see something!" I tell Dr. Ford when I see him for a checkup a week after I've come to the new place. I can't call it home. I don't know what it looks like—I remember the bones I saw—but that's different. I don't know what it looks like now.

"Describe what you see," he says.

I do. I tell him how my vision is an ever-shifting landscape. Figures, shapes, forms, that dissolve like mirages.

"I'm afraid it's your imagination. It happens when we've recently lost something vital, like an appendage. People who've lost a leg or an arm, for example, sometimes momentarily believe it's still there. Vision can be like that, too."

"Can't I have actually seen something?" I hear the note of hysteria in my voice and cringe.

"I'm sorry, but that's not possible, Sarah. Your optic nerve is damaged beyond repair. But don't worry. These phantom visions will stop. And you will get used to it. I want you to talk to someone. "Here," he says.

There's a tap on my hand. I open my palm where he leaves something thin and sharp-edged. A card.

"Dr. Khan's a great therapist and a good friend and colleague. She's from England, too, you know."

Yes. So that will make me want to pour my heart out to her.

I thank him and leave. Dan's waiting outside. He's like my guide dog, leading me everywhere and anywhere. Poor Dan, he's lost his life, too, and he'd only just got it back.

He's as let down as I felt when I tell him Dr. Ford's verdict.

"You're wrong about one thing, you know." It's night. Dan and I sit on the sofa with the lights off. I'm seeing ghosts again and I want to believe that it's because of the lights, that I have some light perception despite the cold hard facts drilled into my head by Dr. Ford.

"What am I wrong about?"

"There are other ways to make memories. Your vision is only one of your five senses. You'll figure it out, Sarah. I know you will."

But I've already figured it all out once before, I want to yell and whine. I've built my life out of naught once before. I should have died on the streets long ago. But somehow, by some miracle, I made it through school and got to Oxford on scholarship. Then, once Barbara died, I moved to the States and started over. I made a living here. I survived by my wits.

All I can think right now is that I can't do it all over again—I'm not strong enough. I don't share Dan's confidence, so I say nothing. The unfairness of it all makes me want to hide in a corner and weep.

I push him to go home. He's been bunking at my place ever since I've come home from the hospital.

"I'll manage, Dan. I have to."

"Okay. Keep the phone charged, handy. Don't leave it lying around—have a dedicated space for it so you can find it as soon as you need it. Casserole and pasta are in the fridge."

He gathers me in a hug before he leaves. "I can stay if you want me to."

"For how long, Dan? I have to learn to live by myself again. And you've got a life."

He scoffs.

"Well, you will if you don't spend all your time here. I'll be fine. I'll call if I need something."

"See you tomorrow," he says.

I shut the door and walk into the blackness of the room. Two paces in, I stub my toe, hard, against the passageway base molding.

I scream and hop into the living room, then trip over the sofa and fall into it headfirst. The next moment, I want to reach into my pocket, take out the phone, and beg Dan to come back. But I don't. I get up, walk back to the door by putting my hand out to the flat surfaces and edges of the back wall and try again. This time I pay attention, and will myself to use my nose, ears, and hands.

I'm walking down 21st Street. Dan's just dropped me off. I'm thinking about packing and I'm planning the move in my head when I start to suffocate. Clawlike fingers squeeze my neck. "Wallet, now!" a voice whisper-screams into my ear.

"Please," I start to beg. They squeeze my neck harder until my eyes begin to pop out of their sockets and explode.

I wake up in a furious panic. I flail until I'm entangled in the comforter. Then I begin to calm down. *I'm safe*, I tell myself, weeping, *I'm safe*. But I can't go back to sleep. Not now, with the memory hanging around my neck so close, it's starting to cut off my oxygen. I manage to step into the living room and fall onto the sofa. There's a comforting aroma from the side table. It's the plants Celia brought me.

In a flash, I'm back on the street, the car heading straight at me, my head pushed into the ground until I can taste the earth. My tether to life. I hung on and on endlessly on the taste of that soil. Earth. *I belong here. I can't die, not now,* I'd thought. *I have plans.*

I pluck the potted plant out of its base. A rain-rich, earthy scent floods my nostrils. I reach into the soil with one hand and grab a fistful. It's blissful. Soft, fresh, warm, full of life.

I can't think what makes me do it. But the second I cram the handful of soil in my mouth, chew, and swallow, I know it's the start of something unhealthy.

AUDREY: NOW

"THANKS FOR THE RIDE HOME, DETECTIVE."

"No problem. Cabs can be tricky to find at this time of night."

I should be relieved that I've finally told them the truth, but they're no closer to finding Sarah, or who killed Kelly. My brain feels as though someone physically wrung it out. "Your partner hates me, doesn't she?" I ask, as the car lurches to a halt, presumably at a stoplight.

"To be fair, she hates everyone."

"Still . . ."

The engine vrooms again. "We have to look at everybody closely, Audrey. It doesn't help that all we get are lies, which wastes valuable time we could have spent chasing the right leads."

"I'll be glad once all this is over."

"You've been at this a long time, haven't you? Did finding Adam Briggs help trace the money you lost or even your clients'?"

"Yes, it did."

"How did you find Sar—Grace Foley?"

I sigh. "Not easily. It took months and a whole team of people who use state-of-the-art technology to trace her. But the starting point was that image of her in a bank. Those two knew what they were doing. Once we had enough info, I analyzed and traced their pattern. They would pick a city, set up muggings, steal info, and when they started to feel the heat, they'd steal a couple of identities, shed their previous avatars, and start over. When my identity was stolen, she was Amy Larson and Adam was Tobias Hill—the names registered in the hotel where they were staying."

"You think Adam's the mugger?"

"I don't know. But something tells me he's too smart to take that risk. He'd have outsourced it to someone local, already in the game. I can't be sure. In the end, though, there's always a mistake. Grace held on to her old driver's license and social security number, and that's how I traced her origin to Harrisburg."

"And how did you manage to get your hands on that?"

I picture his reaction if I tell him how I broke into Sarah's home, rifled through her things, and stole from her. Sympathetic or not, I doubt he'd let it slide. And that's perhaps what I like about him, but not enough to own up. "I-I can't say."

"Oh? Why not?"

A mild panic starts to build when I remember one of the things learned from Sarah. Mystery. I can feel Greene's eyes on me, awaiting an answer. I shrug and smile. I don't know if he sees it; he says nothing, but I know he's still watching me.

"Well, that was careless of her to hang on to incriminating documents."

"More like sentimental."

"And what were you planning to do once you found her?"

"The goal, always, was to find the money. It took us a while to figure out that Adam had been the brains behind the identity theft operation. We could find no trace of him, so our only hope was that she would lead us to him. We thought of tailing her, watching her movements. But since she was used to keeping her guard up, we couldn't risk spooking her. If I moved here as a neighbor, though, she might not suspect me. I couldn't pass up the opportunity to get close enough to her to start digging."

The car slows and the engine quiets down. I assume we've reached Shore Drive.

"I'm guessing it was you who put the GPS tracker on her car."

I purse my lips and smile. I don't want to admit to any illegal activity, however minor the offense.

"Weren't you worried that she'd figure out who you were?"

"I'm only an accountant, not an actress. So of course I was petrified I'd slip up or that she'd catch on to who I was."

"But the reward outweighed the risk?"

"Something like that," I say. "Thanks for the lift." I unbuckle and reach for the handle.

"Don't hesitate to call me if you need anything. My cell is 920-234-5580."

"That's kind of you," I say.

"You're not going to program it into your phone?"

"Oh, I will," I say, smiling. I get out of the car and hear the wind chimes. He's dropped me right outside my townhome today.

He accompanies me to the door. "Take care, Audrey, or should I be calling you Sarah?"

"Audrey is fine. It's my legal name, after all."

"Okay. Bye, Audrey."

"Goodbye, Detective."

I reach for the outer zipper of my purse, drag it back, and find the keys. I plunge the key in and twist it. The weight that's been pressing on me since the night I discovered the body lifts when I cross the threshold. Weary but relieved, my shoulders sag when I hang my bag and stow away my cane. In some bizarre way, it's as though I've taken off a mask, and I'm not certain how comfortable I am without it. It's only a name, but it's felt like an invisible wall I could hide behind. Now the wall has been torn down.

As I pad to the kitchen, I thumb in Detective Greene's number into my phone and set it in its usual spot on the countertop. From the stove, I grab the kettle, fill it, and turn it on. My throat is raw, as though I've screamed my lungs out for hours. The kettle starts up its gentle *whoosh*. I'm about to open the cabinet and reach for a teacup when the floor above presses a gentle creak into the ceiling. I freeze and listen. Another little creak reaches my ears. My blood runs cold when I realize I've been so pre-occupied that not only have I not armed the house, but I've also forgotten to lock the front door.

It's too late to worry about that. Someone's already in the house. I rush to the corner by the sink where I've placed the phone.

"Put it down," a voice says, a moment later.

The familiar twang makes my heart stutter in my chest. "Sarah!"

"I'd do as I'm told. There's a gun in my hand."

The phone slips from my hand and drops to the counter.

To my shock, it isn't fear that overwhelms me. It's anger. "Where the hell have you been these past three days? The police have been looking for you."

It comes to me all of a sudden. *She* was my intruder the night I found Kelly dead. Only she knew how I activated and deactivated the alarm. She must have waited until the police left, and then slipped in when I was in the shower. "After you left here, I mean," I add.

"Oh, very clever. I was right under your nose, and you didn't even know." It's funny. She calls me clever when she's the smart one. She knew I'd smell her, so she was careful enough not to wear her signature per-fume. But in her anxiety over Nicole, she wouldn't have considered how smoking might trigger the alarm or even that I might find the cigarette butts she left behind.

I sigh. "Where *did* you go after you left here?"

"You remember Ben, from the café? I've been hiding out at his place."

The anger I've barely stowed away snakes around me once again. "I thought you were dead!"

"And that would have suited you fine, wouldn't it?"

"What?"

"I know, Audrey. I've been watching you and I heard that detective call you Sarah. But I knew even before then that you were lying about *something*."

I'm struck dumb for a moment. Then, I rally. *I'm* the victim. She's the one who stole my name, my life, but it's so typical of her to make it sound as though it's my fault.

"Yeah, *I'm* Sarah. Or I was before you stole my identity, my life. When I started looking for y—"

"I don't *care* about all that right now, Audrey. Where is Nicole?"

I edge toward the sink.

"What—? The police took custody of her the night I found you—well, I thought it was you at the time."

"Took custody? She's a *thing* to you, something you could use to bargain with me? Is that why you moved in here? To take revenge on me by threatening me with her?"

"Of course not! That's not what I meant. She was taken away by the police first and then by Child Protective Services, but I have no idea where she is."

"You're lying. You know exactly where she is and you're going to tell me right now!"

As slowly as I possibly can, I reach behind me with one hand grasping the drawer pull.

"Ah. Ah. Don't be an idiot. I won't hesitate to pull the trigger."

I gulp and freeze.

"Where *is* she, Audrey? Where have they taken my daughter?"

"I swear, I have no idea. You've got to trust me."

She scoffs and laughs, a low, gravelly groan. "Trust you? You've been lying to me from the beginning!"

"That's rich, coming from you. You've no idea—do you—how many lives you've ruined?"

She lets out a little growl that startles me. "I'll ruin as many lives as it takes to get Nicole back."

"You have only yourself to blame for losing her."

"You shouldn't provoke someone with a gun." Her voice is too close. I stiffen when something pokes my ribs.

"I'm telling you the truth. I don't know where Social Services placed her. There was some talk of reaching your sister in Pennsylvania to see if she'd take Nicole in."

"What? No! I need her back now. Call that detective who dropped you and ask him."

"And what makes you think he'll tell me?"

"Persuade him, lie, I don't care!

"Here," she says, and reaches for something. There's a scrape. "What's this?" she screams a second later. "Who have you called?" I wince, feeling her spittle fly right into my face.

A spasm of fear squeezes my lungs when I hear the clipped chirp of the call-end button.

"Tell me," she says, with a low growl in my ear. "Who did you call?"

The front door opens. My phone chimes to alert me.

"Audrey?" Detective Greene calls out.

Grace tenses beside me as he walks toward us. I freeze when she presses the gun into my ribs. Can he see it? What if he aggravates her?

"Drop it, Grace." I should be relieved that he has spotted the gun, but I panic even more. A minute ago, she was angry and desperate, but now she's cornered, she could become reckless. I whimper.

"Shut up," she snarls in my ear. Her hand doesn't move.

"I want my daughter. Where is Nicole?"

"Drop it and I'll tell you," Greene says.

"No!" she shouts, making me jump with terror. Against my side, her hand is shaking, with rage, or fear, I can't tell. "I want her back *right now*!"

"Listen to him, Grace. The only way you can ever see Nicole now is if you cooperate with the police and tell them why you killed Kelly. If it was self-defense—"

"No! You're not going to pin that on me. It's all your fault!" she says, and pushes the gun deeper into my flesh. I wince when the muzzle pokes my rib. "First, she started harassing me with phone calls. Even after I told her she was mistaken, that I *was* Sarah Connelly, just not the one she was looking for, she wouldn't leave me alone. I got worried that I wasn't safe here anymore. The only reason I even asked you to find Adam was because I didn't know how to deal with Kelly. I should never have trusted you. I dragged him into this because of you."

I stifle a gasp. So *that's* why she wouldn't let me into the house. Adam was already here the day before I found Kelly's body.

"What happened, Grace? Why did he kill her?" Greene asks.

"After Adam got here, I told him about Kelly. He was spooked, too, and we decided it was time to leave town. I'd just put Nicole in her car seat and was about to grab a few things for her but then that woman, Kelly, turned up here. As soon as I let her in and she saw Adam and me, she went all quiet. She tried to play it cool, said she did have the wrong Sarah after all, but we knew something was wrong. She was about to walk away and Adam . . . just reacted. He picked up one of Ronnie's clubs and hit her on the head with it. He didn't mean it, I swear. But when she didn't wake up, he panicked. He said we had to leave immediately. Nicole was crying her head off upstairs. I was about to get her, but then *you* turned up. Adam went crazy! He grabbed my hand and dragged me out through the patio door before I could get her, and it's *your* fault—"

The force of her voice makes me shudder. Grace is crying, hysterical.

"Where's Adam, Grace?" Greene asks.

She sniffles. "You'll never catch him."

"He's left you to take the blame, hasn't he?" Greene asks.

"It's not like that. He wouldn't do that to me." The desperation in her voice makes my heart lurch. She's quite alone now, no comrade, or partner in crime. Adam's left her holding the bag. "He wanted me to go *with* him but I couldn't leave Nicole behind. I had to come back for her . . ."

"Don't protect him, Grace. If you ever want to see Nicole again, you're going to have to give yourself up," I say.

When we hear the whine of sirens, I feel the violent tremor in her hand against my chest. My heart hammers. A simple pull of a finger, a twitch, and I could end up with a giant hole in my chest.

"I'd listen to her if I were you. There's only one way out of this, Grace. Come on, I'll take you to her. She hasn't been sleeping well, you know. Don't you want to see her? She's only ten minutes away . . ." Detective Green's voice is gentle and mesmerizing, like a lullaby.

"Y-you're lying." She starts to cry again.

"No. I promise I'll bring you straight to her. C'mon," he says.

Standing so close to me, I can feel deep sobs rack her body. Finally, her hand slips away from my ribs. Just as I start to ease up, there's a deafening *bang* and I'm moving sideways, falling, falling into a fathomless gorge. All I can think while trying to claw and scratch my way up is, *Not like this. I've lost so much. I can't let her take any more from me—*

Then I slam into the floor.

AUDREY: NOW

"You're okay," someone is saying to me. "You're not hurt."

For a moment, I think I'm dreaming it, but a sturdy arm lifts me. "You're fine," Detective Novak says.

"W-what happened?"

"You're safe. You passed out. The gun in her hand went off by accident. Your floor's got a hole in it, though."

"Better it than me," I say, shuddering. "Where is she?"

"Outside. We've got her," Greene says.

"And are you going to take her to Nicole?"

There's silence.

"We've already called Social Services to bring Nicole to the station," Novak says.

"You're lucky I was only just a street away after dropping you when I got your call," Greene says.

I'm so winded, all I can do is nod. A couple of seconds is all I had to dial his number before Grace, unaware I was already on the call with him, demanded I drop the phone. I thank my stars that he turned the car around and drove right back. If not . . . but I can't think that way. I'm here now. I'm *still* here.

The sun is out, from the heat flooding into the living room, and I want to bathe in it.

I walk into the strange silence of my closet and look for something to wear. My fingers graze the clothes on hangers. I stop when I touch the soft cotton of a summer dress I haven't worn in a long while. I change out of the T-shirt and shorts I'm wearing and slip on the dress. It falls over my curves and stops where the hem tickles the backs of my knees.

I'm about to turn around and head out when Sarah . . . Grace's voice pops into my head. *You're going to go out like that? At least wear some lipstick!*

She'd have been right. It's funny how I still hear her hanging around in my head like Barbara. At least my mother's dead. Grace isn't. But in a way, I suppose she is, to me. Over time, I've created this image of her in my head that's bloated and enlarged until it felt as though she was all I could see. That image is gone. It's blank where she used to be. Sarah is dead, buried.

I pull open the drawer below the mirror of my dresser and reach for lipstick. I pick the center one, a pinky red, the sales assistant had said, and dab it onto my lips, pursing them together to spread out the color.

I close my eyes and try to picture myself. Are my cheeks flushed with the warmth of summer? Is my long, dark hair cascading down my back the way I imagine it? Does my new nose become my old face? Is my scar visible in this light?

I don't know. Once my brain stopped bleeding, the bandages came off, and with them, the realization I had lost more than my vision. Half of my old face was gone, trampled and smashed under the car. With each hospital visit, reconstructive surgery covered another bit of the old and exposed me with a new veneer. I'll never know what I look like now. I open my eyes and stare at where the mirror sits. A gilt-haired woman with high cheekbones, a straight, sharp nose, and green eyes framed by sandy lashes and angled eyebrows stares back at me. A shimmering figure, the one I've always been able to see behind the woman every-one else sees. But also, something more. Something that wasn't there before. Another layer or dimension, a mix of the new me and the me that Grace lived.

Along with this layer comes a revelation that's been building up ever since I moved to No. 4 Shore Drive. When the thought finally forms, it leaves me stunned. In some ways, Sarah had more fun playing me than I did being me.

I make a silent promise to myself. No more holding back, no more saving everything for the future while missing out on the present. I reach underneath the hangers for the jute and cream linen wedges and lace them onto my ankles. Downstairs, I grab the keys and my cane from its spot by the door and step out into the sun. A summery breeze caresses my skin as I lock up. I swivel toward No. 5 for a moment. Then I turn around and walk to the end of the block to cross the street, my hair fluttering in the wind. A car pulls up. I wait until I can hear it chug away, but it stops a little ahead. My phone rings. I'm informed by Siri that it's Sherman.

"Hi, you," I say, after I pick up.

"Are you out?"

"I just stepped out for a walk. Why?"

"Hang on. Turn around," he says.

"Why?" I ask again.

"Because I'm down the road in a car."

"Audrey," a familiar voice calls out. A car door slams shut.

A smile tugs at my lips as I turn back and walk toward the voice.

"It's *so* good to see you," he says, and pulls me into a hug. I soften into his massive form and look up at him.

"Wanna go for a stroll?"

"Of course! What a day," he says. I take his arm as we turn into the walking path.

"It's so lovely here."

"Isn't it?" I ask. I've been waiting for him to visit, but with Sarah around, I didn't think it was safe on many levels. That's why I saved Dan's number under his middle name, Sherman. I couldn't risk having her connect me to any names she might have come across when she stole my identity.

We're on a bench near the lighthouse. The sun is on us. Its warmth climbs up my body and sinks into my skin.

"I can't believe it's over."

He places an arm around my shoulder. "You've done it."

"*We've* done it, Dan. When I set out to move here a year ago, I never thought I could pull it off."

"I didn't doubt you."

"I did. I doubted myself. One afternoon of deceiving Anne and a ten-minute hack into Fortitude's servers wasn't adequate preparation. Not for deception on such a scale as the one I was about to pull off—live as the new me, right under the nose of the person who stole my life."

"I never doubted your intentions, either."

I scoff. "There was a moment on the afternoon I last met Sarah. I don't know what came over me. It was as though all these months' anger built up inside me like a pressure cooker. And when she casually dismissed ruining Priya's life, I almost lost it and blew up."

"You're missing the point. You *didn't* lose it. In the end, you've held it together and achieved something I can only dream of doing. You've created a whole new life for yourself."

"All thanks to Anne," I say, grateful for her persistent push to keep my interview with Greg. After I found out the blindness was permanent I had all but given up hope. It was Anne who convinced me I was the person for the role Aegis had been looking to fill—with or without vision. "So what if you can't see? It's your brain that matters, Sarah. You can still use that," she'd said in her no-nonsense way.

In the silence, I think about how it isn't only my life that's changed. Dan quit his job with Fortitude and started working for Aegis, too. He had to go back to school for a while to enable the career change, as did I. Celia is now part-owner of Tcheznich & Co. And Norman is the senior auditor.

None of us are the same people we were four years ago.

"How's Celia?"

"The same. Oh, her son was born last week, Tobias."

My jaw drops as my eyes round with warmth. "What! That's amazing!" Instantly, I remember Nicole.

"Hey, you okay?" Dan asks. I realize my face is wet.

I wipe my eyes and sniffle. "I miss Nicole. Poor kiddo. Prison visits aren't the same thing as having a mother around."

"You started to care for them, didn't you?"

I can hear the hurt in his voice. He's affronted on my behalf. "I *know*. It's stupid, isn't it? She took everything from me. I should be livid with her. And I was, often. But look how her life has turned out. According to Greene, she's been on the run for a long time."

"What for?"

"There's a warrant out on her for aggravated assault. She got into a fight trying to save her sister from rape. She hit her sister's attacker with a crowbar apparently, putting him in the hospital for months. She was hurt too, in the process. Remember that scar I told you about? She had no choice but to go on the run looking for a fresh start with a new identity and that's how she found Adam before the two made it into a scheme. And now she's lost the only thing that mattered to her."

"Wow," Dan says, after a pause. "We've known next to nothing about the pair of them for so long and now all this information is a little overwhelming."

I nod.

"Knowing you, it's *not* stupid that you started to care for her and Nicole. You've always been that person. That'll never change. Even if you've dyed your hair brown and look different now with your shiny new nose and jaw."

"I'm hurt. I thought you liked my new nose! At least I won't have to worry about my blond roots showing anymore."

He laughs. "True. But you do make a good brunette. And it is a great nose. They did you justice. It's the name I can't get used to. I still think of you as Sarah sometimes."

His admission disarms me. "I know. It's been strange for me to call someone else *Sarah*. Want to hear something weird? It hadn't occurred to me until I changed my name to Audrey that I was never a Sarah—that name never quite fit me. I've become Audrey. I *feel* like an Audrey now. Just as I'll always think of her as Sarah and not Grace."

"Any word on Adam?"

"Nothing. Even if they did find him, I doubt they'd tell me. He's probably long gone by now. He's wanted for murder. I wouldn't be hanging around if I were him." I shudder, remembering how I'd found Kelly with her smashed head and Nicole, alone in the bedroom, crying.

"Hey." Dan puts an arm around me. "It's over."

We're sitting in companionable silence, listening to the rhythmic *swish-swash* of the river when Dan says, "Martin asked me to move in with him."

I gasp. "Dan! That's fantastic, if that's what you want as well."

"It is. I mean, Martin's a great guy."

"And you've known him for two years now."

"Two years and three months," he corrects me.

I smile, cock an eyebrow up at him. "I sense a 'but' coming."

"But," Dan says, his tone lilting upward, amused, "I want to take things a bit slow."

"That's understandable. You've been hurt before. If Martin's serious about you, I'm sure he'll understand."

"He might. *If* I ever work up the courage to tell him."

"Dan!" I nudge his side with my elbow. "Okay. You know I wouldn't dream of interfering, but here are my two cents. Life is too short.

I've always known that in a way, but that night after I got mugged, it sank into me. Life is too fleeting. I begged to stay alive that night. And I was lucky to get a second chance. What could happen, like the worst-case scenario, if you move in with him? That you aren't cut out for each other? But you won't know that until you do move in with him. If you like him, and you're serious about him, don't wait too long to tell him."

"You've changed. You've become more . . . open."

"Believe it or not, I think Grace has rubbed off on me."

I lie in bed, my head heavy with thoughts since the call from Detective Greene. Hoyt Security couldn't confirm that it *was* Grace who used the patio door to come and go from my house. There's no camera on that entrance. I would have noted it sooner, if, after the break-in, I hadn't panicked. It's obvious now, but at the time, I assumed the intruder had left the cigarettes on purpose, to scare me. But I should have connected it to Grace, who used to smoke before Nicole was born. Over the months, I assumed the smell on her was because of Ronnie, or Brian, but now I know she started smoking again. She must have lit up and simply forgotten I'd smell or find them. She must have been tearing her hair out, not being able to be with Nicole, wondering if she was all right.

Even more surprising than realizing that she was my intruder the second time was learning that Grace was also responsible for the other break-ins in our neighborhood. I didn't believe Greene when he told me, but the clues were there then as well. When Bob asked me about the perfume I was wearing, *her* perfume, I should have known right away. And Greene confirmed that they found all the stolen items except Bob's photo frame in Grace's closet. Of course, she had the keys to my house, in case of some emergency, so she's the first person I should have suspected, but why would she break in when she was here half the time anyway?

But I understand, I think. She'd been heavily pregnant then and bored to death. She missed the adrenaline rush of stealing, of starting over. It had all been mere mischief to her, at our expense.

It's all moot now, anyway. She's not going to be getting into trouble any time soon. I'm quite conscious of *my* guilt over my own little mischief, breaking into her home a couple of times, even if it had been worth it.

I toss and turn, restless, sad, and empty, like a vital part of my existence is gone. The last time I felt so empty, Mac had broken up with me. It's Detective Greene and his questions.

"What will you do now?" he'd asked.

My glib answer fades away. I can't picture it, a future without my anger, my simultaneous hatred and fondness for a woman who stole my life—a bizarre mix even I can't begin to understand. There's no one left to hate. A huge driving force for my existence, a path to finding my client's money as well as my money, is over. I've found it.

Then why can't I move on?

I pick up the phone and fidget with it in my hand. The last time we spoke, Mac helped find the account where Kelly had stashed away the embezzled money. I hadn't even called to thank her later. I couldn't. I twirl the phone. No. It's been four years. She wouldn't want to hear from me after all this time.

I feel the weight of the phone as time ticks by. *Oh, what the hell.* I hit DIAL before I can change my mind.

"Hello?"

I frown. Then I cringe. Shit. I've called the home number. But it would seem even more suspicious if I don't speak.

"Liz? Hi. It's Aud—Sarah."

Silence. "Sarah, hi." Liz never warmed to me, so I expect no different, but her hesitance now makes me regret calling Mac even more.

"How are you?"

She scoffs. "Okay."

"Is McKenzie around?? May I speak to her?"

"She's not here, Sarah, but then, you know that."

I sit up straighter and gather the comforter to me, an odd sensation slinking into my spine as I do.

"Is Mac out somewhere? Sorry. I should have tried her cell."

"You can stop with the pretense, Sarah. You know she doesn't live with me anymore."

"What? No. I didn't know. Since when?"

"As if I'd believe that."

"Liz, I didn't know. Are you okay?"

"Of course. It's been four years since we split."

A dull ringing starts at the back of my head. "I'm sorry. It's been—" I nearly say it's been four years since I've spoken to Mac, but it sounds awful, given what she's told me. "It's been a long while since we've talked."

"Somehow, I find that hard to believe."

"Why?"

"Because when she split up with me, she . . . she said it was because of you."

"Because of me?" I repeat dully.

"Look . . . I'm the last person who would want to tell you this, but why don't you speak to her?"

I gulp. "I can't," I whisper.

"She can't even look me in the eye because she's thinking about you. You're clearly still missing her. Just stop being an idiot and talk to her!"

Liz's forcefulness reminds me of Grace for a moment. It's exactly what she would have said if she were here.

"Okay," I say. I sound lame. I know it. She knows it.

"Good," she says, and hangs up.

I think about my advice to Dan—that he should take the plunge—and look at me now. Such a coward.

"So? Stop being one and call her," Grace would have said.

I sigh and pick up the phone. My heart clenches when the dial tone connects.

When a familiar voice says, "McKenzie," my mouth goes dry and something flutters in my stomach.

"Mac?"

Silence. Then, a hesitant, "Yes?"

"It's me."

ACKNOWLEDGMENTS

THERE WAS A TIME AS I WAS WRITING THIS MANUSCRIPT WHEN I WOULD picture the finished version with a captivating cover, a grab-me title, and I would dream of acknowledging all the help I've had along the way, and I would think, *But that's light years away; I don't know how my story is going to turn out yet.* I told myself I would be ever so lucky to get to do these things, so I should keep writing, get to that finish line.

Well, I'm one fortunate gal to have this opportunity to express my gratitude. I had no idea how many people would be involved or the extraordinary effort and help it takes to push a manuscript from its first draft to the spotless, shining book that goes out into the world.

To the two people without whom I wouldn't have made it past that first draft—Mum and Dad, always my first readers—thanks for enduring *all* my drafts, and for the late-night SOS chats that began with plot loopholes, character (and my) crises, and imposter syndrome, and ended in the hope that I could fix them all. Without your unfaltering conviction in me, there would have been no subsequent drafts. Thank you for always being there for me.

To my amazing literary agent Jennifer Weis: Thank you for being my stalwart champion. Your enthusiasm and love for the characters and this story mean the world to me. You steered my manuscript to the best possible narrative. I feel lucky every day to have you on my side, as well as Noah Rosenzweig and the entire team at Ross Yoon Agency.

To my editor extraordinaire at Union Square & Co., Claire Wachtel, who took on this book with an enthusiasm that continues to marvel me: Thank you for being kind, and above all, for your faith in me and this novel. Your insight and forensic attention to detail brought out what matters in the story. I treasure your notes, particularly the one that simply said in the margin, "Really?" A huge thank-you to executive editor Barbara Berger, whose sharp, eagle-eyed approach made the book shine; to Melissa Farris for the clever cover design; and to Rich Hazelton for the interior design. I would also like to thank the team at Union Square & Co. for their enthusiasm and support for this book.

Many people said I was "brave" to represent a main character who is blind. I don't think that that courage should be attributed to me at all. To Mimzy Reiner: I'm immensely grateful and appreciative of you and your comprehensive guide on how to represent a blind character with authenticity via your blog, *Late Night Writing Advice*. Mimzy, you are a star, and a wonderful writer.

A beta-reader's function is to tell you what works and what doesn't, but to receive detailed comments with reasoning is a privilege, and I'm so grateful to my friends who read, critiqued, and encouraged me: Sravani Hotha, Paula Minydzac, Jay DiNitto, Dan Micco (thanks for letting me pick your brain about the law and its procedures, and for answering my many, many questions), from the Shut Up & Write critique group. Thanks to all the beta readers I found via Writers' HQ's Swipe Right: Tavia Allan, Emma Claridge, Julieta Moss, Ben Wakefield, Robyn Wilson, Katie Rodwell, Laura Kitney, Kirsti Sinclair, and Mark Feakins. Your invaluable feedback strengthened my writing and my story.

I couldn't have done it without the incredible support and encouragement of Writers' HQ, run by the brilliant Sarah Lewis and Jo Gatford. A massive thank-you to the Writers' HQ pen-and-word-wielding army, particularly Fiona McKay and Sumitra Singam, who lend their support, cheer me on with their wit and wisdom, and put up with my moaning. A huge thanks to the amazing Writers' HQ retreat hosts Kathy Hoyle, Melissa Stirling Reid, Veronique Kootstra, and A R-H. Your constant encouragement, positivity, and, not to forget, the tarot prompts saw the edits on this book through to the end. The Writers' HQ Friday Flash Face-Off expanded my writing world like none other. If you are a writer, go check out Writers' HQ's FFO. I promise, it will change your world, too.

To the communities of Retreat West; Sisters in Crime (and their spectacular write-ins); Crime Writers of Color; South Asian Flash Writers Group; and the Inner Circle Writers' Group, particularly, Grant Hudson, who once pulled me out of a deep abyss in the early days and instilled in me the first roots of resilience, thank you for your humor and support that kept me sane through it all, and for your generosity with sharing research tips and writing insights. A special shout-out to writer friends, my Twitter writing community, and friends from other walks of life: Bonnie Gilbery, Chelsea Abdullah (thanks for walking me patiently through various publishing scenarios and prospects), and Lazaro Pacheco.

Thanks also to all the libraries, booksellers, BookStagrammers, BookTokkers, BookTubers, book blogs, podcast hosts, and book clubs for your support.

I'd like to say a massive thank-you to my family, as well as my husband Viv's family, for encouraging and supporting my every idea and cheering me along the way. To Hema, my twin from another mother, your unwavering love and faith in me is everything. Thank you to the friends who have always stuck by and showed up for me: in particular, Shriti Suvarna and Archana Pania—my special people. My eternal gratitude to the SGI Community, who are always with me in my every endeavor.

To you, my readers, who hold this book in your heart, my sincere gratitude.

Last, but never the least, to Viv, my sounding board, devil's advocate, partner in life and in crime, draft counter, idea explorer, fact-checker, story critiquer, cheerleader, and one-man fan club at a time when all this was nothing but a pipe dream: Thank you for who you are, for your endless patience, and for putting up with me.